P9-DWZ-620

Where'd You Go, BERNADETTE

ALSO BY MARIA SEMPLE

This One Is Mine

Today Will Be Different

Where'd You Go, BERNADETTE

A NOVEL

MARIA SEMPLE

BACK BAY BOOKS
Little, Brown and Company
NEW YORK BOSTON LONDON

Copyright © 2012 by Maria Semple
Reading group guide copyright © 2013 by Maria Semple and Little, Brown and Company
"Dear Mountain Room Parents" originally appeared in *The New Yorker*.
Excerpt from *Today Will Be Different* copyright © 2016 by Maria Semple

Back Bay Books / Little, Brown and Company
Hachette Book Group
1290 Avenue of the Americas, New York, NY 10104

Originally published in hardcover by Little, Brown and Company, August 2012
First Back Bay paperback edition, April 2013

Back Bay Books is an imprint of Little, Brown and Company, a division of Hachette Book Group, Inc. The Back Bay Books name and logo are trademarks of Hachette Book Group, Inc.

The publisher is not responsible for websites (or their content) that are not owned by the publisher.

The Hachette Speakers Bureau provides a wide range of authors for speaking events. To find out more, go to hachettespeakersbureau.com or call (866) 376-6591.

ISBN 978-1-64385-268-3

Printed in the United States of America

For Poppy Meyer

WHERE'D YOU GO, BERNADETTE

The first annoying thing is when I ask Dad what he thinks happened to Mom, he always says, "What's most important is for you to understand it's not your fault." You'll notice that wasn't even the question. When I press him, he says the second annoying thing, "The truth is complicated. There's no way one person can ever know everything about another person."

Mom disappears into thin air two days before Christmas without telling me? Of course it's complicated. Just because it's complicated, just because you think you can't ever know everything about another person, it doesn't mean you can't try.

It doesn't mean I can't try.

PART ONE

Mom Versus the Gnats

MONDAY, NOVEMBER 15

Galer Street School is a place where compassion, academics, and global connectitude join together to create civic-minded citizens of a sustainable and diverse planet.

Student: Bee Branch

Grade: Eight

Teacher: Levy

KEY

S   Surpasses Excellence

A   Achieves Excellence

W   Working towards Excellence

Geometry	S
Biology	S
World Religion	S
Music	S
Creative Writing	S
Ceramics	S
Language Arts	S
Expressive Movement	S

COMMENTS: Bee is a pure delight. Her love of learning is infectious, as are her kindness and humor. Bee is unafraid to ask questions. Her goal is always deep understanding of a given topic, not merely getting a good grade. The other students look to Bee for help in their studies, and she is always quick to respond with a smile. Bee exhibits extraordinary concentration when working alone; when working in a group, she is a quiet and confident leader. Of special note is what an accomplished flutist Bee continues to be. The year is only a third over, but already I am mourning the day Bee graduates from Galer Street and heads out into the world. I understand she is applying to boarding schools back east. I envy the teachers who get to meet Bee for the first time, and to discover for themselves what a lovely young woman she is.

*

That night at dinner, I sat through Mom and Dad's "We're-so-proud-of-you"s and "She's-a-smart-one"s until there was a lull.

"You know what it means," I said. "The big thing it means."

Mom and Dad frowned question marks at each other.

"You don't remember?" I said. "You told me when I started Galer Street that if I got perfect grades the whole way through, I could have anything I wanted for a graduation present."

"I do remember," Mom said. "It was to ward off further talk of a pony."

"That's what I wanted when I was little," I said. "But now I want something different. Aren't you curious what it is?"

"I'm not sure," Dad said. "Are we?"

"A family trip to Antarctica!" I pulled out the brochure I'd been sitting on. It was from an adventure travel company that does cruises to exotic places. I opened it to the Antarctica page and passed it across the table. "If we go, it has to be over Christmas."

"This Christmas?" Mom said. "Like in a month?" She got up and started stuffing empty take-out containers into the bags they'd been delivered in.

Dad was already deep into the brochure. "It's their summer," he said. "It's the only time you can go."

"Because ponies are cute." Mom tied the handles in a knot.

"What do you say?" Dad looked up at Mom.

"Isn't this a bad time for you because of work?" she asked him.

"We're studying Antarctica," I said. "I've read all the explorers' journals, and I'm doing my presentation on Shackleton." I started wiggling in my chair. "I can't believe it. Neither of you are saying no."

"I was waiting for you," Dad said to Mom. "You hate to travel."

"I was waiting for you," Mom said back. "You have to work."

"Oh my God. That's a yes!" I jumped out of my chair. "That's a yes!" My joy was so infectious that Ice Cream woke up and started barking and doing victory laps around the kitchen table.

"Is that a yes?" Dad asked Mom over the crackling of plastic take-out containers being crammed into the trash.

"That's a yes," she said.

*

TUESDAY, NOVEMBER 16

From: Bernadette Fox
To: Manjula Kapoor

Manjula,

Something unexpected has come up and I'd love it if you could work extra hours. From my end, this trial period has been a lifesaver. I hope it's working for you, too. If so, please let me know ASAP because I need you to work your Hindu magic on a huge project.

OK: I'll stop being coy.

You know I have a daughter, Bee. (She's the one you order the medicine for and wage valiant battle with the insurance company over.) Apparently, my husband and I told her she could have anything she wanted if she graduated middle school with straight A's. The straight A's have arrived—or should I say straight S's, because Galer Street is one of those liberal, grades-erode-self-esteem-type schools (let's hope you don't have them in India)—and so what does Bee want? To take a family trip to Antarctica!

Of the million reasons I don't want to go to Antarctica, the main one is that it will require me to leave the house. You might have figured out by now that's something I don't much like to do. But I can't argue with Bee. She's a good kid. She has more character than Elgie and I and the next ten guys combined. Plus she's applying to boarding school for next fall, which she'll of course get into because of said A's. Whoops, S's! So it would be in pretty bad taste to deny Buzzy this.

The only way to get to Antarctica is by cruise ship. Even the smallest one has 150 passengers, which translates into me being trapped with 149 other people who will uniquely annoy the hell out of me with their rudeness, waste, idiotic questions, incessant yammering, creepy food requests, boring small talk, etc. Or worse, they might turn their curiosity toward me, and expect pleasantry in return. I'm getting a panic attack just thinking about it. A little social anxiety never hurt anyone, am I right?

If I give you the info, could you pretty please take over the paperwork, visas, plane tickets, everything involved with getting we three from Seattle to the White Continent? Is this something you have time for?

Say yes,
Bernadette

Oh! You already have credit card numbers to pay for airfare, trip, and accoutrements. But in terms of your salary, I'd like you to take it directly out of my personal account. When Elgie saw the Visa charge for your work last month—even though it wasn't much money—he wasn't thrilled that I'd hired a virtual assistant from India. I told him I wouldn't be using you anymore. So, if we could, Manjula, let's keep our romance an illicit one.

*

From: Manjula Kapoor
To: Bernadette Fox

Dear Ms. Fox,

It would be my pleasure to assist you with your family travel plans to Antarctica. Attached please find the contract for moving forward on a full-time basis. Where indicated, please include your bank routing number. I look forward to our continued collaboration.

Warm regards,
Manjula

*

Invoice from Delhi Virtual Assistants International

Invoice Number: BFB39382
Associate: Manjula Kapoor

40 hours a week at $0.75 USD/hr.
TOTAL: $30.00 USD
Invoice Due in Full upon Receipt

WEDNESDAY, NOVEMBER 17
Letter from Ollie Ordway ("Ollie-O")

CONFIDENTIAL:
TO GALER STREET SCHOOL PARENT ASSOCIATION

Dear Parents,

It was terrific to meet you last week. I'm thrilled to have been brought in to consult for the wonderful Galer Street School. Head of School Goodyear promised a motivated Parent Association, and you didn't disappoint.

Let's **talk turkey**: in three years you're losing your lease on your current location. Our goal is to **launch a capital campaign** so you will be able to purchase a larger, more suitable campus. For those of you who couldn't attend the meeting, here's the **drill-down**:

I conducted an off-site consisting of 25 parents in the Seattle area with an income of $200K+ and whose children are entering kindergarten. The **headline** is that Galer Street is considered a **second-tier school**, a fallback option for those who don't get accepted to their first-choice school.

Our objective is to **move the needle** on Galer Street and kick it up into the **First-Choice Cluster** (FCC) for Seattle's elite. How do we achieve this? What is the **secret sauce**?

Your mission statement says Galer Street is based on global "connectitude." (You people don't just think **outside the box**, you think **outside the dictionary**!) You received some impressive **big-media** coverage for the cows you bought for the Guatemalans and the solar cookstoves you sent to the African villagers. While raising **small sums of money** for people you've never met is commendable, you need to start raising **large sums of money** for your own children's private school. To do this, you must emancipate yourselves from what I am calling **Subaru Parent** mentality and start thinking more like **Mercedes Parents**. How do Mercedes Parents think? My research indicates the following:

1. The choice of private schools is both **fear-based** and **aspirational**. Mercedes Parents are afraid their children won't get "the best education possible," which has nothing to do with actual education and everything to do with the number of other Mercedes Parents at a school.

2. When applying to kindergarten, Mercedes Parents have their **eyes on the prize**. And that prize is **Lakeside School**, alma mater of Bill Gates, Paul Allen, et al. Lakeside is considered *the* feeder school to the Ivy League. Let me rock it straight: the first stop on this **crazy train** is **Kindergarten Junction**, and nobody gets off until it pulls into **Harvard Station**.

Head of School Goodyear took me on a tour of your current campus at the industrial park. Apparently, Subaru Parents have no problem sending their children to a school adjacent to a **wholesale seafood distributor**. Let me assure you, Mercedes Parents do.

All roads lead to raising the money to buy a new campus. The best way to achieve it is to pack the incoming kindergarten class with **Mercedes Parents**.

Grab your crampons because we have an uphill climb. But fear not: **I do underdog**. Based on your budget, I have devised a **two-pronged action plan**.

The first **action item** is a **redesign** of the Galer Street **logo**. Much as I love clip-art handprints, let's try to find an image that better articulates **success**. A coat of arms divided into four, with images of the Space Needle, a calculator, a lake (as in Lakeside), and something else, maybe some kind of ball? I'm just throwing out some ideas here, nothing's set in stone.

The second **action item** is to hold a **Prospective Parent Brunch (PPB)**, which we aim to fill with Seattle's elite, or, as I have grown fond of saying, **Mercedes Parents**. Galer Street parent Audrey Griffin has generously offered to host this gathering at her lovely home. (Best to keep away from the fishery.)

Attached please find a spreadsheet listing Seattle **Mercedes Parents**. It is imperative that you go over this list and tell me who you can deliver to the PPB. We're looking for the **watershed get** we can then **squawk** as **leverage** toward securing other **Mercedes Parents**. When they all see one another, it will alleviate their fears about Galer Street being a second-tier school and the applications will roll in.

Meanwhile, back at the ranch, I'm working on the invite. Get me those names ASAP. We need to take this brunch at the Griffins' house live before Christmas. Saturday, December 11, is my target date. This puppy has all the ingredients of an epic **kilt lifter**.

Cheers,

Ollie-O

*

Note from Audrey Griffin to a blackberry abatement specialist

Tom,

I was out in my garden, cutting back the perennials and planting some winter color in preparation for a school brunch we're hosting on December 11. I went to turn the compost and got attacked by blackberry vines.

I'm shocked to see that they have returned, not only in the compost pile, but in my raised vegetable beds, greenhouse, and even my worm bin. You can imagine my frustration, especially since you charged me a small fortune to remove them three weeks ago. (Maybe $235 isn't a lot for you, but it's a lot for us.)

Your flyer said you guarantee your work. So, please, could you come back and remove all the blackberries by the 11th, this time for good?

Blessings, and help yourself to some chard,

Audrey

*

Note from Tom, the blackberry abatement specialist

Audrey,

I did remove the blackberries on your property. The source of the vines you're talking about is your neighbor's house at the top of the hill. Their blackberries are the ones coming under your fence and into your garden.

To stop them, we could dig a trench at your property line and pour a concrete barrier, but it would need to be five feet deep, and that would be costly. You could also keep on top of them with weed killer, which I'm not sure you want to do because of the worms and the vegetables.

What really has to happen is the neighbor at the top of the hill has to eradicate their vines. I've never seen so many blackberries growing wild in the city of Seattle, especially on Queen Anne Hill, with your home prices. I saw a house on Vashon Island where the whole foundation was cracked by blackberry vines.

Since the neighbor's bushes are on a steep hillside, they're going to need a special machine. The best one is the CXJ Hillside Side-Arm Thrasher. I don't have one of those myself.

Another option, and a better one in my opinion, is large pigs. You can rent a couple, and in a week's time, they'll pull out those blackberries by the roots and then some. Plus, they're dang cute.

Do you want me to talk to the neighbor? I can go knock on the door. But it looks like nobody lives there.

Let me know.

Tom

*

From: Soo-Lin Lee-Segal
To: Audrey Griffin

Audrey,

I told you I'm starting to take the shuttle bus in to work, right? Well, guess who I rode in with this morning? Bernadette's husband, Elgin Branch. (I know why *I* have to save money by taking the Microsoft Connector. But Elgin Branch?) I wasn't certain it was him at first, that's how little we all see of him at school.

So you're going to love this. There was only one seat available, and it was next to Elgin Branch, an inside one between him and the window.

"Excuse me," I said.

He was furiously typing on his laptop. Without looking up, he moved his knees to the side. I know he's a Level 80 corporate VP, and I'm just an admin. But most gentlemen would stand up to let a woman through. I squeezed past him and sat down.

"Looks like we're going to finally be getting some sunshine," I said.

"That would be great."

"I'm really looking forward to World Celebration Day," I said. He looked a little frightened, like he had no idea who I was. "I'm Lincoln's mom. From Galer Street."

"Of course!" he said. "I'd love to chat, but I've got to get this email out." He grabbed some headphones from around his neck, put them over his ears, and returned to his laptop. And get this — his headphones weren't even plugged in! They were those sound-canceling ones! The whole ride to Redmond he never spoke to me again.

Now, Audrey, for the past five years we always figured Bernadette was the ghastly one. Turns out her husband is as rude and antisocial as she is! I was so miffed that when I got to work, I Googled Bernadette Fox. (Something I can't believe I've waited until now to do, considering our unhealthy obsession with her!) Everyone knows Elgin Branch is team leader of Samantha 2 at Microsoft. But when I looked *her* up, nothing appeared. The only Bernadette Fox is some architect in California. I checked all combinations of her name—Bernadette Branch, Bernadette Fox-Branch. But our Bernadette, Bee's mom, doesn't exist as far as the Internet is concerned. Which, these days, is quite an accomplishment in itself.

On another topic, don't you love Ollie-O? I was crushed when Microsoft ten-percented him last year. But if that hadn't happened, we'd never have been able hire him to rebrand our little school.

Here at Microsoft, SteveB just called a town hall for the Monday after Thanksgiving. The rumor mill is going crazy. My PM asked me to book a meeting room for the hours just prior, and I'm hard-pressed to find one. That can mean only one thing: another round of layoffs. (Happy holidays!) Our team leader heard some scuttlebutt that our project was getting canceled, so he found the biggest email thread he could, wrote "Microsoft is a dinosaur whose stock is going to zero," then hit Reply All. Never a good thing. Now I'm worried they're going to punish the whole org and that I won't land well. Or I might not land at all! What if that meeting room I booked was for my own firing?

Oh, Audrey, please keep me, Alexandra, and Lincoln in your prayers. I don't know what I'd do if I got managed out. The benefits here are gold-plated. If I still have a job after the holidays, I'll be happy to cover some of the food costs for the prospective parent brunch.

Soo-Lin

THURSDAY, NOVEMBER 18

Note from Audrey Griffin to the blackberry abatement specialist

Tom,

You'd *think* nobody lives in that big old haunted house above us, judging by the state of their yard. In fact, someone does. Their daughter, Bee, is in Kyle's class at Galer Street. I'd be thrilled to raise the subject of her blackberry bushes with the mother at pickup today.

Pigs? No pigs. Do take some chard, though.

Audrey

*

From: Bernadette Fox
To: Manjula Kapoor

I'm ecstatic you said yes!!! I've signed and scanned everything. Here's the deal with Antarctica. It will be three of us, so get two rooms. Elgie has a ton of miles on American, so let's try for three tickets that way. Our winter break dates are December 23 through January 5. If we have to miss a little school, that's fine. And the dog! We must find someplace willing to board a 130-pound, perpetually damp dog. Ooh—I'm late picking up Bee at school. Again, THANK YOU.

FRIDAY, NOVEMBER 19

Note from Ms. Goodyear sent home in our weekend folders

Dear Parents,

Word has spread about the incident at pickup yesterday. Luckily, nobody was hurt. But it gives us the opportunity to pause and revisit the rules outlined in the Galer Street handbook. (Italics mine.)

Section 2A. Article ii. There are two ways to pick up students.

By Car: Drive your vehicle to the school entrance. Please be mindful not to block the loading dock for Sound Seafood International.

On Foot: Please park in the north lot and meet your children on the canal path. *In the spirit of safety and efficiency, we ask that parents on foot do not approach the drive-up area.*

It always inspires me that we have such a wonderful community of parents who are so engaged with one another. However, the safety of our students is always top priority. So let's use what happened to Audrey Griffin as a teachable moment, and remember to save our conversations for coffee, not the driveway.

Kindly,
Gwen Goodyear
Head of School

*

Emergency-room bill Audrey Griffin gave to me to give to Mom

Patient name: Audrey Griffin
Attending Physician: C. Cassella

Emergency Room Visitation Fee	900.00
X Ray (Elective, NOT COVERED)	425.83
Rx: Vicodin 10MG (15 tablets, 0 refills)	95.70
Crutch Rental (Elective, NOT COVERED)	173.00
Crutch Deposit:	75.00
TOTAL	1,669.53

Notes: Visual inspection and basic neurological examination revealed no injury. Patient in acute emotional distress, demanded X ray, Vicodin, and crutches.

*

From: Soo-Lin Lee-Segal
To: Audrey Griffin

I heard Bernadette tried to run you over at pickup! Are you OK? Should I come by with dinner? WHAT HAPPENED?

*

From: Audrey Griffin
To: Soo-Lin Lee-Segal

It's all true. I needed to talk to Bernadette about her blackberry bushes, which are growing down her hill, under my fence, and invading my garden. I was forced to hire a specialist, who said Bernadette's blackberries are going to destroy the foundation of my home.

Naturally, I wanted to have a friendly chat with Bernadette. So I walked up to her car while she was in the pickup line. Mea culpa! But how else are you ever going to get a word with that woman? She's like Franklin Delano Roosevelt. You see her only from the waist up, driving past. I don't think she has once gotten out of her car to walk Bee into school.

I tried talking to her, but her windows were rolled up and she pretended not to see me. You'd think she was the first lady of France, with her silk scarf flung just so and huge dark glasses. I knocked on her windshield, but she drove off.

Over my foot! I went to the emergency room and got an incompetent doctor, who refused to accept that there was anything wrong with me.

Honestly, I don't know who I'm more furious at, Bernadette Fox or

Gwen Goodyear, for calling me out in the Friday Folder. You'd think *I* did something wrong! And mentioning me, but not Bernadette, by name! I created the Diversity Council. I invented Donuts for Dads. I wrote Galer Street's mission statement, which that fancy company in Portland was going to charge us ten thousand dollars for.

Maybe Galer Street is happy renting in an industrial park. Maybe Galer Street doesn't want the stability of owning its new campus. Maybe Gwen Goodyear would like me to cancel the Prospective Parent Brunch. I have a call in to her now. I'm not the least bit happy.

The phone is ringing. It's her.

MONDAY, NOVEMBER 22
Note from Ms. Goodyear sent home in the Monday Messenger

Dear Parents,

This is to clarify that Bernadette Fox, Bee Branch's mother, was driving the vehicle that ran over the other parent's foot. I hope you all had a wonderful weekend despite the rain.

Kindly,

Gwen Goodyear

Head of School

*

If someone had asked me, I could have told them what happened at pickup. It took me awhile to get in the car because Mom always brings Ice Cream and lets her sit in the front. Once that dog gets the front seat, she does not like to give it up. So Ice Cream was doing the thing she does when she wants to get her way, which is to go completely rigid and stare straight ahead.

"Mom!" I said. "You shouldn't let her get in the front—"

"She just jumped in." Mom pulled Ice Cream's collar and I shoved her butt and after a lot of grunting, Ice Cream finally got in the back. But she didn't sit on the seat like a normal dog. She stood on the floor squished behind the front seat, with this miserable look on her face, like, See what you guys make me do?

"Oh, stop being such a drama queen," Mom said to her.

I got buckled in. Suddenly Audrey Griffin started running toward the car all stiff and out of rhythm. You could just tell she hadn't run in about ten years.

"Oh, boy," Mom said. "What is it now?"

Audrey Griffin's eyes were wild, and she had a big smile as usual, and she was shaking a piece of paper at us. Her gray hair was coming out of its ponytail, and she was wearing clogs, and under her down vest you could see the pleats on her jeans bulging out. It was hard not to watch.

Señora Flores, who was on traffic duty, gave us the signal to keep it moving because there was a huge line of cars and the Sound Seafood guy was videotaping the traffic jam. Audrey motioned for us to pull over.

Mom was wearing dark glasses like she always does, even when it rains. "For all that gnat knows," Mom muttered, "I don't see her."

We drove off and that was that. I know for a fact we didn't run over anybody's foot. I love Mom's car, but riding in that thing is like "The Princess and the Pea." If Mom had run over something as big as a human foot, it would have set off the air bags.

*

Tuesday, November 23

From: Bernadette Fox

To: Manjula Kapoor

Attached please find a scan of an emergency room bill I suppose I should pay. One of the gnats at Galer Street claims I ran over her foot at pickup. I would laugh at the whole thing, but I'm too bored. See, that's why I call the mothers there "gnats." Because they're annoying, but not so annoying that you actually want to spend valuable energy on them. These gnats have done everything to provoke me into a fight over the past nine years — the stories I could tell! Now that Bee is graduating and I can smell the barn, it's not worth waging a gnat battle over. Could you check our various insurance policies to see if something covers it? On second thought, let's just straight-up pay the bill. Elgie wouldn't want our rates rising over something so trifling. He's never understood my antipathy toward the gnats.

All this Antarctica stuff is fantastic! Get us two Class B Queen rooms. I'm scanning our passports, where you'll find our birthdates, exact spelling of names, and all that other good stuff. I've thrown in driver's licenses and SS numbers just to be safe. You'll see on Bee's passport that her given name is Balakrishna Branch. (Let's just say I was under a lot of stress, and it seemed like a good idea at the time.) I realize that her plane ticket has to read "Balakrishna." But when it comes to the boat — nametag, passenger list, etc. — please move heaven and earth to make sure the divine child is listed as "Bee."

I see there's a packing list. Why don't you get us three of everything. I'm a women's medium, Elgie a men's XL, not for his girth but because he's six foot three without an ounce of flab, God bless him. Bee is small for her age, so why don't you get her whatever would fit a ten-year-old.

If you have questions about size and style, send us several to try on, as long as returns require no more from me than leaving a box outside for the UPS guy. Also, get all suggested books, which Elgie and Bee will devour, and which I will intend to devour.

I'd also like a fishing vest, one replete with zippered pockets. Back when I actually enjoyed leaving the house, I sat on a plane next to an environmentalist who spent his life zigzagging the globe. He had on a fishing vest, which contained his passport, money, glasses, and film canisters—yes, film, it was that long ago. The genius part: everything's in one place, it's handy, it's zipped in, plus you can whip it off and plop it down on the X-ray belt. I always said to myself: next time I travel, I'm going to get me one of those. My time has come. You'd better get two.

Have it all shipped to the manse. You're the best!

*

From: Manjula Kapoor
To: Bernadette Fox

Dear Ms. Fox,

I have received your instructions regarding the packing list and will proceed accordingly. What is manse? I do not find it in any of my records.

Warm regards,

Manjula

*

From: Bernadette Fox
To: Manjula Kapoor

You know what it's like when you go to Ikea and you can't believe how cheap everything is, and even though you may not *need* a hundred tea lights, my God, they're only ninety-nine cents for the whole bag? Or: Sure, the throw pillows are filled with a squishy ball of no-doubt toxic whatnot, but they're so bright and three-for-five-dollars that before you know it you've dropped five hundred bucks, not because you needed any of this crap, but because it was so damn *cheap?*

Of course you don't. But if you did, you'd know what Seattle real estate was like for me.

I came up here on a whim, pretty much. We'd been living in L.A. when Elgie's animation company was bought by Big Brother. Whoops, did I say Big Brother? I meant Microsoft. Around the same time, I'd had a Huge Hideous Thing happen to me (which we definitely do not need to get into). Let's just say that it was so huge and so hideous that it made me want to flee L.A. and never return.

Even though Elgie didn't *need* to relocate to Seattle, Big Brother strongly recommended it. I was more than happy to use it as an excuse to hightail it out of La-La Land.

My first trip up here, to Seattle, the realtor picked me up at the airport to look at houses. The morning batch were all Craftsman, which is all they have here, if you don't count the rash of view-busting apartment buildings that appear in inexplicable clumps, as if the zoning chief was asleep at his desk during the sixties and seventies and turned architectural design over to the Soviets.

Everything else is Craftsman. Turn-of-the-century Craftsman, beautifully restored Craftsman, reinterpretation of Craftsman, needs-some-love Craftsman, modern take on Craftsman. It's like a hypnotist put everyone from Seattle in a collective trance. *You are getting sleepy, when you wake up you will want to live only in a Craftsman house, the year won't matter to you, all that will matter is that the walls will be thick, the windows tiny, the rooms dark, the ceilings low, and it will be poorly situated on the lot.*

The main thing about this cornucopia of Craftsmans: compared to L.A., they were Ikea-cheap!

Ryan, the realtor, took me to lunch downtown at a Tom Douglas restaurant. Tom Douglas is a local chef who has a dozen restaurants, each one better than the last. Eating at Lola—that coconut cream pie! that garlic spread!—made me believe I could actually be happy making a life for myself in this Canada-close sinkhole they call the Emerald City. I blame you, Tom Douglas!

After lunch, we headed to the realtor's car for the afternoon rounds. Looming over downtown was a hill crammed with, say what, Craftsman houses. At the top of the hill, on the left, I could discern a brick building with a huge yard overlooking Elliott Bay.

"What's that?" I asked Ryan.

"Straight Gate," he said. "It was a Catholic school for wayward girls built at the turn of the century."

"What is it now?" I said.

"Oh, it hasn't been anything for years. Every so often some developer tries to convert it to condos."

"So it's for sale?"

"It was supposed to be converted into *eight* condos," he said. Then, his eyes began to pirouette, sensing a sale. "The property is three whole acres, mostly flat. Plus, you own the entire hillside, which you can't build on, but it does ensure privacy. Gatehouse—which is what the developers renamed it because Straight Gate seemed antigay—is about twelve thousand square feet, loaded with charm. There is some deferred maintenance, but we're talking crown jewel."

"How much are they asking?"

Ryan gave a dramatic pause. "Four hundred thousand." He watched with satisfaction as my jaw dropped. The other houses we'd seen were the same price, and they were on tiny lots.

Turns out the huge yard had been deeded to open space for tax pur-
poses, and the Queen Anne Neighborhood Association had designated
Straight Gate a historic site, which made it impossible to touch the exte-
rior or interior walls. So the Straight Gate School for Girls was stuck in
building-code limbo.

"But the area is zoned for single-family residences," I said.

"Let's take a look-see." Ryan shoved me into his car.

In terms of layout, it was kind of brilliant. The basement—where
the girls were penned, it appeared, from the dungeon door that locked
from the outside—was certainly creepy and depressing. But it was five
thousand square feet, which left seven thousand feet above-grade, a
swell size for a house. On the ground floor was a kitchen opening onto a
dining room—pretty fabulous—a huge receiving area that could be
our living room, and a couple of small offices. On the second floor was
a chapel with stained-glass windows and a row of confessionals. Perfect
for a master bedroom and closet! The other rooms could be a kid's
room and a guest room. All that was required was cosmetic: weather-
proofing, refinishing, paint. A cinch.

Standing on the back portico, facing west, I noticed ferry boats glid-
ing like snails along the water.

"Where are they going?" I asked.

"Bainbridge Island." Ryan answered. No dummy, he added, "Lots of
people have second homes out there."

I stayed an extra day and grabbed a beach house, too.

*

From: Manjula Kapoor
To: Bernadette Fox

Dear Ms. Fox,

The items on the packing list will be shipped to the Gate Avenue address.

Warm regards,
Manjula

*

From: Bernadette Fox
To: Manjula Kapoor

Oh! Could you make dinner reservations for us on Thanksgiving? You can call up the Washington Athletic Club and get us something for 7 PM for three. You *are* able to place calls, aren't you? Of course, what am I thinking? That's all you people do now.

I recognize it's slightly odd to ask you to call from India to make a reservation for a place I can see out my window, but here's the thing: there's always this one guy who answers the phone, "Washington Athletic Club, how may I direct your call?"

And he always says it in this friendly, flat...Canadian way. One of the main reasons I don't like leaving the house is because I might find myself face-to-face with a Canadian. Seattle is crawling with them. You probably think, U.S./Canada, they're interchangeable because they're both filled with English-speaking, morbidly obese white people. Well, Manjula, you couldn't be more mistaken.

Americans are pushy, obnoxious, neurotic, crass—anything and everything—the full catastrophe as our friend Zorba might say. Canadians are none of that. The way *you* might fear a cow sitting down in the middle of the street during rush hour, that's how *I* fear Canadians. To Canadians, everyone is equal. Joni Mitchell is interchangeable with a secretary at open-mic night. Frank Gehry is no greater than a hack pumping out McMansions on AutoCAD. John Candy is no funnier than Uncle Lou when he gets a couple of beers in him. No wonder the only Canadians anyone's ever heard of are the ones who have gotten the hell out. Anyone with talent who stayed would be flattened under an avalanche of equality. The thing Canadians don't understand is that some people are extraordinary and should be treated as such.

Yes, I'm done.

If the WAC can't take us, which may be the case, because Thanksgiving is only two days away, you can find someplace else on the magical Internet.

*

I was *wondering* how we ended up at Daniel's Broiler for Thanksgiving dinner. That morning, I slept late and came downstairs in my pajamas. I knew it was going to rain because on my way to the kitchen I passed a patchwork of plastic bags and towels. It was a system Mom had invented for when the house leaks.

First we lay out plastic bags under the leaks and cover them with towels or moving blankets. Then we put a spaghetti pot in the middle to catch the water. The trash bags are necessary because it might leak for hours in one place, then move over two inches. Mom's pièce de résistance is putting an old T-shirt inside the spaghetti pot to muffle the drip-drip-drip. Because that can drive you crazy when you're trying to sleep.

It was one of the rare mornings when Dad was around. He'd

gotten up early to go cycling, and he was sweaty, standing at the counter in his goony fluorescent racing pants, drinking green juice of his own making. His shirt was off, and he had a black heart-rate monitor strapped across his chest, plus some shoulder brace he invented, which is supposedly good for his back because it pulls his shoulders into alignment when he's at the computer.

"Good morning to you, too," he said disapprovingly.

I must have made some kind of face. But I'm sorry, it's weird to come down and see your Dad wearing a bra, even if it is for his posture.

Mom came in from the pantry covered with spaghetti pots. "Hello, Buzzy!" She dropped the pots with a huge clang. "Sorry-sorry-sorry. I'm really tired." Sometimes Mom doesn't sleep.

Dad tap-tap-tap-tapped across the floor in his bicycle shoes and plugged his heart-rate monitor into his laptop to download his workout.

"Elgie," Mom said, "when you get a chance, I'll need you to try on some waterproof boots for the trip. I got you a bunch to choose from."

"Oh, great!" He tap-tap-tapped into the living room.

My flute was on the counter and I played some scales. "Hey," I asked Mom, "when you were at Choate, was the Mellon Arts Center there yet?"

"Yes," Mom said, once more laden with pots. "It was the one and only time I was ever onstage. I played a Hot Box Girl in *Guys and Dolls.*"

"When Dad and I went to visit, the tour girl said Choate has a student orchestra, and every Friday people from Wallingford actually pay to see the concerts."

"That's going to be so great for you," Mom said.

"If I get in." I played some more scales, then Mom dropped the pots again.

"Do you have any idea how strong I'm being?" she erupted. "How much my heart is breaking that you'll be going off to boarding school?"

"You went to boarding school," I said. "If you didn't want me to, you shouldn't have made it sound so fun."

Dad pushed open the swing door, wearing muck boots with tags hanging off them. "Bernadette," he said, "it's amazing, all this stuff you've gotten." He put his arm around her and gave her a squeeze. "What, are you spending every waking hour at REI?"

"Something like that," Mom said, then turned back to me. "See, I never thought through the actual implication of you applying to boarding schools. I.e., that you'd be leaving us. But really, it's fine with me if you run off. I'll still see you every day."

I glowered at her.

"Oh, didn't I tell you?" she said. "I'm going to move to Wallingford and rent a house off campus. I already got a job working in the Choate dining hall."

"Don't even joke," I said.

"Nobody will know I'm your mother. You won't even have to say hi. I just want to look at your gorgeous face every day. But a little wave every now and then would sure warm a mum's heart." She did that last part sounding like a leprechaun.

"Mom!" I said.

"You have no choice in it," she said. "You're like the Runaway Bunny. There's no way for you to get away from me. I'll be lurking behind the sneeze guards with my plastic gloves, serving hamburgers on Wednesdays, fish on Fridays—"

"Dad, make her stop."

"Bernadette," he said. "Please."

"Both of you think I'm joking," she said. "Fine, think that."

"What are we doing for dinner tonight anyway?" I asked.

Something flashed on Mom's face. "Hold on." She went out the back door.

I grabbed the TV remote. "Aren't the Seahawks playing Dallas today?"

"It's on at one," Dad said. "How about we hit the zoo and come back for the game."

"Cool! We can see that new baby tree kangaroo."

"Want to ride bikes?"

"Will you be on your recumbent bike?" I asked.

"I think so." Dad made his hands into fists and twirled them. "These hills make it tough on my wrists—"

"Let's drive," I said quickly.

Mom returned. She wiped both hands on her pants and took a gigantic breath. "Tonight," she declared, "we are going to Daniel's Broiler."

"Daniel's Broiler?" Dad said.

"Daniel's Broiler?" I repeated. "You mean that totally random place on Lake Union with the tour buses that always advertises on TV?"

"That's the one," Mom said.

There was a silence. It was broken by a huge "Ha!" which was Dad. "In a million years," he said, "I'd never have thought you'd pick Daniel's Broiler for Thanksgiving."

"I like to keep you guessing," she said.

I used Dad's phone and texted Kennedy, who was with her mom on Whidbey Island. She was totally jealous we were going to Daniel's Broiler.

There was a piano player and they gave you free refills on lemonade, and the chocolate cake was a huge slab, they call it Death by Chocolate, and it was even bigger than the colossal slice you get at P. F. Chang's. When I got to school on Monday, everyone was all "No way, you got to go to Daniel's Broiler for Thanksgiving? That's so cool."

MONDAY, NOVEMBER 29
Note from Tom

Audrey,

I don't need chard. I need you to pay your bill. Otherwise, I will have to start lien proceedings.

*

Note from Audrey Griffin

Tom,

I find it rich indeed that *you* are threatening liens against *me*. My husband, Warren, who works in the DA's office, finds it especially amusing because *we* could take *you* to small claims court and easily win. Before it gets to that, I donned my thinking cap and came up with a friendlier solution. Please write an estimate for removing my neighbor's blackberries. If you need to get one of those machines, fine. Whatever it takes, as long as it doesn't literally involve swine.

Once I have this estimate in hand, I will pay you for your past work in full. But I'm hosting a very important school brunch in less than two weeks and I need my yard back.

WEDNESDAY, DECEMBER 1
Note from Tom

Audrey,

For a job this size, you'll definitely need the Hillside Thrasher. But my guy prefers not to use it until after the rains. The earliest he could start is May. For an estimate, we'd need to gain access to the neighbor's property. Did you ever talk to them that day? Do you have their phone number?

＊

Note from Audrey Griffin

Tom,

I feel like I am living in cuckooville. In ten days, Seattle's elite are descending on my home for a momentous school function and will want to enjoy my backyard. I can't have their clothing shredded by pricker bushes. May is not OK. One month from now is not OK. I don't care if you need to rent the Hillside Thrasher yourself. I need those blackberries gone by December 11.

As for gaining access to the neighbor's property for an estimate, she is very prickly, no pun intended. My suggestion is we meet at my house on Monday at 3PM sharp. I know for a fact that's when she'll be at school picking up her daughter. We can quickly climb through a hole in the side fence and look at her blackberry bushes.

＊

Excerpt from my report on Sir Ernest Shackleton

The Drake Passage is the body of water between the southern tip of South America at Cape Horn, Chile, and the Antarctic continent. The five-hundred-mile passage is named after the sixteenth-century privateer Sir Francis Drake. There is no significant land at the latitudes of the Drake Passage. This creates the unimpeded circular flow of the Antarctic Circumpolar Current. As a result, the Drake Passage is the roughest and most feared water in the world.

*

From: Bernadette Fox
To: Manjula Kapoor

The things you learn from eighth graders when you ask rhetorical questions like, What are you doing in school these days?

For instance, did you know the difference between Antarctica and the Arctic is that Antarctica has land, but the Arctic is just ice? I knew Antarctica was a continent, but I figured there was land up north, too. Also, did you know there are no polar bears in Antarctica? I didn't! I thought we'd be watching from our boat as poor put-upon polar bears attempted to leap from one melting iceberg to another. But you'll have to go to the North Pole for that sad spectacle. It's *penguins* that populate the South Pole. So if you had some idyllic image of polar bears frolicking with penguins, disabuse yourself now, because polar bears and penguins are literally on different ends of the earth. I suppose I should get out more.

Which brings me to the next thing I didn't know. Did you have any idea that getting to Antarctica requires crossing the Drake Passage? Do you know that the Drake Passage is the most turbulent body of water on the entire planet? Well, I do, because I just spent the last three hours on the Internet.

Here's the thing. Do you get seasick? People who don't get seasick have no idea what it's like. It's not just nausea. It's nausea plus losing the will to live. I warned Elgie: All that matters during those two days is that he keep me away from guns. In the throes of seasickness, blowing my brains out would be an easy call.

Ten years ago I saw a documentary on the siege of that Moscow theater. After just forty-eight hours of the terrorists confining the hostages to their seats with no sleep, the lights blazing, and being forced to pee in their pants—although if they had to shit, they could do so in the orchestra pit—well, more than a few hostages just stood up and walked to the exit knowing they'd get shot in the back. Because they were DONE.

My point is this. I'm getting really scared about the trip to Antarctica. And not just because I hate people, which, for the record, I still do. I just don't think I can make it across the Drake Passage. If it weren't for Bee, I'd certainly cancel the trip. But I can't let her down. Maybe you can find me something really strong for seasickness. And I don't mean Dramamine. I mean *strong*.

On another topic: I fully expect you to be charging me for the time it takes to read all my rambling emails!

*

**Letter from Bruce Jessup,
dean of admissions at Choate**

Dear Bee,

After a careful review of an outstanding group of Early Decision applicants, it is our great pleasure to offer you admission to Choate Rosemary.

We thoroughly enjoyed learning about your academic achievements and your varied interests during our review process. Your scores and assessments were so outstanding, in fact, that our director of studies, Hillary Loundes, has sent a letter under separate cover to your parents discussing your unique enrollment opportunities.

For now, let us warmly congratulate you on surviving this extremely competitive process. I have absolutely no doubt that you will find your classmates as stimulating, challenging, and engaging as we find you.

Sincerely,

Bruce Jessup

✳

**Letter from Hillary Loundes,
director of studies at Choate**

Dear Mr. and Mrs. Branch,

Congratulations on Bee's acceptance to Choate Rosemary. As you know better than anyone, Bee is an extraordinary young woman. So extraordinary, in fact, that I am recommending she skip third form (ninth grade) and enter Choate Rosemary in the fourth form (tenth grade).

This year, Choate Rosemary will accept one in ten applicants. Almost without exception, each candidate, like Bee, has excellent SSAT scores and near perfect GPAs. You may wonder how we wade through this sea of academic sameness consisting of grade and recommendation inflation to find students who will truly thrive at Choate Rosemary.

Since the late 1990s, our admissions department has been working with Yale's PACE (Psychology of Abilities, Competencies, and Expertise) Center to develop a hard measure of the soft skills required to adjust to the academic and social challenges of boarding school. The result of this work is something unique to the admissions process at Choate Rosemary, the Choate Self-Assessment.

It was on her CSA that Bee truly separated herself from the pack. In this new vocabulary of success, there are two words we like to use when describing our ideal student. Those words are "grit" and "poise." Your daughter tested off the charts for both.

As we all know, the worst thing that can happen to a gifted child is for her to grow bored. Therefore, we think it is in Bee's best interest to enter the fourth form.

Boarding tuition is $47,260. To guarantee Bee's place, please submit the enrollment contract and deposit by January 3.

I look forward to discussing this further. Above all, welcome to Choate Rosemary!

Sincerely,

Hillary Loundes

＊

From: Bernadette Fox
To: Manjula Kapoor

Do you hear the weeping all the way in India? Bee was accepted to Choate! Truly, I blame Elgie and myself, for regaling Bee with our boarding school adventures. Elgie went to Exeter; I went to Choate. It was nothing but brilliant kids, Grateful Dead concerts, and innovative ways to prevent your dorm room from reeking of bong water: what wasn't to like? A gigantic part of me does want my daughter sprung from the dreary provinciality of Seattle. And Bee is dying to go. So I have no choice but to cowboy up and not make this all about me.

Elgie is composing a letter about not wanting Bee to skip a grade. But that's not your concern. Please pay the deposit from our joint account. Any word on the seasickness medicine? I'm kind of freaking out.

More later, but I'm late picking up Bee and I can't find the dog.

＊

"OK," Mom said that day, as soon as I got in the car, "we have a problem. Ice Cream got into my closet, the door shut behind her, and I can't open it. She's stuck."

If that sounds weird, it isn't. Our house is old. All day and night it cracks and groans, like it's trying to get comfortable but can't, which I'm sure has everything to do with the huge amount of water it absorbs any time it rains. It's happened before that a door all of a sudden won't open because the house has settled around it. This was the first time Ice Cream was involved.

Mom and I raced home and I flew upstairs calling, "Ice Cream, Ice Cream." In Mom and Dad's bedroom, there's a row of confessionals they use as closets. The doors are rounded and pointy at the top. Behind a door, Ice Cream was barking, not a scared whimpering bark, but a playful bark. Trust me, she was laughing at us.

There were tools all over the floor and also some two-by-fours, which are always on hand in case we need to secure tarps to the roof. I pulled the door handle, and there was no give whatsoever.

"I tried everything," Mom said. "The fascia is totally rotted. See there? How the beam is sagging?" I knew Mom fixed up houses before I was born, but she was talking as if she were a whole different person. I didn't like it. "I tried to raise the doorframe with a jack," she said, "but I couldn't get enough leverage."

"Can't we just kick it in?" I said.

"The door opens out..." Mom drifted off in thought, then had an idea. "You're right. We'll have to kick it open, from the inside. Let's climb up the house and go in through the window." Now, that sounded fun.

We ran down the stairs and got a ladder from the shed and dragged it across the squishy lawn to the side of the house. Mom put down some plywood as a base for the ladder. "OK," she said, "you hold it. I'll climb up."

"She's my dog," I said. "You hold the ladder."

"Absolutely not, Bala. It's too dangerous."

Mom took off her scarf and wrapped it around her right hand, then began her ascent. It was funny seeing her in her Belgian shoes and Capri pants climbing up the paint-splattered ladder. She punched the stained glass with her protected hand and unlatched the window, then climbed in. An eternity passed.

"Mom!" I kept calling. The rotter didn't even stick her head out. I was so drenched and annoyed that I didn't care. I put my foot on the ladder. It was totally secure. I scrambled up superquick because what would have made me lose my balance was Mom catching me halfway up and yelling. I took me about eight seconds and I climbed in the window without slipping.

Ice Cream had no reaction when she saw me. She was more interested in Mom, who was karate-kicking the door, and karate-kicking the door, and karate-kicking the door. "Gaaah," Mom cried with each kick. Finally, the door skidded open.

"Nice job," I said.

Mom jumped. "Bee!" She was furious, and got furiouser when there was a loud crash outside. The ladder had fallen away from the house and was lying across the lawn.

"Whoops," I said. I gave Ice Cream a huge hug and breathed in her musty scent for as long as I could without passing out. "You are the worst dog ever."

"This came for you." Mom handed me a letter. The return address was the Choate seal. "Congratulations."

Mom had dinner delivered early and we drove out to celebrate with Dad. As we zoomed across the floating bridge over Lake Washington, my mind was wild with images of Choate. It was so vast and clean, and the buildings so majestic, red brick with ivy on the sides. It's what I imagined England would look like. Dad and I had visited in the spring when the tree branches were heavy with flowers and ducklings glided across sparkling ponds. I'd never seen a place so picturesque except for jigsaw puzzles.

Mom turned to me. "You're allowed to be happy about going away, you know."

"It's just weird."

I love Microsoft. It's where I went to day care, and when the sun was out they'd load us into big red wagons and pull us around to visit our parents. Dad made a treasure machine. I still don't understand how it worked, but when it was time to get picked up, you got to put in a coin and out would drop a treasure, matched perfectly to you. A boy who liked cars would get a Hot Wheels. Not just any Hot Wheels, but one he didn't already have. And if a girl was into baby dolls, she would get a bottle for her baby doll. The treasure machine is now on display in the Visitor Center because it's an early example of facial recognition technology, which is what Dad was doing in L.A. when Microsoft bought him out.

We parked illegally, and Mom swanned across the Commons carrying the take-out bags, with me at her heels. We entered Dad's building. Looming above the receptionist was a jumbo digital clock that counted down:

119 DAYS
2 HOURS
44 MINUTES
33 SECONDS

"That's what they call a *ship clock*," Mom explained. "It's how long until Samantha 2 ships. They put it up as motivation. No comment."

The same clock was in the elevator, the hallways, and even the bathrooms. It ticked down that whole meal in Dad's office, where we sat on the inflatable balls he uses instead of chairs, our take-out containers wobbling precariously on our knees. I was telling them about all the different kinds of penguins we were going to see on the trip.

"You want to know the coolest part?" Mom chimed in. "There isn't assigned seating at the dining room, and they have tables for four. That means the three of us can sit down and if we pile the extra chair with our gloves and hats, nobody can sit with us!"

Dad and I looked at each other, like, Is she joking?

"And penguins," Mom quickly added. "I'm wildly excited about all those penguins."

Dad must have told everyone we were coming, because people kept walking by and peeking through the glass, but acting like they weren't, which is what it must feel like to be famous.

"I wish this was more of a celebration," Dad said, glancing at his email. "But I have a video conference with Taipei."

"That's OK, Dad," I said. "You're busy."

*

From Dad

Dear Ms. Loundes,

First off, we're thrilled that Bee has been accepted to Choate. While I'm an Exonian myself, my wife, Bernadette, always said her happiest days were spent at Choate, and Bee has wanted to attend ever since she was a little girl.

Secondly, thank you for the kind words about Bee. We agree, she's extraordinary. However, we are strenuously opposed to her skipping a grade.

I have just looked over her application, and I realize there is no way you would know the essential fact about Bee: she was born with a heart defect, which required a half-dozen surgeries. As a result, she spent her first five years on and off at Seattle Children's Hospital.

Bee entered kindergarten on schedule, even though her little body was having difficulty keeping up. (She was in the zero percentile for height and weight during this time; she is still struggling to catch up, as you saw for yourself.) Yet her profound intelligence was already making itself known. Teachers encouraged us to get Bee tested. Really, though, Bernadette and I had no interest in the gifted-child industry. Perhaps because we both went to prep school and Ivy League universities ourselves, we did not fetishize them like other Seattle parents. Our primary concern was that our daughter know a modicum of normalcy after the sickening circumstances of her first five years.

It was a decision that has richly benefited Bee. We found a wonderful neighborhood school, Galer Street. Sure, Bee was "ahead" of the other kids in her class. In response, she took it upon herself to teach the slower kids to read and write. To this day, Bee stays after school and helps in homework lab. She didn't mention that on her application, either.

Choate has marvelous facilities. I'm certain Bee will find more than enough to keep her from "growing bored."

While we're on the subject, please indulge me while I tell you the story of the first and last time Bee ever claimed she was bored. Bernadette and I were driving Bee and a friend, both preschoolers, to a birthday party. There was traffic. Grace said, "I'm bored."

"Yeah," Bee mimicked, "I'm bored."

Bernadette pulled the car over, took off her seat belt, and turned around. "That's right," she told the girls. "You're bored. And I'm going to let you in on a little secret about life. You think it's boring now? Well, it only gets more boring. The sooner you learn it's *on you* to make life interesting, the better off you'll be."

"OK," Bee said quietly. Grace burst into tears and never had a play-date with us again. It was the first and last time Bee ever said she was bored.

We look forward to meeting you in the fall, when Bee arrives with her fellow third formers.

Sincerely,

Elgin Branch

＊

I am not sick! I was born with hypoplastic left heart syndrome, OK? It's a congenital condition where the mitral valve, left ventricle, aortic valve, and aorta don't develop completely and which required me to have three open-heart surgeries plus three more because of complications. The last surgery was when I was five. I know I'm supposed to be so smart, but guess what? I don't remember any of it! And double-guess what? I'm totally fine now, and have been for *nine and a half years*. Just take a time-out and ponder that. For two-thirds of my life I've been totally normal.

Mom and Dad bring me back to Children's every year for an echocardiogram and X rays that even the cardiologist rolls her eyes at because I don't need them. Walking through the halls, Mom is always, like, having a Vietnam flashback. We'll pass some random piece of art hanging on the wall and she'll grab onto a chair and say, Oh, God, that Milton Avery poster. Or, gulping a big breath, That ficus tree had origami cranes hanging on it that awful Christmas. And then she'll close her eyes while everyone just stands there, and Dad hugs her really tight, tears flooding his eyes, too.

All the doctors and nurses come out of their offices hailing me like the conquering hero, and the whole time I'm thinking, Why? They show me pictures of when I was a baby tucked into the hospital bed wearing a little cap, like I'm supposed to remember it. I don't even know what the point of any of it is besides I'm totally fine now.

The only thing now is I'm short and don't have breasts, which is annoying. Plus my asthma. Lots of doctors said I could have asthma even if I was born with a good heart. It doesn't keep me from doing anything like dancing or playing the flute. I don't have the thing where you wheeze. I have the even grosser thing where any time I get sick, even if it's a stomach virus, it's followed by two weeks of disgusting phlegm, which I have no choice but to cough up. I'm not saying it's the most pleasant thing to be sitting across from, but if you care about how it feels to me, I'll tell you that I barely notice it.

The nurse at school, Mrs. Webb, is totally ridiculous the way she's obsessed with my cough. I swear, on the last day of school I want to pretend to drop dead in her office just to freak her out. I seriously think that every day Mrs. Webb leaves Galer Street and it's a day I didn't die on her watch, she feels this soaring relief.

I'm totally off-task. Why did I even start writing all this? Oh, yeah. I'm not sick!

Thursday, December 2

From: Soo-Lin Lee-Segal
To: Audrey Griffin

You have been very dear *not* to ask me how the Microsoft town hall went. I'm sure you're dying to know if I was a casualty of the epic downsizing that has been all over the papers.

This was a top-to-bottom RIF, a ten percent haircut. In the old days, a reorg meant a hiring spree. Now it means layoffs. As I might have told you, my project was about to be canceled, and my PM got a little unhinged and flamed half of Microsoft. I maniacally checked meeting room reservations and the jobs website, trying to glean *something* about my future. Our top people landed at Windows Phone and Bing. When I tried to get answers from my PM about me, all I received in response was eerie silence.

Then, yesterday afternoon, I got pinged by an HR rep who wanted to see me in the meeting room down the hall the next day. (I had seen that appointment. I had no idea it was for me!)

Before I got out the teapot and threw myself a pity party, I dropped everything and found the nearest Victims Against Victimhood meeting, which helped enormously. (I know you're a huge skeptic when it comes to VAV, but they are my rock.)

I drove myself to work this morning because I didn't want the added indignity of having to load a bunch of boxes onto the Connector. I showed up in the meeting room, where the HR woman calmly informed me that our entire team, except for those who already left for Bing and Windows Phone, were being RIFed.

"However," she said, "you rank so well that we'd like to assign you to a special project located in Studio C."

Audrey, I just about fell over. Studio C is on the new Studio West campus, and their work is the most high profile at Microsoft. Good news: I'm getting *promoted!* Bad news: the new product I'm working on is in high gear, and I'll be expected to work weekends. It's a hush-hush project. I don't even know its name yet. Bad news: I may not be able to make the Prospective Parent Brunch. Good news: I'll definitely be able to pay for the food.

Talk soon, and go Huskies!

*

From: Ollie-O
To: Prospective Parent Brunch Committee

REAL-TIME ⚡ FLASH!
We're up to 60 RSVPs! I'm just **throwing out some fertilizer**, but:
Pearl Jam. I hear they've got kids entering kindergarten. If we get one of
them — **it doesn't have to be the singer** — I can **grow** it.

*

From: Audrey Griffin
To: Soo-Lin Lee-Segal

Great news about the promotion! I'll gladly take you up on your offer to
pay for the food. I still have enough green tomatoes in the greenhouse
to fry up for appetizers, plus dill, parsley, and cilantro for aioli. I've
stored two bushels of apples and want to make my rosemary tarte tatin
for dessert. For the main course, how about we get that traveling pizza
oven to cater? They can set up in the backyard, which frees up my
kitchen.

Ollie-O was right about buzz being "viral." Today at Whole Foods,
a woman I didn't even recognize recognized *me* and said she was looking forward to my brunch. Judging from the contents of her shopping
cart — imported cheese, organic raspberries, fruit wash spray — she is
the exact quality of parent we need at Galer Street. I saw her in the parking lot. She was driving a Lexus. Not a Mercedes, but close enough!

Did you hear? Shipping a sick child off to boarding school! Why am
I not surprised?

*

That day, I had a hall pass because our music teacher, Mr. Kangana, asked me to accompany the first graders for the song they were performing for World Celebration Day, and he needed me for rehearsal. I was at my locker getting my flute, and who did I run into, but Audrey Griffin. She was hanging some prayer rugs the third graders had woven for the art auction.

"I hear you're going to boarding school," she said. "Whose idea was that?"

"Mine," I said.

"I could never send Kyle to boarding school," Audrey said.

"I guess you love Kyle more than my mom loves me," I said, and played my flute as I skipped down the hall.

*

From: Manjula Kapoor
To: Bernadette Fox

Dear Ms. Fox,

I have researched medicines for motion sickness. The strongest remedy available by prescription in the U.S. is called ABHR transdermal cream. It is a composite of Ativan, Benadryl, Haldol, and Reglan, formulated into a cream for topical application. It was devised by NASA to administer to the cosmonauts to combat motion sickness in outer space. It has since been embraced by the hospice community to use on terminally ill cancer patients. It would be my sincere pleasure to send you links to various message boards that sing the high praise of ABHR cream. However, I must warn you, there are accompanying photographs of gravely ill patients, which you may find disturbing. I have taken the initiative to research the obtainment of ABHR cream. It is available only through "compound pharmacies." We do not have these in India. Apparently, they are widely used in the U.S. I have found a doctor who will call in a prescription. Please advise me how you wish to proceed.

Warm regards,

Manjula

*

To: Manjula Kapoor
From: Bernadette Fox

If it's good enough for astronauts and cancer patients, it's good enough for me! Call it in!

*

Note from Audrey Griffin

Tom,

Here's the check for your past work. To confirm, we'll meet at my place Monday afternoon and pop up the hill to the house with the blackberry bushes. I understand your hesitation about entering the neighbor's property uninvited. But I know for a fact nobody will be there.

*

MONDAY, DECEMBER 6

That day, we had art sixth period, and I had gunk in my throat, so I stepped into the hall to spit it in the water fountain, which is what I always did when I was in art. Who turned the corner as I was hawking it up? Mrs. Webb, the nurse. She got all panicked that I was spreading germs, which I tried to explain I wasn't, because white phlegm is *dead* germs. Ask a real doctor and not some office administrator whose only justification for calling herself a nurse isn't nursing school but a box of Band-Aids she keeps in her desk.

"I'll get my backpack," I grumbled.

I'd like to point out that Mr. Levy, my biology and homeroom teacher, has a daughter who has viral-induced asthma like me, and she plays travel hockey, so he knows my cough is no big deal. In a million years he would never send me to Mrs. Webb's office. When I get gunk in my throat, it's easy to tell because I'll be answering a question and my voice will start cutting out like a bad cell-phone connection. Mr. Levy will do this thing where he passes me a tissue behind his back. Mr. Levy is really funny. He lets the turtles walk around the classroom, and once he brought in liquid nitrogen and started freezing our uneaten lunch.

I didn't feel that bad about Mom having to pick me up early, because it was already sixth period. The thing I mainly felt bad about was that I wouldn't get to tutor at homework lab. The fourth graders were doing a debate, and I was helping them prepare. Their class was studying China, and the debate was going to be *pro and con* Chinese occupation of Tibet. Have you ever heard of such a thing? Galer Street is so ridiculous that it goes beyond PC and turns back in on itself to the point where fourth graders are actually having to debate the *advantages* of China's genocide of the Tibetan people, not to mention the equally devastating cultural genocide. I wanted them to say that one of the pros was that Chinese occupation is helping with the world food shortage because there are fewer Tibetan mouths to feed. But Mr. Lotterstein overheard me and told me I'd better not dare.

There I was, sitting on the overpass steps in the rain. (We weren't allowed to wait in the office ever since Kyle Griffin was sent there one day, and when nobody was looking he went through the Galer Street directory and started calling all the parents from the main office number. So when the parents looked at their cell phones, it said there was an incoming call from Galer Street. They'd answer, and Kyle screamed, "There's been an accident!" and hung up. From then on, all the kids had to wait outside.) Mom drove up. She didn't even ask how I was because she knows Mrs. Webb is totally annoying. On the drive home, I started playing my new flute. Mom never lets me play in the car because she's afraid someone might crash into us and my flute will impale me into the seat. I find that ridiculous, because how could that even happen?

"Bee—" Mom said.

"I know, I know." I put the flute away.

"No," Mom said. "Is that new? I've never seen it before."

"It's a Japanese flute called a *shakuhachi*. Mr. Kangana lent it to me from his collection. The first graders are going to sing for the parents on World Celebration Day and I'm going to accompany them. Last week, I went to rehearse, and they were just standing there singing. It was my idea they should do a little elephant dance, so I get to choreograph it."

"I didn't know you're choreographing a dance for the first graders." Mom said. "That's a huge deal, Bee."

"Not really."

"You need to tell me these things. Can I come?"

"I'm not sure when it is." I knew she didn't like coming to school, and probably wouldn't, so why pretend.

We got home, and I went up to my room, and Mom did what she always did, which was go out to the Petit Trianon.

I don't think I've mentioned the Petit Trianon yet. Mom likes to get out of the house during the day, especially because Norma and her sister come to clean, and they talk really loudly to each other from room to room. Plus the gardeners come inside to weed-whack. So Mom got an Airstream trailer and had a crane lower it into the backyard. It's where her computer is, and where she spends most of her time. I was the one who named it the Petit Trianon, after Marie Antoinette, who had a whole mini-estate built at Versailles, where she could go when she needed a break from Versailles.

So that's where Mom was, and I was upstairs starting my homework, when Ice Cream began barking.

From the backyard, I heard Mom's voice. "Can I help you with something?" she said, all dripping with sarcasm.

There was an idiotic little shriek.

I went to the window. Mom was standing on the lawn with Audrey Griffin and some guy in boots and overalls.

"I didn't think you would be home," Audrey sputtered.

"Apparently." Mom's voice was superbitchy. It was pretty funny.

Audrey started short-circuiting about our blackberry bushes and her organic garden and the guy who had a friend with a special machine and something that needed to get done this week. Mom just listened, which made Audrey talk even faster.

"I'll be happy to hire Tom to remove my blackberry bushes," Mom finally said. "Do you have a card?" A long painful silence as the guy searched his pockets.

"It seems like we're done," Mom said to Audrey. "So why don't you go back through the same hole in the fence you crawled in, and keep out of my cabbage patch." She spun around and marched back into the Petit Trianon and shut the door.

I was, like, Go Mom! Because here's the thing. No matter what people say about Mom now, she sure knew how to make life funny.

*

From: Bernadette Fox
To: Manjula Kapoor

Attached, please find information for a fellow who "abates" blackberry vines. (Can you believe there's such a thing?!) Contact him and tell him to do who-what-when-where-how he needs. I'll pay for it all.

*

Five minutes later, Mom followed it up with this:

From: Bernadette Fox
To: Manjula Kapoor

I need a sign made. 8 feet wide by 5 feet high. Here's what I want it to read:

PRIVATE PROPERTY

NO TRESPASSING

Galer Street Gnats

Will Be Arrested

and Hauled Off to Gnat Jail

Make the sign itself the loudest, ugliest red, and the lettering the loudest, ugliest yellow. I'd like it placed on the western edge of my property line, at the bottom of the hill, which will be accessible once we've *abated* the despised blackberries. Make sure the sign is facing toward the neighbor's yard.

*

TUESDAY, DECEMBER 7

From: Manjula Kapoor
To: Bernadette Fox

I am confirming that the sign you would like fabricated is *eight feet wide* by *five feet high*. The gentleman I have contracted remarked it is unusually large and seems out of proportion for a residential area.

Warm regards,
Manjula

*

From: Bernadette Fox
To: Manjula Kapoor

You bet your bindi that's how big I want it.

*

From: Manjula Kapoor
To: Bernadette Fox

Dear Ms. Fox,

The sign has been ordered and will be erected the same day Tom completes the abatement work.

Also, I am pleased to inform you I have found a doctor willing to write a prescription for ABHR cream. The only compound pharmacy in Seattle that will fill it, unfortunately, does not deliver. I inquired about messenger services, but, alas, the pharmacy insists that you pick up the prescription because they are required by law to review the side effects with you in person.

Attached please find the address of the pharmacy and a copy of the prescription.

Warm regards,

Manjula

*

FRIDAY, DECEMBER 10

From: Bernadette Fox
To: Manjula Kapoor

I'm heading down to the pharmacy now. Not a terrible thing to be getting out of the house while this infernal machine with spikes, telescoping arms, and vicious rotors is chewing up my hillside and spraying mulch everywhere. Tom has literally lashed himself on top of the beast so he doesn't get bucked off. I wouldn't be surprised if it starts spitting fire.

Oh! The fishing vests arrived. Thank you! Already, I've tucked away my glasses, car keys, cell phone. I may never take this thing off.

*

From: Soo-Lin Lee-Segal
To: Audrey Griffin

As Ollie-O would say...**REAL-TIME ⚡ FLASH!**

I told you I was being made admin of a new team? I just found out the team is Samantha 2, headed by none other than Elgin Branch!

Audrey, my body is a cauldron of emotions right now! When Elgin unveiled Samantha 2 at the TED conference in February, it caused a near riot on the Internet. In less than a year, his is the fourth-most-watched TEDTalk of all time. Bill Gates recently said his favorite project in the whole company is Samantha 2. Last year, Elgin was given a Technical Recognition Award, Microsoft's highest honor. The Samantha 2 guys, and Elgin in particular, are like rock stars around here. You go over to Studio West and you can tell by their swagger they're on Samantha 2. *I* know I'm good at my job, but to be put on Samantha 2 means everyone here knows it, too. It's a giddy feeling.

Then there's Elgin Branch himself. His rudeness and arrogance that day on the Connector, it was a slap in the face that still stings. Wait until you hear what happened this morning.

I went to HR to get my new key card and office assignment. (In ten years, this is the first time I've had a window office!) I was unpacking my photos, mugs, and snow baby collection when I looked up and saw Elgin Branch across the atrium. He wasn't wearing any shoes, just socks, which I found odd. I caught his eye and waved. He vaguely smiled, then kept walking.

I decided to be proactive (one of the three P's that serve as the interpersonal foundation for Victims Against Victimhood) and initiate our first face-to-face meeting in our new roles as manager and admin.

Elgin was at his stand-up desk, his hiking boots in a tangle at his feet. Immediately, I was struck by the number of patent cubes haphazardly piled around the office. (Anytime a developer patents something, he receives a ceremonial cube, a cute thing we do at MS.) My last GM had four. On Elgin's windowsill alone there were twenty, not to mention those that had fallen on the floor.

"Is there something I can do for you?" he said.

"Good morning." I straightened myself. "I'm Soo-Lin Lee-Segal, the new admin."

"Nice to meet you." He held out his hand.

"We've actually met. I have a son, Lincoln, at Galer Street, in Bee's class."

"I'm sorry," he said. "Of course."

The Dev lead, Pablo, popped his head in. "It's a beautiful day, neighbor." (Everyone on the team teases Elgin with Mr. Rogers references. It's a quirk of Elgin's, apparently, that as soon as he gets inside, like Mr. Rogers, he removes his shoes. Even on his TEDTalk, which I just rewatched, Elgin is standing there in his socks. In front of Al Gore and Cameron Diaz!) "We're on for noon," Pablo went on. "We have a third-party meeting in South Lake Union. How about we turn it into lunch downtown? Wild Ginger?"

"Great," answered Elgin. "It's next to the light rail station. I can go straight to the airport." I had seen on the Samantha 2 calendar that Elgin has an out-of-town presentation tomorrow.

Pablo turned, and I introduced myself. "Hooray!" he said. "Our new admin! Man, we've been dying around here without you. How about you join us for lunch?"

"You must have heard my stomach growling," I chirped. "I have a car. I can drive us downtown."

"Let's take the 888 Shuttle," Elgin said. "I'm going to need the Wi-Fi to get some emails out."

"The 888 Shuttle it is," I said, insulted at the rejection but a little consoled because the 888 Shuttle is for VPs and up, and this will be my first opportunity to ride it. "Wild Ginger at noon. I'll make a reservation."

So here I am now, dreading the meal on what should be the happiest day of my life. Oh, Audrey, I hope your day is going better than mine.

*

From: Audrey Griffin
To: Soo-Lin Lee-Segal

Who cares about Elgin Branch? I care about you. I'm so proud of everything you've overcome since the divorce. Finally, you're getting the recognition you deserve.

My day is going dandy. A machine is ripping out all the blackberry vines from Bernadette's hill. It has put me in such soaring spirits that I am able to laugh off an incident at Galer Street that otherwise might have landed me in a snit.

Gwen Goodyear grabbed me this morning and asked to speak privately in her office. Who was sitting there in a big leather chair with his back to me? Kyle! Gwen shut the door and went behind her desk. There was a chair next to Kyle, so I sat down.

Gwen opened her drawer. "We found something in Kyle's locker yesterday." She held up an orange pill bottle. It had my name on it—it was the Vicodin prescription I got after Our Lady of Straight Gate tried to plow me over in her car.

"What's that doing here?" I said.

"Kyle?" Gwen said.

"I don't know," said Kyle.

"Galer Street has a zero-tolerance drug policy," Gwen said.

"But it's *prescription* medicine," I said, still not understanding her point.

"Kyle," Gwen said. "Why was it in your locker?"

I did not like where this was going. Not one bit. I told her: "I went to the emergency room thanks to Bernadette Fox. I left *on crutches*, if you remember. I asked Kyle to hold my purse, and the prescription medicine. Good Lord."

"When did you realize your Vicodin was missing?" Gwen asked.

"Not until this moment," I said.

"Why is the bottle empty? Let Kyle answer this, Audrey." She turned to Kyle. "Kyle, why is it empty?"

"I don't know," Kyle answered.

"I'm sure it was empty when we got it," I said. "You know how understaffed they are over at the UW Medical. They probably forgot to fill it. Are we done yet? Maybe you haven't heard, but I'm hosting a party tomorrow for sixty prospective parents." I got up and left.

Now that I write this, I'd like to know what *Gwen Goodyear* was doing in Kyle's locker. Don't they have locks on them? Isn't that why they're called lockers?

*

All our lockers have combination locks built into the doors. It's a total drag to turn the little dials back and forth a million times whenever you need to get something. Everyone hates it. But Kyle and the juvies figured out a way around it, which is to smash the locks until they break off. Kyle's locker door is permanently ajar. That's what Ms. Goodyear was doing in Kyle's locker.

*

From: Bernadette Fox
To: Manjula Kapoor

It was the first time I had been downtown in a year. I immediately remembered why: the pay-to-park meters.

Parking in Seattle is an eight-step process. Step one, find a place to park (gooood luuuuck!). Step two, *back* into the angled parking space (who ever innovated *that* should be sentenced to the chokey). Step three, find a ticket dispenser that *isn't* menacingly encircled by a stinky mosaic of beggars/bums/junkies/runaways. This requires step four, crossing the street. Oh, plus you've forgotten your umbrella (there goes your hair, which you stopped worrying about toward the end of the last century, so that's a freebie). Step five, slide your credit card into the machine (small miracle if you've found one that hasn't been filled with epoxy by some misguided malcontent). Step six, return to your car (passing aforementioned putrid gauntlet, who heckle you because you didn't give them money on the way there — oh, and did I mention, they all have shivering dogs?). Step seven, affix the ticket to the proper window (is it passenger-side for back-in angle parking? or driver-side? I would read the rules on the back of the sticker but can't because WHO THE HELL BRINGS READING GLASSES TO PARK THEIR CAR?). Step eight, pray to the God you don't believe in that you have the mental wherewithal to remember what the hell it was you came downtown for in the first place.

Already I wished a Chechen rebel would shoot me in the back.

The compound pharmacy was cavernous, wood-paneled, and home to a few poorly stocked shelves. In the middle of it sat a brocade sofa, over which hung a Chihuly chandelier. The place made no sense at all, so already I was pretty much a wreck.

I approached the counter. The girl was wearing one of those white headdresses that look like a nun's hat without the wings. I have no idea what ethnicity that made her, but there are tons of them here, especially working at rental-car places. One of these days, I really need to ask.

"Bernadette Fox," I said.

Her eyes met mine, then flashed mischief. "One moment." She stepped onto a platform and whispered something to another pharmacist. He lowered his chin and examined me severely over his spectacles. Both he and the girl descended. Whatever was about to happen, they had decided beforehand it was a two-person job.

"I received the prescription from your doctor," said the gentleman. "It was written for seasickness, for a cruise you'll be taking?"

"We're going to Antarctica over Christmas," I said, "which requires crossing the Drake Passage. The statistics about the speed of the swirling water and the heights of the swells would shock you if I told you. But I can't, because I'm hopeless when it comes to remembering numbers.

Plus, I'm trying really hard to block it out. I blame my daughter. I'm only going because of her."

"Your prescription is for ABHR," he said. "ABHR is basically Haldol with some Benadryl, Reglan, and Ativan thrown in."

"Sounds good to me."

"Haldol is an antipsychotic." He dropped his reading glasses into his shirt pocket. "It was used in the Soviet prison system to break prisoners' wills."

"And I'm only discovering it now?" I said.

This guy was proving resistant to my many charms, or else I am without charm, which is probably the case. He continued. "It has some severe side effects, tardive dyskinesia being the worst. Tardive dyskinesia is characterized by uncontrollable grimacing, tongue protrusion, lip smacking…"

"You've seen those people," the Flying Nun gravely added. She held a contorted hand up to her face, cocked her head, then shut one eye.

"You obviously don't get seasick," I said. "Because a couple of hours of that is a day at the beach by comparison."

"Tardive dyskinesia can last forever," he said.

"Forever?" I said weakly.

"The likelihood of tardive dyskinesia is about four percent," he said. "It increases to ten percent for older women."

I blew out really hard. "Oh, man."

"I spoke to your doctor. He wrote you a prescription for a scopolamine patch for motion sickness, and Xanax for anxiety."

Xanax, I had! Bee's battalion of doctors had always sent me home with Xanax or some sleeping pill. (Have I mentioned? I don't sleep.) I never took them, because the one time I did, they left me nauseous and not feeling like myself. (I know, that should have been a selling point. What can I say? I've grown accustomed.) But the problem with the Xanax and the hundreds of other pills I had squirreled away was this: they were currently jumbled together in a Ziploc bag. Why? Well, once, I was thinking about OD'ing, so I dumped the contents of every prescription bottle into my two hands — they didn't even fit, that's how many I had — just to eyeball to see if I could swallow them all. But then I cooled off on the whole idea and dumped the pills in a baggie, where they languish to this day. Why did I want to OD? you're probably wondering. Well, so am I! I don't even remember.

"Do you have some kind of laminated chart of what the pills look like?" I asked the pharmacist. My thinking was, maybe I could figure out which ones were Xanax and return them to their proper container. The poor guy looked baffled. Who can blame him?

"Fine," I said. "Give me the Xanax and that patch thing."

I removed myself to the brocade couch. It was murderously uncomfortable. I put my leg up and leaned back. That was more like it. It was a fainting couch, I now realized, and wanted to be lain upon. Hovering over me was the Chihuly chandelier. Chihulys are the pigeons of Seattle. They're everywhere, and even if they don't get in your way, you can't help but build up a kind of antipathy toward them.

This one was all glass, of course, white and ruffly and full of dripping tentacles. It glowed from within, a cold blue, but with no discernible light source. The rain outside was pounding. Its rhythmic splatter only made this hovering glass beast more haunting, as if it had arrived with the storm, a rainmaker itself. It sang to me, Chihuly...Chihuly. In the seventies, Dale Chihuly was already a distinguished glassblower when he got into a car accident and lost an eye. But that didn't stop him. A few years later, he had a surfing mishap and messed up his shoulder so badly that he was never able to hold a glass pipe again. That didn't stop him, either. Don't believe me? Take a boat out on Lake Union and look in the window of Dale Chihuly's studio. He's probably there now, with his eye patch and dead arm, doing the best, trippiest work of his life. I had to close my eyes.

"Bernadette?" said a voice.

I opened my eyes. I had fallen asleep. This is the problem with never sleeping. Sometimes you actually do, at the worst times: like this time: in public.

"Bernadette?" It was Elgie. "What are you doing asleep in here?"

"Elgie—" I wiped the drool off my cheek. "They wouldn't give me Haldol, so I have to wait for Xanax."

"*What?*" He glanced out the window. Standing on the street were some Microsoft people I vaguely recognized. "What are you wearing?"

He was referring to my fishing vest. "Oh, this. I got it from the Internet."

"Could you please stand up?" he said. "I have a lunch. Do I need to cancel it?"

"God, no!" I said. "I'm fine. I didn't sleep last night and just dozed off. Go, do, be."

"I'm going to come home for dinner. Can we go out to dinner tonight?"

"Aren't you going to D.C.—"

"It can wait," he said.

"Yeah, sure," I said. "Buzz and I will pick a place."

"Just me and you." He left.

And this is when it began to unravel: I could swear one of the people waiting for him outside was a gnat from Galer Street. Not the one who's hassling us about the blackberries, but one of her flying monkeys. I blinked to make sure. But Elgie and his group had been absorbed into the lunch rush.

My heart was really thumping. I should have stayed and popped one of those Xanax. But I couldn't stand to be in that compound pharmacy anymore, trapped with the icy portent. I blame you, Dale Chihuly!

I fled. I had no idea which way I was pointed, where I was even headed. But I must have gone up Fourth Avenue, because the next thing I knew, I was standing outside the Rem Koolhaas public library.

I had stopped, apparently. Because a guy approached me. A graduate student, he looked like. Completely nice, nothing mean or threatening about him.

But he recognized me.

Manjula, I have no idea how. The only photograph of me floating around was one taken twenty years ago, right before the Huge Hideous Thing. I am beautiful, my face radiating with confidence, my smile bursting with the future of my choosing.

"Bernadette Fox," I blurted.

I am fifty, slowly going mad.

This can't make sense to you, Manjula. It doesn't have to. But you see what happens when I come into contact with people. It doesn't bode well for the whole Antarctica thing.

*

Later that day, Mom picked me up. Maybe she was a little quiet, but sometimes that happens, because on the way to school she listens to "The World" on PRI, which is usually a downer, and that day was no exception. I got into the car. A terrible report was on about the war in the Democratic Republic of Congo, and how rape was being used as a weapon. All the females were getting raped, from baby girls, six months old, all the way to eighty-year-old grandmothers, and every age in between. More than one thousand women and girls were getting raped *each month*. It had been going on for *twelve years* and nobody was doing anything about it. Hillary Clinton had gone there and promised to help, which gave everyone hope, but then all she did was give money to the corrupt government.

"I can't listen to this!" I smacked the radio off.

"I know it's horrific," Mom said. "But you're old enough. We live a life of privilege in Seattle. That doesn't mean we can literally switch off these women, whose only fault was being born in the Congo during a civil war. We need to bear witness." She turned the radio back on.

I crumpled in my seat and fumed.

"The war in Congo rages on with no end in sight," the announcer said. "And now comes word of a new campaign by the soldiers, to find the women they have already raped and re-rape them."

"Holy Christ on a cross!" Mom said. "I draw the line at re-raping." And she turned off NPR.

We sat in silence. Then, at ten of four, we had to turn the radio back on because Fridays at ten of four is when we listen to our favorite person ever, Cliff Mass. If you don't know who Cliff Mass is, well, he's this thing me and Mom have, this awesome weather geek who loves weather so much you have no choice but to love him in return.

Once, I think I was ten, and I was home with a babysitter while Mom and Dad went to Town Hall for some lecture. The next morning, Mom showed me a picture on her digital camera. "Me and guess who?" I had no idea. "You're going to be so jealous when you find out." I made a mean face at her. Mom and Dad call it my Kubrick face, and it was a glowering face I made when I was a little baby. Mom finally screamed, "Cliff Mass!"

Oh my God, can someone please stop me before I write more about Cliff Mass?

Here's my point: first, because of the re-raping, and second, because Mom and I were so in love with Cliff Mass, of course we didn't talk much on the way home that day, so I couldn't have known she was traumatized.

We pulled in the driveway. There were a bunch of giant trucks on the side street, and one was parked on our loop to keep the gate open. Workmen were coming and going. It was hard to make out what exactly was going on through the rain-smeared windshield.

"Don't ask," Mom said. "Audrey Griffin demanded we get rid of the blackberries."

When I was little, Mom brought me to see *The Sleeping Beauty* at the Pacific Northwest Ballet. In it, an evil witch puts a curse on the princess, which makes her fall asleep for one hundred years. A gentle fairy protects the sleeping princess by enveloping her in a forest of briars. During the ballet, the princess is sleeping as thorny branches grow thicker around her. That's what I felt like in my bedroom. I knew our blackberry vines were buckling the library floor and causing weird lumps in the carpet and shattering basement windows. But I had a smile on my face, because while I slept, there was a force protecting me.

"Not *all of them!*" I cried. "How could you?"

"Don't get all peevish on me," she said. "I'm the one taking you to the South Pole."

"Mom," I said, "we're not going to the South Pole."

"Wait, we're not?"

"The only place tourists go is the Antarctic Peninsula, which is like the Florida Keys of Antarctica." It's shocking, but Mom genuinely didn't seem to know this. "It's still zero degrees," I continued. "But it's a teeny-tiny part of Antarctica. It's like someone saying they're going to Colorado for Christmas, and then you ask them, How was New York? Sure, it's the United States. But it's just totally ignorant. Please tell me you knew that, Mom, but you forgot because you're tired."

"Tired *and* ignorant," she said.

*

From: Soo-Lin Lee-Segal
To: Audrey Griffin

Before you write me off as the Girl Who Cried Real-Time Flash!, listen to this.

As I told you, Elgin, Pablo, and I had a lunch meeting downtown. Elgin insisted we take the 888 Shuttle. (Which, it turns out, is no different from the Connector. All these years I'd imagined the doors opening and it looking like the inside of a genie's bottle or something.) There was construction downtown, so when we got to the corner of Fifth and Seneca, traffic had completely stopped. Elgin said it would be faster to walk. It was pouring buckets, but it wasn't my place to argue so I followed them off the shuttle.

Now, Audrey, you're always talking about God's plan. For the first time, I understand what you mean. I would have thought God was forsaking me when he made me walk three blocks in the pouring rain. But it turns out there was something on that third block that God intended me to see.

Elgin, Pablo, and I were scurrying along Fourth Avenue, heads down, clutching closed our hoods over our faces. I happened to glance up, and what do I see? Bernadette Fox asleep in a pharmacy.

I repeat, Bernadette Fox just lying on a couch with her eyes closed in the middle of a compound pharmacy. She might as well have been in the window at Nordstrom for all of Seattle to see. She wore dark glasses, trousers and loafers, a men's shirt with silver cuff links, and some kind of vest underneath her raincoat. Also, she was clutching a fancy purse with one of her silk scarves tied to it.

Pablo and Elgin were up ahead on the corner, turning in circles, wondering where I had gone. Elgin spotted me and marched over, looking irate.

"I—" I stammered, "I'm sorry—" It was my first day on the job. Whatever was going on with Bernadette, I wanted no part of it. I ran to catch up, but it was too late. Elgin had already looked in the window. His face went white. He pulled open the door and went inside.

By this time, Pablo had come over. "Elgin's wife is asleep in there," I explained.

"It's really coming down," Pablo said. He smiled and refused to turn his head toward the pharmacy.

"I already know what I'm going to order for lunch," I said. "The salt-and-pepper calamari. It's not on the menu, but they make it for you if you ask."

"Sounds good," he said. "I'm probably going to have to check out the menu before I order."

Finally, Elgin came out, looking shaky. "Change my flight to D.C.," he said. "I want to leave in the morning."

I wasn't completely up to speed on Elgin's schedule. But I did know his presentation was in D.C. at four p.m. I opened my mouth to explain that with the time difference—

"Just—" he said.

"Fine."

Then, wouldn't you know, a Connector passed by. Elgin darted into traffic and stopped it. He conferred with the driver, then waved me over. "He's taking you back to Redmond," Elgin said. "S-plus me my new itinerary."

What choice did I have? I boarded the shuttle. Pablo did bring me back an order of salt-and-pepper calamari, but it didn't travel well.

*

From: Audrey Griffin
To: Soo-Lin Lee-Segal

This will have to be quick because I'm up to here with party prepara-
tions. The real "flash update" is that you're starting to realize that God
is driving the bus. (In your case, literally. Honk, honk!) I'd love to talk
to you more about it sometime. Coffee, maybe? I can come out to
Microsoft.

*

**Email from the guy outside the library to
his architecture professor at USC**

From: Jacob Raymond
To: Paul Jellinek

Dear Mr. Jellinek,

Remember how I told you I was going to Seattle on a pilgrimage to
see the public library, and I joked that I'd let you know if I had a Bernadette Fox sighting? Well, guess who I saw outside the public library?

Bernadette Fox! She was about fifty, her hair was brown and wild.
The only reason I looked twice was because she was wearing a fishing
vest, which is something you notice.

There's the one picture of Bernadette Fox taken about twenty years
ago when she won her award. And you hear all the speculation about
her, how she moved to Seattle and became a recluse or went crazy. I had
a really strong feeling it was her. Before I could say anything, she
abruptly volunteered, "Bernadette Fox."

I started gushing. I told her I was a graduate student at USC, and had visited Beeber Bifocal every time they opened it to the public, and that our winter project is a competition to reinterpret the Twenty Mile House.

I suddenly realized I had said too much. Her eyes were vacant. Something was seriously wrong with her. I wanted to get a picture of me with the elusive Bernadette Fox. (Talk about a profile pic!) But then I thought better of it. This woman has given me so much already. The relationship has been one-way, and still I want to take *more?* I bowed to her with my hands in prayer position and walked into the library, leaving her standing outside in the rain.

I feel bad because I think I might have messed her up. Anyway. In case you were wondering: Bernadette Fox is walking around Seattle in the middle of winter wearing a fishing vest.

See you in class,

Jacob

*

Mom and Dad went out to dinner that night without me, to some Mexican place in Ballard, which was fine because Friday is when a bunch of us go to Youth Group and they have fried shrimp, plus they let us watch a movie, which was *Up*.

Dad left at five in the morning to catch a plane because he had Samantha 2 business at Walter Reed.[1] Claire Anderssen was having a

---

1 I'm not divulging any proprietary Microsoft information when I say this. Microsoft is built on ideas, and you can't just go blabbing those ideas, even to your family, because they might blab it to Kennedy, who blabs it to her dad, and even though he works at Amazon, he used to work at Microsoft and knows people, who he tells, and Dad hears about it, and you learn your lesson. Normally I'd never say where Dad was going on business, but I looked it up on the Internet, and there's a video of his presentation at Walter Reed hospital that afternoon, so it's totally public.

party on Bainbridge Island, and I wanted to go out to our house there, plus I wanted Kennedy to spend the night. Kennedy gets on Dad's nerves, and there was no way we could have a sleepover if he was there, so I was happy he was gone.

Mom and I had a plan. We'd catch the 10:10 to Bainbridge, and Kennedy would take the passenger ferry after gymnastics, which she tried to get out of, but her mom wouldn't let her.

SATURDAY, DECEMBER 11
Cliff Mass blog post

This storm is turning into a complex weather event. I will need some time to describe it because the media is not fully comprehending its implications. The cloud band leading the approaching weather system hit western Washington yesterday afternoon. The latest high-resolution computer models show sustained winds of 40–50 mph with gusts of 70–80 mph and the low going north of us instead of the southern trajectory predicted earlier.

On the radio yesterday, I expressed extreme skepticism at yesterday's track for the low center, and the latest satellite pictures confirm that the center of the low will cross southern Vancouver Island and move into British Columbia. Such a position allows warm, moist air to move right into western Washington with the potential for heavy rain.

Yesterday, the media shrugged off my serious weather warnings for Seattle as a Henny Penny false alarm. *This is no false alarm.* The unforeseen storm path has allowed a low-pressure system to move north of Puget Sound and warm temperatures to abound.

In Seattle, warm temperatures, associated with moist, Pine-apple Express air, have already produced a rainfall of two inches between 7 PM yesterday and 7 AM this morning. I am now going out on a limb and projecting that this flow will stagnate over Puget Sound and the deluge will continue for hours. We are in the midst of a most notable weather show.

*

See, that's what I mean about loving Cliff Mass. Because, basically, all he's saying is it's going to rain.

*

From: Ollie-O
To: Prospective Parent Brunch Committee

REAL-TIME ⚡ FLASH!

The day of the PPB has come. Unfortunately, our biggest get, **the sun**, is going to be a no-show. Ha-ha. That was my idea of a joke.

It's imperative we **run tight**. It would be **death-dealing** for Galer Street if the prospectives felt their time was being wasted, especially during the **holiday shopping season**. Our objective is for the **Mercedes Parents** to see and be seen, and then spring them so they can storm U Village and take advantage of these astonishing **fifty-percent-off store-wide sales.**

10:00–10:45 — MPs arrive. Drinks and food passed.
10:45 — Mr. Kangana and parent Helen Derwood arrive with kin-dergarteners, who enter, quiet as **church mice**, through side door and situate themselves for marimba performance.

10:55 — Gwen Goodyear gives short welcoming speech, then directs MPs to sunroom. Mr. Kangana leads kindergarteners in marimba performance.

11:15 — Closing remarks.

Gwen Goodyear will be stationed at the door, **bidding adieux**, and handing out Galer Street swag. There is no way to overemphasize the importance of this. Just because they're **Mercedes Parents** doesn't mean they're not highly receptive to **free shit**. (Excuzey-moi!)

Cheers!

*

From: Soo-Lin Lee-Segal
To: Audrey Griffin

GOOD LUCK TODAY! I just spoke with Pizza Nuovo. The rain doesn't affect their wood-burning oven. They will set up a tent in the backyard. I'm stuck in Redmond because Elgin is making a presentation in another city and he wants me at my desk to troubleshoot any glitches. No comment.

*

From: Ollie-O
To: Prospective Parent Brunch Committee

Crisis. Enormous billboard hovering over Audrey's house. Erected overnight by **crazy neighbor**. (Fellow Galer Street parent?) Audrey hysterical. Husband calling city attorney. I don't do **black swan**.

*

From: Helen Derwood, PhD
To: Galer Street Kindergarten Parents
Cc: Galer Street All-School List

Dear Parents,

I assume your little ones have told you snippets about the shocking events at today's brunch. No doubt you are concerned and confused. As the only kindergarten parent in attendance, I've been inundated with phone calls asking what really happened.

As many of you know, I'm a counselor at Swedish Medical Center, specializing in post-traumatic stress disorder (PTSD). I went to New Orleans after Katrina and still make frequent trips to Haiti. With the permission of Head of School Goodyear, I am writing both as a parent and PTSD counselor.

It's important to root our discussion in the facts. You dropped off your children in front of Galer Street. From there, we boarded the bus, and Mr. Kangana drove us to the Queen Anne home of Audrey and Warren Griffin. Despite the rain, the setting was lovely. The planters were full of colorful flowers, and the smell of burning wood filled the air.

A gentleman by the name of Ollie-O greeted us and directed us to the side entrance, where we were asked to remove our raincoats and rain boots.

The brunch was in full swing. There were approximately fifty guests in attendance, who all appeared to be enjoying themselves. I noted palpable tension coming from Gwen Goodyear, Audrey Griffin, and Ollie-O, but nothing a kindergartener would be able to detect.

We were led to the sunroom, where Mr. Kangana had set up his marimbas the night before. The children who had to go potty did, then kneeled behind their instruments. The shades were drawn, leaving the room quite dark. The children had difficulty locating their mallets, so I began to raise the shades.

Ollie-O materialized and grabbed my hand. "That's a nonstarter." He turned on the lights.

The guests packed in for the performance. After a short introduction by Gwen Goodyear, the children started in with "My Giant Carp." You would have been so proud! It was going delightfully. About a minute in, however, a commotion erupted in the backyard, where the caterers were.

"Holy s——!" someone shouted from outside.

A few guests reacted with good-natured titters. The children hardly noticed, they were so absorbed in their music. The song ended. All the little eyes were on Mr. Kangana, who counted them into their next song, "One, two, three—"

"F——!" someone else shouted.

This was *not* OK. I dashed through the laundry room to the back door, with the intention of shushing the raucous caterers. I turned the handle. A strong, dull, *consistent* pressure pushed the door toward me. Immediately sensing a terrible force of nature on the other side, I attempted to close the door. The inhuman force wouldn't allow it. I stuck my foot against the bottom of the door. I heard an ominous creak. The hinges began pulling loose from the frame.

Before I could compute any of this, the marimba music suddenly stopped. A series of pops and pings erupted from the sunroom. A child squealed in distress.

I abandoned the threat at the door and hurtled to the sunroom, where I was met by the shattering of glass. The children were running, screaming, from their instruments. With none of their own parents to run to for comfort, the kindergarteners collectively burrowed into the crowd of prospective parents, who in turn were trying to squeeze through the one small door leading to the living room. It's a small miracle nobody was trampled.

My daughter, Ginny, ran to me and hugged my legs. Her back was wet...and muddy. I looked up. The shades were now eerily raised of their own accord.

And then came the mud. In it sloshed, through the broken windows. Thick mud, watery mud, rocky mud, mud with beveled-glass shards, mud with window muntins, mud with grass, mud with barbecue utensils, mud with a mosaic birdbath. In a flash, the sunroom windows were gone, and in their place, a gaping, mud-oozing hole.

Adults, children, everyone, was trying to outrun the wreckage, which now included furniture. I stayed behind with Mr. Kangana, who was attempting to rescue the marimbas he had brought with him as a young boy when he emigrated from his beloved Nigeria.

Then, as suddenly as it began, the mud stopped. I turned. An upside-down billboard was flat against the hole in the sunroom, forming a dam. I have no clue as to where this billboard originated, but it was bright red and vast enough to cover what had been a wall of windows.

PRIVATE PROPERTY

NO TRESPASSING

Galer Street Gnats

Will Be Arrested

and Hauled Off to Gnat Jail

By now, the guests were flying out the front door and screeching off in their cars. Mud-caked servers and chefs were milling around, viciously whooping as if this were the most hilarious thing they'd ever seen. Mr. Kangana was swimming in mud, scooping up marimbas. Gwen Goodyear was in the foyer, trying to keep a brave face as she handed out Galer Street gear. Ollie-O was in a semicatatonic state, uttering nonsensical phrases like "This is not biodegradable—the downstream implications are enormous—the optics make for rough sledding—going forward—" before getting stuck on the words "epic fail," which he kept repeating.

Most incredible, perhaps, Audrey Griffin was running down the street, *away* from her home. I called after her, but she had turned the corner.

I alone was left to care for thirty traumatized kindergarteners.

"OK," I rallied. "Let's everyone find their boots and raincoats!" I recognize now this was the wrong thing to say, as it only drew attention to the impossibility of such a task. Further, these children were in their socks, some even barefoot, and there was broken glass everywhere.

"Nobody move." I collected every cushion I could find and laid a path out the front door to the sidewalk. "Walk on these cushions, and line up against the hedge."

If there's one thing kindergarteners understand, it's how to line up. One by one, I carried each child down the street to the bus, which I drove back to Galer Street.

This is why your children were returned to you shoeless, jacketless, covered in mud, and full of fantastic stories.

Now let me speak to you as a PTSD specialist.

"Trauma" can be loosely described as any event a person experiences which he perceives as being a threat to his life. This can take as little as 1/18th of a second. In the immediate aftermath of trauma, children might demonstrate fear or confusion. I took the time to carry each child to the bus so that I had the opportunity to physically connect with them. Research has shown how healing touch can be immediately following trauma, especially with children.

During the walk to the bus, I was able to listen, express curiosity, and simply "be" with each child. I was also able to observe them for early indications of PTSD. I am happy to report that your children appeared to be coping very well. Their greatest concern was whether they'd get their rain gear back, and how it would be returned to them. I answered every question as honestly as I could. I told them we'd do our best to recover their belongings, which would probably be dirty, but the mommies would try to clean them.

The good news is this was a single traumatic incident, and therefore the chances of developing PTSD are minor. The bad news is that PTSD can surface months or even years after an event. I feel it is my responsibility as a doctor to let you know some symptoms of PTSD that may occur in your child:

- worry about dying
- bed-wetting, nightmares, insomnia
- reverting to thumb sucking, baby talk, and diaper
   wearing
- physical complaints for which there is no underlying
   physical cause
- withdrawal from family and friends
- refusal to attend school
- sadistic, violent behavior

If you notice any of these symptoms now or within the next several years, it is important you immediately notify a specialist and tell them about the events at Audrey Griffin's house. I'm not saying this will happen. The chances are very much against it.

I have offered Gwen Goodyear my counseling services for both kindergarten classes. We are still weighing whether to have an all-school assembly, a kindergarten-only gathering, or a parent forum to collectively process this traumatic event. I'd like to hear your feedback.

Sincerely,

Helen Derwood, PhD

*

So you understand fully, here's how freakish the weather was that morning: it was the first time since 9/11 that ferry service was suspended.

Mom and I had breakfast at Macrina, then hit Pike Place Market for our usual Saturday rounds. Mom waited in the car while I ran to the flying fish guy for salmon, Beecher's for cheese, and the butcher for dog bones.

I was going through an *Abbey Road* phase because I had just read a book about the last days of the Beatles, and I spent most of breakfast telling Mom about it. For instance, that medley on the second side, it was originally conceived as individual songs. It was Paul's idea to string them together in the studio. Also, Paul knew exactly what was going on when he wrote, "Boy, you're going to carry that weight." It's about how John wanted the Beatles to break up, but Paul didn't. Paul wrote, "Boy, you're going to carry that weight" right at John. He was saying, "We've got a good thing going. If this band breaks up, it's all on you, John. You sure you want to live with that?" And the final instrumental at the end, where the Beatles trade off leads on guitar, and which has Ringo's only drum solo? You know how it always seems like this tragic, intentional farewell to the fans and you picture the Beatles dressed like hippies playing that last part of *Abbey Road* all looking at one another, and you think, Oh, man, they must have been crying so hard? Well, that whole instrumental was also constructed by Paul in the studio after the fact, so it's just a bunch of fake sentimentality.

Anyway, when we got to the ferry dock, the line was all the way out the loading lot, under the viaduct, and across First Avenue. We had never seen it that long. Mom parked in line, turned off the engine, and walked through the pelting-down rain to the booth. She returned and said a storm drain on the Bainbridge side had flooded the ferry terminal. Three boats were backed up, full of cars waiting to unload. It sounded totally chaotic. But all you can do when it comes to ferries is get in line and hope.

"When's that flute performance?" Mom said. "I want to come see you."

"I don't want you to come." I was hoping she'd forgotten about it.

She dropped her jaw all the way down.

"The words to it are too cute," I explained. "You might die of cuteness."

"But I want to die of cuteness! It's my favorite thing, to die of cuteness."

"I'm not telling you when it is."

"You are such a rotter," she said.

I popped in a CD of *Abbey Road*, which I'd burned that morning, and cranked it. I made sure only the front speakers were on because Ice Cream was asleep in the back.

Of course, the first song is "Come Together." It starts with that great weird "shoomp" and the bass part. And when John started singing "Here come old flattop . . . ," what happened, but Mom knew every single word of the song! Not just every word, but every cadence. She knew every "all right!" and "aww!" and "yeaaaah." And it kept going, song after song. When "Maxwell's Silver Hammer" started, Mom said, "Yuck, I always thought this was totally sophomoric." Still, what did she do? She sang every single word of that, too.

I hit the pause button. "How do you even know this?" I demanded.

"*Abbey Road*?" Mom shrugged. "I don't know, you just know it." She unpaused the CD.

When "Here Comes the Sun" started, what happened? No, the sun didn't come out, but *Mom* opened up like the sun breaking through the clouds. You know how in the first few notes of that song, there's something about George's guitar that's just so hopeful? It was like when Mom sang, she was full of hope, too. She even got the irregular clapping right during the guitar solo. When the song was over, she paused it.

"Oh, Bee," she said. "This song reminds me of you." She had tears in her eyes.

"Mom!" This is why I didn't want her to come to the first-grade elephant dance. Because the most random things get her way too full of love.

"I need you to know how hard it is for me sometimes." Mom had her hand on mine.

"What's hard?"

"The banality of life," she said. "But it won't keep me from taking you to the South Pole."

"We're not going to the South Pole!"

"I know. It's a hundred below zero at the South Pole. Only scientists go to the South Pole. I started reading one of the books."

I wiggled out my hand and hit play. Here's the funny part. When I burned the CD, I didn't uncheck the thing iTunes defaults to when it asks if you want two seconds between songs. So when it came to the awesome medley, Mom and I sang along to "You Never Give Me Your Money," then "Sun King," which Mom knew, even the Spanish part, and she doesn't even speak Spanish, she speaks French.

And then the two-second gaps started.

If you don't understand how tragic and annoying this is,

seriously, start singing along to "Sun King." Toward the end, you're singing all sleepy in Spanish, gearing up to start grooving to "Mean Mr. Mustard," because what makes the end of "Sun King" *so great* is you're drifting along, but at the same time you're anticipating Ringo's drums, which kick in on "Mean Mr. Mustard," and it turns funky. But if you *don't* uncheck the box on iTunes, you get to the end of "Sun King" and then—

HARSH DIGITAL TWO-SECOND SILENCE.

And during "Polythene Pam," right after the "look out," it— GAPS OUT—before "She Came in Through the Bathroom Window." Seriously, it's torture. During all this, Mom and I were howling. Finally, the CD ended.

"I love you, Bee," Mom said. "I'm trying. Sometimes it works. Sometimes it doesn't."

The ferry line hadn't moved. "I guess we should just go home," I said. It was a bummer because Kennedy never wanted to spend the night in Seattle because our house scares her. Once, she swore she saw a lump in one of the rugs move. "It's alive, it's alive!" she screamed. I told her it was just a blackberry vine growing through the floorboards, but she was convinced it was the ghost of one of the Straight Gate girls.

Mom and I headed up Queen Anne Hill. Mom once said the ganglia of electric bus wires overhead were like a Jacob's ladder. Every time we drove up, I imagined reaching my fanned fingers up into the web and pulling them through the roof in a cat's cradle.

We turned into our driveway. We were halfway through the gate. And there was Audrey Griffin walking up to our car.

"Oh, boy," Mom said. "Déjà vu all over again. What is it now?"

"Watch out for her foot," I said, totally joking.

"Oh, no!" Mom's voice kind of barfed out the words. She covered her face with her hands.

"What?" I said. "What?"

Audrey Griffin wasn't wearing a jacket. Her pants were covered in mud from the knee down, and she was barefoot. There was mud in her hair, too. Mom opened her door without turning off the car. By the time I got out, Audrey Griffin was screaming.

"Your hillside just slid into my home!"

I was like, *what?* Our yard was so big, and the end of our lawn was so far down, I couldn't see what she was talking about.

"During a party," Audrey continued, "for prospective Galer Street parents."

"I had no idea—" Mom's voice was all shaky.

"*That* I believe," Audrey said, "because you are totally uninvolved in the school. Both kindergarten classes were there!"

"Was anyone hurt?" Mom said.

"Thank the Lord, no." Audrey had a crazy smile. Mom and I share a fascination with what we call happy-angry people. This display of Audrey Griffin's had just become the best version of that ever.

"OK. That's good." Mom sighed a huge sigh. "That's good." I could tell she was trying to convince herself.

"Good?!" Audrey shrieked. "My backyard is six feet high in mud. It broke windows, destroyed plants, trees, hardwood floors, ripped my washer and dryer out of the wall!" Audrey was talking really fast and taking lots of breaths. It was like with each item she ticked off, the needle on her happy-angry meter was moving more and more to the right. "My barbecue is gone. My window treatments are ruined. My greenhouse crushed. Seedlings killed. Specimen apple trees that have taken *twenty-five years* to establish, pulled up by the roots. Japanese maples flattened. Heirloom roses gone. The fire pit that I tiled myself is gone!"

Mom was sucking in the corners of her mouth to keep a smile

from forming. I had to quickly look down so I wouldn't crack up. But any perverse humor we might have found in the situation suddenly ended.

"And that sign!" Audrey said with a growl.

Mom's face dropped. She could barely utter the words "The sign."

"What sign?" I asked.

"What kind of person puts up a sign—" Audrey said.

"I'll have it taken down today," Mom said.

"What sign?" I repeated.

"The mud took care of that for you," Audrey told Mom. I'd never noticed how light green Audrey Griffin's eyes were until they bugged out at my mother.

"I'll pay for everything," Mom said.

Here's something about Mom: she's bad with annoyances, but great in a crisis. If a waiter doesn't refill her water after she's asked three times, or she forgets her dark glasses when the sun comes out, look out! But when it comes to something truly bad happening, Mom plugs into this supreme calm. I think she got it from all those years half living at Children's because of me. I'm just saying, when things are bad, there's nobody better to have in your corner than Mom. But this calm of hers seemed only to set Audrey Griffin off worse.

"Is that all everything is about for you?! Money?!" The madder Audrey got, the sparklier her eyes became. "Up here in your gigantic house looking down on all of us, writing checks, but never deigning to come off your throne and honor us with your presence?"

"You're obviously emotional," Mom said. "You need to remember the work I had done on the hillside was at your insistence, Audrey. I used your guy and had him do it on the day you specified."

"So none of it is your responsibility?" Audrey clucked. "That's mighty convenient for you. How about the sign, then? Did I make you put that up, too? Really, I'm curious."

"What sign?!" I started to get scared with all the talk of the sign.

"Buzz," Mom turned to me. "I did something really stupid. I'll tell you about it."

"This poor child," Audrey said bitterly. "With everything she's had to go through."

"Whaa—?" I said.

"I'm truly sorry about the sign," Mom stated emphatically to Audrey. "I did it on impulse the day I found you on my lawn with your gardener."

"You're blaming *me?*" Audrey said. "Isn't this just fascinating!" It was like her happy needle had busted through the danger zone and was now entering uncharted territory where no happy-angry person has gone before. I, for one, was frightened.

"I'm blaming myself," Mom said. "I'm just making the point that there is a larger context to what happened today."

"You think a gentleman coming to your house to give you an estimate for yard work, which is legally required by city code, is equivalent to putting up a billboard, traumatizing both kindergarten classes, jeopardizing Galer Street enrollment, and destroying my home?"

"The sign was a reaction to that," Mom said. "Yes."

"Wooowww," Audrey Griffin said, spreading the word up and down like a roller coaster. Her voice was so full of hate and craziness that it pierced my skin. My heart began racing in a scary way it never had before.

"This is really interesting." Audrey widened her eyes. "So *you* think putting up a hateful billboard over my home is an *appropriate* reaction to getting an estimate for yard work." She pointed her finger in eight different directions during that last sentence. "I think I understand."

"It was an *overreaction*," Mom told Audrey with renewed calm. "Don't forget you were trespassing on my property."

"So basically," Audrey exploded, "you're insane!" Her eyes fluttered spastically. "Golly, I was always wondering. Now I have my answer." Her face froze in demented wonder and she started clapping her hands really fast and small.

"Audrey," Mom said. "Don't stand there and pretend you haven't been playing this game, too."

"I don't play games."

"How about getting Gwen Goodyear to send out that letter about me running over your foot? What was that?"

"Oh, Bernadette," Audrey said, shaking her head sadly. "You really need to stop being so paranoid. Perhaps if you interacted more with people, you'd realize we're not a bunch of scary bogeymen who are out to get you." She held up both hands and clawed the air.

"I think we're done," Mom said. "Again, I want to apologize for the sign. It was a stupid mistake and I intend to take full responsibility, in terms of money, in terms of time, in terms of Gwen Goodyear and Galer Street." Mom turned and walked around the front of the car. When she was about get in, Audrey Griffin started up again, like a movie monster come back to life.

"Bee never would have been accepted to Galer Street if they knew she lived in this house," Audrey Griffin said. "Ask Gwen. Nobody realized you were the people from L.A. who came to Seattle and bought a twelve-thousand-square-foot building in the middle of a charming neighborhood and called it *your home*. Where we're standing now? Within a four-mile radius is the house *I* grew up in, the house *my mother* grew up in, and the house *my grandmother* grew up in."

"That I believe," Mom said.

"My great-grandfather was a fur trapper in Alaska," Audrey said. "Warren's great-grandfather bought furs from him. My point is, you come in here with your Microsoft money and think you belong. But you don't belong. You never will."

"Say amen to that."

"None of the other mothers like you, Bernadette. Do you realize we had an eighth-grade moms-and-daughters Thanksgiving on Whidbey Island, but we didn't invite you and Bee? But I hear you had a wonderful holiday at *Daniel's Broiler!*"

My breath kind of stopped then. I was standing there, but it was like Audrey Griffin had knocked the wind out of me. I reached for the car to steady myself.

"That's it, Audrey." Mom took about five steps toward her. "Fuck you."

"Fine," Audrey said. "Drop the f-bomb in front of a child. I hope that makes you feel powerful."

"I'll say it again," Mom said. "Fuck you for bringing Bee into this."

"We love Bee," Audrey Griffin said. "Bee is a terrific student and a wonderful girl. It just goes to show how resilient children are because she's turned out so well in spite of it all. If Bee were my daughter, and I know I'm speaking for every mother at Whidbey Island, we'd never ship her off to boarding school."

I finally caught enough of my breath to say, "I want to go to boarding school!"

"Of course you do," Audrey said to me, all full of pity.

"It was my idea!" I screamed, just so furious. "I already told you that!"

"No, Bee," Mom said. She wasn't even looking at me. She just held up her hand in my direction. "It's not worth it."

"Of course it was your idea," Audrey Griffin said to me, poking her head around Mom, and boinging her eyes. "Of course you want to go away. Who can blame you?"

"You don't talk to me that way!" I screamed. "You don't know me!" I was soaking wet and the car was running this whole time, which is a waste of gas, and both doors were open so the rain was pouring in and ruining the leather, plus we were parked on the loop so the gate kept trying to shut but then opening again, and I was worried the motor would burn out, and Ice Cream was just stupidly watching from the back with her mouth open and tongue hanging out, like she didn't even sense we needed protecting, plus *Abbey Road* was playing "Here Comes the Sun," which was the song Mom said reminded her of me, and I knew I'd never listen to *Abbey Road* again.

"Oh, God, Bee, what's wrong?" Mom had turned and seen that something was the matter with me. "Talk to me, Buzz. Is it your heart?"

I pushed Mom off me and slapped Audrey across her wet face. I know! But I was just so mad.

"I pray for you," Audrey said.

"Pray for yourself," I said. "My mother's too good for you and those other mothers. *You're* the one everyone hates. Kyle is a juvie who doesn't do sports or any extracurriculars. The only friends he has are because he gives them drugs and because he's funny when he's making fun of you. And your husband is a drunk who has three DUIs but he gets off because he knows the judge, and all you care about is that nobody finds out, but it's too late because Kyle tells the whole school everything."

Audrey said quickly, "I am a Christian woman so I will forgive that."

"Give me a break," I said. "Christians don't talk the way you talked to my mother."

I got into the car, shut the door, turned off *Abbey Road,* and just started whimpering. I was sitting in an inch of water, but I didn't care. The reason I was so scared had nothing to do with a sign or a stupid mudslide or because Mom and I didn't get invited to stupid Whidbey Island, like we'd ever want to go anywhere with those jerks in a million years, but because I knew, I just knew, that now everything was going to be different.

Mom got in and shut the door. "You're supercool," she said. "You know that?"

"I hate her," I said.

What I didn't say, because I didn't need to, because it was implied, and really, I can't tell you why, because we'd never kept secrets from him before, but me and Mom both just understood: we weren't going to tell Dad.

Mom wasn't the same after that. It wasn't the day in the compound pharmacy. Mom had bounced back. I was there in the car with her singing to *Abbey Road.* And I don't care what Dad or the doctors or the police or anybody says, it was Audrey Griffin screaming at Mom that made her never the same again. And if you don't believe me:

*

Email sent five minutes later

From: Bernadette Fox
To: Manjula Kapoor

Nobody can say I didn't give it the college try. But I just can't go through with it. I can't go to Antarctica. How I'll ever extract myself, I'm not sure. But I have faith in us, Manjula. Together we can do anything.

*

From Dad to Dr. Janelle Kurtz,
a shrink at Madrona Hill

Dear Dr. Kurtz,

My friend Hannah Dillard sang your praises regarding her husband, Frank's, stay at Madrona Hill. From what I understand, Frank was struggling with depression. His inpatient treatment at Madrona Hill, under your supervision, did him wonders.

I write you because I too am deeply concerned about my spouse. Her name is Bernadette Fox, and I fear she is very sick.

(Forgive my shambolic penmanship. I'm on an airplane, and my laptop battery is dead so I've taken up a pen for the first time in years. I'll press on, as I think it's important to get everything down while it's fresh in the memory.)

I'll begin with some background. Bernadette and I met about twenty-five years ago in Los Angeles, when the architecture firm for which she worked redesigned the animation house for which I worked. We were both from the East Coast and had gone to prep school. Bernadette was a rising star. I was taken by her beauty, gregariousness, and insouciant charm. We married. I was working on an idea I had for computer animation. My company was bought by Microsoft. Bernadette ran into trouble with a house she was building and abruptly declared herself through with the L.A. architecture scene. To my surprise, she was the engine behind our move to Seattle.

Bernadette flew up to look at houses. She called to say she had found the perfect place, the Straight Gate School for Girls, in Queen Anne. To anyone else, a crumbling reform school might seem an odd place to call home. But this was Bernadette, and she was enthusiastic. Bernadette and her enthusiasm were like a hippo and water: get between them and you'll be trampled to death.

We moved to Seattle. I was swallowed whole by Microsoft. Bernadette became pregnant and had the first of a series of miscarriages. After three years, she passed the first term. At the beginning of her second term, she was put on bed rest. The house, which was a blank canvas on which Bernadette was to work her magic, understandably languished. There were leaks, strange drafts, and the occasional weed pushing up through a floorboard. My concern was for Bernadette's health—she didn't need the stress of a remodel, she needed to stay put—so we wore parkas inside, rotated spaghetti pots when it rained, and kept a pair of pruning shears in a vase in the living room. It felt romantic.

Our daughter, Bee, was born prematurely. She came out blue. She was diagnosed with hypoplastic left heart syndrome. I imagine that having a sick child can knit a husband and wife together, or rip them apart. In our case, it did neither. Bernadette immersed herself so thoroughly in Bee's recovery that it became her every fiber. I worked even longer hours and called it a partnership: Bernadette would call the shots; I'd pay for them.

By the time Bee entered kindergarten, she was healthy, if unusually small for her age. I always assumed this was when Bernadette would return to her architecture practice or, at the very least, fix up our house. Leaks had become holes in the roof; windows with small cracks had become cardboard-and-duct-tape panels. Once a week, the gardener weed-whacked under the rugs.

Our home was literally returning to the earth. When Bee was five, I was in her room playing restaurant. She took my order, and after lots of furious activity in her miniature kitchen, she brought me my "lunch." It was damp and brown. It smelled like dirt, but fluffier. "I dug it up," she remarked proudly, and pointed to the wood floor. It was so damp from the years of rain, Bee could literally dig into it with a spoon.

Once Bee was settled into kindergarten, Bernadette showed no interest in fixing up the house, or in any kind of work. All the energy she had once channeled so fearlessly into architecture, she turned toward fulminating about Seattle, in the form of wild rants that required no less than an hour to fully express.

Take five-way intersections. The first time Bernadette commented on the abundance of five-way intersections in Seattle, it seemed perfectly relevant. I hadn't noticed it myself, but indeed there were many intersections with an extra street jutting out, and which required you to wait through an extra traffic light cycle. Certainly worthy of a conversation between a husband and wife. But the second time Bernadette went off on the same topic, I wondered, Is there something *new* she wishes to add? But no. She was just complaining with renewed vehemence. She asked me to ask Bill Gates why he'd still live in a city with so many ridiculous intersections. I came home and she asked if I'd asked him yet. One day she got a map of old Seattle and explained that there were once six separate grid systems, which, over time, bled together without a master plan. One night, on the way to a restaurant, she drove miles out of our way to show me where three of the grids met, and there was an intersection with seven streets coming out. Then she timed it while we waited at the stoplight. The helter-skelter layout of Seattle streets was just one of Bernadette's greatest hits.

Some nights I'd be asleep in bed. "Elgie," she'd say, "are you awake?"

"I am now."

"Doesn't Bill Gates know Warren Buffett?" she'd say. "And doesn't Warren Buffett own See's Candy?"

"I guess."

"Great. Because he needs to know what's happening at the Westlake

Plaza. You know how See's Candy has a policy where they hand out free samples? Well, all those horrible runaways have caught on. So today I had to wait thirty minutes, in a line *out the door*, behind bums and drug addicts who didn't buy anything but demanded their free sample, and then went to the end of the line for another."

"So don't go to See's Candy anymore."

"Believe me, I won't. But if you see Warren Buffett around Microsoft, you should tell him. Or tell me, and I can tell him."

I tried engaging her, tuning her out, asking her to stop. Nothing worked, especially asking her to stop, which would only tack ten minutes onto that particular rant. I began to feel like a hunted animal, cornered and defenseless.

Remember, for the first several years of living in Seattle, Bernadette was pregnant, or had recently miscarried. As far as I knew, these moods were hormonal swings, or a way of processing grief.

I encouraged Bernadette to make friends, but that would only trigger a diatribe about how she had tried, but nobody liked her.

People say Seattle is one of the toughest cities in which to make friends. They even have a name for it, the "Seattle freeze." I've never experienced it myself, but coworkers claim it's real and has to do with all the Scandinavian blood up here. Maybe it *was* difficult at first for Bernadette to fit in. But eighteen years later, to still harbor an irrational hatred of an entire city?

I have a very stressful job, Dr. Kurtz. Some mornings, I'd arrive at my desk utterly depleted by having to endure Bernadette and her frothing. I finally started taking the Microsoft Connector to work. It was an excuse to leave the house an hour earlier to avoid the morning broadsides.

I really did not intend for this letter to go on so long, but looking out airplane windows makes me sentimental. Let me jump to the incidents of yesterday which have prompted me to write.

I was walking to lunch with some colleagues when one pointed to Bernadette, asleep on a couch in a pharmacy. For some reason she was wearing a fishing vest. This was especially strange because Bernadette insists on wearing stylish clothes, in protest against everyone else's terrible taste in fashion. (I'll spare you the specifics of that delightful rant.) I hurried inside. When I finally roused Bernadette, she said quite matter-of-factly that she was waiting for a Haldol prescription.

Dr. Kurtz, I don't have to tell you. Haldol is an antipsychotic. Is my wife under the care of a psychiatrist who's prescribing Haldol? Is she obtaining it illegally? I haven't the faintest clue.

I was so alarmed that I rescheduled my business trip so we could have dinner, just the two of us. We met at a Mexican restaurant. We ordered, and I immediately broached the subject of Haldol. "I was surprised to see you at the pharmacy today," I said.

"Shhh!" She was eavesdropping on the table behind us. "They don't know the difference between a burrito and an enchilada!" Bernadette's face tightened as she strained to listen. "Oh my God," she whispered. "They've never heard of *mole*. What do they look like? I don't want to turn around."

"Just...people."

"What do you mean? What kind of—" She couldn't contain herself. She quickly turned. "They're covered in tattoos! What, you're so cool that you ink yourself head-to-toe, but you don't know the difference between an enchilada and a burrito?"

"About today—" I started.

"Oh, yeah," she said. "Was that one of the gnats you were with? From Galer Street?"

"Soo-Lin is my new admin," I said. "She has a son in Bee's class."

"Oh, boy," Bernadette said. "It's all over for me."

"What's all over?" I asked.

"Those gnats have always hated me. She's going to turn you against me."

"That's ridiculous," I said. "Nobody hates you—"

"Shh!" she said. "The waiter. He's about to take their order." She leaned back and to her left, closer, closer, closer, her body like a giraffe's neck, until her chair shot out from under her and she landed on the floor. The whole restaurant turned to look. I jumped up to help. She stood up, righted the chair, and started in again. "Did you see the tattoo one of them had on the inside of his arm? It looked like a roll of tape."

I took a gulp of margarita and settled into my fallback option, which was to wait her out.

"Know what one of the guys at the drive-through Starbucks has on his forearm?" Bernadette said. "A *paper clip!* It used to be so daring to get a tattoo. And now people are tattooing *office supplies* on their bodies. You know what I say?" Of course this was rhetorical. "I say, dare *not* to get a tattoo." She turned around again, and gasped. "Oh my God. It's not just *any* roll of tape. It's literally Scotch tape, with the green-and-black plaid. This is too hilarious. If you're going to tattoo tape on your arm, at least make it a generic old-fashioned tape dispenser! What do you think happened? Did the Staples catalogue get delivered to the tattoo parlor that day?" She stuck a chip into the guacamole and it broke under the weight. "God, I hate the chips here." She dug into the guacamole with a fork and took a bite. "What were you saying?"

"I'm curious about the medicine they wouldn't fill for you at the pharmacy."

"I know!" she said. "A doctor wrote me a prescription, and it turned out to be Haldol."

"Is it your insomnia?" I asked. "Haven't you been sleeping?"

"Sleep?" she asked. "What's that?"

"What was the prescription for?"

"Anxiety," she said.

"Are you seeing a psychiatrist?" I asked.

"No!"

"Do you want to see a psychiatrist?"

"God, no!" she said. "I'm just anxious about the trip."

"What specifically are you so anxious about?"

"The Drake Passage, people. You know how it is."

"Actually," I said, "I don't."

"There's going to be a lot of people. I'm not good when exposed to people."

"I think we need to find someone you can talk to."

"I'm talking to you, aren't I?"

"A professional," I said.

"I tried that once. It was a complete waste." She leaned in and whispered. "OK, there's a guy in a suit standing at the window. This is the fourth time I've seen him in three days. And I will promise you one thing. If you look now, he won't be there."

I turned around. A man in a suit disappeared down the sidewalk.

"What did I say?" she said.

"Are you telling me you're being followed?"

"It's unclear."

Fishing vests, sleeping in public, antipsychotic medication, and now men following her?

When Bee was two, she developed a strange attachment to a novelty book Bernadette and I had bought years ago from a street vendor in Rome.

ROME Past and Present
A Guide
To the Monumental Centre of Ancient Rome
With Reconstructions of the Monuments

It has photographs of present-day ruins, with overlays of how they looked in their heyday. Bee would sit in her hospital bed, hooked up to her monitors, and flip back and forth among the images. The book had a puffy red plastic cover that she'd chew on.

I realized I was now looking at Bernadette Past and Present. There was a terrifying chasm between the woman I fell in love with and the ungovernable one sitting across from me.

We returned home. While Bernadette slept, I opened her medicine cabinet. It was crammed with prescription bottles written by an array of doctors for Xanax, Klonopin, Ambien, Halcion, trazodone, and others. All the bottles were empty.

Dr. Kurtz, I don't pretend to understand what's wrong with Bernadette. Is she depressed? Manic? Hooked on pills? Paranoid? I don't know what constitutes a mental breakdown. Whatever you want to call it, I think it's fair to say my wife is in need of serious attention.

Hannah Dillard spoke so highly of you specifically, Dr. Kurtz, and all you did to help Frank though his rough patch. If I remember correctly, at the outset Frank was resistant to treatment, but he soon embraced your program. Hannah was so impressed that she's now a member of your board.

Bernadette, Bee, and I are scheduled to go to Antarctica in two weeks. Bernadette obviously does not want to go. I now think it might be a better idea if Bee and I go to Antarctica, just the two of us, while Bernadette checks into Madrona Hill. I can't imagine Bernadette will be too keen on the idea, but it's clear to me she needs some supervised R&R. I am anxious to hear your thoughts.

Sincerely,
Elgin Branch

PART TWO

Bernadette Past and Present

Architecture competition sponsored by
the Green Builders of America

FOR IMMEDIATE RELEASE:

Green Builders of America
and the Turner Foundation announce:

20 × 20 × 20: The Twenty Mile House
Twenty Years Later
Twenty Years in the Future

Deadline for submission: February 1

Bernadette Fox's Twenty Mile House no longer stands. There are few photos of it, and Ms. Fox is purported to have destroyed all plans. Still, its relevance grows with each passing year. To celebrate the twentieth anniversary of the Twenty Mile House, the Green Builders of America, in conjunction with the Turner Foundation, invite architects, students, and builders to submit designs to reenvision and rebuild the Twenty Mile House and, in doing so, open a dialogue for what it means to "build green" in the next twenty years.

The challenge: Submit plans for a 3-bedroom, 4,200-sf single-family residence at 6528 Mulholland Drive in Los Angeles.

The only restriction is the one Ms. Fox placed on herself: *Every material used must come from within twenty miles of the building site.*

The winner: Will be announced at the GBA/AIA gala at the Getty Center and be awarded a $40,000 prize.

SATURDAY, DECEMBER 11
**From Paul Jellinek, professor of architecture at USC,
to the guy Mom ran into on the street outside the library**

Jacob,

Because you've taken an interest in Bernadette Fox, here's a bit of a hagiography from the not-yet-published February issue of *Artforum*. They asked me to vet it for glaring mistakes. In case you have an impulse to contact the writer with news of your Bernadette Fox sighting, please don't. Bernadette has obviously made a choice to get lost, and it seems to me we should respect it.

Paul

✳

PDF of *Artforum* article

"Saint Bernadette:
The Most Influential Architect You've Never Heard Of"

The Architects and Builders Association of America recently polled three hundred architectural graduate students and asked them which architects they admire most. The list is what you'd expect — Frank Lloyd Wright, Le Corbusier, Mies van der Rohe, Louis Kahn, Richard Neutra, Rudolf Schindler — with one exception. Tucked among the great men is a woman who is virtually unknown.

Bernadette Fox is extraordinary for many reasons. She was a young woman practicing solo in a male-dominated profession; she received a MacArthur grant at thirty-two; her handmade furniture stands in the permanent collection of the American Folk Art Museum; she is considered a pioneer of the green building movement; the only house she ever built no longer stands; she dropped out of architecture twenty years ago and has designed nothing since.

Alone, any of these attributes would make an architect noteworthy. Taken together, an icon was born. But who was Bernadette Fox? Was she forging the way for young women architects to come? Was she a genius? Was she green before there was green? Where is she now?

Artforum spoke with the handful of people who worked closely with Bernadette Fox. What follows is our attempt to unlock one of architecture's true enigmas.

Princeton in the mideighties was the front line in the battle for the future of architecture. The modernist school was firmly established, its acolytes lauded and influential. The postmodernists, led by Princeton faculty member Michael Graves, were mounting a serious challenge. Graves had just built his Portland Public Service Building, its wit, ornamentation, and eclecticism a bold rejection of the austere, minimalist formality of the modernists. Meanwhile, deconstructivists, a more confrontational faction, were banding together. Led by former Princeton professor Peter Eisenman, deconstructivism rejected both modernism and postmodernism in favor of fragmentation and geometric unpredictability. Students at Princeton were firmly expected to pick sides, take up arms, and shed blood.

Ellie Saito was in Bernadette Fox's class at Princeton.

ELLIE SAITO: For my thesis I designed a teahouse for the visitors center at Mount Fuji. It was essentially a pulled-apart cherry blossom made of exploding pink sails. I was defending my design during review. I was taking it from all sides. And Bernadette looked up from her knitting and asked, "Where are they going to put their shoes?" We all just looked at her. "Aren't people supposed to take off their shoes in teahouses?" Bernadette said. "Where will they put them?"

Fox's preoccupation with the prosaic caught the attention of Professor Michael Graves, who hired her to work in his New York office.

ELLIE SAITO: Bernadette was the only one in the whole class he hired. It was a big blow.

MICHAEL GRAVES: I'm not looking to hire an architect with a huge ego and huge ideas. I'm the one with a huge ego and huge ideas. I want someone who has the ability to carry out my ideas and solve the problems I throw at them. What struck me about Bernadette was the joy she took in tasks that most students would find beneath them. Architecture isn't a profession usually chosen by egoless worker bees. So when you're looking to hire, and you see a talented one, you grab her.

Fox was the most junior member of a group assigned to the Team Disney Building in Burbank. Her first job was typical grunt work, laying out bathrooms in the executive wing.

MICHAEL GRAVES: Bernadette was driving everyone insane. She wanted to know how much time the executives spent in their offices, how often they'd be in meetings, at what time of day, how many people would be in attendance, the ratio of men to women. I picked up the phone and asked her what the hell she was doing.

She explained, "I need to know what problems I'm solving with my design."

I told her, "Michael Eisner needs to take a piss, and he doesn't want everyone watching."

I'd like to say I kept her around because I recognized the talent that would emerge. But really, I liked the sweaters. She knitted me four, and I still have them. My kids keep trying to steal them. My wife wants to give them to Goodwill. But I won't part with them.

The Team Disney Building was repeatedly delayed because of the permitting process. During an all-firm meeting, Fox presented a flowchart on how to game the building department. Graves sent her to Los Angeles to work on-site.

MICHAEL GRAVES: I was the only one sad to see her go.

In six months, the Team Disney job ended. Graves offered Fox a job back in New York, but she liked the freedom of the Los Angeles architecture scene. On a recommendation from Graves, Fox was hired by the firm of Richard Meier, already at work on the Getty Center. She was one of a half-dozen young architects charged with sourcing, importing, and quality-checking the sixteen thousand tons of travertine from Italy which would sheathe the museum.

In 1988, Fox met Elgin Branch, a computer animator. They married the next year. Fox wanted to build a house. Judy Toll was their realtor.

JUDY TOLL: They were a darling young couple. Both very smart and attractive. I kept trying to put them in a house in Santa Monica, or the Palisades. But Bernadette was fixated on getting a piece of land where she could design something herself. I showed them an abandoned factory in Venice Beach that was being sold for land value.

She looked around and said it was perfect. To my shock, she was talking about the building itself. The only one more surprised than I was the husband. But he trusted her. The wives always make these decisions anyway.

Fox and Branch bought the former Beeber Bifocal Factory. Soon thereafter, they went to a dinner party and met the two most influential people in Fox's professional life: Paul Jellinek and David Walker. Jellinek was an architect and professor at SCI-Arc.

PAUL JELLINEK: It was the day she and Elgie closed on Beeber Bifocal. Her enthusiasm for it lit up the whole party. She said the factory was still filled with boxes of old bifocals and machinery that she wanted to "do something with." The way she was talking, all wild and fuzzy, I had no idea she was a trained architect, let alone a darling of Graves.

David Walker was a contractor.

DAVID WALKER: Over dessert, Bernadette asked me to be her contractor. I said I'd give her some references. She said, "No, I just like you," and she told me to come by that Saturday and bring some guys.

PAUL JELLINEK: When Bernadette said she was working on the Getty travertine, I totally got it. A friend of mine was on travertine duty, too. They had these talented architects reduced to being Inspector 44 on an assembly line. It was soul-destroying work. Beeber was Bernadette's way of reconnecting to what she loved about architecture, which was building stuff.

The Beeber Bifocal Factory was a three-thousand-square-foot cinder-block box with eleven-foot ceilings topped by a clerestory. The roof was a series of skylights. Transforming this industrial space into a home consumed the next two years of Fox's life. Contractor David Walker was there every day.

DAVID WALKER: From the outside, it looked like some junky thing. But you walk in and it's full of light. That first Saturday I show up with some guys like Bernadette asks. She has no plans, no permits. Instead, she's got brooms and squeegees and we all go to work sweeping the floor and cleaning the windows and skylights. I ask her if I should order a dumpster. She practically shouts, "No!"

She spends the next week taking everything in the building and laying it out on the floor. There's thousands of bifocal frames, boxes of lenses, bundles of flattened cardboard boxes, plus all the machinery for cutting and polishing lenses.

Every morning I show up, she's already there. She's wearing this backpack with yarn coming out of it, so she can knit while she's standing. And she's just knitting and looking at everything. It reminded me of being a kid and dumping out a bunch of Legos on the carpet. And you just sit there and stare before you have any idea what you're going to make.

That Friday, she takes home a box of wire bifocal frames. Monday, she returns and she's knitted them all together with wire. So you have this awesome chain mail with glasses embedded in it. And it's strong, too! So Bernadette puts the guys to work, with clippers and pliers, turning thousands of old bifocal frames into screens, which she uses as interior walls.

It was hilarious to see these macho guys from Mexico sitting in chairs and knitting out in the sun. They loved it, though. They'd play their ranchera music on the radio and gossip like a bunch of ladies.

PAUL JELLINEK: Beeber Bifocal just kind of evolved. It's not like Bernadette had a big idea going in. It started with knitting the glasses together. And then came the tabletops made out of lenses. Then the table bases made out of machinery parts. It was fucking great. I'd come by with my students and give them extra credit if they'd help.

There was a back room piled ceiling-to-floor with catalogues. Bernadette glued them together until they were solid four-foot-by-four-foot cubes. One night we all got drunk and took a chain saw to them and cut out seats. They became the living room furniture.

DAVID WALKER: Pretty soon it became obvious that the point was to avoid any runs to the hardware store and use only what was on the premises. It became kind of a game. I don't know if you could call it architecture, but it sure was fun.

PAUL JELLINEK: Back then, architecture was all about the technology. Everyone was switching from drafting boards to Auto-CAD; all anyone wanted to talk about was prefab. People were building McMansions to within six inches of the lot line. What Bernadette was doing was completely outside the mainstream. In some ways, Beeber Bifocal's roots lie in hobo art. It's a very crafty house. The feminists are going to kill me on this, but Bernadette Fox is a very feminine architect. When you walk into Beeber Bifocal, you're overwhelmed by the care and the patience that was put into it. It's like walking into a big hug.

At her day job at the Getty, Fox was growing indignant at the waste of shipping ton after ton of travertine from Italy only to have it refused by her superiors for minor inconsistencies.

PAUL JELLINEK: One day, I mentioned to her that the city's Department of Cultural Affairs had just bought an empty lot next to the Watts Towers, and they were interviewing architects for a visitors center.

Fox spent a month secretly designing a fountain, museum, and a series of viewing platforms made from the Getty's rejected travertine.

PAUL JELLINEK: She made the connection because the Watts Towers were constructed out of other people's garbage. Bernadette designed these nautilus-shaped viewing platforms, which echoed the fossils in the travertine and the whorls of the Watts Towers.

When Fox presented her plan to the Getty management, they quickly and unequivocally shot her down.

PAUL JELLINEK: The Getty was interested in one thing: getting the Getty built. They didn't need some low-level employee telling them what to do with their extra material. Plus, can you imagine the PR? It's not good enough for the Getty, but it's good enough for South Central? Who needs that headache?

Richard Meier and Partners were unable to find Fox's drawings in their Getty Center archives.

PAUL JELLINEK: I'm sure Bernadette just threw them away. The important thing to come out of it—and she knew it—was that she had forged a distinct point of view, which was, simply, to waste nothing.

Fox and Branch moved into the Beeber Bifocal House in 1991. Fox was restless for another project.

JUDY TOLL: Bernadette and her husband had poured everything into that glasses factory they were living in, and she didn't have much money to spend. So I found her a scrubby piece of land on Mulholland in Hollywood, near Runyon Canyon. It had a flat pad and a great view of the city. The piece of land next to it was also for sale. I suggested they buy that, too, but they couldn't afford it.

Fox committed to building a house using only materials from within a twenty-mile radius. That didn't mean going to a Home Depot a mile away and buying steel from China. The materials all had to be sourced locally.

DAVID WALKER: She asks me if I'm up for the challenge. I tell her, Sure.

PAUL JELLINEK: One of the smartest things Bernadette did was hook up with Dave. Most contractors can't work without plans, but he could. If the Twenty Mile House demonstrates anything, it's what a genius she was with permits.

When it comes to Bernadette, everyone teaches Beeber and Twenty Mile. I teach her permits. It's impossible to look at the plans she submitted to plan-check without cracking up. It's pages and pages full of official-looking documentation that contain virtually no information. It was different back them. It was before the building boom, before the earthquake. You could just go down to the building department and talk to the top guy.

Ali Fahad was the top guy at the Los Angeles Department of Building and Safety.

ALI FAHAD: Of course I remember Bernadette Fox. She was a charmer. She wouldn't deal with anybody but me. My wife and I had just had twins, and Bernadette came with hand-knit blankets and hats for them both. She'd sit, we'd have tea, she'd explain what she wanted to do with her house, and I'd tell her how to do it.

PAUL JELLINEK: See! Only a woman could do something like that.

Architecture has always been a male-dominated profession. Until the emergence of Zaha Hadid in 2005, one was hard-pressed to name a famous female architect. Eileen Gray and Julia Morgan are sometimes mentioned. Mainly, female architects stood in the shadows of their famous male partners: Ann Tyng to Louis Kahn, Marion Griffin to Frank Lloyd Wright, Denise Scott Brown to Robert Venturi.

ELLIE SAITO: That's what drove me so crazy about Bernadette at Princeton. To be one of two women in the whole architecture department, and you spend your time knitting? It was as bad as crying during review. I felt it was important, as a woman, to go toe-to-toe with the men. Any time I tried to talk to Bernadette about this, she had no interest.

DAVID WALKER: If we needed something welded, I'd bring a guy in and Bernadette would explain to him what she'd want, then the guy gave *me* the answer. But it never bothered Bernadette. She wanted to get her house built, and if that meant some sub disrespecting, it was fine with her.

PAUL JELLINEK: That's why Dave was so important. If Bernadette was just a woman standing on-site trying to get metal welded, she'd have gotten eaten alive. And don't forget, she was thirty. Architecture is one of the few professions where age and experience are actually considered assets. To be a young woman on her own, building a house essentially without plans, well, that just wasn't done. I mean, even Ayn Rand's architect was a guy.

After receiving a building permit for a three-bedroom, four-thousand-square-foot, glass-and-steel box with a detached garage and guesthouse, Fox began construction on the Twenty Mile House. A cement factory in Gardena supplied the sand, which Fox mixed on-site. For steel, a recycling yard in Glendale contacted Fox if beams came in. (Materials from a dump were deemed OK, even if the materials themselves originated from outside the twenty-mile radius.) A house down the street was being torn down; its

*dumpster was a great source for materials. Tree trimmers provided
wood, which would be used for cabinets, flooring, and furniture.*

ELLIE SAITO: I was in L.A. on my way to Palm Springs to meet
with some prefab developers. I stopped by the Twenty Mile
House. Bernadette was all laughter, in overalls and a tool belt,
speaking broken Spanish to a bunch of workers. It was infectious. I rolled up my Issey Miyake and helped dig a trench.

*One day, a convoy of trucks pulled into the adjacent lot. The
property had been purchased by Nigel Mills-Murray, the TV
magnate from England, best known for his smash game show
You Catch It, You Keep It. He had hired a British architect to
design a fourteen-thousand-square-foot Tudor-style white marble
mansion Fox dubbed the White Castle. Initially, the relationship
between the two crews was cordial. Fox would go to the White Castle and borrow an electrician for an hour. An inspector was about
to revoke the White Castle's grading permit, and Fox talked him
out of it.*

DAVID WALKER: The building of the White Castle was like a
movie in fast motion. Hundreds of workers descended on the
place and worked around the clock, literally. Three crews a day
working eight-hour shifts.

There's a story that during the filming of *Apocalypse Now*,
Francis Ford Coppola had a sign on his trailer: "Fast, Cheap,
Good: Pick Two." That's the way it is with houses. Me and Bernadette, we definitely picked "cheap" and "good." But, man,
we were slow. The White Castle, well, they picked "fast" and
"fast."

The White Castle was ready to move into before Fox and Walker had closed the walls on the Twenty Mile House.

DAVID WALKER: The *You Catch It, You Keep It* guy starts coming by, doing walk-throughs with the decorator. One day, he decides he doesn't like the brass hardware. He has every handle, doorknob, hinge, and bathroom fixture switched out.

For us, it was like Christmas came early. The next day, Bernadette is literally standing in the White Castle's dumpster when the English guy pulls up in his Rolls-Royce.

Nigel Mills-Murray did not respond to several interview requests. His business manager did.

JOHN L. SAYRE: Who *would* like to drive up and find a neighbor digging through his trash? Nobody, that's who. My client would have been happy to discuss a fair price for his fixtures. But the woman didn't ask. She just entered his property and stole from him. Last time I checked, that was illegal.

Overnight, Mills-Murray erected a razor-wire fence and posted a twenty-four-hour security guard at the entrance to the driveway. (The White Castle and the Twenty Mile House shared a driveway. Technically, it was an easement deeded to the White Castle over the Twenty Mile House's property. This would become an important factor in the year to come.)

Fox became obsessed with getting the discarded hardware. When a truck arrived at the White Castle to remove the dumpster, she jumped in her car and followed it to a traffic light. She gave the driver a hundred bucks to salvage Mills-Murray's hardware.

DAVID WALKER: She thought it was too tacky to use in the house. She decided to solder the pieces together with wire, like in the old days, and turn it into her front gate.

Mills-Murray called the police, but no charges were filed. The next day, the gate was gone. Fox was convinced Mills-Murray had stolen it, but she had no proof. With Fox's job at the Getty winding down, she quit and devoted all her energies to the Twenty Mile House.

PAUL JELLINEK: I definitely noticed a different energy once Bernadette quit. I'd show up with students, and all she'd talk about was the White Castle and how ugly it was, how much they wasted. It was all true, but it had nothing to do with architecture.

The White Castle was finally completed. Its crowning touch was a million dollars' worth of California fan palms planted along the shared driveway, each lowered into place by helicopter. Fox became furious that her entry now looked like a Ritz-Carlton. She complained, but Mills-Murray sent over the title report clearly specifying that his easement over her property was for "ingress and egress" and "landscaping decisions and maintenance."

DAVID WALKER: Twenty years later, any time I hear the words "easement," "ingress," or "egress," I still get sick to my stomach. Bernadette would not stop ranting about it. I started to wear a Walkman so I could tune her out.

Mills-Murray decided to christen his new home by hosting a lavish Oscar after-party. He hired Prince to play in the backyard. Lack of parking is always an issue along Mulholland Drive, so

Mills-Murray hired a valet. The day before the party, Fox eaves-dropped on Mills-Murray's assistant as she walked the driveway with the head valet, figuring out where to park a hundred cars. Fox notified a dozen towing companies that cars were going to be illegally parked on her driveway.

During the party, while the valets snuck into the backyard to watch Prince perform "Let's Go Crazy," Fox waved in the idling fleet of tow trucks. In a flash, twenty cars were towed. When a raging Mills-Murray confronted Fox, she calmly produced the property title, which stated the driveway was for "ingress and egress." Not parking cars.

PAUL JELLINEK: Elgie and Bernadette were living at Beeber Bifocal at the time, with the idea they would move into the Twenty Mile House and start a family. But Elgie was growing distraught by what the neighbor feud was doing to Bernadette. There was no way he was going to move into that house. I told him to wait, that things might change.

One April morning in 1992, Fox received a phone call. "Are you Bernadette Fox?" the voice asked. "Are you alone?"

The caller told her she'd been awarded a MacArthur "genius" grant. It had never before been given to an architect. The $500,000 grant is awarded to "talented individuals who have shown extraordinary originality and dedication in their creative pursuits and a marked capacity for self-direction."

PAUL JELLINEK: A friend of mine in Chicago who was affiliated with the MacArthur Foundation—I don't even know how, the whole thing's so mysterious—asked me what I thought was the most exciting thing going on in architecture. I told him the truth—Bernadette Fox's house. Who the hell knew what she was exactly—an architect, an outsider artist, a lady who liked working with her hands, a glorified dumpster-diver. I just knew her houses felt good to walk into.

It was '92, and there was talk of green architecture, but this was before LEED, before the Green Building Council, a decade before *Dwell*. Sure, environmental architecture had been around for decades, but beauty wasn't a priority.

My friend from Chicago came out with a big group. No doubt they expected some ugly-ass yurt made out of license plates and tires. But when they walked into the Twenty Mile House, they started laughing, that's how gorgeous it was. A sparkling glass box with clean lines, not an inch of drywall or paint. The floors were concrete; the walls and ceiling, wood; the counters, exposed aggregate with bits of broken glass for translucent color. Even with all those warm materials, it felt lighter inside than outside.

That day, Bernadette was building the garage, pouring concrete into forms and doing tilt-up walls. The MacArthur guys took off their suit jackets, rolled up their sleeves, and helped. That's when I knew she'd won it.

Receiving this recognition enabled Fox to let go of the Twenty Mile House and put it on the market.

JUDY TOLL: Bernadette told me she wanted to list the house and look for another piece of property without a shared driveway. Having Nigel Mills-Murray next door was very good for her property values. I snapped some pictures and told her I'd run some comps.

When I got to my office, I had a message on my answering machine. It was from a business manager I worked with often, who had heard the house was for sale. I told him we wouldn't be listing it for a couple of months, but he was an architecture buff and wanted to own the house that won the "Genius award."

We ate at Spago to celebrate, me, Bernadette, and her darling husband. You should have seen the two of them. He was so proud of her. She had just won a big award and made a killing on the house. What husband wouldn't be proud? During dessert, he took out a little box and gave it to Bernadette. Inside was a silver locket with a yellow photograph inside, of a severe and disturbed-looking girl.

"It's Saint Bernadette," Elgie said. "Our Lady of Lourdes. She had visions, eighteen in all. You had your first vision with Beeber Bifocal. You had your second vision with the Twenty Mile House. Here's to sixteen more."

Bernadette started crying. I started crying. He started crying. The three of us were in a puddle when the waiter came with the check.

At that lunch, that's when they decided to go to Europe. They wanted to see Lourdes, home of Saint Bernadette. It was all just so sweet. They had the whole world ahead of them.

Bernadette still needed to get the house photographed for her portfolio. If she waited a month, it would give the garden time to fill in. So she decided to do it after they returned. I called the buyer and asked if this was acceptable. He said, Yes, of course.

PAUL JELLINEK: Everyone thinks I was so close to Bernadette, but I really didn't talk to her all that much. It was the fall and I had a new group of students. I wanted to show them the Twenty Mile House. I knew Bernadette had gone to Europe. Still, I did what I always did, left a message to say I'd be stopping by the Twenty Mile house with my class. I had a key.

I turned off of Mulholland and saw that Bernadette's gate was open, which was the first weird thing. I drove up and got out of my car. It took me a second to understand what I was seeing: a bulldozer was demolishing the house! Three bulldozers, actually, pushing into walls, breaking glass, crunching beams, just smashing and flattening the furniture, lights, windows, cabinets. It was so fucking loud, which made it more confusing.

I had no idea what was going on. I didn't even know she'd sold the house. I ran up to one of the bulldozers and literally pulled the guy off and screamed at him, "What the hell are you doing?" But he didn't speak English.

There were no cell phones back then. I had my students form a chain in front of the bulldozers, then I drove as fast as I could to Hollywood Boulevard, to the nearest pay phone. I called Bernadette and got her answering machine. "What the hell are you doing?" I screamed into it. "I can't believe you didn't tell me. You don't just go off to Europe and destroy your house!"

Jellinek wasn't at the office two weeks later when Fox left the following message, which he still has, and he plays for me. "Paul," says a woman's voice. "What's going on? What are you talking about? We're back. Call me." Fox then called her realtor.

JUDY TOLL: She asked if anything was wrong with the house. I told her I didn't know if Nigel had done anything with it. She said, "Who?" I said, "Nigel." Again, she said, "Who?!" but this time she shrieked it. I said, "The gentleman who bought your house. Your neighbor, Nigel, with the television show where they drop expensive things from a ladder and if you catch it, you keep it. He's English."

"Wait a second," Bernadette said. "A friend of yours named *John Sayre* bought my house."

Then I realized, of course, she didn't know! While she was in Europe, the business manager had me transfer title over to Nigel Mills-Murray. I had no idea, but the business manager was buying it for his client, Nigel Mills-Murray. That happens all the time, celebrities buy houses in the names of their business managers and then transfer title. For privacy, you know.

"Nigel Mills-Murray was the buyer all along," I told Bernadette.

There was silence, and then she hung up the phone.

The Twenty Mile House, which had taken three years to complete, had been demolished in a day. The only pictures that exist are the ones realtor Judy Toll took with her point-and-shoot. The only plans are the comically incomplete ones Fox submitted to the building department.

PAUL JELLINEK: I know she's considered the big victim in all of this. But the Twenty Mile House getting destroyed was nobody's fault but Bernadette's.

There was an outpouring of grief in architecture circles as word spread that the house had been demolished.

PAUL JELLINEK: Bernadette went AWOL. I had a ton of architects sign a letter, which ran in the paper. Nicolai Ouroussoff wrote a nice editorial. The Landmark Commission got serious about preserving modern architecture. So that was something good that came out of it.

I tried calling her, but she and Elgie sold Beeber Bifocal and left town. I can't imagine. I just can't imagine. It makes me sick to think about it. I still drive by the site. There's nothing there.

Bernadette Fox never built another house. She moved to Seattle with her husband, who got a job at Microsoft. When the AIA made Fox a fellow, she didn't attend the ceremony.

PAUL JELLINEK: I'm in a weird position when it comes to Bernadette. Everyone looks to me, because I was there, and I never gave her the chance to alienate me. But she built only two houses, both for herself. They were great buildings, that's not what I'm saying. I'm saying it's one thing when you build a house with no client, no budget, and no time constraints. What if she had to design an office building, or a house for someone else? I don't think she had the temperament. She didn't get along with most people. And what kind of architect does that make you?

It's because she produced so little that everyone is able to canonize her. Saint Bernadette! She was a young woman in a man's world! She built green before there was green! She was a master furniture maker! She was a sculptor! She called out the Getty on its wasteful ways! She founded the DIY movement! You can say anything you want, and what's the evidence against it?

Getting out when she did was probably the best thing that could have happened for her reputation. People say that Nigel Mills-Murray destroying the Twenty Mile House caused Bernadette to go crazy. I think, Yeah, crazy. Crazy like a fox.

An Internet search produces no clues as to what Fox is up to these days. Five years ago, there was an auction item listed in a brochure for the Galer Street School, a private school in Seattle. It read, "CUSTOM TREE HOUSE: Third-grade parent Bernadette Fox will design a tree house for your child, supply all materials, and build it herself." I contacted the head of school about this auction item. She emailed back: "According to our records, this auction item received no bids and went unsold."

Monday, December 13
From Mom to Paul Jellinek

Paul,

Greetings from sunny Seattle, where women are "gals," people are "folks," a little bit is a "skosh," if you're tired you're "logy," if something is slightly off it's "hinky," you can't sit Indian-style but you *can* sit "crisscross applesauce," when the sun comes out it's never called "sun" but always "sunshine," boyfriends and girlfriends are "partners," nobody swears but someone occasionally might "drop the f-bomb," you're allowed to cough but only into your elbow, and any request, reasonable or unreasonable, is met with "no worries."

Have I mentioned how much I hate it here?

But it is the tech capital of the world, and we have this thing called "the Internet," which allows us to do something called a "Google search," so if we run into a random guy outside the public library and he starts talking about an architecture competition in L.A. inspired by let's say, *oneself*, we can type that information into the aforementioned "Google search" and learn more.

You little rotter, Paul. Your fingerprints are all over that Twenty

Mile House redux. Why do you love me so? I've never understood what you saw in me, you big lunk.

I suppose I should be honored or angry, but really the word would be nonplussed. (I just looked that up in the dictionary, and you know what's funny? The first definition is "so surprised and embarrassed one doesn't know how to react." The second definition is "not at all disturbed." No wonder I never know how to use it! In this case, I'm using it in the latter context.)

Paul Jellinek. How the hell are you? Are you mad at me? Longing for me because life's just not the same without me? Nonplussed, in either the first or second sense of the word?

I believe I owe you a return phone call.

You probably wonder what I've been doing for the last twenty years. I've been resolving the conflict between public and private space in the single-family residence.

I'm joking! I've been ordering shit off the Internet!

By now you've figured out that we moved to Seattle. Elgie was hired by Microsoft. MS, as it's known on the inside. You've never seen a more acronym-happy company than Microsoft.

My intention was never to grow old in this dreary upper-left corner of the Lower Forty-eight. I just wanted to leave L.A. in a snit, lick my considerably wounded ego, and when I determined that everyone felt sufficiently sorry for me, unfurl my cape and swoop in to launch my second act and show those bastards who the true bitch goddess of architecture really is.

But then: Elgie ended up loving it here. Who knew that our Elgin had a bike-riding, Subaru-driving, Keen-wearing alter ego just waiting to bust out? And bust out it did, at Microsoft, which is this marvelous Utopia for people with genius IQs. Wait, did I say Microsoft is marvelous and Utopian? I meant to say sinister and evil.

There are meeting rooms everywhere, more meeting rooms than offices, which are all teeny-tiny. The first time I beheld Elgie's office, I gasped. It was hardly larger than his desk. He's now one of the biggest guys there, and still his office is minuscule. You can barely fit a couch long enough to nap on, so I ask, What kind of office is that! Another oddity: there are no assistants. Elgie heads a team of 250, and they all share one assistant. Or admins, as they're called, accent on the "ad." In L.A., someone half as important as Elgie would have two assistants, and assistants for *their* assistants, until every bright son or daughter of anyone west of the 405 was on the payroll. But not at Microsoft. They do everything themselves through specially coded portals.

OK, OK, calm down, I'll tell you more about the meeting rooms. There are maps on every wall, which is perfectly normal, right, for businesses to have a map on the wall showing their territories or distribution routes? Well, on Microsoft's walls are maps of the world, and in case you're still unclear about their dominion, under these maps are the words: THE WORLD. The day I realized their goal was WORLD DOMINATION, I was out at Redmond having lunch with Elgie.

"What's Microsoft's mission, anyway?" I asked, wolfing down a piece of Costco birthday cake. It was Costco Day on campus, and they were signing people up for discounted membership, using free sheet cake as enticement. No wonder I get confused and sometimes mistake the place for a marvelous Utopia.

"For a long time," Elgie answered, not eating cake because the man has discipline, "our mission was to have a desktop computer in every house in the world. But we essentially accomplished that years ago."

"So what's your mission now?" I asked.

"It's..." He looked at me warily. "Well," he said, looking around. "That's not something we talk about."

See, a conversation with anyone at Microsoft ends in either one of two ways. This is the first way—paranoia and suspicion. They're even terrified of their own wives! Because, as they like to say, it's a company built on information, and that can just walk out the door.

Here's the second way a conversation with an MS employee ends. (MS — oh, God, they've got me doing it now!) Let's say I'm at the playground with my daughter. I'm bleary-eyed, pushing her on the swings, and one swing over there's an outdoorsy father — because fathers only come in one style here, and that's outdoorsy. He has seen a diaper bag I'm carrying which isn't a diaper bag at all, but one of the endless "ship gifts" with the Microsoft logo Elgie brings home.

OUTDOORSY DAD: You work at Microsoft?

ME: Oh, no, my husband does. (Heading off his next question at the pass) He's in robotics.

OUTDOORSY DAD: I'm at Microsoft, too.

ME: (Feigning interest, because really, I could give a shit, but wow, is this guy chatty) Oh? What do you do?

OUTDOORSY DAD: I work for Messenger.

ME: What's that?

OUTDOORSY DAD: You know Windows Live?

ME: Ummm...

OUTDOORSY DAD: You know the MSN home page?

ME: Kind of...

OUTDOORSY DAD: (Losing patience) When you turn on your computer, what comes up?

ME: The *New York Times.*

OUTDOORSY DAD: Well, there's a Windows home page that usually comes up.

ME: You mean the thing that's preloaded when you buy a PC? I'm sorry, I have a Mac.

OUTDOORSY DAD: (Getting defensive because everyone there is lusting for an iPhone, but there's a rumor that if Ballmer sees you with one, you'll get shitcanned. Even though this hasn't been proven, it hasn't been *disproven* either.) I'm talking about Windows Live. It's the most-visited home page in the world.

ME: I believe you.

OUTDOORSY DAD: What's your search engine?

ME: Google.

OUTDOORSY DAD: Bing's better.

ME: No one said it wasn't.

OUTDOORSY DAD: If you ever, *once*, went to Hotmail, Windows Live, Bing, or MSN, you'd see a tab at the top of the page that says "Messenger." That's my team.

ME: Cool! What do you do for Messenger?

OUTDOORSY DAD: My team is working on an end-user, C Sharp interface for HTML5…

And then they kind of trail off, because at some point in every conversation, there's nobody in the world smart enough to dumb it down.

It turns out, the whole time in L.A., Elgie was just a guy in socks searching for a carpeted, fluorescent-lit hallway in which to roam at all hours of the night. At Microsoft, he found his ideal habitat. It's like he was back at MIT pulling all-nighters, throwing pencils into ceiling tiles, and playing vintage Space Invaders with foreign-accented code monkeys. When Microsoft built their newest campus, they made it the home of Elgie's team. In the atrium of his new building, there's a sandwich shop with the sign BOAR'S HEAD FINEST DELI MEATS SERVED HERE. The moment I saw that, I knew I'd never see him again.

So here we are in Seattle.

First off, whoever laid out this city never met a four-way intersection they didn't turn into a five-way intersection. They never met a two-way street they didn't suddenly and for no reason turn into a one-way street. They never met a beautiful view they didn't block with a twenty-story old folks home with zero architectural integrity. Wait, I think that's the first time the words "architectural" and "integrity" have ever been used together in a discussion of Seattle.

The drivers here are horrible. And by horrible, I mean they don't realize I have someplace to be. They're the slowest drivers you ever saw. If someone is at a five-way stoplight, and growing old while they're waiting for the lights to cycle through, and finally, finally it's time to go, you know what they do? They start, then put on their brakes in the middle of the intersection. You're hoping they lost a half a sandwich under their seat and are digging for it, but no. They're just slowing down because, hey, it *is* an intersection.

Sometimes these cars have Idaho plates. And I think, What the hell is a car from Idaho doing here? Then I remember, That's right, we *neighbor* Idaho. I've moved to a state that neighbors Idaho. And any life that might still be left in me kind of goes poof.

My daughter did an art project called a "step book," which started with the universe, then opened up to the solar system, then the Earth, then the United States, then Washington State, then Seattle—and I honestly thought, What does Washington State have to do with her? And I remember, that's right, we *live* here. Poof.

Seattle. I've never seen a city so overrun with runaways, drug addicts, and bums. Pike Place Market: they're everywhere. Pioneer Square: teeming with them. The flagship Nordstrom: have to step over them on your way in. The first Starbucks: one of them hogging the milk counter because he's sprinkling free cinnamon on his head. Oh, and they all have pit bulls, many of them wearing handwritten signs with witticisms such as I BET YOU A DOLLAR YOU'LL READ THIS SIGN. Why does every beggar have a pit bull? Really, you don't know? It's because they're *badasses*, and don't you forget it.

I was downtown early one morning and I noticed the streets were full of people pulling wheelie suitcases. And I thought, Wow, here's a city full of go-getters. Then I realized, no, these are all homeless bums who have spent the night in doorways and are packing up before they get kicked out. Seattle is the only city where you step in shit and you pray, Please God, let this be dog shit.

Anytime you express consternation as to how the U.S. city with more millionaires per capita than any other would allow itself to be overtaken by bums, the same reply always comes back. "Seattle is a compassionate city."

A guy named the Tuba Man, a beloved institution who'd play his tuba at Mariners games, was brutally murdered by a street gang near the Gates Foundation. The response? Not to *crack down on gangs* or anything. That wouldn't be compassionate. Instead, the people in the neighborhood redoubled their efforts to "get to the root of gang violence." They arranged a "Race for the Root," to raise money for this dunderheaded effort. Of course, the "Race for the Root" was a triathlon, because God forbid you should ask one of these athletic do-gooders to partake in only *one* sport per Sunday.

Even the mayor gets in on the action. There was a comic-book store in my neighborhood that demonstrated great courage by putting a sign in the window indicating that nobody with pants pulled below their buttocks would be allowed in. And the mayor said he wanted to get to *the root* of why kids sag their pants. The fucking mayor.

And don't get me started on Canadians. It's a whole thing.

Remember when the feds busted in on that Mormon polygamist cult in Texas a few years back? And the dozens of wives were paraded in front of the camera? And they all had this long mouse-colored hair with strands of gray, no hairstyle to speak of, no makeup, ashy skin, Frida Kahlo facial hair, and unflattering clothes? And on cue, the *Oprah* audience was shocked and horrified? Well, they've never been to Seattle.

There are two hairstyles here: short gray hair and long gray hair. You go into a salon asking for hair color, and they flap their elbows and cluck, "Oh, goody, we never get to do color!"

But what really happened was I came up here and had four miscar-riages. Try as I might, it's hard to blame that one on Nigel Mills-Murray.

Oh, Paul. That last year in L.A. was just so horrible. I am so ashamed of my behavior. I've carried it with me to this day, the revulsion at how vile I became, all for a stupid house. I've never stopped obsessing about it. But just before I completely self-immolate, I think about Nigel Mills-Murray. Was I really so bad that I deserved to have *three years of my life* destroyed for some rich prick's practical joke? So I had some cars towed, yes. I made a gate out of trash doorknobs. I'm an artist. I won a Mac-Arthur grant, for fuck's sake. Don't I get a break? I'll be watching TV and see Nigel Mills-Murray's name at the end. I'll go nuts inside. He gets to keep creating, and I'm the one who's still in pieces?

Let's inventory the toy chest: shame, anger, envy, childishness, self-reproach, self-pity.

The AIA gave me that nice honor years back, there's this 20 × 20 × 20 thing, an *Artforum* reporter tried to talk to me about some article. Those things just make it worse, you see. They're booby prizes because everyone knows I am an artist who couldn't overcome failure.

Just last night, I woke up to pee. I was half asleep, with no concept of myself, a blank, and then the data started reloading—*Bernadette Fox*—*Twenty Mile House destroyed*—*I deserved it*—*I'm a failure.* Fail-ure has got its teeth in me, and it won't stop shaking.

Ask me about the Twenty Mile House now, I'm a twister of noncha-lance. *That old thing? Who cares?* It's my false front, and I'm sticking to it.

When the miscarriages started, Elgie was there for me, leaning in.

"It's all my fault," I'd say.

"No, Bernadette," he'd say. "It's not your fault."

"I deserve this," I'd say.

"Nobody deserves this."

"I can't make anything without destroying it," I'd say.

"Please, Bernadette, that's not true."

"I'm a monster," I'd say. "How can you possibly love me?"

"Because I know you."

What Elgie didn't know was that I was using his words to help me heal from an even deeper grief than the miscarriages, a grief I couldn't admit to: grief over the Twenty Mile House. Elgie still doesn't know. Which just adds to my bottomless, churning shame, that I have become so demented and dishonest, a stranger to the most brilliant and honorable man I've ever met.

The only thing you can blame Elgie for is he makes life look so damn simple: do what you love. In his case, that means working, spending time with his family, and reading presidential biographies.

Yes, I've hauled my sorry ass to a shrink. I went to some guy here, the best in Seattle. It took me about three sessions to fully chew the poor fucker up and spit him out. He felt terrible about failing me. "Sorry," he said, "but the psychiatrists up here aren't very good."

I bought a house when we got here. This crazy reform school for girls with every building restriction conceivable attached. To make something of it would require Harry Houdini ingenuity. This, of course, appealed to me. I truly intended to recover from the body blow of the Twenty Mile House by making a home for me and Elgie and the baby I was always pregnant with. Then I'd sit on the toilet and look down, my upper body a capital C, and there it was, blood on my underpants, and I'd weep to Elgie all over again.

When I finally stayed pregnant, our daughter's heart hadn't developed completely, so it had to be rebuilt in a series of operations. Her chances for survival were minuscule, especially back then. The moment she was born, my squirming blue guppy was whisked off to the OR before I could touch her.

Five hours later, the nurse came around and gave me the shot to dry up my milk. The surgery had been botched. Our baby wasn't strong enough to endure another one.

Here's what inconsolable looks like: me sitting in my car in the parking lot of Children's Hospital, all the windows rolled up, wearing my hospital gown, twelve inches of pads between my legs and Elgie's parka over my shoulders, Elgie standing outside in the dark, trying to make me out through fogged windows. I was all torture and adrenaline. I had no thoughts, no emotions. Inside me roiled something so terrible that God knew he had to keep my baby alive, or this torrent within me would be unleashed on the universe.

Ten in the morning, a knock on the windshield. "We can see her now," Elgie said. That's when I met Bee. She was sleeping peacefully in her incubator, a little blue loaf with a yellow cap on, the sheets perfectly stretched across her chest. There were wires and tubes stuck on and in every piece of her. Beside her towered a rack of thirteen monitors. She was plugged into every one. "Your daughter," the nurse said. "She's been through a lot."

I understood then that Bee was *other* and that she had been entrusted to me. You know those posters of baby Krishna, "Balakrishna," as he's known, the incarnation of Vishnu, the creator and destroyer, and he's fat and happy and *blue?* That's what Bee was, the creator and the destroyer. It was just so obvious.

"She's not going to *die*," I said to the nurses, like they were the stupidest people on earth. "She's Balakrishna." The name was put on her birth certificate. The only reason Elgie played along was because he knew the grief counselor was scheduled to meet with us in an hour.

I asked to be left alone with my daughter. Elgie once gave me a locket of Saint Bernadette, who had eighteen visions. He said Beeber Bifocal and Twenty Mile were my first two visions. I dropped to my knees at Bee's incubator and grabbed my locket. "I will never build again," I said to God. "I will renounce my other sixteen visions if you'll keep my baby alive." It worked.

Nobody in Seattle likes me. The day I got here, I went to Macy's to buy a mattress. I asked if someone could help me. "You're not from around here, are you?" the lady said. "I can tell from your energy." What kind of energy was that? That I asked to be helped by a mattress saleslady in a mattress department?

I can't tell you the number of times I've been in the middle of a perfunctory conversation, and someone will say, "Tell us what you *really* think." Or "Maybe you should switch to decaf." I blame the proximity to Canada. Let's leave it at that; otherwise I'll get onto the subject of Canadians, and that's something you seriously don't have time for.

I recently made one friend, though, a woman named Manjula, who runs my errands for me all the way from India. She's virtual, but it's a start.

The motto of this city should be the immortal words spoken by that French field marshal during the siege of Sebastopol, *"J'y suis, j'y reste"*—"I am here, and here I shall remain." People are born here, they grow up here, they go to the University of Washington, they work here, they die here. Nobody has any desire to leave. You ask them, "What is it again that you love so much about Seattle?" and they answer, "We have everything. The mountains and the water." This is their explanation, mountains and water.

As much as I try not to engage people in the grocery checkout, I couldn't resist one day when I overheard one refer to Seattle as "cosmopolitan." Encouraged, I asked, "Really?" She said, Sure, Seattle is full of people from all over. "Like where?" Her answer, "Alaska. I have a ton of friends from Alaska." Whoomp, there it is.

Let's play a game. I'll say a word, and you say the first word that pops into your head. Ready?

ME: Seattle.

YOU: Rain.

What you've heard about the rain: it's all true. So you'd think it would become part of the fabric, especially among the lifers. But *every time it rains*, and you have to interact with someone, here's what they'll say: "Can you believe the weather?" And you want to say, "Actually, I *can* believe the weather. What I can't believe is that I'm actually having a conversation about the weather." But I don't say that, you see, because that would be instigating a fight, something I try my best to avoid, with mixed results.

Getting into fights with people makes my heart race. *Not* getting into fights with people makes my heart race. Even sleeping makes my heart race! I'm lying in bed when the thumping arrives, like a foreign invader. It's a horrible dark mass, like the monolith in *2001*, self-organized but completely unknowable, and it enters my body and releases adrenaline. Like a black hole, it sucks in any benign thoughts that might be scrolling across my brain and attaches visceral panic to them. For instance, during the day I might have mused, Hey, I should pack more fresh fruit in Bee's lunch. That night, with the arrival of The Thumper, it becomes, I'VE GOT TO PACK MORE FRESH FRUIT IN BEE'S LUNCH!!! I can feel the irrationality and anxiety draining my store of energy like a battery-operated racecar grinding away in the corner. This is energy I will need to get through the next day. But I just lie in bed and watch it burn, and with it any hope for a productive tomorrow. There go the dishes, there goes the grocery store, there goes exercise, there goes bringing in the garbage cans. There goes basic human kindness. I wake up in a sweat so thorough I sleep with a pitcher of water by the bed or I might die of dehydration.

Oh, Paul, do you remember that place down the street from the Twenty Mile House, on La Brea, with the rosewater ice cream and they'd let us have meetings there and use their phone? I'd love you to meet Bee.

I know what you're wondering: When on earth do I find time to shower? I don't! I can go for days. I'm a mess, I don't know what's wrong with me. I've gotten into a dispute with a neighbor—yes! again!—and this time, in retaliation, I put up a sign and inadvertently destroyed her house. Can you fucking believe it?

The tale of woe begins in kindergarten. The school Bee attends is wild about parental involvement. They're always wanting us to sign up for committees. I never do, of course. One of the parents, Audrey Griffin, approached me in the hall one day.

"I see you didn't sign up for any committees," she said, all smiles and daggers.

"I'm not so much into committees," I said.

"What about your husband?" she asked.

"He's even less into them than I am."

"So neither of you believes in community?" she asked.

By now, a gaggle of moms was circling, relishing this long-overdue confrontation with the sick girl's antisocial mom. "I don't know if community is something you do or don't *believe* in," I answered.

A few weeks later, I went into Bee's classroom and there was a thing up called the Wonderwall. On it, kids wrote questions like, "I wonder what children in Russia eat for breakfast?" or "I wonder what makes an apple red or green?" I was bursting with cuteness when I came upon the following, "I wonder why all the parents except one volunteer in the classroom?" Written by Kyle Griffin, spawn of the trout.

I never liked this kid, Kyle. In kindergarten, Bee had one hell of a scar blazing the length of her chest. (It's melted away with time, but back then, it was a beaut.) One day, Kyle saw Bee's scar and called her "Caterpillar." I wasn't thrilled when Bee told me, of course, but kids are cruel, and Bee wasn't even that upset. I let it go. The principal, who knew this kid was a bad seed, used Bee as cover and convened a bullying forum.

A year later, still miffed after the Wonderwall, I got over my bad self and actually signed up for my first volunteer job, as a parent driver for a school visit to Microsoft. I was in charge of four kids: Bee and three others, including this kid Kyle Griffin. We were walking past a bunch of candy machines. (Microsoft has candy machines everywhere, set so that without putting in money you can push a button and candy will come out.) Young Goodman Griffin, because his default is low-grade destruction, whacked a machine. A candy bar dropped down. So he just started banging the shit out of the machines, and all the kids joined in, including Bee. Candy and soda tumbled to the floor, the kids screaming, jumping up and down. It was too fabulous, something out of *A Clockwork Orange*. Just then, another group of kids, chaperoned by the principal herself, happened upon our mini-droog rampage. "Which one of you started this?" she demanded.

"Nobody started it," I said. "It's my fault."

What does Kyle do, but raise his hand and rat himself out. "It was me." His mother, Audrey, has hated me ever since, and she's gotten the other moms in on the action.

So why didn't I switch schools? The other good schools I could have sent Bee to...well, to get to them, I'd have to drive past a Buca di Beppo. I hated my life enough without having to drive past a Buca di Beppo four times a day.

Are you bored yet? God, I am.

In a nutshell: Once when I was a kid, there was an Easter egg hunt at the country club, and I found a golden egg, which entitled me to a baby bunny. My parents weren't at all amused. But they grimly bought a hutch and we set up the bunny in our apartment on Park Avenue. I named the rabbit Sailor. That summer, I went away to camp, and my parents repaired to Long Island, leaving Sailor in the apartment with instructions for the maid to feed him. We returned at the end of August to find that Gloria had run off two months prior, with the silverware and Mom's jewelry. I ran to Sailor's hutch to see if he'd made it through alive. He was backed into the corner, shivering, and in the most wretched condition: he had become so malnourished that his fur had grown horribly long, his body's attempt to compensate for his slow metabolism and low temperature. His claws were an inch long, and worse, his front teeth had curled over his lower lip so he could hardly open his mouth. Apparently, rabbits need to be chewing on hard things like carrots; otherwise their teeth will grow. Terrified, I opened the cage door to hug little Sailor, but, in a spastic fury, he started scratching my face and neck. I still have the scars. Without anyone attending to him, he had gone feral.

That's what's happened to me, in Seattle. Come at me, even in love, and I'll scratch the hell out of you. 'Tis a piteous fate to have befallen a MacArthur genius, wouldn't you say? Poof.

But I do love you,
Bernadette

TUESDAY, DECEMBER 14
From Paul Jellinek

Bernadette,

Are you done? You can't honestly believe any of this nonsense. People like you must create. If you don't create, Bernadette, you will become a menace to society.

Paul

PART THREE

Menace to Society

Tuesday, December 14
Griffin family Christmas letter

'Twas the week before Christmas
When all through the house
So much mud began flowing,
Our things it did douse.

We moved to the Westin
But did not despair
When we saw that the rooms here
Are beyond compare.

Warren dons a fine bathrobe,
And I in my cap,
Each eve we head poolward
For long winter laps.

At night we love nestling
All snug in our beds
While visions of room service
Dance in our heads.

So whatever you've heard
Which has given you fright,
We Griffins are fine.
Have a swell Christmas night!

*

From: Soo-Lin Lee-Segal
To: Audrey Griffin

Audrey,

I've been a nervous wreck trying to track you down after I heard about the mudslide. But I just now received your fabulous Christmas letter. That's why you've been so quiet. You were busy turning lemons into lemonade!

Who knew the Westin was so luxurious? They must have fixed it up since I was there. If you ever get bored, I insist you move in with us. After the divorce, I converted Barry's office into a guest room and added a Murphy bed, where you and Warren can sleep, although it's a smidge tight with my new treadmill. Kyle can bunk with Lincoln and Alexandra. But be warned, we'll all have to share the one bathroom.

Samantha 2 ships in three months, so of course Elgin Branch decides now is the perfect time to go to Antarctica, the only place on the planet with no Internet. It's my responsibility to make sure things run smoothly while he's off-grid. I must admit, though, there's something thrilling about remaining completely unruffled in the midst of his mercurial demands.

You should've seen him this morning. He chewed out some women from marketing. I'm no fan of those marketing gals myself, traipsing around the world staying at five-star hotels. Still, I took Elgin aside afterward.

"I'm sure you had your hands full at home this weekend," I said. "But you must remember, we're all working toward the same goal." Boy, did that silence him. Score one for us, Audrey!

*

WEDNESDAY, DECEMBER 15

From: Audrey Griffin
To: Soo-Lin Lee-Segal

Oh, Soo-Lin!

I must confess, the Westin is nothing like I described in my holiday verse. Where do I begin?

All night self-closing doors slam, the plumbing chugs whenever a toilet is flushed, and any time someone takes a shower, it sounds like a teakettle whistling in my ear. Families of foreign tourists save their conversations until they're standing outside our door. The mini-fridge rattles and hums so much you think it's about to spring to life. Garbage trucks screech and collect dumpsterfuls of clanging bottles at 1 AM. Then the bars let out, and the streets fill with people yelling at one another in gravelly, drunken voices. All the talk involves cars. "Get in the car." "I'm not getting in the car." "Shut up, or you're not getting in the car." "Nobody tells me I can't get into my own car."

That's a lullaby compared to the alarm clock. The housekeeper must run her rag along the top of it when she cleans, so it's been going off every night at a different wee hour. We finally unplugged the flippin' thing.

Then, last night at 3:45, the *smoke alarm* started chirping. But the maintenance man was AWOL. Just as we were adjusting to this nerve-grating sound, the radio alarm in the *next room* went off! Full-blast, half-static, half-Mexican talk radio. If you ever wondered what the walls at the Westin are made of, I have your answer: tissue paper. Warren sleeps like a log, so he was useless.

I got dressed to go hunt for someone, anyone, to help. The elevator door opened. You wouldn't believe the band of degenerates that tumbled out. They looked like those horrible runaways who gather across from the Westlake Center. There were a half-dozen of them, full of the most unspeakable piercings, neon-colored hair shaved in unflattering patches, blurry tattoos top-to-bottom. One fellow had a line across his neck imprinted with the words CUT HERE. One gal wore a leather jacket, on the back of which was safety-pinned a teddy bear with a bloody tampon string hanging out of it. I couldn't make this up.

I finally tracked down the night manager and expressed my dissatisfaction with the unsavory element they allow into their establishment.

Poor Kyle, who's two rooms over, is feeling the stress. His eyes are always bloodshot from the lack of sleep. I wish we owned stock in Visine!

On top of all this, Gwen Goodyear is trying to haul in Warren and me for yet another Kyle summit. Considering our circumstances, you'd think she'd give us a grace period before cranking up that boring old tune. I know Kyle's not the most academically minded, but Gwen has had it in for him ever since Candy-machine-gate.

Oh, Soo-Lin, just writing this transports me to the halcyon days when we were happily collecting outrages about Bernadette! What simple times those were.

*

From: Soo-Lin Lee-Segal
To: Audrey Griffin

You want to be transported back? Well, Audrey, buckle your seat belt. I just had the most devastating conversation with Elgie Branch, and you'll be shocked to learn what I just did.

I'd put Elgie in a conf. room for an 11 AM all-hands. I was running around fulfilling laptop requests, expediting furniture exchanges, authorizing battery orders. I even found a missing ball for the foosball game. All I can say about life at Mister Softy is: when it rains it pours. When I got to my office—did I mention, I finally have a window office!—no less than six coworkers told me Elgie had come by looking for me, in person. He'd written a note on my door for everyone to see, asking if we could have lunch. He signed it EB, but some joker had come by and changed it to "E-Dawg," one of his many nicknames.

As I headed out, he appeared at my door, wearing shoes.

"I thought we could bicycle," he said. It was such a nice day, we decided to get some sandwiches at the deli downstairs and bike to a nice spot off campus.

Because I'm new to Samantha 2, I didn't realize we have a dedicated fleet of bicycles. Elgie is quite an acrobat. He put one foot on the pedal and skated along with the other, then swung it over the seat. I haven't been on a bike in years, and I'm afraid it showed.

"Is something wrong?" Elgie said when I veered off the path and onto the lawn.

"I think the handlebars are loose." It was the damndest thing. I couldn't keep the bike pointing straight! As I got back on, Elgie stood on his bike with both feet on the pedals and jiggled so he didn't fall over. You think that's easy? Try it sometime.

I finally got the hang of it, and we zoomed along. I'd forgotten the freedom that comes with riding a bicycle. The wind was fresh against my face, the sun was shining, and the trees were still dripping from the storm. We rode through the Commons, where people were taking their lunch outside, enjoying the sunshine and the Seahawks cheerleaders, who were doing a demonstration on the soccer field. I could feel the curious eyes upon me. Who's that? What's *she* doing with Elgin Branch?

A mile away, Elgie and I found a church with a lovely fountain courtyard and some benches. We unpacked our sandwiches.

"The reason I asked you to lunch," he said, "is what you said this morning about having my hands full at home. You were referring to Bernadette, weren't you?"

"Oh—" I was shocked. Work is work. It was very disorienting for me to switch gears.

"I'm wondering if you've noticed anything different about her recently." Elgie's eyes welled up with tears.

"What's wrong?" I took his hand, which I know probably sounds forward, but I did it out of compassion. He looked down, then gently extracted his hand. It was fine, really.

"If something's wrong," he said, "it's my fault as much as it is hers. It's not like I'm around. I'm always working. I mean, she's a great mother."

I didn't like the way Elgie was talking. Thanks to Victims Against Victimhood, I have grown expert at detecting the signs of being victimized by emotional abuse: confusion, withdrawal, negotiating reality, self-reproach. At VAV, we don't help newcomers, we CRUSH them.

C: Confirm their reality.

R: Reveal our own abuse.

U: Unite them with VAV.

S: Say sayonara to abuse.

H: Have a nice life!

I launched into the saga of Barry's failed businesses, his trips to Vegas, his Intermittent Explosive Disorder (which was never diagnosed, but which I'm convinced he suffers from), and finally how I found the strength to divorce him, but not before he successfully drained our life savings.

"About Bernadette...," he said.

My face flushed. I *had* been talking a lot about myself and VAV, which I have been known to do. "I'm sorry," I said. "How can I help?"

"When you see her at school, how does she seem? Have you noticed anything?"

"Well, to be honest," I said carefully, "from the beginning...Bernadette didn't seem to value community."

"What does that have to do with anything?"

"The underlying principle of Galer Street is community. It's not *written* anywhere that parents have to participate. But the school is built on unspoken assumptions. For instance, I am in charge of classroom volunteers. Bernadette has never once signed up. Another thing, she never walks Bee into the classroom."

"That's because you drive up and drop off the kids," Elgie said.

"You *can* do that. But most mothers prefer to walk their children into the classroom. Especially if you're a stay-at-home mom."

"I guess I'm not understanding," he said.

"The foundation of Galer Street is parent participation," I pointed out.

"But we write a check each year, on top of tuition. Isn't that participation enough?"

"There's *financial* participation, and there's the other, more *meaningful* participation. Like traffic duty, baking healthy snacks for Talent Night, brushing hair on Picture Day."

"I'm sorry," he said. "But I'm with Bernadette on this—"

"All I'm trying to do—" I felt my voice rising and took a breath. "I'm trying to give you a context for the tragedy this weekend."

"What tragedy?" he said.

Audrey, I thought he was joking. "Haven't you been getting the emails?"

"What emails?" Elgie asked.

"From Galer Street!"

"God, no," he said. "I asked to be taken off those lists years ago... hang on. What are you talking about?"

I proceeded to tell him about Bernadette erecting that billboard and destroying your home. Hand to God: he knew nothing! He just sat there, taking it all in. At one point, he dropped his sandwich and didn't even bother to pick it up.

My phone alarm beeped. It was 2:15, and he had a 2:30 skip 1:1.

We bicycled back. The sky was black, except for a brilliant white cloud patch where rays of sunshine broke through. We rode in a darling neighborhood of little bungalows cuddled together. I love the gray-green-putty colors against the leafless cherry trees and Japanese maples. I could feel the crocus, daffodil, and tulip bulbs underground, gaining strength, patiently enduring our winter, waiting to burst forth for another glorious Seattle spring.

I held my hand out and whooshed it through the thick, healthy air. What other city has given birth to the jumbo jet, the Internet super-store, the personal computer, the cellular phone, online travel, grunge music, the big-box store, *good coffee?* Where else could somebody like me ride bikes alongside the man with the fourth-most-watched TEDTalk? I started laughing.

"What's wrong?" Elgie asked.

"Oh, nothing." I was remembering how crushed I was when my father couldn't afford to send me to USC and instead I went to the UW. I'd hardly been out of Washington State. (And I still have never seen New York City!) Suddenly I didn't care. Let everyone else travel all over the world. What they're searching for in Los Angeles and New York and everywhere else is something I already have right here in Seattle. I want it all to myself.

✳

From: Audrey Griffin
To: Soo-Lin Lee-Segal

Do you think I woke up this morning and drank a big cup of stupid? Wouldn't it be convenient if Elgin Branch knew nothing of his wife's swath of destruction? I shared your tale with Warren, who suspected the same thing as me: Elgin Branch is attempting to establish a paper

trail so when we sue him for everything he's worth, he can claim igno-
rance. Well, that trick won't work. Why don't you tell that to E-Dawg
next time you're littering at a house of God? He didn't receive any of the
emails! What a pantload!

*

From: Audrey Griffin
To: Gwen Goodyear

Please check the all-school email list and confirm that Elgin Branch is
on it. I'm not talking about Bernadette, but Elgin Branch specifically.

*

It was Kennedy's birthday that night, and her mother works nights,
so Mom and I did what we always do, which is take Kennedy out for
a birthday dinner. That morning at drop-off, Kennedy was waiting
for me and Mom to pull up.

"Where are we going, where are we going?" Kennedy said.

Mom rolled down her window. "The Space Needle restaurant."

Kennedy screamed with joy and started jumping up and down.

First Daniel's Broiler, and now this? "Mom," I said. "Since when
did you get so supercool about restaurants?"

"Since now."

On the way to homeroom, Kennedy had a hard time containing
her excitement.

"Nobody *ever* goes to the Space Needle restaurant!" she shrieked.
Which is true, because even though it's at the top and it revolves —
which should make it the only restaurant you'd ever go to — it's
totally touristy and the food is expensive. Then Kennedy did her
growl thing, and tackled me.

It had been at least ten years since I'd been to the Space Needle restaurant, and I'd forgotten how awesome it is. We ordered, then Mom reached into her purse and whipped out a pencil and piece of white cardboard. In the middle, she'd written in different-colored markers, MY NAME IS KENNEDY AND I'M TURNING FABULOUS FIFTEEN.

"Huh?" Kennedy said.

"You've never been here, have you?" Mom asked Kennedy, then turned to me. "And you don't remember, do you?" I shook my head. "We put this on the windowsill." She propped the card against the glass. "And we put a pencil next to it. While the restaurant revolves, everyone will write something, so when it comes back around, you'll have a card full of birthday wishes."

"That's so cool!" Kennedy said at the same time that I said, "That's no fair!"

"We can come here for your birthday next year, I promise," Mom said.

The birthday card slowly left us, and, oh, we had so much fun. We did the one thing that Kennedy and I always do when we're with Mom, which is talk about Youth Group. Mom was raised Catholic and became an atheist in college, so she completely freaked out when I started going to Youth Group. But I only went because it was Kennedy's idea. Kennedy's mom spends half her life at Costco, so they have these huge bags of candy bars and drums of licorice at home. Plus, they have a giant TV with every cable channel, which means I spent a lot of time at Kennedy's house eating candy and watching *Friends*. But then one day Kennedy started thinking she was fat and wanted to go on a diet, and she was, like, "Bee, you can't eat licorice because I don't want to get fat." Kennedy is totally crazy like that, and we always have the craziest conversations. So she made this huge declaration that we weren't allowed to go to her house anymore because it makes her fat and instead we had to go to Youth Group. She called it her "Youth Group diet."

I kept it secret from Mom as long as I could, but when she found out she was furious because she thought I was going to turn into a Jesus freak. But Luke and his wife, Mae, who run Youth Group, aren't into that at all. Well, OK, they're a little into that. But their Bible talk lasts only, like, fifteen minutes, and when they're done we have two hours to watch TV and play games. I kind of feel sorry for Luke and Mae because they're all excited to have half of Galer Street coming over on Fridays. But they have no idea there's nowhere else to go because Friday is the one day there's no sports or extracurriculars, and all we really want to do is watch TV.

Still, Mom hates Youth Group, which Kennedy thinks is the most hilarious thing in the world. "Hey, Bee's Mom," Kennedy said. That's what she calls Mom. "Have you ever heard of poop in the stew?"

"Poop in the stew?" Mom said.

"We learned about it in Youth Group," Kennedy said. "Luke and Mae did a puppet show about drugs. And the donkey was, like, 'Well, just one little puff of marijuana can't hurt.' But the lamb said, 'Life is stew, and pot is poop. If someone stirred even a teeny-tiny bit of poop in the stew, would you really want to eat it?'"

"And those featherheads wonder why people are fleeing the church? Puppet shows for teenagers—" Before Mom could totally go off, I grabbed Kennedy's hand.

"Let's go to the bathroom again," I said. The bathroom is in the part of the restaurant that doesn't revolve, so when you return, your table isn't where you left it. That time, we were walking back, all like, "Where did our table go?" and we finally spotted Mom.

Dad was there, too. He was wearing jeans, hiking boots, and a parka, and he still had his Microsoft badge around his neck. Some things you just know. And I just knew Dad had found out about the mudslide.

"Your dad is here!" Kennedy said. "I can't believe he came to my birthday party. That is so nice." I tried to stop Kennedy, but she squirmed away and bolted over.

"Those blackberries were the only thing holding up the hillside," Dad was saying. "You knew that, Bernadette. Why on earth would you denude an entire hillside in the middle of the wettest winter on record?"

"How did you find out?" Mom said. "Let me guess. Your admin is pouring poison in your ears."

"Keep Soo-Lin out of this," Dad said. "She's the only reason it's even feasible for me to leave for three weeks."

"If you're interested in the truth," Mom said, "I had the blackberries removed in accordance with the specifications of Bugs Meany."

"Bugs Meany from *Encyclopedia Brown*?" Kennedy said. "That's so awesome!"

"Will you stop treating this as a joke?" Dad told Mom. "I look at you, Bernadette, and I'm scared. You won't talk to me. You won't go to a doctor. You're better than this."

"Dad," I said, "stop freaking out."

"Yeah, really," Kennedy said. "Happy birthday to me."

There was a moment of quiet, then me and Kennedy burst into giggles. "I'm, like, happy birthday to me," Kennedy said, which triggered another fit of laughter.

"The Griffins' house caved in," Dad said to Mom. "They're living at a hotel. Is this something we're going to have to pay for?"

"Mudslides are considered an act of God, so the Griffins' insurance covers it."

It was like Dad was a crazy person who had come into the Space Needle waving a loaded gun, and then he turned it on me. "Why didn't *you* tell me, Bee?"

"I don't know," I said quietly.

"Goody, goody gumdrops!" Kennedy said. "Here comes my birthday card!" She grabbed my arm really hard and squeezed it.

"Could you please take some Ritalin and shut up?" I said.

"Bee!" Dad snapped. "What did you just say? You don't talk to people like that."

"It's OK," Mom told Dad. "It's how they talk to each other."

"No, it's not!" He turned to Kennedy. "Kennedy, I need to apologize for my daughter."

"For what?" she asked. "Here comes my card!"

"Dad," I said. "Why do you even care? You don't even like Kennedy."

"He doesn't?" Kennedy said.

"Of course I like you, Kennedy. Bee, how could say such a thing? What's going on with this family? I just came here to have a conversation."

"You came here to yell at Mom," I said. "Audrey Griffin yelled at her already. You weren't even there. It was horrible."

"Get it, get it!" Kennedy climbed over me and grabbed her birthday card.

"It's not about yelling at Mom —" Dad became flustered. "This is a conversation between me and your mother. It was my mistake to interrupt Kennedy's birthday dinner. I didn't know when I'd have the time otherwise."

"Because you're always working," I mumbled.

"What's that?" Dad demanded.

"Nothing."

"I'm working for *you,* and for *Mom,* and because the work I'm doing has the potential to help millions of people. I'm working *especially* long hours now so I can take you to Antarctica."

"Oh, no!" Kennedy shrieked. "I hate this thing." She was about to rip up her card, but I grabbed it out of her hand. It was full of patches of different writing. There were a few "Happy Birthday"s. But mostly the card was covered with things like "Jesus is our savior. Remember our Lord Jesus died for our sins." Plus passages from the Bible. I started laughing. And then Kennedy started crying, which she does sometimes. Really, the thing to do is just let it pass.

Mom snatched the card. "Don't worry, Kennedy," she said. "I'm going to go hunt down those Jesus freaks."

"No, you are not," Dad said to Mom.

"Do it," Kennedy said, suddenly perky. "I want to watch."

"Yeah, Mom, I want to watch, too!"

"I'm leaving," Dad said. "Nobody cares, nobody listens, nobody wants me here. Happy birthday, Kennedy. Good-bye, Bee. Bernadette, go ahead, embarrass yourself, attack people who have actually found some meaning in their lives. We'll continue this when you get home."

When we drove up to the house, the light in their bedroom was on. Mom headed straight out to the Petit Trianon. I went inside. The floorboards above me creaked. It was Dad, getting out of bed, walking to the top of the stairs.

"Girls," he called down. "Is that you?"

I held my breath. A whole minute passed. Dad walked back to the bedroom, then to the bathroom. The toilet flushed. I grabbed Ice Cream by her flabby neck and we slept with Mom out in the Petit Trianon.

And Mom didn't hunt down the Jesus freaks at the restaurant. But she did write, "IT'S A CHILD'S BIRTHDAY. WHAT THE HELL IS WRONG WITH YOU PEOPLE?" and set it on the window, and as we left, it started to go around.

*

Thursday, December 16

From: Gwen Goodyear
To: Audrey Griffin

Good morning, Audrey. I checked with Kate Webb, and she does remember Bernadette and Elgin Branch requesting to be opted out of all Galer Street emails back when Bee first enrolled. I double-checked myself and indeed they are not on any of the lists we currently employ.

On another topic, I'm glad to see you're settled and that your Internet connection is working. Per my last three unanswered emails, Mr. Levy feels it's imperative that we sit down and have a talk about Kyle. I can work around your schedule.

Kindly,
Gwen

*

That morning in homeroom, we were doing vocabulary lightning round, where Mr. Levy throws out a word and points to someone and they have to use that word in a sentence. Mr. Levy said, "Sheathe," and pointed at Kyle. And Kyle said, "Sheathe my dick." We have never laughed so hard. That is *so* why Mr. Levy wanted to have a conference with Audrey Griffin. Because even though it was totally funny, I can also see why it's kind of bad.

*

From: Soo-Lin Lee-Segal
To: Audrey Griffin

I have chosen to disregard the tone of your previous nasty-gram and chalk it up to the stress of your living conditions. Audrey, you have Elgie all wrong.

This morning, I got on the Connector at my usual stop and settled into a seat in the back. Elgie boarded a few stops later, looking like he hadn't slept. He lit up when he saw me. (I think he'd forgotten I'd signed us up for the same Connector.)

Did you know he's from a prominent family in Philadelphia? Not that he would come out and say such a thing. But as a boy, he spent all his summers in Europe. I was embarrassed to admit that I'd never left the United States.

"We'll have to change that, won't we?" he said.

Don't jump to any conclusions, Audrey! He said that rhetorically. It's not like he's planning on taking me on a trip to Europe or anything.

He went to boarding school. (On that topic, it seems you and I were simply misinformed. People like me and you, who were born in Seattle and went to the UW, we lack the…I don't want to use the word *sophistica-tion*…but we lack the *something* to understand this broader worldview.)

When Elgie asked about me, I was flustered because I've led such a dull life. The only thing I could think of that is remotely interesting is how my father went blind when I was seven and that I had to take care of him.

"No kidding," Elgie said. "So you communicated in sign language?"

"Only when I was feeling cruel," I retorted. Elgie was confused. "He was *blind*," I said, "not deaf."

We both broke up laughing. Someone quipped, "What is this, the Belltown Connector?" It's an inside joke—the Belltown Connector is notoriously raucous, much more so than the Queen Anne Connector. So it was a combination of Get-A-Room and a reference to what fun they have on the Belltown Connector. I'm not sure my explanation helps you get the humor. Maybe you had to be there.

We turned to the subject of work. Elgie was anxious about the amount of time he was taking off for Christmas.

"You keep calling it a month," I said. "It's twenty-seven days. Twelve of which are Christmas vacation, when Microsoft clears out anyway. Six days are weekends. You have five travel days, where you'll be in hotels with Internet access, I checked. That leaves you out of touch for a total of nine. That's like having a bad flu."

"*Wow*," he said. "I can actually breathe."

"Your only mistake was telling the team you were leaving in the first place. I could have covered for you, and nobody would have known."

"I told them before you came along," he said.

"Then you're forgiven."

Most wonderful was that by the time we arrived, Elgie's spirits were buoyed. Which made me happy, too.

✳

From Ms. Goodyear, hand-delivered to the Westin

Audrey and Warren,

A disturbing allegation has been presented to me regarding Kyle. A parent came to me a month ago with an accusation that Kyle had been selling drugs to students in the hallways. I refused to believe it, for your sake as much as Kyle's.

Yesterday, however, another parent found twenty pills in her child's backpack. These pills have been identified as OxyContin. Under questioning, the student pointed to Kyle as the source. The student has been allowed to continue classes for the next week, with the understanding he/she will receive treatment over winter break. I need to speak to you and Warren immediately.

Kindly,

Gwen Goodyear

*

From: Audrey Griffin
To: Gwen Goodyear

You're going to have to do better than that if you wish to implicate Kyle in a Galer Street drug ring. Warren is curious about how a legal prescription for Vicodin written to *me*, which I asked Kyle to carry because *I was on crutches due to an injury sustained on your campus*—something I never considered holding Galer Street liable for, even though the statute of limitations gives me plenty of time to change my mind—has anything to do with twenty OxyContin? Was my name on those pills too?

Speaking of Warren, he's looking into the legality of letting a student who's a known drug abuser finish out the semester. Isn't that a threat to the other students? I'm asking out of curiosity.

If you're so hell-bent on placing blame, I suggest you look in the mirror.

*

From: Audrey Griffin
To: Soo-Lin Lee-Segal

Excuse me for not responding sooner. But it has taken me an hour to pull my jaw off the floor. I'm spending Christmas in a hotel and you're lauding my tormentor? Last time I checked my calendar, it was the middle of December, not April first.

*

From: Soo-Lin Lee-Segal
To: Audrey Griffin

Let me clarify. Elgin Branch walking down the aisle of the Microsoft Connector is like Diana Ross walking through her adoring audience, that time we saw her in Las Vegas. People literally *reach out and touch him*. I'm not sure Elgie knows any of them, but he's led so many gigantic meetings, and been on so many teams, that his face is familiar to hundreds, if not thousands, of MS employees. Last year when he won Outstanding Technical Leadership, which is awarded to the *ten* greatest visionaries in a company of 100,000, they hung a huge banner of his face from Building 33. He raised more money than anyone to be dunked in the dunk tank for the company-wide giving campaign. Not to mention his TEDTalk, which is number four on the list of all-time most-watched TEDTalks. No wonder he wears sound-canceling headphones. Otherwise, people would be climbing over one another to get some face time with him. Frankly, it stuns me that he takes the Connector to work at all.

My point is, it would have been wholly unprofessional for us to launch into Bernadette's transgressions with everyone straining to listen in.

*

From: Audrey Griffin
To: Soo-Lin Lee-Segal

I don't give a fig about Ted. I don't know who he is and I don't care what he says during this talk you refuse to shut up about.

*

From: Soo-Lin Lee-Segal
To: Audrey Griffin

TED stands for Technology, Entertainment, and Design. The TED conference is an exclusive meeting of the most brilliant minds in the world.
It's held once a year, in Long Beach, and it's an enormous privilege to be
chosen to give a talk. Here's a link to Elgie's TEDTalk.

*

Dad's TEDTalk *was* a really big deal. All the kids at school knew
about it. Ms. Goodyear had Dad come to give the whole school a live
demonstration. It's hard to believe Audrey Griffin had never heard
of it.

*

**Live-blog transcript of Dad's TEDTalk posted
by the blogger Masked Enzyme**

4:30 PM AFTERNOON BREAK

Half hour to go until Session 10: "Code and Mind," the last
one of the day. The gals at the Vosges chocolate booth really out-
did themselves for this break, passing out truffles with bacon.
Hot buzz: at the end of Session 9, while Mark Zuckerberg droned
on about some education initiative that nobody gave a shit
about, the Vosges girls started frying their bacon, and the smell
wafted into the auditorium. This got everyone murmuring
excitedly, "Do you smell bacon? I smell bacon." Chris bolted out
and must have torn into the Vosges girls, who now have mascara

dripping down their cheeks. Chris has always had his *detrac-tors* and this sure didn't help.

4:45 PM PEOPLE FILING INTO AUDITORIUM FOR SESSION 10

• Ben Affleck having his picture taken with Murray Gell-Mann. Dr. Gell-Mann arrived this morning, driving up to the valet in his Lexus with New Mexico plates reading QUARK. Nice touch, nice man.

• While we were on break, the stage was transformed into a living room, or maybe a college dorm. La-Z-Boy recliner, TV set, microwave, vacuum. A robot, too!

• Jesus Christ, there's a robot onstage. It's a cute one—four feet high, anthropomorphic. Hourglass shape. Dare I say, a sexy robot? Hmmm, program says next speaker is a dancer from Madagascar discussing her creative process. What's the robot for, then? Will there be some kind of African-lesbian-robot-living-room dance? Stay tuned, this might get good.

• Guy with eye patch and Nehru jacket who gave deranged talk last year about floating cities just sat down where Al Gore usually sits. No reserved seats at TED, natch, but Al Gore has sat in the third row, right aisle, dating back to Monterey, and everyone knows it. You don't just go plop down in Al Gore's spot.

• Jane doing housekeeping announcements. Gift bag pickup closes tonight. Last chance to test-drive Tesla. Luncheon tomorrow with (the awesome) E. O. Wilson for an update on his TED wish, the Encyclopedia of Life.

• Al Gore just entered, talking with Sergey Brin's parents. They're so cute and tiny and don't speak great English.

• All eyes on the veep, waiting to see how he reacts to the fact that his seat is taken. Nehru jacket offers to move, but Al Gore declines. Nehru hands Al Gore a business card! What a dirty trick. He's practically booed by the audience, but nobody will admit to being that interested. Al Gore takes business card with a smile. I heart Al Gore.

5 PM CHRIS TAKES THE STAGE

Announces that before the African lady, there will be a surprise talk, a mind-bender, he promises, on brain-computer interface. People snap out of their truffle-and-bacon haze. Chris introduces Elgin Branch from...wait for it...Microsoft Research. Research *is* the only half-decent group at MS, but really? Microsoft? Audience deflating. Energy dissipating.

5:45 PM HOLY CRAP

Disregard snarkiness of 5 PM post. Give me a second...I'm going to need some time...

7 PM SAMANTHA 2

Thanks for your patience. This talk won't post on the TED website for a month. In the meantime, let me try to do it justice. Big shout-out to my blogging pal TEDGRRRL for letting me transcribe her phone video.

5 PM Branch puts on headset. On the big screen:

ELGIN BRANCH

(You've gotta feel for these guys who have only five minutes. They're all rushing and nervous.)

5:01 PM Branch: "Twenty-five years ago, my first job was testing code for a research team at Duke. They were attempting to merge mind and computer."

5:02 PM Clicker doesn't work. Branch hits it again. And again. Branch looking around. "This isn't working," he says to everyone and no one.

5:03 PM Branch bravely soldiering on without video. "They sat two rhesus monkeys in front of a video screen with joysticks, which controlled a little animated ball. Every time the monkeys used the joysticks to move the ball in a basket, they were rewarded with a treat." He clicks again and again and looks around. Nobody is coming to help. This is ridiculous! The guy's a good sport. David Byrne stormed offstage this morning when his audio blew.

5:05 PM Branch: "That was supposed to be a video of the pioneering Duke study. In it, you'd see a pair of monkeys with two hundred electrodes implanted into their brains' motor cortex. They look like those grow-her-hair Barbies with the crown of their heads cut open and a bunch of wires cascading down. It's pretty grisly. It's probably best that I can't show you. Anyway, it was an early instance of brain-computer interface, or BCI." He clicks the clicker again. "I had a really good slide explaining how it worked."

IMHO, the guy should be angrier about this! It's a technology conference, and they can't get the clickers to work?

5:08 PM Branch: "After the monkeys had mastered using the joysticks to move the balls, the researchers disconnected the joysticks. The monkeys fiddled with the joysticks for a couple seconds, but recognized they no longer worked. They still wanted their treats, so they sat there, staring at the screen, and *thought about* moving the balls into the baskets. At this point, the electrodes implanted into their motor cortexes were activated. They diverted the monkeys' 'thoughts' to a computer, which we had programmed to interpret their brain signals and act on their thoughts. The monkeys realized they could move the ball just by *thinking about it*—and they received their treats. The most amazing thing, when you watch the video—" Branch squints into the spotlight. "Do we have the video? It would be great to see the video. Anyway, what's remarkable is how quickly the monkeys mastered moving the balls with their thoughts. It took them about fifteen seconds."

5:10 PM Branch squints into the audience. "They tell me I have one minute left."

5:10 PM Chris jumps onstage and apologizes. He's pissed about the clicker. We all are. This Branch guy is nice and low-key. And he's said nothing about the robot!

5:12 PM Branch: "The job ended. Years later, I found my way to Microsoft. In robotics." Crowd cheers. Branch squints. "What?" He obviously has no idea how excited we've all become about that damn robot.

5:13 PM Branch: "I went to work on the voice-activated personal robot you see in front of you." A rumble from the audience. Who cares if Craig Venter just announced he'd synthesized arsenic-based life in a test tube. Give us a *Jetsons*-style robot any day!

5:13 PM Branch continues, "Let's say I'm in the mood for some popcorn. I say, 'Samantha!'" The robot lights up. "We named her Samantha after the character on *Bewitched*." Laughter. "Samantha, please bring me some popcorn." You have to see this guy Branch. He's very sweet and unassuming—wearing jeans, T-shirt, and no shoes. He looks like he just rolled out of bed.

5:14 PM Samantha glides to the microwave, opens the door, and removes a bag of popcorn. Branch: "We had to pre-pop that, like one of the cooking shows." The robot rolls to Branch and hands him a bag of popcorn. Applause. Branch: "Thank you, Samantha." Robot replies, "You're welcome." Laughter. Branch: "It's cute, basic, voice-activated technology."

5:17 PM A voice from the front row says, "Can I have some of that?" It's David Pogue. Branch: "Okay, ask her." Pogue: "Samantha, bring me some popcorn." The robot doesn't move. Branch: "Say please." Pogue: "Come on!" Laughter. Branch: "I'm serious. My daughter was eight when I was working on Samantha and she accused me of being a bully. So I programmed it in. Please. It's literally the magic word." Pogue: "Samantha, bring me some popcorn... *please?*" Hilarity ensuing! The robot rolls to the edge of the stage and reaches out, but drops the bag of popcorn before Pogue can grab it. It spills all over the stage.

5:19 PM Branch: "It's Microsoft. We had some bugs." A thunderclap of laughter from the audience. Branch looks offended. "It wasn't that funny."

5:21 PM Branch: "We taught Samantha five hundred commands. We could have taught her five hundred more, but what kept holding us back was her thousands of moving parts. She lacked marketplace agility and was too expensive to scale up. Eventually, the Samantha project was canceled." Everyone in the audience goes *awww*. Branch: "What are you people? A bunch of geeks?" Instant TED classic!

5:23 PM A guy meanders onto the stage carrying a new clicker. Halfway across, he stops and hitches up his pants. Branch: "Take your time." Huge laughter.

5:24 PM Branch: "So Samantha was canceled. But then I remembered those monkeys at Duke. And I thought, Hmmm, the complicating factor in creating a personal robot is the robot itself. Maybe we could just *lose the robot.*"

5:25 PM Branch's clicker finally works, so he starts the slideshow. First image is monkeys with wires coming out of their heads. Audience gasps, some scream. Branch: "Sorry, sorry!" Branch turns off slideshow.

5:26 PM Branch: "According to Moore's law, the number of transistors that can be placed on an integrated surface doubles every two years. So in twenty years' time, what once was that horrible image…became this…" He clicks through to a slide showing a person's shaved head with what looks like a computer chip under the skin.

5:26 PM Branch: "Which became this…" He holds up a football helmet with a Seahawks sticker on it. On the inside are electrodes with wires coming out. "You could just put it on and nothing had to be wired into your brain."

5:27 PM Branch puts down the helmet and reaches into his pocket. "Which became this." He holds up something that looks like a Band-Aid. "TEDsters, meet Samantha 2."

5:27 PM Branch sticks the Band-Aid on his forehead, just under his hairline. He sits down in the La-Z-Boy. Branch: "I'm going to throw in something real-time for the skeptics." He pulls the lever and the chair reclines.

5:29 PM Weird sound. A vacuum has started up! It's moving on its own, coming over and vacuuming up popcorn. Branch is lying down with his eyes open, concentrating on the popcorn. Vacuum turns off. Branch turns to face the TV.

5:31 PM TV turns on by itself. Channels changing. It stops at a Lakers game.

5:31 PM Big screen changes to Outlook. A blank email opens. The cursor goes to the TO: field. It's writing on its own! BERNADETTE. The cursor jumps to the message field: TED TALK WENT WELL. CLICKER DIDN'T WORK. TOO BAD NOBODY HERE KNOWS POWERPOINT. DAVID POGUE IS KIND OF UNCOORDINATED. P.S.: LAKERS LEADING BY 3 AT THE HALF.

The place is on its feet. What can best be described as a roar is coming from the audience. Branch gets up and pulls the "Band-Aid" off his forehead and holds it up.

5:32 PM Branch: "In March, we ship Samantha 2 to Walter Reed hospital. Go to the Microsoft website today and watch a video of paralyzed veterans using Samantha 2 to cook for themselves in a smart kitchen, watch TV, work on a computer, even care for a pet. At Samantha 2, our goal is to help our wounded veterans live independent and productive lives. The possibilities are endless. Thank you."

The audience goes ape-shit. Chris has taken the stage and is hugging Branch. Nobody can believe what they just saw.

*

Voilà. There it is, Samantha 2.

*

From: Audrey Griffin
To: Soo-Lin Lee-Segal

I've had enough of you. Do you understand? Enough!

*

From Dr. Janelle Kurtz

Dear Mr. Branch,

I have received your inquiry regarding your wife. Perhaps I have misread your intent, but what you genially refer to as "supervised R&R," which you fear Bernadette won't "be too keen on," is, in practicality, asking that she be detained against her will at Madrona Hill.

The procedure for such extreme action is detailed in the Involuntary Treatment Act, Title 71, Chapter 5, Section 150, of the Revised Code of Washington. Per the ITA, in order for a County Designated Mental Health Professional to place an individual on an involuntary hold, the CDMHP must thoroughly evaluate the person and determine if they are an imminent danger to themselves, others, or property, due to a psychiatric illness.

If you believe your wife poses such a threat, you must immediately call 911 and have her taken to an emergency room. There she will be assessed. If it is determined that Bernadette does present such a threat, she will be asked to voluntarily seek appropriate treatment. If your wife refuses, her civil liberties will be suspended and she will be transferred to a state-licensed psychiatric hospital and put on an ITA hold for up to seventy-two hours. From that point, it's up to the courts.

Madrona Hill, on Orcas Island, is unique in that along with our renowned inpatient and residential treatment, we operate the only private psych ER in the state. Therefore, I witness the devastating effects of involuntary commitment every day. Families are ripped apart. Police, lawyers, and judges get involved. It goes on public record, for all future employers and financial institutions to see. Because it is so costly in terms of blood, treasure, and emotion, involuntary commitment should be considered only after every other option has been exhausted.

As you describe it, your wife's behavior is cause for concern. I was surprised to learn that she isn't in therapy. That seems like a logical first step. I'd be happy to suggest some wonderful psychiatrists in your area who could meet Bernadette and ask the proper questions so she can receive appropriate treatment. Don't hesitate to call if this is a path you choose to pursue.

Sincerely,

Dr. Janelle Kurtz

*

IM exchange between Dad and Soo-Lin
during a staff meeting

Soo-LinL-S: Everything OK? You seem distracted.

ElginB: Starting to question my sanity. Home stuff.

Soo-LinL-S: If you were to share your stories about Bernadette at a VAV meeting, you couldn't get through two sentences without getting TORCHed. TORCH stands for: Time Out, Reality CHeck!

Soo-LinL-S: Any time a speaker slips into the abuser's story— for instance, if I were to say something like "I know I'm always tired and all I want to talk about is work," which is what Barry used to accuse me of—someone stands up and TORCHes them by yelling, "Time Out, Reality CHeck!"

Soo-LinL-S: It teaches us to separate *our* reality from our abuser's story, which is the first step toward halting the abuse cycle.

Soo-LinL-S: I know you'll be uncomfortable with some of the VAV terminology. I was, too. I thought, I'm not being *abused* by Barry.

Soo-LinL-S: But at VAV, our definition of abuse is intentionally broad and esteem-positive. We are victims, make no mistake about it, but we want to move beyond victim*hood*, which is a subtle yet important distinction.

Soo-LinL-S: Elgie, you are a Level 80 at the most successful company in the world. You've vested out three times. You have a daughter who's thriving academically despite several heart surgeries.

SOO-LINL-S: Your TEDTalk is ranked number four on the all-
time most-watched list *yet you live with a woman who has no
friends, destroys homes, and falls asleep in stores?*

SOO-LINL-S: I'm sorry, Elgie, you are hereby TORCHed.

ELGINB: Thanks for this, but I kind of have to concentrate. Will
read more carefully after meeting.

*

FRIDAY, DECEMBER 17

From: Bernadette Fox
To: Manjula Kapoor

I'm back! Did you miss me? You know how I said I was going to come
up with a way to get out of going to Antarctica?

What if I had emergency surgery?

My dentist, Dr. Neergaard, keeps insisting I get all four wisdom
teeth removed, which I haven't been in any rush to do.

But how about I call up Dr. Neergaard and ask him to remove all four
wisdom teeth *the day before the trip?* (And when I say how about *I* call up
Dr. Neergaard and ask him to remove all four wisdom teeth the day
before the trip, what I really mean is how about *you* call up Dr. Neergaard
and ask him to remove all four wisdom teeth the day before the trip?)

I can claim it was an emergency, and that I'm devastated, but the
doctor forbids me from flying. That way, husband and daughter can go
on the trip themselves and nobody blames me.

Dr. Neergaard's number is below. Schedule my surgery for December 23, any time after 10. (There's a school recital that morning, and
Bee is doing the choreography. The little rotter has forbidden me from
going, but I checked online and found out when it is.) My plan is this:
I'll go to school, then pretend I'm going Christmas shopping.

The next time anyone sees me, I'll look like a chipmunk. I'll claim my teeth had been aching and I popped by Dr. Neergaard's. The next thing I knew, he had removed four wisdom teeth and now I can't go to Antarctica. Here in America, we call that a win-win.

MONDAY, DECEMBER 20
From Marcus Strang of the FBI

Dear Mr. Branch,

I am the regional director of the Internet Crime Complaint Center (IC3), working in partnership with the Department of Homeland Security. My department within the IC3 tracks advance fee schemes and identity fraud.

You have come to our attention because of a charge on a Visa card billed to you dated 10/13, in the amount of $40, to a company calling itself Delhi Virtual Assistants International. This company does not exist. It is a shell company for a crime syndicate working out of Russia. We have spent the last six months building a case against them. A month ago, we were granted a warrant, which allowed us to track emails between your wife, Bernadette Fox, and one "Manjula."

In the course of this correspondence, your wife has turned over credit card information, bank wiring instructions, social security numbers, drivers license numbers, addresses, passport numbers, and photographs of you, herself, and your daughter.

You are apparently unaware of this activity. Your wife suggests in one email to "Manjula" that you had forbidden her from using the services of Delhi Virtual Assistants International.

This matter is delicate and urgent. Yesterday "Manjula" asked for power of attorney while your family is away in Antarctica. We were able to intercept this email before it was delivered to your wife. Judging from her past behavior, we had every reason to believe she would sign it without hesitation.

As you read this letter, I will be landing in Seattle. I will be at the Microsoft Visitor Center at noon, where I expect you to meet me and offer your full cooperation.

In the next three hours, it is imperative that you do not share this information with anyone, especially your wife, who has proven herself to be an unreliable actor.

The warrant obtained was for all your wife's emails in the past three months containing the word "Manjula." There were literally hundreds. I have selected the twenty most relevant and have also included a lengthy one from her to a Paul Jellinek. Please familiarize yourself with them prior to my arrival. I suggest you clear your calendar for the rest of the day and week.

I look forward to meeting you at the Visitor Center. With your full cooperation, we are hoping to keep Microsoft out of it.

Yours,
Marcus Strang

P.S.: We all love your TEDTalk. I'd love to see the latest on Samantha 2 if time permits.

PART FOUR

Invaders

Police report filed by night manager at the Westin Hotel

STATE OF WASHINGTON
CIRCUIT COURT
KING COUNTY

STATE OF WASHINGTON -vs.- Audrey Faith Griffin

I, Phil Bradstock, an officer with the Seattle Police Department, having been first duly sworn in, on oath, state that:

The above-named defendant on December 20, in the City of Seattle, Washington, while in a public place, did engage in indecent, abusive, boisterous, or otherwise disorderly conduct, under circumstances in which such conduct tended to cause or provoke a disturbance contrary to RCW 9A.84.030 c2, and did commit Assault in the Fourth Degree as defined in RCW 9A.36.041, both Misdemeanors, and upon conviction may be fined not more than One Thousand Dollars ($1,000) or imprisoned not more than thirty (30) days, or both.

This information is based upon the testimony of the complainant STEVEN KOENIG, night manager at the Westin Hotel in downtown Seattle. I find the testimony of Steven Koenig to be both truthful and reliable.

1. On Monday, December 20, at approximately 2 AM, Steven Koenig reports that he was on duty as the night manager of the Seattle Westin Hotel when he received a call from guest AUDREY GRIFFIN in Room 1601, complaining of noise emanating from Room 1602.

2. Mr. Koenig reports that he checked the registration list and found Room 1602 to be unoccupied.

3. Mr. Koenig reports that when he conveyed the above information to Ms. Griffin, she became irate and demanded that he investigate in person.

4. Mr. Koenig reports that upon exiting the elevator on the 16th floor, he heard loud voices, laughter, rap music, and what he described as "partying."

5. Mr. Koenig reports that he detected traces of smoke and an uncharacteristic odor in the hallway, which in his opinion was "weed."

6. Mr. Koenig reports that he tracked the noise and smell to Room 1605.

7. Mr. Koenig reports that he knocked on the door and identified himself, at which time the music was turned off and all noise ceased. The momentary silence was followed by giggling.

8. Mr. Koenig reports that Ms. Griffin, wearing a hotel robe, approached him in the hallway and strongly suggested he was knocking on the wrong door, as Room 1605 belonged to her son, Kyle, who was asleep.

9. Mr. Koenig reports that after he explained to Ms. Griffin that Room 1605 was the source of the noise, she then expressed her low opinion of him, using words such as "idiot," "moron," and "incompetent dummy."

10. Mr. Koenig reports that he advised Ms. Griffin of Westin policy regarding verbal abuse. Ms. Griffin then expressed her low opinion of the Westin facility with terms such as "dump," "fleabag," and "pig hole."

11. Mr. Koenig reports that while Ms. Griffin's negative assessment continued, her husband, WARREN GRIFFIN, appeared in the hallway, squinting and wearing boxer shorts.

12. Mr. Koenig reports that Mr. Griffin's attempts to quiet his wife were met with resistance and verbal abuse.

13. Mr. Koenig reports that while in the process of trying to quiet both husband and wife, Mr. Griffin belched, emitting a "nasty stench."

14. Mr. Koenig reports that Ms. Griffin "got in her husband's face" regarding his abuse of alcohol and insatiable appetite for steak.

15. Mr. Koenig reports that Mr. Griffin went back inside Room 1601 and slammed the door.

16. Mr. Koenig reports that while Ms. Griffin was engaged in stating her extreme displeasure with "the person who invented alcohol" to the closed door of 1601, he stuck his master key in the lock of 1605.

17. Mr. Koenig reports that "out of nowhere, my head jerked back" because "that crazy bitch" (Ms. Griffin) had grabbed hold of his hair and yanked, causing him distress and pain.

18. Mr. Koenig reports that he radioed for Seattle PD, and while he was on the radio, Ms. Griffin entered Room 1605 and emitted a scream.

19. Mr. Koenig reports that he entered Room 1605 and counted nine individuals: Ms. Griffin's son, KYLE GRIFFIN, and assorted Seattle street youth.

20. Mr. Koenig reports that he observed a variety of drug paraphernalia, including, but not limited to, "bongs, bindles, rolling papers, prescription drug bottles, roach clips, one-hitters, pinchies, rigs, works, spoons, and an 'epic vape.'" A visual scan of the room indicated no controlled substances other than "shake and seeds on the mini-fridge."

21. Mr. Koenig reports that Ms. Griffin commenced approximately five minutes of hysterically expressing disappointment at her son's choice of friends.

22. Mr. Koenig reports that the subdued response on the part of Kyle Griffin and his companions indicated that "they were totally wasted."

23. Mr. Koenig reports that Ms. Griffin suddenly lunged at a girl with a teddy bear safety-pinned to the back of the her jacket.

NARRATIVE CONTINUATION BY OFFICER:

Upon arrival, I identified myself as Seattle PD. I attempted to pull Ms. Griffin off the teddy bear, which appeared to be causing her acute distress. I informed Ms. Griffin that if she did not lower her voice and step into the hallway with me, I would have to put her in handcuffs. Ms. Griffin started screaming at me with profanity, "I'm a model citizen. These druggies are the ones breaking the law and corrupting my son." I grabbed hold of her left arm. Ms. Griffin screamed profanities at me while I placed her in handcuffs. Ms. Griffin attempted to pull away, saying, "Take your damn hands off me, you can't touch me, I didn't do anything wrong." She threatened that her husband was a DA and she would use the hotel's video surveillance to prove I was holding her in custody without probable cause and she would make sure the video was "all over the evening news." I explained that she was only being temporarily detained while I attempted to ascertain what was going on. Two backup security officers arrived and, with the assistance of my partner, Officer Stanton, escorted the non–hotel residents off the premises. At that point, the complainant related the hair-pulling incident. Ms. Griffin strenuously denied it. I asked Mr. Koenig if he wished to press charges. Ms. Griffin interjected sarcastically, to the effect of "Whoop-de-doo, it's my word against his. Who is a judge going to believe? The wife of a DA or the crowned king of the pig hole?" Mr. Koenig stated that he did wish to press charges.

Based on the information above, I, Officer Phil Bradstock, ask that the defendant be made to answer to the charges.

*

From: Audrey Griffin
To: Soo-Lin Lee-Segal

Hello, stranger! It turns out you were right. Hotel living has finally lost its luster. I'm taking you up on your offer to host us chez Lee-Segal. Don't worry! I know you're busy with your big new job, and I wouldn't dream of inconveniencing you.

I looked for you at drop-off today. Lincoln told me you're working such long hours you don't even have a Christmas tree! I'm going to swing by my garage and grab my bins of decorations. I'll have your house trimmed by the time you return. Don't try to stop me. You know Christmas is my favorite holiday!

How's this for irony? Remember when you were divorcing Barry, and Warren handled the whole thing for you gratis, saving you thirty thousand dollars? Remember when you literally sobbed in gratitude, promising you'd make it up to us? Here's your chance! I'll let myself in with the key under the cupid.

One question. What do you want for dinner? I'm going to have a feast waiting when you get home.

Blessings, you!

*

From: Elgin Branch
To: Soo-Lin Lee-Segal

I realize that everything you just learned in that meeting with Agent Strang was an awful lot to lay on you, way outside your job description. But I was completely overwhelmed and couldn't face that briefing alone. As stunned as I was, and as stunned as I still am, I'm also incredibly grateful that Agent Strang finally allowed you to be present. I'm even more grateful to you for standing by my side.

*

Handwritten note from Soo-Lin

Elgie,

My job is to see that S2 runs smoothly. Knowing the particulars of your situation allows me to better perform my job. I am honored you trust me. I promise I won't let you down. From here on, let's not correspond electronically about B.

SL

*

Handwritten answer from Dad

Soo-Lin,

I just got off the phone with Dr. Kurtz. If "harm to others" is one of the requirements, we have it in spades, with Audrey Griffin's foot and the mudslide. B's talk of overdosing on pills surely constitutes "harm to self." Dr. Kurtz is coming by tomorrow to discuss committing Bernadette.

EB

*

From: Soo-Lin Lee-Segal
To: SAMANTHA 2 TEAM (Undisclosed Recipients)

EB will be dealing with a personal matter that requires his full attention. All meetings to go forward as scheduled. EB to be kept apprised electronically.

Thanks!

*

From: Soo-Lin Lee-Segal
To: Audrey Griffin

NOT A GOOD TIME for you to stay with us. Emergency at work. I've already paid Maura to pick up Lincoln and Alexandra from school and stay through the week. She's in the spare bedroom. I'm so, so sorry. Maybe a different hotel? A short-term rental house? I'll help you look.

*

From: Audrey Griffin
To: Soo-Lin Lee-Segal

I called Maura and told her you wouldn't be needing her. She moved back to her apartment.

Your home looks fantastic. The inflatable Santa is waving hello to the passersby, and the windowsills are edged with "snow." Joseph, Mary, and baby Jesus are stuck in the lawn, along with my sign, WE SAY MERRY CHRISTMAS. I should be the one thanking *you*.

*

From Dad to the dean of admissions
at Choate

Dear Mr. Jessup,

As you know, I received a letter from Hillary Loundes regarding Bee's acceptance to Choate next fall. When I first read Ms. Loundes's suggestion that Bee skip a grade, my instinct was to say no. However, Ms. Loundes's wise words have stayed with me. I now concur that it is in Bee's best interest that her immersion in Choate's academic abundance commence immediately. Since Bee is currently working beyond the third-form level, I ask that you consider admitting her this January—yes, in a month—as a third-former.

If my memory serves me, at Exeter there were always students who left midyear and others who took their place. If we are to proceed, I'd like to start with the paperwork as quickly as possible, so Bee's transition can be a smooth one. Thank you.

Sincerely,
Elgin Branch

*

From Dad to his brother

From: Elgin Branch
To: Van Branch

Van,

I hope this finds you well. I know it's been a while since we spoke, but a family emergency has come up, and I was wondering if you could come to Seattle on Wednesday and stay a couple of days. I'll send you a ticket and get you a hotel room. Let me know.

Thanks,
Elgie

TUESDAY, DECEMBER 21
A flurry of emails between Uncle Van and Dad

Elgie,

Ahoy there, stranger. Sorry, but I don't think I'll be able to make it to your parts. Christmas is a busy time for me. Let's take a rain check. (You probably hear that a lot in Seattle.)

Mahalo,
Van

*

Van,

Maybe I didn't make it clear. This is an emergency involving my family. I'll cover all costs and any lost wages. The dates are Dec. 22 through Dec. 25.

*

Bro,

Maybe *I* was the one who didn't make it clear. I have a life in Hawaii. I have responsibilities. I can't hop on a plane just because you decide to grace me with your first email in five years and invite me to spend Christmas in a hotel.

*

Van,

You're a fucking house sitter. Bernadette is sick. Bee doesn't know. I need you to spend the day with Bee while I get Bernadette help. I know we've lost touch, but I want Bee to be with family. I apologize if the hotel offer appeared brusque. My house is a shambles. The guest room has been boarded up for years because of a hole in the floor that nobody bothered to repair. It all relates to Bernadette's illness. Come on.

*

Elgie,

I'll do it for Bee. Book me on the direct flight out of Kona. There's one first-class seat left, and it would be sweet if you could nab it. There's a Four Seasons that shows availability in junior suites facing the water. I found someone to cover for me so there's no rush flying me back.

*

Authorization Request Submitted by Dr. Janelle Kurtz

REQUEST TO BILL FOR OFF-ISLAND APPOINTMENT
RE: BERNADETTE FOX/ELGIN BRANCH

Bernadette Fox was brought to my attention on December 12. Her husband, Elgin Branch, a friend of board member Hannah Dillard, wrote me a long-winded and highly emotional letter inquiring about involuntary commitment (Attachment #1).

Mr. Branch's description of his wife suggested social anxiety, medication-seeking behavior, agoraphobia, poor impulse control, untreated postpartum depression, and possible mania. If I were to take him at his word, I'd posit a dual diagnosis of substance abuse and bipolar type two.

I wrote back to Mr. Branch, explained the law, and suggested his wife seek therapy (Attachment #2).

Yesterday I received a call from Mr. Branch requesting a face-to-face meeting. He spoke of new developments with his wife, including suicidal ideation.

I find Mr. Branch's call curious, if not suspicious, for the following reasons.

1. TIMING: In my reply to Mr. Branch, I spelled out that in order to have his wife involuntarily committed, she would have to prove imminently harmful to herself or others. Within days, he claims to be in possession of such evidence.

2. RESISTANCE TO SEEK THERAPY: Mr. Branch seems fixated on having Ms. Fox committed at Madrona Hill. Why wouldn't he first seek outpatient therapy for his wife?

3. SECRECY: Mr. Branch refuses to divulge specific information over the phone, instead insisting we meet in person.

4. URGENCY: On the phone today, Mr. Branch begged me to see him immediately, ideally at his office.

Taken together, I have reason to question Mr. Branch's motives and credibility. However, I feel I must follow up. Madrona Hill has twice been notified of Ms. Fox's behavior. Since suicide was explicitly mentioned, it is now a matter of liability. Further, Mr. Branch's tenacity suggests he will not stop contacting me until we meet.

I will be in Seattle lecturing at the UW. I have arranged to meet Mr. Branch at his office this evening. I recognize that this is an unusual arrangement, but I am happy to make the extra effort for the friend of a board member. My hope is to convince Mr. Branch to look elsewhere for more appropriate treatment for his wife.

I told him my rate was $275/hr plus time and a half for travel. He understands that we do not bill insurance and that my trip to his office is most likely not covered.

*

From: Audrey Griffin
To: Soo-Lin Lee-Segal

Hey you! I got gingerbread houses to decorate after school. When will you be home? I want to know when to pop the roast in the oven.

*

From: Soo-Lin Lee-Segal
To: Audrey Griffin

As I said, I'm superbusy at work, so I won't be back for dinner. But my mouth is watering just thinking about your famous roast!

*

From: Audrey Griffin
To: Soo-Lin Lee-Segal

Don't think I can't take a hint. How about I get in my car and deliver you a plate myself?

*

From: Soo-Lin Lee-Segal
To: Audrey Griffin

How about you don't? Thanks, though!

*

That Tuesday, I was in my room doing homework when the phone rang twice, which meant someone was at the gate, and which also signaled dinner. I pushed *7 to open the gate, then went downstairs and met the courier. I was psyched to see he had bags from Tilth. I brought the food to the kitchen. Dad was standing there, grinding his jaw.

"I thought you were working," I said. The last couple of nights he hadn't come home, and I figured he was pulling all-nighters because of Antarctica.

"I want to see how you're faring," he said.

"Me?" I said. "I'm fine."

Mom came in from the Petit Trianon and kicked off her rain boots. "Hey, look who's home! I'm glad. I ordered too much food."

"Hi, Bernadette." Dad didn't hug Mom.

I peeled back the edges of the take-out containers and set them in front of our chairs at the kitchen table.

"Let's do plates tonight." Mom got china from the pantry, and I slid the food onto the nice dishes.

But Dad just stood there, his parka zipped. "I have some news. Van is coming tomorrow."

Uncle Van was my only uncle and therefore my favorite uncle. Mom had a nickname for him, which was Van "Are You Going to Eat the Rest of That?" Branch. He lives in Hawaii, in a caretaker's cottage on a huge estate that belongs to a Hollywood movie producer. The Hollywood producer was hardly ever there, but he must have OCD because he pays Van to go to the house every day and flush the toilets. The Hollywood producer also has a house in Aspen, and one winter the pipes froze and the toilets overflowed and wrecked a bunch of antiques so he's totally paranoid about it happening again, even though pipes can't freeze in Hawaii. So, as Mom likes to point out, Van flushes toilets for a living. Once we went to Hawaii, and Van took me on a tour of the estate and let me flush the toilets, which was funny.

"What's Van coming here for?" I asked.

"Good question." Mom was now standing frozen, the same as Dad.

"A visit," Dad said. "I thought he could dog-sit while we were away. Why, Bernadette? Do you have a problem with that?"

"Where's he going to stay?" Mom asked.

"The Four Seasons. I'm going to pick him up at the airport tomorrow. Bee, I'd like you to come with me."

"I can't," I said. "I'm going to see the Rockettes Christmas show with Youth Group."

"His plane gets in at four," Dad said. "I'll pick you up at school."

"Can Kennedy come?" I said, and added a big smile.

"No," he said. "I don't like being in the car with Kennedy. You know that."

"You're no fun." I threw him my meanest Kubrick face and started eating.

Dad stomped into the living room, the door banging against the counter. A second later came a thud, followed by swearing. Mom and I ran in and turned on the lights. Dad had crashed into a ton of boxes and suitcases. "What the hell is all this crap?" he asked, jumping up.

"It's for Antarctica," I said.

UPS boxes had been arriving at a terrifying clip. Mom had three packing lists taped to the wall, one for each of us. All the boxes were half-opened and spilling with parkas, boots, gloves, and snow pants, in various stages of unwrap, hanging out like tongues.

"We've pretty much got everything." Mom stepped expertly among the boxes. "I'm waiting on zinc oxide for you." She pointed her foot in the direction of one huge black duffel. "I'm trying to find Bee one of those face masks in a color she likes—"

"I see my suitcase," Dad said. "I see Bee's suitcase. Where's your suitcase, Bernadette?"

"It's right there," Mom said.

Dad walked over and picked it up. It just hung there like a deflated balloon. "Why isn't there anything in it?" he asked.

"What are you even doing here?" Mom said.

"What am I even doing here?"

"We were about to have dinner," she said. "You didn't sit down. You didn't take off your coat."

"I have an appointment back at the office. I'm not staying for dinner."

"Let me get you some fresh clothes, at least."

"I have clothes at the office."

"Why did you drive all the way home?" she said. "Just to tell us about Van?"

"Sometimes it's nice to do things in person."

"So stay for dinner," Mom said. "I'm not understanding this."

"Me neither," I said.

"I'll do things my way," Dad said. "You do things your way." He walked out the front door.

Mom and I stood there, waiting for him to come back in, all embarrassed. Instead, we heard his Prius glide over the gravel and onto the street.

"I guess he really did just come home to tell us about Van," I said.

"Weird," said Mom.

WEDNESDAY, DECEMBER 22
Report by Dr. Kurtz

PATIENT: Bernadette Fox

BACKGROUND: Per my authorization request dated 12/21, I had arranged to meet Elgin Branch at the Microsoft campus. Since that request, in which I expressed skepticism of Mr. Branch, my opinion of him and his motives has dramatically changed. In an attempt to illuminate this about-face I will go into inordinate detail regarding our meeting.

NOTES ON MEETING: My lecture at the UW had wrapped up sooner than expected. Hoping to catch the 10:05 ferry, I arrived half an hour early. I was directed to Mr. Branch's administrator's office. Sitting at the desk was a woman in a raincoat with a foil-covered plate in her lap. I asked for Mr. Branch. This woman explained she was a friend of the administrator's and had come to surprise her with dinner. She said everyone was in a meeting in the big theater downstairs.

I said I, too, had come on personal business. She noticed the Madrona Hill ID clipped to my briefcase and said something to the effect of "Madrona Hill? Hi-ho, I'll say that's personal business!"

The administrator arrived and practically screamed when she saw me talking to her friend with the food plate. She pretended that I was a Microsoft employee. I tried to signal the administrator that I had already identified myself otherwise, but she quickly hustled me into a conference room and pulled down the shades. The administrator handed me a classified FBI file and left. I am unable to divulge its contents other than the salient facts pertaining to Ms. Fox's mental state:

• she ran over a mother at school

• she had a billboard erected outside this woman's home to taunt her

• she hoards prescription medicine

• she suffers from extreme anxiety, grandiosity, and suicidal thoughts.

Mr. Branch arrived, appearing agitated, due to the fact that he was keeping everyone late downstairs and they had hit a programming bug just before he came up. I promised I would be quick and handed him a list of some wonderful psychiatrists in the area. Mr. Branch was incredulous. He strongly believed the FBI file contained adequate proof to qualify his wife for inpatient treatment.

I expressed my concern at his determination to put his wife on an involuntary hold. He assured me he merely wanted to get her the best care possible.

Mr. Branch's administrator knocked and asked if Mr. Branch had reviewed a code fix. Mr. Branch looked at his cell phone and shuddered. Apparently, forty-five emails had come in while we were talking. He said, "If Bernadette doesn't kill me, Reply All will." He scrolled through the emails and barked some code talk about submitting a change list, which his administrator furiously copied down before dashing out.

After a spirited back-and-forth in which Mr. Branch accused me of dereliction of duty, I acknowledged that his wife might be suffering from adjustment disorder, which, I explained, is a psychological response brought on by a stressor, and it usually involves anxiety or depression. The stressor in his wife's case appears to be a planned trip to Antarctica. In extreme cases, a person's coping mechanisms can be so inadequate that the stressor causes a psychotic break.

Mr. Branch almost collapsed with relief that I had finally confirmed there was something wrong with his wife.

The administrator entered again, this time joined by two men. There was more jargon involving deploying a code fix.

After they left, I told Mr. Branch that the recommended treatment for adjustment disorder is psychotherapy, not a psychiatric hold. I bluntly stated that it is wholly unethical and completely unheard of for a psychiatrist to place a person on an

ITA hold without meeting them first. Mr. Branch assured me he was not fixated on having her taken away in a straitjacket, and he asked if there was perhaps an intermediate step.

For the third time, the administrator knocked. Apparently, Mr. Branch's fix had worked, and the meeting was over. More people entered the conference room, and Mr. Branch went through a priority list for tomorrow.

I was struck by the *intensity* of it all. I've never seen a group of people so self-motivated, working at such a high level. The pressure was palpable, but so was the camaraderie and love for the work. Most striking was the reverence paid to Mr. Branch, and his joking, egalitarian nature, even under extreme stress.

At one point, I noticed Mr. Branch was in his stocking feet, and I realized: he was the man in the TEDTalk! The one where you stick a computer chip to your forehead and you never have to move a muscle for the rest of your life. It's an extreme version of what I find an alarming trend toward reality avoidance.

After everyone left, it was just me, Mr. Branch, and the administrator. I suggested that because Ms. Fox appears to be self-medicating for anxiety, I could refer him to one of my able colleagues who specializes in drug interventions. Mr. Branch was grateful. But because nobody but me could be privy to this FBI file, he asked if I would consider conducting the intervention myself. I said yes.

I emphasized the importance of Mr. Branch getting some sleep. His administrator said she'd booked a hotel room for him, and would drive him there herself.

*

The next afternoon Dad picked me up at school and we drove to the airport.

"Are you still excited about Choate?" he asked.

"Yeah," I said.

"I'm really, really glad to hear that," Dad said. Then, "Do you know what a lame-duck president is?"

"Yeah."

"That's what it was like for *me,* right after *I* got accepted to Exeter. I felt like I was stuck treading water at middle school. I bet that's how you feel right now."

"Not really."

"A lame-duck president is when a president has been voted out of office—"

"I know what it is, Dad. What does it have to do with Choate? All the other kids are leaving Galer Street and going to another school in the fall like me. So it's like saying the day you start eighth grade, the whole year is a lame-duck year. Or when you turn fourteen, it's a lame-duck year until you turn fifteen."

That quieted him down for a few minutes. But he started back up. "I'm happy to hear you're enjoying Youth Group," he said. "If you're drawing strength from your time there, I want you to know I fully support it."

"Can I spend the night at Kennedy's?"

"You've been spending a lot of time at Kennedy's," he said, all concerned.

"Can I?"

"Of course you can."

We drove past the rail yards on Elliott Bay with the huge orange cranes that look like drinking ostriches standing sentry over thousands of stacked shipping containers. When I was little, I asked Mom what all those containers were. She said ostrich eggs filled with Barbie dolls. Even though I don't play with Barbies anymore, it still gets me excited to think of that many Barbies.

"I'm sorry I haven't been around much." It was Dad again.

"You're around."

"I'd like to be around more," he said. "I *am* going to be around more. It's going to start with Antarctica. The two of us are going to have such a good time there."

"The three of us." I got out my flute and played the rest of the way to the airport.

Uncle Van was supertan, his face craggy, and he had whitish peeling lips. He wore a Hawaiian shirt, flip-flops, an inflatable sleeping pillow around his neck, and a big straw hat with a bandanna around it that said THE HANGOVER.

"Bro!" Van gave Dad a big hug. "Where's Bee? Where's your little girl?"

I waved.

"*You're* a big girl. My niece, Bee, is a little girl."

"I'm Bee," I said.

"No way!" He held up his hand. "High-five for growing."

I limply slapped him five.

"I come bearing gifts." He removed his straw hat and shucked off more straw hats from under it, each with a HANGOVER bandanna. "One for you." He put one on Dad's head. "One for you." He put one on my head. "One for Bernadette."

I snatched it. "I'll give it to her." It was so hideous, I had to give it to Kennedy.

As Van stood there smearing ChapStick across his gross lips, I thought, I hope nobody sees me at the zoo with this guy.

*

Presentation by Dr. Kurtz to her supervisor

PATIENT: Bernadette Fox

INTERVENTION PLAN: I presented my patient background to Drs. Mink and Crabtree, who specialize in drug interventions. They concurred that due to the component of substance abuse, it is appropriate to stage an intervention. While I am not formally trained in drug interventions, because of the unique circumstances described in my patient background I have decided to lead it myself.

JOHNSON MODEL VS. MOTIVATIONAL INTERVENTION: For the last decade, Madrona Hill has been moving away from the Johnson Model of "ambush-style" intervention in favor of the more inclusive Miller-and-Rollnick "motivational" approach, which studies have shown to be more effective. However, due to the secrecy dictated by the FBI, the Johnson Model was chosen.

PREPARATORY MEETING: Mr. Branch and I met at Dr. Mink's Seattle office this afternoon. Dr. Mink conducted many Johnson-style interventions in the 1980s and '90s, and walked us through its steps.

1. Forcefully "present reality" to the patient.

2. Family members express love for the patient in their own words.

3. Family members detail the damage the patient has caused.

4. Family members guarantee support in treatment of patient.

5. Family members and health professional explain negative consequences if patient refuses treatment.

6. Patient given opportunity to voluntarily seek treatment.

7. Immediate transfer of patient to treatment center.

All hopes are that Bernadette Fox will admit to her illness and check herself into Madrona Hill voluntarily.

*

That night, I went to the *Radio City Christmas Spectacular* with Youth Group. The first part, with the Rockettes, was annoying. All it was, was piped-in music while the Rockettes kicked. I thought they would have at least sung, or done some other kind of dancing. But they just kicked in a line facing one direction. They kicked in a line facing the other direction. They kicked in a line with the whole line twirling, to songs like "It's Beginning to Look a Lot Like Christmas" and "I Saw Mommy Kissing Santa Claus." The whole thing was junk. Kennedy and I both were like, Why?

Intermission came. There was no reason to go to the lobby because nobody had any money, which meant the best we could do was drink water out of the fountain. So me and all the Youth Group kids stayed at our seats. As the audience filed back in, the ladies in hair helmets, caked-on makeup, and blinking Christmas pins all started bubbling with excitement. Even Luke and Mae, who chaperoned us, were standing in front of their seats, staring at the red curtain.

The theater went dark. A star was projected on the curtain. The audience gasped and clapped way too enthusiastically just for a star.

"Today is the most sacred day for all mankind," boomed a scary voice. "It is the birth of my son, Jesus, the king of kings."

The curtain flew open. Onstage was a manger with a real-life baby Jesus, Mary, and Joseph. "God" narrated, in the most ominous way, the story of the Nativity. Shepherds came out with live sheep, goats, and donkeys. With every new animal that trotted out, there were fresh "oohs" and "aahs."

"Haven't any of these people ever been to a petting zoo?" Kennedy said.

Three wise men entered on a camel, elephant, and ostrich. Even I was like, OK, that's cool, I didn't know ostriches would let you ride them.

Then a big black woman walked out, which kind of broke the spell, because she was wearing a supertight red dress, the kind you see at Macy's.

"*O holy night,*" she started.

Ecstatic gasps sprung up all around me.

"*The stars are brightly shining,*" she sang. "*It is the night of our dear Savior's birth. Long lay the world / In sin and error pining / Till he appeared and the spirit felt its worth.*" Something about the tune made me close my eyes. The words and music filled me with a warm glow. "*A thrill of hope / The weary world rejoices / For yonder breaks / A new and glorious morn.*" There was a pause. I opened my eyes.

"*Fall on your knees!*" she sang, full of startling, loud joy. "*O hear the angels' voices!*"

"*O niiiiight divine,*" more voices joined in. A chorus was now onstage, above baby Jesus, fifty of them, all black people, dressed in sparkly clothes. I hadn't even seen them arrive. The glow inside me started to harden, which made it difficult to swallow.

"*O night when Christ was born. O niiiiight diviiiiiine! O night! O night Divine!*"

It was so weird and extreme that I got disoriented for a second, and it was almost a relief when it was over. But the music kept going. I knew I had to brace myself for the next wave. Across the top of the stage, words appeared on a digital scroll. Like the chorus, it just seemed to have materialized. Red-dot words glided across...

TRULY HE TAUGHT
US TO LOVE ONE ANOTHER...
HIS LAW IS LOVE
AND HIS GOSPEL IS PEACE.

A low rumble surrounded me. It was people in the audience rising to their feet, joining in, singing.

CHAINS SHALL HE BREAK
FOR THE SLAVE HE IS OUR BROTHER...
AND IN HIS NAME
ALL OPPRESSION SHALL CEASE.

I couldn't see the words anymore because of the people in front of me. I stood, too.

SWEET HYMNS OF JOY
IN GRATEFUL CHORUS RAISE WE,
WITH ALL OUR HEARTS
WE PRAISE HIS HOLY NAME.

Everyone in the audience started raising their arms halfway up and wiggling their fingers like they were doing jazz hands.

Kennedy had put the HANGOVER bandanna on. "What?" she said, and crossed her eyes. I shoved her.

Then, the main black lady, who hadn't been singing that loudly but letting the chorus do all the work, suddenly stepped forward.

"Chriiiist is the Lord!" her voice roared, as the sign flashed:

CHRIST IS THE LORD!

It was so joyful and unapologetically religious, I realized that these people, "churchy" people, as Mom called them, were actually oppressed, and only now could they open up because they were safely among other churchy people. The ladies who looked so nice with their special hairdos and Christmas sweaters, they didn't care how bad their voices were, they were joining in, too. Some threw their heads back and even closed their eyes. I raised my hands, to see how it felt. I let my head drop back and my eyes close.

THEN EVER, EVER PRAISE WE.

I was baby Jesus. Mom and Dad were Mary and Joseph. The straw was my hospital bed. I was surrounded by the surgeons and residents and nurses who helped me stay alive when I was born blue and if it weren't for them I would be dead now. All those people I didn't even know, I couldn't pick them out of a lineup if I had to, but they had worked their whole lives to get the knowledge that ended up saving my life. It was because of them that I was in this magnificent wave of people and music.

O NIGHT DIVINE! O NIGHT! O NIGHT DIVINE!

There was a jab at my side. It was Kennedy punching me.

"Here." She handed me her HANGOVER bandanna because tears were burning down my cheeks. "Don't turn all Jesus on me."

I ignored her and threw my head back. Maybe that's what religion is, hurling yourself off a cliff and trusting that something bigger will take care of you and carry you to the right place. I don't know if it's possible to feel everything all at once, so much that you think you're going to burst. I loved Dad so much. I was sorry I was so mean to him in the car. He was just trying to talk to me, and I didn't know why I couldn't let him. Of course I noticed he was never home. I had noticed it for years. I wanted to run home and hug Dad, and ask him to please not be away so much, to please not send me off to Choate because I loved him and Mom too much, I loved our house and Ice Cream and Kennedy and Mr. Levy too much to leave. I felt so full of love for everything. But at the same time, I felt so hung out to dry there, like nobody could ever understand. I felt so alone in this world, and so loved at the same time.

The next morning, Kennedy's mom came in to wake us. "Shit," she said. "You're going to be late." She threw a bunch of breakfast bars at us and went back to bed.

It was eight fifteen. World Celebration Day started at eight forty-five. I quickly got dressed and ran down the hill and across the overpass without stopping. Kennedy is always late to school, and her Mom doesn't even care, so she stayed and ate cereal and watched TV.

I ran straight to the equipment room, where Mr. Kangana and the first graders were doing a final rehearsal. "I'm here," I said, waving my *shakuhachi*. "Sorry." The little kids looked so sweet in their Japanese kimonos. They started climbing on me like monkeys.

Through the wall, Ms. Goodyear announced us, and we entered the gym, which was packed with parents aiming video cameras. "And now," she said, "we'll have a performance by the first graders. Playing along is eighth grader Bee Branch."

The first graders lined up. Mr. Kangana gave me the signal and I played the first few notes. The kids started singing.

> *Zousan, zousan*
> *O-ha-na ga na-ga-I no ne*
> *So-yo ka-a-san mo*
> *Na-ga-I no yo*

They did a great job, singing in unison. Except for Chloe, who had lost her first tooth that morning and stood there frozen, sticking her tongue into the slot where her tooth had been. We took a pause, and then it was time to sing the song in English, with my choreography. The first graders began singing and moving like elephants, their hands clasped and arms hanging down like swaying trunks.

> *Little elephant, little elephant*
> *You have a very long nose.*
> *Yes, sir, my mama has a long nose, too.*

Just then I had a feeling. There she was, Mom, standing in the doorway, wearing her huge dark glasses.

> *Little elephant, little elephant*
> *Tell me who do you love.*
> *Oh, you know it's my mama that I love.*

I laughed because I knew Mom would think it was funny that now *I* was the one crying. I looked up. But she was gone. It was the last time I saw her.

FRIDAY, DECEMBER 24
From Dr. Janelle Kurtz

To the Board of Directors,

I would like to inform you that I hereby resign from my position as director of psychiatry at Madrona Hill. I love my job. My colleagues are like family. However, as Bernadette Fox's admitting psychiatrist, and in light of the tragic and mysterious events surrounding her intervention, it is a decision I must make. Thank you for the many wonderful years and for the opportunity to serve.

Sincerely,

Dr. Janelle Kurtz

*

Dr. Kurtz's report on Mom's intervention

PATIENT: Bernadette Fox

We were planning to confront Ms. Fox at her dentist's office, where she had a 10 AM appointment. Dr. Neergaard was informed of our plan and had set aside an empty office for our use. Elgin Branch's brother, Van, was to pick up the daughter, Bee, at school and go to the zoo until further notification.

We did not want Ms. Fox to see her husband's car at the dentist's office when she arrived. Therefore, it was decided that Mr. Branch and I would meet at his home and take my car to Dr. Neergaard's office.

THE FOX/BRANCH RESIDENCE: It is the former home of the Straight Gate School for Girls, a grand but decrepit brick building sitting on an immense sloping lawn overlooking Elliott Bay. The inside is in shocking disrepair. Rooms are boarded up. It is dark and damp, with a musty smell so overpowering I could taste it. That a family with significant income would live in such deteriorating conditions suggests a lack of self-respect, ambivalence about their financial/social superiority, and poor reality testing.

I arrived at the Branch residence at 9 AM and found several cars, including a police car, parked haphazardly in the driveway. I rang the doorbell. Ms. Lee-Segal, Mr. Branch's administrator, opened the door. She explained that she and Mr. Branch had just arrived. FBI Agent Marcus Strang was in the middle of informing them that "Manjula," the Internet assistant, had stolen all his miles on American Airlines last week.

Mr. Branch was shocked that Agent Strang was only telling him this now. Agent Strang explained that they did not take the threat seriously, as Internet thieves usually don't leave their basement, let alone hop on planes. But last night the miles had been used to purchase a one-way ticket from Moscow to Seattle, with the plane arriving tomorrow. Further, "Manjula" had been sending emails to Ms. Fox, asking her to confirm that she'd be alone in the house while Mr. Branch and his daughter were in Antarctica.

Mr. Branch practically buckled in shock and had to find a wall for support. Ms. Lee-Segal rubbed his back and assured him his wife would be safe at Madrona Hill on Orcas Island. I reiterated that there was no such guarantee, that I would have to evaluate Ms. Fox before I could place her on an involuntary hold.

Mr. Branch began to misdirect his rage and powerlessness onto me, accusing me of bureaucratese and stonewalling.

Ms. Lee-Segal interrupted, pointing out we were late for Dr. Neergaard's. I asked Agent Strang if the intervention would place us in any physical danger, considering "Manjula" was on the loose. He assured us we were safe and that ample police protection was in place. Quite shaken, we all headed out the front door when, suddenly, from behind, we heard a woman's voice.

"Elgie, who are all these people?"

It was Bernadette Fox. She had just entered through the kitchen.

A quick visual assessment indicated an attractive woman in her early fifties, of medium height and medium build, with no makeup and a pale but healthy complexion. She wore a blue raincoat and, underneath it, jeans, a white nubby cashmere sweater, and loafers with no socks. Her long hair appeared brushed and tied back with a scarf. There was nothing about her appearance that indicated she did not care for herself. Indeed, she came off as well groomed and chic.

I turned on my tape recorder. What follows is a transcript:

FOX: Is it Bee? Nothing happened to Bee. I just saw her at school—

BRANCH: No, Bee is fine.

FOX: Then who are these people?

DR. KURTZ: My name is Dr. Janelle Kurtz.

BRANCH: You're supposed to be at the dentist, Bernadette.

FOX: How did you know that?

DR. KURTZ: Let's have a seat.

FOX: Why? Who are you? Elgie—

BRANCH: Shall we do it here, doctor?

DR. KURTZ: I suppose—

FOX: Do what here? I don't like this. I'm leaving.

DR. KURTZ: Bernadette, we're here because we care about you and we want you to get the help you need.

FOX: Exactly what kind of help? Why are the police outside? And why the gnat?

DR. KURTZ: We'd like you to sit down so we can present you with the reality of your situation.

FOX: Elgie, please ask them to leave. Whatever this is, let's talk about it privately. I mean it. These people don't belong here.

BRANCH: I know everything, Bernadette. So do they.

FOX: If this is about Dr. Neergaard…if he told you…if somehow you found out…I canceled the appointment ten minutes ago. I'm going on the trip. I'm going to Antarctica.

BRANCH: Bernadette, please. Stop lying.

FOX: Check my phone. See? Outgoing calls. Dr. Neergaard. Dial him yourself. Here—

BRANCH: Dr. Kurtz, should we—

DR. KURTZ: Bernadette, we are concerned for your ability to care for yourself.

FOX: Is this a joke? I really don't understand. Is this about Manjula?

BRANCH: There is no Manjula.

FOX: What?

BRANCH: Agent Strang, could you—

FOX: *Agent* Strang?

AGENT STRANG: Hi. From the FBI.

BRANCH: Agent Strang, since you're here, could *you* perhaps explain to my wife the havoc her actions have wreaked?

AGENT STRANG: If this has all of a sudden turned into an intervention, that's not really my thing.

BRANCH: I just want—

AGENT STRANG: Outside the pay grade.

BRANCH: Manjula is an alias for an identity-theft ring operating out of Russia. They have been posing as Manjula as a way to capture all of our personal banking information. Not only that, they're coming to Seattle to make their move while Bee and I are in Antarctica. Is that right, Agent Strang?

AGENT STRANG: Pretty much.

FOX: I don't believe it. I mean, I do believe it. What kind of move?

BRANCH: Oh, I don't know! Cleaning out our bank accounts, brokerage accounts, property title, which shouldn't be that hard because you've handed them all our personal information and passwords! Manjula even requested power of attorney.

FOX: That's not true. I haven't heard back from her for days. I was getting ready to fire her.

BRANCH: That's because the FBI has been intercepting the emails and responding as you. Don't you get it?

DR. KURTZ: Yes, that's a good idea, Bernadette, for you to sit down. Let's all sit down.

FOX: Not there—

DR. KURTZ: Oh!

FOX: It's wet. Sorry, there's a leak. God, Elgie, I completely fucked up. Did she take everything?

BRANCH: Thank God, nothing yet.

LEE-SEGAL: (WHISPERS: NOT AUDIBLE)

BRANCH: Thank you. I forgot! She cashed in our miles!

FOX: Our miles? I'm sick about this. I'm sorry, I'm just in shock.

DR. KURTZ: Now that we're comfortable…ish. Oh! My skirt.

FOX: Is the couch wet? Sorry. It's that orange color because the flashing on the roof is rusted and the water drips through. It usually washes out with lemon juice and salt. Who are you?

DR. KURTZ: Dr. Janelle Kurtz. It's quite all right. Bernadette, I'd like to keep presenting reality. Because the FBI gained access to your email account, we were able to see that you pondered suicide in the past. You stashed pills for future suicide attempts. You tried to run over a mother at school.

FOX: Don't be ludicrous.

LEE-SEGAL: (SIGHS HEAVILY)

FOX: Oh, shut up. What the hell are you doing here anyway? Will someone open a window and let the gnat out?

BRANCH: Stop calling her that, Bernadette!

FOX: Forgive me. Could someone get the *admin* out of my living room?

DR. KURTZ: Ms. Lee-Segal, it *would* be a good idea for you to leave.

BRANCH: She can stay.

FOX: Really? She can stay? How's that?

BRANCH: She's a friend—

FOX: What kind of friend? She is not a friend of this marriage, I'll guarantee you that.

BRANCH: You're not in charge now, Bernadette.

FOX: Wait a second, what is that?

LEE-SEGAL: What?

FOX: Sticking out of the bottom of your pants.

LEE-SEGAL: Me? Where?

FOX: It's a pair of underwear. You've got panties sticking out of your jeans!

LEE-SEGAL: Oh—I have no idea how they got there—

FOX: You're a Seattle-born secretary and you have no place in this house!

DR. KURTZ: Bernadette is right. This is for family only.

LEE-SEGAL: I'm happy to go.

AGENT STRANG: How about I go, too? I'll be right outside.

(GOOD-BYES AND THE FRONT DOOR OPENING AND CLOSING)

FOX: Please proceed, Captain Kurtz—sorry, *Dr. Kurtz.*

DR. KURTZ: Bernadette, your aggression toward your neighbor led to the destruction of her home and possible PTSD of thirty children. You have no intention of going to Antarctica. You planned on getting four wisdom teeth removed to prevent it. You willingly turned over personal information to a criminal, which could have led to financial ruin. You are incapable of even the most basic human interaction, relying on an Internet assistant to buy groceries, schedule appointments, and conduct all basic household duties. Your home is worthy of condemnation by the building department, which indicates to me serious depression.

FOX: Are you still "presenting reality" to me? Or can I say something?

MALE VOICE: Get 'im!

KURTZ/BRANCH: (PANICKED NOISES)

(WE TURNED TO SEE A MAN IN A LONG COAT STARING AT HIS PHONE)

BRANCH: Who are you?!

DETECTIVE DRISCOLL: Detective Driscoll. Seattle P.D.

FOX: He's been there the whole time. I passed him on my way in.

DETECTIVE DRISCOLL: Sorry. I got a little excited. Clemson picked off a pass and ran it in. Pretend I'm not here.

DR. KURTZ: Bernadette, Elgin would like to begin by expressing his love for you. Elgin...

BRANCH: What the hell is wrong with you, Bernadette? I thought you were even more upset than I was about those miscarriages. But, really, the whole time all you cared about was some stupid house? What you went through with the Twenty Mile House—I go through shit like that ten times a day at Microsoft. People get over things. It's called bouncing back. You won a MacArthur grant. Twenty years later you're still nursing the injustice of a fight you had with some English asshole, a fight you brought upon yourself? Do you realize how selfish and self-pitying that is? Do you?

DR. KURTZ: OK. So. It's important to acknowledge there's a lot of hurt. But let's stay in the here and now. Elgin, why don't you try *expressing your love* for Bernadette. You had mentioned what a wonderful mother—

BRANCH: And you're back there in your Airstream lying to me left and right, outsourcing your life, *our lives*, to India? Don't I get a vote in that? You're afraid of getting seasick when we're crossing the Drake Passage? There's a way to deal with it. It's called a scopolamine patch. You don't arrange to get *four wisdom teeth removed* and lie to me and Bee about it. People die getting their wisdom teeth pulled. But you'll do it just to avoid small talk with strangers? What the hell is Bee going to think when she hears this? And all because you're a "failure"? How about a wife? How about a mother? What happened to coming to your husband? Why do you have to spill your guts out to some architect you haven't seen for twenty years? God, you're sick. You make me sick, and you're sick.

DR. KURTZ: Another example of love is a hug.

BRANCH: You've gone insane, Bernadette. It's like aliens came down and replaced you with a replica, but the replica is a drag-queen demented version of you. I became so convinced of this that one night while you slept I reached across and felt your elbows. Because I thought, No matter how good they made the replica, they wouldn't have gotten the pointy elbows right. But there they were, your pointy elbows. You woke up when I did that. Do you remember?

FOX: Yes, I remember.

BRANCH: When I caught myself, I realized, Oh my God, she's going to take me with her. Bernadette has gone crazy, but I will not let her pull me down with her. I'm a father. I'm a husband. I'm team leader of over 250 people who rely on me, whose *families* rely on me. I refuse to plunge off the cliff with you.

FOX: (SOUND OF CRYING)

BRANCH: And for this you hate me? You mock me as a simpleton because I love my family? Because I love my job? Because I love books? When did this contempt for me start, Bernadette? Do you have an exact date? Or do you have to check with your Internet assistant who you pay seventy-five cents an hour but is actually the Russian Mafia, who has cashed in all our miles and is heading to Seattle to kill you? Jesus, I have to stop talking!

DR. KURTZ: How about we put a pin in love, and let's move on to the *damage* that Bernadette's behavior has caused.

BRANCH: Are you joking? The damage she has caused?

FOX: I know the damage.

DR. KURTZ: Great. Next is...I forgot what's next. We covered reality, love, damage...

DETECTIVE DRISCOLL: Don't look at me.

DR. KURTZ: Let me check my notes.

DETECTIVE DRISCOLL: Is this a good time to ask, is this anyone's coffee? I put mine down somewhere…

DR. KURTZ: The guarantee of support!

BRANCH: Of course I'll support you. You're my wife. You're Bee's mother. We're all lucky there's a dime left to our names so I can pay for this support.

FOX: I'm sorry, Elgie. I don't know how I can make it up to you. You're right, I need help. I'll do anything. Let's start by spending time in Antarctica, just the three of us, no computers, no work—

BRANCH: How about you *don't* blame this on Microsoft?

FOX: I'm just saying the three of us, our family, without any distractions.

BRANCH: I'm not going to Antarctica with you. I'd throw you overboard the first chance I got.

FOX: Is the trip canceled?

BRANCH: I'd never do that to Bee. She's been reading books and doing reports on Antarctica for the last year.

FOX: I'm confused, then…

DR. KURTZ: Bernadette, I'd like to suggest that we work together over the next several weeks.

FOX: You're going on the trip with us? That's so exotic.

DR. KURTZ: No, I'm not. You need to concentrate on getting yourself better, Bernadette.

FOX: I still don't quite know how you fit in.

DR. KURTZ: I'm a psychiatrist at Madrona Hill.

FOX: Madrona Hill? The loony bin? Jesus Christ! You're shipping me off to a loony bin? Elgie! You're not!

DETECTIVE DRISCOLL: Shit, are you?

BRANCH: Bernadette, you need help.

FOX: So you're going to take Bee to Antarctica and lock me up at Madrona Hill? You can't do that!

DR. KURTZ: We'd like you to come voluntarily.

FOX: Oh Jesus. Is that why Van is here? To keep Bee distracted with snow leopards and carousel rides while you're locking me up?

BRANCH: You still have no concept of how ill you are, do you?

FOX: Elgie, look at me. I'm in the weeds. I can get myself out. We can get out of this together. For us. For Bee. But I won't work with these invaders. I'm sorry, but I've had to pee since I got here. Or do I need doctor's approval?

DR. KURTZ: Go right ahead—

FOX: God, it's *you!* It's him! Elgie!

BRANCH: What?

FOX: The guy I said was following me at the restaurant that night? This is him! You've been following me, right?

DETECTIVE DRISCOLL: You weren't supposed to know. But yes.

FOX: The point of all this is I'm supposed to be crazy. But I'm just so relieved that he *has* been following me, because now at least I know I'm not insane.

(BATHROOM DOOR CLOSING). (LONG SILENCE)

DR. KURTZ: I did tell you interventions aren't my forte.

BRANCH: Bernadette *was* being followed. What if she did call Dr. Neergaard to cancel? Shouldn't we at least check?

DR. KURTZ: As we discussed, doubt is a natural, even *necessary* component of interventions. Remember, your wife will not get help of her own volition. We want to prevent her from hitting rock bottom.

BRANCH: Isn't that what this is now? Rock bottom?

DR. KURTZ: Rock bottom is death. This is to raise the bottom for Bernadette.

BRANCH: How is this good for Bee?

DR. KURTZ: Her mother is getting help.

BRANCH: Jesus.

DR. KURTZ: What is it?

BRANCH: Her bag. A couple of nights ago, only my bag and Bee's were packed. This is Bernadette's bag. Now it's packed.

DETECTIVE DRISCOLL: What are you saying?

BRANCH: Dr. Kurtz, this proves she *was* planning to go! Maybe she did become overreliant on the Internet and got caught up in a scam. People get their identities stolen all the time. They don't get sent to the crazy house—

DR. KURTZ: Mr. Branch—

(KNOCKING ON BATHROOM DOOR)

BRANCH: Bernadette. I'm sorry. Let's talk about this.

(KICKING AT DOOR)

DETECTIVE DRISCOLL: We need some backup.

DR. KURTZ: Mr. Branch—

BRANCH: Let go of me. Bernadette! Why isn't she answering? Sir—

DETECTIVE DRISCOLL: Yeah, here.

BRANCH: What if she had pills, or broke a window and slit her wrists....Bernadette!

(FRONT DOOR OPENING)

AGENT STRANG: Is there a problem?

DETECTIVE DRISCOLL: She's been in the bathroom for several minutes, and she's not responding.

AGENT STRANG: Step back. Miss Fox!

(EXTENDED DOOR KICKING)

DETECTIVE DRISCOLL: She's not here. The water is running in the sink.

BRANCH: She's gone?

DR. KURTZ: Is there a window—

AGENT STRANG: It's closed. (WINDOW OPENING) The yard slopes way down. It's too far up for her to have jumped without injury. There's no ledge. I was at the front door. (RADIO STATIC) Kevin, you see anything?

VOICE FROM RADIO: Nobody in or out.

BRANCH: She didn't vanish. You were standing at the bathroom door, weren't you?

DETECTIVE DRISCOLL: I stepped away for a second to look at the suitcase.

AGENT STRANG: Jesus Christ.

DETECTIVE DRISCOLL: He made it sound really exciting.

DR. KURTZ: This is the only door she could have…where does it lead?

BRANCH: The basement. We never open it. It's overgrown with blackberries. Detective, could you help?

(DOOR SCRAPING AGAINST THE FLOOR)

DR. KURTZ: Oh, God, the smell.

DETECTIVE DRISCOLL: Ghhaw.

AGENT STRANG: She obviously didn't go down there—

(SOUND OF MOTOR STARTING)

DR. KURTZ: What is that?

BRANCH: A weed whacker. If she did go into the basement—

DR. KURTZ: There's no way—

(LOUD MOTOR)

DR. KURTZ: Mr. Branch!

Mr. Branch did not make it far into the basement before he fell into the blackberry brambles. He emerged, bloody, his clothes frayed. His left eyelid was torn, and his eye was severely scratched. An ambulance rushed Mr. Branch to the eye clinic at Virginia Mason.

A K9 team searched the premises. There was no sign of Bernadette Fox.

PART FIVE

Dangers Passed

Friday, January 14
From Dad

Bee,

Mrs. Webb called to say your giraffe mug is glazed and ready to pick up. I went by Galer Street, and the first-grade teacher gave me this good-bye poster her class made for you. It's so colorful I thought you'd like to put it up on your dorm room wall. (I'm keeping the mug for myself, though, on the pretense that it might break in the mail!) Everyone at Galer Street sends their love, darling, from the kindergartners on up to Gwen Goodyear.

Seattle is just how you left it. We had three days of sun, but it's raining again now. Still no word from Mom. I remain in close contact with the cell phone and credit card companies. As soon as there's any activity, they'll let me know.

Remember, Bee, this whole situation has nothing to do with you. It's a grown-up problem between your mom and me. It's complicated, and I'm not sure I understand everything that happened. What matters most is that you know how much we both cherish you.

I'm going to D.C. next week for a meeting. I thought I could drive up to Choate, pick you up, and we can make a long weekend out of it in New York. We can stay at the Plaza, just like Eloise.

I miss you terribly. I'm always around for a phone call, or I'd love to Skype, if you ever change your mind about that.

Love,
Dad

*

Fax from Soo-Lin

Dear Audrey,

I hope this finds you well in Arizona. (Utah? New Mexico? All Warren said is you're in the desert at a motel without cell reception or email, darn you!)

I'm not sure how much news of the past month has reached you, so I'll start from the beginning.

As you suspected, long before even I did, Elgie and I were developing a strong bond on Samantha 2. It started, for my part, as an admiration for his genius, then blossomed into much more as he confided in me about his abusive marriage.

The eighth graders are reading Shakespeare, and one of Lincoln's assignments is to memorize a soliloquy. (Tell that to Kyle. He'll be thrilled he's no longer at Galer Street!) Lincoln was given a speech from *Othello*, where the Moor defends the improbable love he and Desdemona share. It's me and Elgie in a nutshell.

> *She loved me for the dangers I had passed*
> *And I loved her that she did pity them.*

Shakespeare always puts it best, doesn't he?

You know that Bernadette disappeared from a drug intervention at her house. Everyone's first concern was that the Russian Mafia had gotten in and kidnapped her. However, we soon learned the Russians had been apprehended switching planes in Dubrovnik. That made the FBI and the police vanish almost as quickly as Bernadette!

Elgie and Bee did not go to Antarctica after all. Elgie had to be treated for a corneal abrasion, and he received stitches on his eyelid. After seventy-two hours, he filed a missing-persons report. To this day, there's still no news of Bernadette.

If you ask me, she was swallowed up by the ghosts of the Straight Gate girls. Did you know Straight Gate wasn't just a "school for wayward girls"? It was a place to lock up *pregnant* girls, and illegal abortions were performed in the basement. And this was where Bernadette chose to raise a baby daughter?

I digress.

Elgie had made contingency plans to send Bee to boarding school in January. Once Bernadette disappeared, he assumed she wouldn't want to go. But Bee insisted.

I asked Elgie to move in, but he still prefers a hotel, which I respect. Lucky me, I have that big dopey dog of theirs, who runs around day and night whimpering for Bernadette, dripping water on everything.

Elgie suggested I look for a bigger house on Queen Anne, which he would pay for. Then Lincoln got accepted to Lakeside. (Oh, did I tell you? We got accepted to Lakeside!) Since Lakeside was going to be the center of our lives for the next four years, I thought, What's keeping us on Queen Anne anyway? Why not Madison Park? It's closer to Lakeside. It's closer to Microsoft. Elgie said fine, as long as the house requires no construction.

I found the most beautiful home, right across from Lake Washington, a charming Craftsman, the one that used to belong to Kurt Cobain and Courtney Love. Lincoln's stock has zoomed up at school, that's for sure!

I quit Microsoft, and thank God. There's about to be another huge reorg. Yes, so soon! Of course, Samantha 2 is protected, but still, Microsoft is not a fun place to be right now. Productivity grinds to a halt with all the rumors.

Upon rereading this letter, I fear it's in terribly bad taste, considering where you are. Where *is* that, anyway?! How is Kyle? I hope you can be happy for me.

Love,
Soo-Lin

SATURDAY, JANUARY 15
Fax from Audrey Griffin

Dear Soo-Lin,

Congratulations on your newfound happiness. You're a wonderful person, and you deserve all the joy your new life has brought to you. May it continue.

I have found serenity myself, in Utah, where Kyle is in wilderness rehab. He's a drug addict and has been diagnosed with ADHD and borderline personality disorder.

We found a wonderful, if arduous, immersion program. The reason we chose Utah is because it's the only state that by law essentially allows you to kidnap your child, so they specialize in these wilderness programs. On the first day, they drove Kyle and a group of kids, blindfolded, twenty miles out into the middle of the desert and dumped them without sleeping bags, food, toothbrushes, or tents, and told them they'd be back for them in a week.

It's not like a reality television show where there are cameras and everyone is being watched. No. These kids are forced to cooperate in order to survive. Many of them, like Kyle, were coming off drugs cold turkey.

Of course, I was terrified. Kyle is incapable of doing anything for himself. You remember those calls when we were having girls' night out. "Mom, the remote is out of batteries." And I'd leave early to go to the store to get him more? How would he survive seven days in the desert? Or worse, I looked around at the other mothers, and I thought, My son is going to kill one of your children.

After a week, the kids were rounded up and brought back to the rehab center. Kyle came back alive, ten pounds lighter, smelling to high heaven, and a tiny bit *meek*.

Warren returned to Seattle, but I couldn't. I checked into a motel that makes the Westin look like the Taj Mahal. The soda machines are covered with metal grating. The sheets were so scratchy, I drove a hundred miles to the nearest Walmart and bought cotton ones.

I started going to Al-Anon meetings, ones that specialize in parents whose kids have substance-abuse problems. I have come to accept that my life has become unmanageable. I always went to church, but this program is deeply spiritual in a way I've never before experienced. I'll leave it at that.

Truthfully, I'm afraid of going back to Seattle. Gwen Goodyear has generously offered to take Kyle back at Galer Street after spring break and let him make up his credits over the summer so he can graduate with his class. But I'm not sure I want to go back just yet. I'm not the same woman who wrote that foolish Christmas poem. At the same time, I'm not sure who I am. I trust God to guide me.

That is very upsetting news about Bernadette. I know she'll turn up. She always has a trick up her sleeve, doesn't she?

Love,

Audrey

SUNDAY, JANUARY 16

From: Soo-Lin
To: Audrey Griffin

Audrey! I'm in the middle of the most horrific nightmare!! I should write to a fellow VAVite. I can't pecause my labtob with all my addresses is dead, and yours is the only email address I know by heart. I'm in an Internet café in South America,, and this keypoard is so dirty and sticky and HORRIPLE and the P makes a B and the B makes a P and the comma sticks and you have to immediately hit packsbace or else the whole email will pe commas! I'd fix the p's and b's put they're charging me py the minute and they don't take credit cards and I had only 20 besos. I'm on a timer and this HUNK OF JUNK combuter shuts off in 2 minutes. I don't want Elgie to know I snuck out so I'm going to tell you as much as I can pefore my money runs out.

They found her!!! They found Pernadette!!!! Yesterday a charge for $1300 from the Antarctic cruise combany showed ub on Elgie's Visa card. Elgie called the travel agent, who confirmed it. Pernadette went to Antarctica without them!!! Her credit card was on file,,,, and pecause the trip was ending,, her card was charged for the incidentals, so Elgie was alerted. The travel agent said the shib was at that very moment heading into the Drake Bassage, returning from Antarctica, and it would land in Ushuaia, Argentina, in 24 hours! Elgie called me and I got us two tickets to go down.

Audrey,,, I'm bregnant!!!! Yes, I'm carrying Elgie's child. I wasn't going to tell you or anyone pecause I'm 40 and it's a geriatric bregnancy. Elgie knows of course and that's really why I quit my job,, so I wouldn't have any added stress and that's also why Elgie is puying a house, not for me and him to live happily ever after, HA HA HA, like I wish, put for his new papy!!! Now that Pernadette is pack in the bicture, what will habben to me? I should have never quit MS! I'm a fool! I was living in a fantasy pupple, stubidly pelieving Elgie and me and the kids would live habbily ever after. What will I do for money? Pernadette hates me. You should have heard the mean things she said to me. I'm terrified of her. She's a witch. I'm in a state of total banic. Elgie doesn't want me here. He almost died when he found out I was coming to Ushuaia,,,, too. He didn't realize I was getting myself a ticket. What was he going to do, turn down the woman who is carrying his papy? Ha ha, no. I'm in Ushuaia,, that's where I am now, writing on this HORRIPLE KEY-POARD!!!!!! I must must must pe right there standing by Elgie's side when Pernadette gets off that shib tomorrow. If HE doesn't tell her I'm bregnant, you petter pelieve I will and

TUESDAY, JANUARY 18
From Bruce Jessup

Dear Mr. Branch,

I tried calling your office, but a recording tells me you're out of the country. It is with great sadness and urgency that I write. After conferring with Bee's adviser and dorm mistress, we unanimously recommend that Bee withdraw from Choate Rosemary immediately, without finishing the academic year.

As you know, we were all thrilled by Bee's sudden arrival. We found her a room at Homestead, one of our more intimate dorms, and a roommate, Sarah Wyatt, a dean's list student from New York.

Yet from Bee's first week, I received reports that she was failing to thrive in the boarding school environment. Teachers said Bee sat in the back and never took notes. I watched her bringing food back to her dorm room instead of eating in the dining hall with the other students.

Then her roommate requested to switch rooms. Sarah complained that Bee was spending study hours watching Josh Groban perform "O Holy Night" on YouTube. Hoping this was a portal into Bee, I sent the chaplain to her dorm. He said he found her apathetic to spiritual discourse.

Yesterday morning I noticed a bounce in Bee's step as she crossed campus. I was greatly relieved until Sarah burst into my office, quite distraught. She told me that a few days earlier she and Bee were in the student activities center getting their mail. In Bee's box was a thick manila envelope with no return address. It was postmarked Seattle. Bee remarked that the writing was unfamiliar. The package contained a sheaf of documents.

Bee jumped up and down as she excitedly read them. Sarah asked what they were, but Bee wouldn't say. Back at the dorm, Bee stopped watching YouTube and told Sarah she was writing "a book" based on these documents.

Yesterday afternoon, while Bee was away, Sarah snuck a peek at Bee's "book." Sarah was so shaken by its contents—in particular, FBI documents marked CONFIDENTIAL—that she ran straight to me.

Based on Sarah's description, Bee has written a narrative connecting the contents of the envelope. They include: FBI documents involving surveillance of your wife, emails between you and your administrator, handwritten notes between a woman and her gardener, the same woman's emergency room bill, back-and-forth from a Galer Street School fundraiser about a disastrous brunch, an article about your wife's architecture career, correspondence between you and a psychiatrist.

My concern is Bee. As you may know, John F. Kennedy attended Choate. While he was here, the headmaster, Seymour St. John, gave a commencement speech in which he uttered the immortal words, "Ask not what Choate can do for you. Ask what you can do for Choate."

Even though it's difficult, here's what I can do for Choate. I can recognize when a student, even one as gifted as Bee, has come to boarding school at a time in her life when she should be home with family. I expect you will agree, and that you will immediately come to Wallingford and take your daughter home.

Sincerely,

Bruce Jessup

WEDNESDAY, JANUARY 19
Fax from Soo-Lin

Audrey,

WARNING: Aliens took over my brain yesterday! It's been such a long time since I've been pregnant that I completely forgot how hormones can make you do crazy things, like run to Argentinean Internet cafés in the middle of the night and write wild, embarrassing emails to friends back home.

Now that I've got my brain back, I will attempt a more levelheaded update of the Bernadette saga. But I must warn you, if the events described in my last (incoherent) email seemed action-packed, they're nothing compared to what transpired over the past forty-eight hours.

After arriving in the middle of the night, Elgie and I awoke in the dreary, wet, little town of Ushuaia. It was summer, but it was not like any summer I'd ever seen. The fog was thick and constant, and the air damper than even the rain forests of the Olympic Peninsula. We had time to kill before Bernadette's boat arrived, so we asked the gentleman at the front desk if there were any sights to see. He said their most famous tourist attraction was a prison. Yes, a prison is their idea of fun. It was decommissioned a while back and is now an art gallery. Thanks, but no thanks. Elgie and I walked straight to the dock to meet Bernadette's boat.

Along the way, I did see some Icelandic poppies, lupine, and fox-gloves, which reminded me of home. I took pictures and will send them to you if you'd like.

The dock stank of fish and was packed with the most unattractive fishing boats and vulgar dockworkers. In Seattle, we park our cruise ships far from the fishing vessels. Not in Argentina!

Elgie and I waited in the "immigration office," four flimsy walls with a framed photograph of Michael Jackson and an X-ray machine that wasn't even plugged in. There were three boxy, ancient-looking pay phones. Lots of international sailors waited in line to call home. It was like the Tower of Babel at that place.

To give you a sense of where Elgie was emotionally during the weeks leading up to this, he vacillated between believing Bernadette would come traipsing through the door and worrying that something terrible had happened. As soon as he learned Bernadette had skedaddled to Antarctica, leaving them all worried sick, well, he was *furious*. I can tell you, I found it a little strange.

"You don't get mad at someone for getting cancer," I said. "She's clearly sick."

"This isn't *cancer*," he said. "She's selfish and weak. Instead of facing reality, she escapes. She escaped from Los Angeles. She escaped into her Airstream. She escaped from any personal responsibility. What did she do when confronted with this fact? She *literally escaped*. And now I'm fucking blind."

Audrey, he isn't blind. My father was blind, so I don't have patience for exaggeration. Elgie just has to wear tape over his left eyeglass lens until his cornea heals, which will be soon.

The H&H *Allegra* finally sailed into port. She's smaller than any cruise vessel I've seen in Seattle, but a real gem, with fresh paint. The dockhands rolled up a set of stairs and the passengers started filing out and going through immigration. Elgie sent word that we were there to see Bernadette Fox. Passengers and more passengers streamed by, but no Bernadette.

Poor Elgie, he was like a dog whimpering by the door for his master to get home. "There she is…," he'd say. Then "No, that's not her. Oh, there she is!" Then all sad, "No, that's not her." The passengers slowed to a trickle, and still we waited.

After a long worrisome gap of no passengers at all, the ship's captain and a few officers walked toward us in a tight pack, talking severely among themselves.

"She didn't," Elgie muttered.

"What?" I said.

"You're *fucking kidding me!*" he said.

"What?" I said, as the captain and his gang entered the immigration hut.

"Mr. Branch," the captain said in a thick German accent. "There seems to be a problem. We can't find your wife."

I'm not kidding, Audrey. Bernadette did it again! Somewhere along the way, she disappeared from the ship.

The captain was really shaken up, you could tell. He'd reported it to the president of the cruise line and promised a thorough investigation. Then it got truly surreal. As we stood there, absorbing this huge bomb that had just been dropped, the captain graciously excused himself. "The next group of passengers is due to arrive," he said. "We must prepare the ship."

The purser, a German woman with bleached-blond hair cut very short, handed us Bernadette's passport with a sheepish smile, as if to say, *I know it isn't much, but it's all we have.*

"Wait a second—" Elgie cried. "Whose responsibility is this? Who's in charge?"

The answer, it turns out, is *nobody*. When Bernadette boarded the ship, she left Argentina (it was stamped right there on her passport), so this wasn't Argentina's problem. But because Antarctica isn't a country, and has no ruling government, Bernadette didn't officially *enter* anyplace when she left Argentina.

"Can I search the boat?" Elgie pleaded. "Or her room?" But some Argentinean official insisted we couldn't board because we didn't have the proper paperwork. The captain then trudged back along the rain-swept dock, leaving us standing there, agape.

"The other passengers," Elgie said, running to the street. But the last bus had already departed. Elgie then made a mad dash toward the ship. He didn't get far because he ran into a pole, which knocked him to the ground. (His depth perception is hinky because of the one dark lens.) By that time, the Argentinean customs agent was standing over Elgie with a gun. My screaming had caused enough of a ruckus for the captain to at least turn around. The sight of Elgie flat on the slimy dock, groaning, "My wife, my wife," with a gun pointed at him, and me jumping up and down, was enough for even a German to take pity. He came back and told us he'd have the ship searched and to wait.

As far as I was concerned, if Bernadette was across the ocean in Antarctica, Antarctica could keep her. Yes, you heard me. If I didn't like that woman before, I *really* didn't like her now that I was pregnant with her husband's baby! The reason I can admit to such craven selfishness is because here's how much I love Elgie: if he wanted to find his wife, then I wanted to find his wife. I swung into full admin mode.

I got in line behind the dozen crew members wanting to call home during their quick turnaround. When it was my turn, I miraculously got through to Agent Strang at the FBI. Elgie and I shared the earpiece as

Agent Strang connected us to a friend of his, a retired maritime lawyer. We explained our dilemma, and he searched the Internet from his end.

Our silence made the waiting sailors more irate by the minute. Finally, the lawyer got back on and explained that the H&H *Allegra* was registered under a "flag of convenience" in Liberia. (I'll save you a trip to the atlas: Liberia is an impoverished, war-torn country in West Africa.) So that was of no comfort or help. The lawyer told us to expect zero cooperation from Harmsen & Heath. In the past, this gentleman had represented families of persons who'd gone missing from cruise ships (who knew that's an industry unto itself?), and it took him years and government subpoenas to obtain so much as a passenger list. The lawyer then explained that if a crime occurred in international waters, the government of the victim has jurisdiction. However, Antarctica is the *one place on the planet* that isn't considered international waters, because it's governed by something called the Antarctic Treaty. He said it looked like we had fallen down a legal rabbit hole. He suggested we try to get the Liberian government to help, or the U.S. government, but we'd have to first convince a judge that the "long-arm statute" applies. He didn't explain what that was because he was late for squash.

Agent Strang was still on the phone, and he said something about us being "shit out of luck." I think he had grown disgusted with Elgie and especially Bernadette, for the trouble they had caused. For some reason he was no fan of mine, either.

Time was ticking. Our only connection to Bernadette was the ship itself, which was leaving in an hour. The fleet of buses returned, this time with a new group of passengers who dismounted and started to wander around snapping pictures.

Thank God the captain kept his word and returned. The ship had been searched top to bottom with a carbon-detecting ray gun that checks for stowaways. But nobody who was *not* a crew member was on board. Elgie asked the captain if he knew of another ship that could take us (us!) to the places Bernadette visited, so we could search for her ourselves. But every ship with ice-breaking capabilities was booked years in advance. Adding to the sheer impossibility of heading out to find her, the Antarctic summer was ending, and the ice was closing up. So even the H&H *Allegra*, on this next trip, wouldn't be going as deep into Antarctica as it had on the previous one.

Trust me when I say nothing could be done.

"Stop! *Warten sie!*" It was the purser, running toward us in her short skirt and ankle-high cowboy boots, waving a notepad. "This was found on the desk." But there was no writing on it. "The pen is pressed down."

Elgie took off his glasses and examined the paper. "It's indented—" he said. "We can send it to a forensic specialist. Thank you! Thank you!" The pad of paper is now in the hands of a lab in Delaware that tests for such things, at huge expense, I might add.

They say hope for the best. But how can you, when the best is that Bernadette was left behind on an iceberg in Antarctica? It's one thing to disappear from Seattle. It's quite another to disappear in a land with no shelter and the coldest temperatures on the planet.

We returned to Seattle this morning in a state of shock. Elgie checked his voicemail and had a bunch of calls from the headmaster at Choate. It seems like something is now up with *Bee*. Elgie wouldn't tell me what. He's on a plane back east to see her, which seems a little sudden.

As for me, I'm trying to focus on the here and now: my pregnancy and furniture for the new house. So many bedrooms, and a full bath for each! We're waiting until I'm safely in my second trimester to tell Alexandra and Lincoln about the new baby. Bee knows nothing of the pregnancy or our trip to Ushuaia. Elgie wants to wait for the captain's report before he sits her down. Bee is scientifically minded, so he thinks it would help to have some facts in front of her.

Anyway, I told you this one would be a doozy. Oh, I miss you, Audrey. Come home soon!

Soo-Lin

THURSDAY, JANUARY 20
Fax from Audrey Griffin

Soo-Lin,

Don't worry about that email from Ushuaia. I've been in much worse shape than that! Don't believe me? I was actually arrested for disturbing the peace one night at the Westin! The charges were dropped. But still, you have nothing on me when it comes to being run amok by emotions. And I didn't even have the very legitimate excuse of pregnancy hormones. Congratulations! You, Elgie, and the baby are in my prayers.

That is very unsettling news about Bernadette. I don't believe for a second that she froze to death in Antarctica. Please do send the captain's report as soon as you receive it. I am quite anxious.

Love,
Audrey

TUESDAY, JANUARY 25
Fax from Soo-Lin

Dear Audrey,

Keep that last letter I wrote you, and frame it, for it is an artifact from a fleeting moment when I could call true happiness my own.

You know how I said Elgie was heading back east to see Bee? Which

I found kind of strange? It turns out Elgie withdrew Bee from Choate. He just returned to Seattle with her in tow!

Remember what a sweet, quiet girl Bee always was? Well, the child is unrecognizable, I tell you, absolutely consumed with hatred. Elgie moved back into the Gate Avenue house to be with her. But Bee refuses to sleep under the same roof as him. The only place she wants to sleep is Bernadette's Airstream. Saint Bernadette!

Elgie is so guilt-ridden, he'll do anything Bee wants. She won't go back to Galer Street? Fine! She refuses to step foot in my home for our weekly dinners? Fine!

You'd never guess the source of all this turmoil. It's the most incredible "book" Bee wrote. She won't let anybody see it, but from what little Elgie will tell me, it's based on emails between you and me, Audrey, plus the FBI report, even handwritten notes between you and the blackberry specialist. I have no idea how Bee got her mitts on all of this. Not to point fingers, but the only person who could possibly have had access is Kyle. (The old Kyle.) Perhaps you can confront him during your next therapy session. I, for one, would like some answers. I'm even paranoid this fax will fall into enemy hands.

Elgie wants Bee to go to Lakeside in the fall. All I can say is she had better get over herself because there is *no way* we're moving that Airstream over to the new house. Can you imagine? We'd be the hillbillies of Madison Park. "We"! As if Elgie would ever want to live together as a family!

I'm sure you think I'm being horribly selfish, but my life has been turned upside down, too! I gave up my job, I'm pregnant at age forty by a man whose life is in turmoil, plus I have terrible morning sickness. The only thing I can hold down is French toast. I've already gained eleven pounds, and I'm not even in my second trimester. When Bee finds out that Bernadette perished, not to mention about the baby, who knows what she'll do?

Here's a letter from the cruise company along with the captain's report, plus the forensic analysis. And those gorgeous pictures I promised of the poppies from Ushuaia. I'm late for a VAV meeting, and boy do I need it.

Love,

Soo-Lin

*

From Elijah Harmsen, President of Harmsen & Heath Adventure Travel

Dear Mr. Branch,

Let me begin by expressing my sincerest condolences to you and Bee for the sudden disappearance of Bernadette. I can only imagine what a shock it must be to lose such an extraordinary woman.

Since Harmsen & Heath was founded by my great-grandfather in 1903, the safety of our passengers has always been our top priority. Indeed, for over a century we have enjoyed an unblemished record.

As promised, I have enclosed a report compiled by Captain Jürgen Altdorf. It is largely based on the electronic signature created by your wife's magnetically coded ID card. It paints a reliable and detailed portrait of her shipboard life: daily disembarkations, purchases in the gift shop, bills from the ship's lounge. Additionally, Captain Altdorf conducted extensive interviews per Harmsen & Heath protocol.

Your wife's last recorded activity occurred on January 5. She went on the morning excursion, and returned safely to the ship, then made some significant charges at the bar. At that point, the H&H *Allegra* headed through the Gerlache Strait. It should be noted that the ocean was unusually turbulent during the next twenty-four hours. We were forced to cancel two planned disembarkations. Out of an abundance of caution, several announcements were made over the PA system, warning passengers not to go out on deck during such severe weather.

I believe the weather conditions and charges made at the Shackleton Lounge will give you a better understanding of your wife's condition on the day she was last seen. While nobody can ever know what really happened, there are inevitable conclusions to be drawn.

While unpleasant to contemplate, the facts may provide a small measure of comfort to you and your daughter during this difficult grieving period.

Sincerely, and with my utmost condolences,

Elijah Harmsen

*

Captain's report

THIS IS A REPORT FILED BY CAPTAIN JÜRGEN GEBHARD ALTDORF OF THE HARMSEN & HEATH *ALLEGRA* BASED ON PARTICULARS FROM ELECTRONIC SIGNATURE OF PASSENGER ID CARD #998322-01 ON 26 DECEMBER VOYAGE FROM USHUAIA, ARGENTINA, TO ANTARCTIC PENINSULA AND REGARDING THE VERIFIED PRESENCE OF MANIFEST PASSENGER #998322-01 BERNADETTE FOX U.S. CITIZEN, WASHINGTON STATE, SEATTLE.

26 DECEMBER 16:33 PASSENGER BOARDED HH *ALLEGRA* ASSIGNED CABIN 322. 26 DECEMBER 18:08 PASSENGER COLLECTED PHOTO ID CARD. 26 DECEMBER 18:30 PASSENGER MARKED PRESENT FOR MUSTER DRILL. 26 DECEMBER 20:05 GIFT SHOP CHARGE $433.09 USD FOR CLOTHING AND TOILETRIES.

27 DECEMBER AT SEA. 06:00 PASSENGER RECEIVED TREATMENT FROM SHIP'S DOCTOR FOR MOTION SICKNESS. 27 DECEMBER PASSENGER NOTIFIED HOUSEKEEPING NOT TO ENTER

ROOM FOR CLEAN OR TURN-DOWN SERVICE UNTIL FURTHER NOTICE. HOUSEKEEPER RECALLS VARIOUS CONTACT WITH PASSENGER IN SHIP HALLWAY AND ENVIRONS. INQUIRY ABOUT CLEANING AND TURN-DOWN SERVICE. PASSENGER REFUSED ALL SERVICE. NO HOUSEKEEPING SERVICE LOGGED FOR DURATION OF JOURNEY.

30 DECEMBER 10:00 PASSENGER DISEMBARKED DECEPTION ISLAND, WHALERS BAY. 30 DECEMBER 12:30 BOARDED SHIP. 30 DECEMBER 13:47 PASSENGER LOGGED OUT NEPTUNE'S BELLOWS. 30 DECEMBER 19:41 BOARDED SHIP.

31 DECEMBER 08:00 PASSENGER DISEMBARKED 70.6S 52.4W WEDDELL SEA. 31 DECEMBER 13:23 LAST PASSENGER TO BOARD.

1 JANUARY 10:10 PASSENGER DISEMBARKS DEVIL ISLAND. PASSENGER REEMBARKS 16:31. 1 JANUARY 23:30 PASSENGER SIGNS FOR 2 PINK PENGUIN DRINKS AT SHACKLETON LOUNGE. 1 BOTTLE WINE CABERNET AT DINNER.

2 JANUARY 08:44 PASSENGER DISEMBARKS DANCO COAST. 2 JANUARY 18:33 REEMBARKS. 2 JANUARY 23:10 1 BOTTLE CABERNET WINE AT DINNER. PASSENGER SIGNS FOR 2 PINK PENGUIN DRINKS, LOUNGE.

3 JANUARY 08:10 DETAILLE ISLAND PASSENGER DISEMBARKS. 3 JANUARY 16:00 PASSENGER BOARDS SHIP. 3 JANUARY 19:36 PASSENGER SIGNS FOR 5 PINK PENGUINS, LOUNGE.

4 JANUARY 08:05 PASSENGER DISEMBARKS PETERMANN ISLAND. 4 JANUARY 11:39 EMBARKS. 4 JANUARY 13:44 PASSENGER SIGNS 1 BOTTLE CABERNET WINE LUNCH. 14:30 PASSENGER DISEMBARKS PORT LOCKROY. 18:30 REEMBARKS. 4 JANUARY 23:30 PASSENGER SIGNS 4 PINK PENGUINS, 4 WHISKEY SOURS, SHACKLETON LOUNGE.

5 JANUARY 08:12 PASSENGER DISEMBARKS NEKO HARBOR. 5 JANUARY 16:22 PASSENGER CARDS IN. 5 JANUARY 18:00 PASSENGER SIGNS 2 BOTTLES WINE, SHACKLETON LOUNGE.

6 JANUARY 05:30 SHIP UNABLE TO ANCHOR DUE TO OCEAN CONDITIONS. 6 JANUARY 08:33 ANNOUNCEMENT MADE, ROUGH SEAS. CONTINENTAL MEAL SERVICE ONLY. 6 JANUARY 18:00 ANNOUNCEMENT MADE, SHACKLETON LOUNGE CLOSING.

15 JANUARY 17:00 PRELIMINARY ROOM CHARGES TOTALED. BILL PLACED IN PASSENGER'S DOOR.

16 JANUARY 16:30 PASSENGER MARKED NOT PRESENT FOR FINAL DISEMBARKATION BRIEFING. 16 JANUARY 19:00 PASSENGER DOES NOT SUBMIT PAYMENT FOR BAR BILL, GIFT SHOP BILL, AND CREW GRATUITY. 16 JANUARY 19:00 PASSENGER DOES NOT RESPOND TO REPEATED PAGES. 16 JANUARY 19:30 PASSENGER DOES NOT ANSWER REPEATED ATTEMPTS TO ENTER CABIN. 16 JANUARY 19:32 PURSER ENTERS CABIN. PASSENGER NOT PRESENT. 16 JANUARY 22:00 EXHAUSTIVE SEARCH OF SHIP DOES NOT LOCATE PASSENGER.

17 JANUARY 07:00 PASSENGERS INTERROGATED BY MYSELF AND PURSER. NO RELEVANT INFORMATION GAINED. PASSENGERS RELEASED. 17 JANUARY 10:00 CARBO THERMAL SCAN REVEALS NO UNACCOUNTED FOR PERSONS.

**PHOTO DOCUMENTATION REVEALS NO PHOTOS OF PASSENGER IN CRUISE PHOTOGRAPHER'S ARCHIVES. NO VIDEO OF PASSENGER FROM SHIP'S VIDEOGRAPHER.

*** SEARCH OF CABIN 322 REVEALS PAD OF PAPER WHICH HAS PER INSTRUCTIONS BEEN TURNED OVER TO USA EXPERT.

*

Report by Tonya Woods, forensic document examiner

Dear Mr. Branch,

Using an Electro-Static Detection Apparatus (ESDA), we analyzed the second-page writing present on several sheets of stationery with the HARMSEN & HEATH *ALLEGRA* letterhead. Due to the *three distinct depths* of indented writing, it is highly probable that a *three-page letter* was written. It is signed, "Love, Mom." This strongly indicates to us that it is a letter written from a mother to a child. The most frequently repeated words are "Audrey Griffin," which appear to have been written at least six times. While we are unable to piece together the whole letter, we are somewhat confident that the letter contains the following phrases:

"Audrey Griffin is the devil."
"Audrey Griffin is an angel."
"Romeo, Romeo."
"I am a Christian."
"Audrey knows."

Please let me know if I can be of further assistance.

Sincerely,
Tonya Woods

*

Fax from Audrey Griffin to her husband

Warren,

I need you to immediately go home and check the answering machine, my mail, and email. I'm urgently looking for anything from Bernadette Fox.

Yes, Bernadette Fox.

For months, you've wanted to know what transpired during those days before Christmas that caused me to capitulate. I have been trying to find the courage to tell you one of these weekends in family therapy. But God has decided he wants me to tell you now.

Those days leading up to Christmas were a nightmare. I was furious at Bernadette Fox. I was furious at Kyle for being such a stinker. I was furious at Soo-Lin for siding with Elgin Branch. I was furious at you for drinking and refusing to move to Soo-Lin's with us. No matter how many gingerbread houses I made, it only increased my fury.

Then one evening I visited Soo-Lin at work. A woman came in and asked for Elgin Branch. I noticed an ID badge from Madrona Hill, the mental institution. I was intrigued, to put it mildly. My interest was further piqued when Soo-Lin lied to me about this woman's identity.

Soo-Lin returned home late that night, and while she slept, I rifled through her bag. In it, I found a classified FBI dossier.

The contents were astonishing. Bernadette had unwittingly given her financial information to an identity-theft operation, and the FBI was conducting a sting. Even more shocking were Post-it notes stuck to the back of the file. They were handwritten, between Elgin and Soo-Lin, suggesting that he was meeting with Madrona Hill because Bernadette was a harm to herself and others. His evidence? That she had run over my foot and destroyed our home.

My sworn enemy was being sent away to a mental institution?! It should have been cause for celebration. Instead, I sat on the hall bench, my whole body quivering. Everything fell away but the truth: Bernadette never ran over my foot. I faked the whole thing. And the mudslide? Bernadette removed the blackberries exactly as I had asked her to do.

A full hour must have passed. I didn't move. I just breathed and stared at the floor. I wish a camera had been trained on me, because it would show what it looks like for a woman to be awakened to the truth. The truth? My lies and exaggerations would be responsible for a mother being locked up.

I dropped to my knees. "Tell me, God," I said. "Tell me what to do."

A calm came over me. A calm that has protected me for the past month. I walked to the twenty-four-hour Safeway, made a copy of every document in that file, plus the Post-it notes, and tucked the originals back into Soo-Lin's bag before anyone was up.

While everything in those documents was true, it was a *partial* truth. I was determined to fill in the story with my own documentation. The next morning, I ransacked our house for every email and note I could find about the mudslide and my "injury," then spent the whole day assembling them chronologically with Bernadette's emails from the FBI file. I knew that my more complete story would absolve Bernadette.

But from what? What had transpired in that meeting between Elgin and the psychiatrist? Was there a plan?

I returned to Soo-Lin's at four in the afternoon. Lincoln and Alexandra were at swim team. Kyle, of course, was zombified, playing video games in the basement. I stepped in front of the TV. "Kyle," I said, "if I needed to read Soo-Lin's email, how would I go about it?" Kyle grunted and went upstairs to the linen closet. A dusty tower computer, giant keyboard, and boxy monitor were on the floor. Kyle set them up on the bed in the guest room and hooked the modem into the phone jack.

An ancient version of Windows loaded, with a turquoise screen, a strange blast from the past! Kyle turned to me. "I'm assuming you don't want her knowing?" "That would be optimal." Kyle went to a Microsoft website and downloaded a program that allows you to remotely take over another person's computer. He had Soo-Lin's password and ID sent to her email program on this computer. With that information, he entered a bunch of numbers separated by periods, and, within minutes, what Soo-Lin sees on her laptop at Microsoft appeared on the screen in front of us. "She's away from her computer, it looks like," Kyle told me, cracking his knuckles. He punched in a few more things. "She's got a signature saying she'll be out of the office for the night. You probably have time."

I didn't know whether to hug him or slap him. Instead, I gave him money and told him to wait outside for Lincoln and Alexandra and take them out for pizza. Kyle was halfway down the stairs when I had an even bigger idea. "Kyle," I called, "you know how Soo-Lin's an admin? Do you think we have enough information to take over, say, her boss's computer?" "You mean Bee's dad?" "Yeah, Bee's dad." "It depends," he said, "if she has access to his in-box. Let me check."

Warren, I'm not joking when I say that within five minutes I was looking at Elgin Branch's computer. Kyle checked his calendar. "He's having dinner with his brother right now, so he'll probably be off-line for at least an hour."

I furiously read correspondence between Elgin and Soo-Lin, his brother, and that psychiatrist. I discovered the plan for an intervention the next morning. I wanted copies of the documents to add to my new, comprehensive narrative, but there was no printer. After everyone was asleep (except Soo-Lin, who'd called to say she wouldn't be coming home that night), Kyle opened two Hotmail accounts and taught me how to take something called a "screen shot" and email the image from one Hotmail account to the other...or something. All I know is, it worked. I printed them out from a computer at the Safeway.

The intervention was happening at Dr. Neergaard's office. I didn't want to interfere with an FBI investigation. But there was no way Bernadette was going to get hauled off to a mental hospital because of my lies. At nine a.m., I headed to the dentist's office. On my way, on a hunch, I drove by Straight Gate.

There was a police car in the driveway as well as Soo-Lin's Subaru. I parked on a side street. Just then, a familiar car zoomed by. It was Bernadette, behind dark glasses. I had to get this file to her. But how would I get past the police?

Of course! The hole in the fence!

I ran down the side street, climbed through the fence, and clambered up the naked hill. (An incredible side note: the blackberries had begun to grow back. All that work for nothing!)

I clawed my way across the watery mud until I reached Bernadette's photinia. I grabbed the branches and hoisted myself up onto the lawn. There was one police officer at the far side of the house, with his back to me. I crept up the lawn to the house. I had no plan. It was just me, the manila envelope in the waist of my pants, and God.

Commando-style, I slithered up the grand stairway along the back of the house and onto the rear portico. Everyone was gathered in the living room. I couldn't hear them, but it was clear from their body language that the intervention was in full swing. Then a figure crossed to the far side of the living room. It was Bernadette. I ran down the steps. A light turned on in a small side window, about twelve feet up. (The side yard slopes down steeply, so from the back of the house the first floor is the equivalent of several stories high.) Crouched down, I ran to it.

Then I tripped over something. I'll be damned, but it was a ladder, lying across the side yard, as if God had placed it there Himself. From that point on, I felt invincible. I knew He was protecting me. I picked up the ladder and stood it against the house. Without hesitation, I climbed up and tapped on the window.

"Bernadette," I whispered. "Bernadette."

The window opened. Bernadette's gobsmacked face was in it. "Audrey?"

"Come."

"But—" She couldn't pick her poison, coming with me or being locked up in a loony bin.

"Now!" I climbed down, and Bernadette followed, but not before she shut the window.

"Let's go to my house," I said. Again she hesitated.

"Why are you doing this?" she asked.

"Because I'm a Christian."

A radio squelched. "Kevin, see anything?"

Bernadette and I made our break across the lawn, dragging the ladder with us.

We skidded down the muddy hill and into our backyard. The floor guys were quite surprised to see us mud creatures stagger through the door. I sent the men home.

I handed Bernadette my completed dossier, which also included a newly published article Kyle had found on the Internet about Bernadette's architecture career. "You should have told me you won a MacArthur grant," I said. "I might have been less of a gnat if I knew you were such a genius."

I left Bernadette at the table. I took a shower, brought her tea. She read, expressionless, with furrowed brow. She spoke only once, to say, "I would have done it."

"Done what?" I asked.

"Given Manjula power of attorney." She turned the last page and took a deep breath.

"There's still boxes of Galer Street gear in the living room if you'd like to change," I said.

"That's how desperate I am." She peeled off her muddy sweater. Underneath, she was wearing a fishing vest. She patted it. Through the mesh pockets, I could see her wallet, cell phone, keys, passport. "I can do anything," she said with a smile.

"That you can."

"Please see that Bee gets this." She slipped the documents back in the envelope. "I know it's a lot. But she can handle it. I'd rather ruin her with the truth than ruin her with lies."

"She won't be ruined," I said.

"I have to ask you a question. Is he fucking her? The admin, your pally, what's her name?"

"Soo-Lin?"

"Yeah," she said. "Soo-Lin. Are she and Elgie—"

"Hard to say."

That was the last I saw of Bernadette.

I returned to Soo-Lin's and reserved a space for Kyle at Eagle's Nest.

I found out Bee was at boarding school. I confirmed it with Gwen Goodyear and sent the envelope of documents to Bee at Choate, with no return address.

I just now learned that Bernadette ended up going to Antarctica, and that she disappeared somewhere on the continent. An investigation was conducted and, reading between the lines, they want everyone to believe Bernadette got drunk and fell overboard. I don't buy it for a second. But I am worried that she might have tried to get word to Bee through me. Warren, I know this is a lot to digest. But please go home and double-check to see if there's anything from Bernadette.

Love,

Audrey

*

Fax from Warren Griffin

Darling,

I'm tremendously proud of you. I'm at the house now. There's no word from Bernadette. I'm sorry. Can't wait to see you this weekend.

Love,

Warren

FRIDAY, JANUARY 28
Fax from Soo-Lin

Audrey,

I got TORCHed at VAV. I am forbidden to return until I "WYP and Read It." (WYP stands for Write Your Part, and it's pronounced, "weep," not "wipe," which we think sounds scatological.) It's an inventory we write, owning our part in our abuse. If I ever find myself slipping into victimhood, I have to TORCH myself. I spent the last three hours WYPing. Here it is, if you're interested.

*

WYP by Soo-Lin Lee-Segal

After I got off to a rocky start as Elgie's admin, our working relationship flourished. Elgie would request the impossible. I would make it happen. I could feel Elgie marvel at my wizardry. It soon became a skyward duet of me doing the best work of my life, and Elgie praising me. I could feel us falling in love.

(TIME-OUT REALITY CHECK: I was falling in love, not Elgie.)

Everything changed the day he asked me to lunch and confided in me about his wife. If he didn't understand you don't speak ill of your spouse to a coworker, especially a coworker of the opposite sex, I certainly did. I tried not to engage. But we had kids in the same school, so the line between work and our personal lives was already blurred.

(TIME-OUT REALITY CHECK: The moment Elgie began speaking ill of his wife, I could have politely ended the conversation.)

Then Bernadette got tangled up in a ring of Internet hackers. Elgie was furious at her, and confided in me, which I interpreted as further proof of his love. One night, when Elgie was planning to sleep at the office, I booked him a room at the Hyatt in Bellevue and drove him there myself. I pulled the car up to the valet.

"What are you doing?" Elgie asked.

"I'm coming in to get you set up."

"Are you sure?" he said, an acknowledgement, to me, that tonight we were going to finally act on our crackling sexual tension.

(TIME-OUT REALITY CHECK: Not only was I completely deluded, I was preying on a emotionally vulnerable man.)

We took the elevator up to his room. I sat down on the bed. Elgie kicked off his shoes and climbed under the covers, fully dressed.

"Could you turn off the light?" he asked.

I turned off the bedside lamp. The room was blackout dark. I just sat there, coursing with desire, barely able to breathe. I carefully swung my feet onto the bed.

"Are you leaving?" he asked.

"No," I said.

Minutes passed. I still maintained an image of where Elgie was on the bed. I could visualize his head, both arms over the covers, his hands clasped just under his chin. More time passed. He was obviously waiting for me to make the first move.

(TIME-OUT REALITY CHECK: Ha!)

I jabbed my hand toward where I pictured his hands to be. My fingers plunged into something moist and soft, then sharp.

"Gaahh—" Elgie said.

I had poked my fingers into his mouth, and he'd reflexively bit me.

"Oh dear!" I said. "I'm sorry!"

"I'm sorry," he said. "Where's your—"

He was groping in the dark for my hand. He found it and laid it on his chest, then covered it with his other hand. Progress! I breathed as quietly as I could and waited for a cue. Another eternity passed. I wiggled my thumb against the top of his hand, pathetically trying to manufacture a spark, but his hand remained stiff.

"What are you thinking?" I finally said.

"Do you really want to know?"

I went wild with excitement. "Only if you feel like telling me," I shot back in my best kittenish banter.

"The most painful part of the FBI file was that letter Bernadette wrote to Paul Jellinek. I wish I could go back in time and tell her I want to know her. Maybe if I'd done that, I wouldn't be lying here right now."

Thank God it was pitch-black, or the room would have started spinning. I got up and drove myself home. I'm lucky I didn't drive myself off the 520 bridge, accidentally or otherwise.

The next day, I went to work. Elgie was scheduled to rehearse his wife's intervention with a psychiatrist off campus. Afterward, his brother was arriving from Hawaii. I went about my business, fixated on a corny fantasy of a bouquet of flowers appearing in my doorway, waving in midair, followed by Elgie, hangdog, professing his love.

Suddenly it was 4 PM, and I realized: Elgie wasn't coming to work at all! Not only that, but tomorrow was the intervention. The following day he'd be off to Antarctica. So I wouldn't be seeing him for weeks! There was no call, no nothing.

I had been configuring a tablet computer for Elgie to take on his trip. On my way home, I dropped it off at the hotel where his brother was staying, and where I had also booked a room for Elgie for the next two nights.

(TIME-OUT REALITY CHECK: I could have had someone else bring it, but I was desperate to see him.)

I left the package at the front desk when I heard, "Hey, Soo-Lin!"

It was Elgie. Just hearing him speak my name made me swoon and filled me with hope. He and his brother invited me to dine with them. What can I say? At that dinner, everything flipped, in part due to the rounds of tequila that Van kept ordering on the basis of tequila's "clear buzz." I don't think I've ever laughed as hard in my life as with the two of them telling stories of their childhood. My eyes would meet Elgie's and we'd hold our glances for an extra second before looking down. After dinner, we all wandered into the lobby.

A singer named Morrissey was staying at the hotel, and a group of ardent young homosexuals had gathered, hoping for a glimpse. They were carrying Morrissey posters, records, boxes of chocolate. Love was in the air!

Elgie and I took a seat on a bench, but Van went upstairs to sleep. As the elevator doors shut on him, Elgie said, "Van's not that bad, right?"

"He's hilarious," I answered.

"Bernadette thinks he's a gigantic loser who keeps hitting me up for money."

"Which is no doubt true," I said, to which Elgie gave an appreciative laugh. Then I handed Elgie the tablet computer. "I can't forget to give you this. I had Gio program it so it wouldn't start until you watched a slideshow."

The slideshow began. It was pictures I'd collected of Elgie during all his years at Microsoft. Him presenting his work in the theater, candid shots of him with Samantha 1, throwing a football with Matt Hasselbeck at the executive picnic back when it was at Paul Allen's ranch, receiving his Technical Recognition Award. Also there were photos of three-year-old Bee sitting in his lap. She'd just been released from the hospital, and you could still see the bandage peeking out the top of her dress. There was one of her in day care, in leg braces, because she'd spent so much of her early years lying in bed that her hips hadn't properly rotated. There was the famous E-Dawg photo, with Elgie in gold chains and a big clock around his neck, making rapper signs.

"It's important to me that you see that every day," I said. "To know that you have another family, at Microsoft. I know it isn't the same. But we love you, too."

(TIME-OUT REALITY CHECK: I cut Bernadette out of a few of those pictures. I also included one of me at my desk, which I Photoshopped to make it look like my face radiated light.)

"I'm not going to cry," Elgie said.

"You can," I said.

"I can, but I won't." We just looked at each other, smiling. He gave a laugh. I did, too. The future was glorious, and it was opening itself up to us.

(TIME-OUT REALITY CHECK: Because we were drunk.)

And then it started to snow.

The walls at the Four Seasons are made of thin pieces of slate, stacked like French pastry, and an edge had ripped a hole in Elgie's parka, releasing feathers, which swirled around us. The Morrissey fans waved their arms around theatrically and started singing one of his songs that went something like "through hail and snow I'd go..." It reminded me of one of my favorite movies, *Moulin Rouge!*

"Let's go upstairs." Elgie took my hand. As soon as the elevator closed, we kissed. We came up for air, and I said, "I was wondering what that would be like."

Sex was awkward. Elgie obviously wanted to get it over with, and then he fell asleep. The next morning, we hurriedly got dressed, looking at the floor. He'd given Van his car, so I drove him home. That's when Bernadette walked in on her intervention.

Bernadette is still out of the picture, and I am pregnant. That sorry night in the hotel was the first and last time we ever had sex. Elgie has promised to take care of me and the baby. But he refuses to live with me. Some days I think all I need to do is give him time. He loves presidential biographies? I named my son Lincoln, after a president. He loves Microsoft? I love Microsoft. We're totally compatible.

(TIME-OUT REALITY CHECK: Elgie will never love me because I fundamentally lack his intelligence and sophistication. He will always love Bee more than our unborn child. He's trying to buy me off with this new house, and I should damn well take it.)

WEDNESDAY, FEBRUARY 2
Fax from Soo-Lin

Audrey,

I went to VAV to read my WYP and I got TORCHed. Again! Not since Frankenstein has such an angry mob descended on a poor suffering creature.

I thought my WYP was pretty frigging honest. But everyone said it was full of self-pity.

In the course of defending myself, I explained that because I was pregnant I was being revictimized by Elgie. That was a mistake. Because in VAV there's no such thing as revictimization: if we're revictimized, it's because we're *allowing* ourselves to be victimized and therefore there's a new abuser, which is our self, so technically no revictimization has taken place. But I pointed out that my baby was being victimized by Elgie, which would mean a new victim, same perp. They actually said it was *me* victimizing my baby. I could almost buy that, but then someone pointed out that because the baby was Elgie's, it was actually *me* victimizing *Elgie*.

"What kind of support group is this?" I exploded. "I'll tell you who's the victim here. It's *me*, and the abusers are you, you church-basement sadists!" I stormed out and got ice cream and cried in my car.

That was the high point.

I returned home and realized it was the one night of the week Elgie comes for dinner. He was already there, helping Lincoln and Alexandra with their homework. I'd made lasagna ahead of time, and the kids had put it in the oven and set the table.

These family dinners are something Elgie resisted at first, but now he actually seems to enjoy them. Listen to this: Bernadette didn't cook, she just ordered take-out. And when they were finished eating, she couldn't be bothered to wash the plates. No, there were drawers in the dining room table, like desk drawers, so Bernadette's big idea was to just open the drawers, pile in the soiled plates and utensils, and shut them. The next day, the maid would empty the dirty dishes from the drawers and wash them. Have you ever heard of such a way of life?

As I was dumping the lettuce into the salad bowl, Elgie whispered, "I forwarded you the captain's report and the lawyer's letter. Did you have time to read them?"

"Why would you ask me?" I slammed the salad and bottle of dressing on the table. "You don't care what I think."

The front door flew open. In hurtled Hurricane Bee, waving Mr. Harmsen's letter and captain's report. "You wish Mom were dead?!"

"Bee—" Elgie said. "Where did you get these?"

"They came in the mail to the house." She stomped her foot and pushed the back of Elgie's chair. "I could take everything else! But all anyone cares about is proving Mom is dead."

"I didn't write that," Elgie said. "That's lawyerspeak from a guy who doesn't want to get sued."

"What happens when Mom comes home and finds out you're eating dinner with people she hated, all *la la la?*"

"If that happens, then *she'll* be the one with the explaining to do," I said. I know, I know, wrong thing.

"You gnat!" Bee spun around and screamed at me. "You're the one who wishes she were dead so you can marry Dad and take his money."

"I'm sorry," Elgie said to me. "She's just grieving."

"I'm grieving over what a jerk you are," Bee told Elgie. "And how you've fallen under the spell of Yoko Ono."

"Lincoln, Alexandra," I said. "Go to the basement and watch TV."

"I'm sure she doesn't mean it that way," Elgie tried to assure me.

"Oh, just keep stuffing your face," Bee hissed at me.

I burst into tears. Of course, she doesn't know I'm pregnant. But still, I told you how terrible the morning sickness has been, Audrey. For some reason, French toast hasn't been enough. I woke up the other night with a craving to put Molly Moon's salted caramel ice cream on it. I bought a carton and started making salted caramel and French toast ice-cream sandwiches. Believe me when I say I should trademark them and start a business. Yesterday Dr. Villar said I'd better watch out, because the baby will be born made of sugar, like a Peep. Who can blame me for crying? I ran upstairs and threw myself on the bed.

After an hour, Elgie appeared. "Soo-Lin," he said. "Are you OK?"

"No!" I howled.

"I'm sorry," he said. "I'm sorry about Bee, I'm sorry about Bernadette, I'm sorry about the baby."

"You're sorry about the baby!" I launched into a whole new round of convulsive sobs.

"That's not what I meant," he said. "It's just all so sudden."

"It's only sudden to *you* because Bernadette had all those miscarriages. When you're a healthy woman, like me, and you make love to a man, you get pregnant."

There was a long silence. Finally, Elgie spoke. "I told Bee we could go to Antarctica."

"You know I can't travel there."

"Just me and Bee," he said. "She thinks it will help her get some closure. It's her idea."

"So of course you'll go."

"It's the only way Bee will let me spend time with her. I miss her."

"Then by all means, go."

"You're an amazing woman, Soo-Lin," he said.

"Gee, thanks."

"I know what you want to hear," he said. "But think about what I've been through, what I'm still going through. Do you really want me saying stuff I'm not sure I mean?"

"Yes!" I was done with dignity.

"The last trip of the season leaves in two days," he finally said. "There's room on the ship. We have a credit that would otherwise expire. It's a lot of money. And I owe it to Bee. She's a good kid, Soo-Lin. She really is."

So that's it. Elgie and Bee leave tomorrow for Antarctica. The whole thing is completely tragic, in my opinion. But what do I know? I'm just a Seattle-born secretary.

Love to you,
Soo-Lin

PART SIX

The White Continent

We arrived in Santiago at six in the morning. I'd never flown first-class before, so I didn't know each seat was its own egg and when you pushed a button, it became a bed. As soon as my seat went totally flat, the stewardess covered me with a crisp white comforter. I must have smiled, because Dad looked over from his seat and said, "Don't get too used to this." I smiled back, but then I remembered I hated him, so I plopped on my eye pillow. They bring you this kind that is filled with flaxseed and lavender, which they microwave, so it's toasty warm and you breathe in relaxation. I slept for ten hours.

There was a massive immigration line at the airport. But an officer waved over Dad and me, and unhooked a chain so we could go straight to an empty window reserved for families with small children. At first, I was annoyed because I'm fifteen. But then I thought, Fine, I'll do cutsies.

The guy wore military fatigues and took forever with our passports. He kept looking at me, in particular, then at my passport. Up, down, up, down. I figured it was my stupid name.

Finally, he spoke. "I like your hat." It was a Princeton Tigers baseball hat they sent Mom when they wanted her to give money. "Princeton," he said. "That's an American university, like Harvard."

"Only better," I said.

"I like tigers." He placed his palm over both of our passports. "I like that hat."

"Me, too." I stuck my chin in my palm. "That's why I'm wearing it."

"Bee," Dad said. "Give him the hat."

"Whaa?" I said.

"Very much I'd like the hat," the guy said, agreeing with Dad.

"Bee, just do it." Dad grabbed my hat, but it was hooked on my ponytail.

"It's my hat!" I covered my head with both hands. "Mom gave it to me."

"She threw it in the garbage," Dad said. "I'll get you another one."

"Get one yourself," I told the guy. "You can order them on the Internet."

"We can order you one," Dad added.

"We will not!" I said. "He's a grown man with a job and a gun. He can do it himself."

The man handed us our stamped passports and gave a shrug, like, It was worth a try. We collected our bags and were funneled into the main part of the airport. A tour guide immediately identified us by the blue-and-white ribbons we tied to our luggage. He told us to wait while everyone else in the group went through immigration. It would be awhile.

"There's no free lunch," Dad said. He had a point, but I acted like I didn't hear him.

Others with blue-and-white ribbons started appearing. These were our fellow travelers. They were mostly old, with wrinkled faces and wrinkle-free travel clothes. And the camera equipment! These people were circling one another like khaki peacocks, presenting their lenses and cameras. In between the preening, they'd pull out cloudy Ziploc bags of dried fruit and tuck little pieces into their mouths. Sometimes I'd catch their curious glances, probably because I was the youngest, and they'd smile all friendly. One of them stared so long I couldn't resist, I just had to say it: "Take a picture. It lasts longer."

"Bee!" Dad puffed.

One thing that was funny: beside a random windowless room, there was a sign depicting a stick figure on its knees under a pointy roof. This was the universal sign for church. Janitors, lunch-counter workers, and taxi drivers would go in and pray.

It was time to board the bus. I waited until Dad found a seat, then sat somewhere else. The highway into the city center ran along a river, which had trash scattered on its bank: soda cans, water bottles, tons of plastic, and food scraps just dumped. Kids were kicking a ball among the trash, running with mangy dogs among the trash, even squatting to wash their clothes among the trash. It was totally annoying, like, Would one of you just pick up the trash?

We entered a tunnel. The guide standing in the front of the bus got on the PA system and started rhapsodizing about when the tunnel was built, who won the contract to build it, how long it took, which president approved it, how many cars go through it every day, etc. I kept waiting for him to reveal its greatness, like maybe it was self-cleaning, or made out of recycled bottles. Nope, it was just a tunnel. Still, you couldn't help but feel happy for the guide, that if things ever got really bad, he'd always have the tunnel.

We went to our hotel, which was a swirling concrete column. In a special conference room, an Austrian lady checked us in.

"Make sure there are *two beds* in our room," I said. I was horrified when I had found out Dad and I would be sharing a room for the entire trip.

"Yes, you have two beds," the lady said. "Here is your *wowcher* for the city tour and transfer to the airport."

"My what?" I asked.

"Your *wowcher*," she said.

"My *what?*"

"Your *wowcher*."

"What's a *wowcher*?"

"Voucher," Dad said. "Don't be such a little bitch." The truth was I didn't understand what the lady was saying. But I was being a little bitch in general, so I let Dad have this one. We got our key and went to our room.

"That city tour sounds fun!" Dad said. You almost have to feel sorry for him with his taped-over lens and desperate attitude, until you remember this whole thing started because he tried to get Mom locked up in a mental hospital.

"Yeah," I said. "Do you want to go on it?"

"I do," he said, all hopeful and touched.

"Have fun." I grabbed my backpack and headed to the pool.

Choate was big and majestic, with ivy-covered buildings and jewels of modern architecture dotted on huge expanses of snowy lawn criss-crossed with boot paths. I had nothing against the place itself. It's just that the people were weird. My roommate, Sarah Wyatt, didn't like me from the start. I think it's because when she left for Christmas break, she was living in a double all by herself. And when she got back, all of a sudden she had a roommate. At Choate, you talked about who your father was. Her dad owned buildings in New York. Every single kid, I'm not kidding, had an iPhone, and most of them had iPads, and every computer I saw was a Mac. When I said my dad worked at Microsoft, they openly mocked me. I had a PC and listened to music on my Zune. What is that thing? people would ask in the most offended way, like I had just taken a huge stinky poop and stuck earbuds into it. I told Sarah my mother was a famous architect who had won a MacArthur genius award, and Sarah said, "She did not." And I said, "Sure she did. Look it up." But Sarah Wyatt didn't look it up, that's how little respect she had for me.

Sarah had thick straight hair and wore expensive clothes, which she liked to explain to me, and any time I said I hadn't heard of one of the stores, she'd emit a little grunt. Marla, her best friend, lived downstairs. Marla talked all the time, and she was funny, I suppose, but she had angry acne, smoked cigarettes, and was on academic probation. Her father was a TV director in L.A., and there was lots of jabber about her friends back home who had famous people for parents. Everyone would gather at her feet as she yakked about how cool Bruce Springsteen is. And I'd think, Of course Bruce Springsteen is cool, I don't need Marla to tell me that. I mean, Galer Street smelled like salmon, but at least the people were normal.

Then one day I went to my mailbox, and the manila envelope arrived. It had no return address, strange block writing that wasn't Mom or Dad's, and no letter saying who it was from, just all the documents about Mom. Then everything was better, because I started writing my book.

I knew something was up, though, one day after classes, when I got back to my room. Our dorm was Homestead, which was a creaky little house in the middle of campus where George Washington had once spent the night, according to a plaque. Oh, I forgot to mention that Sarah had this weird smell, like baby powder, but if the smell of baby powder made you feel sick. It couldn't have been actual perfume, and I never saw any baby powder. To this day I still don't know what it was. Anyway, I opened the front door and I heard some scurrying footsteps overhead. I went upstairs, but our room was empty. I could hear Sarah in the bathroom, though. I sat down at my desk, opened my laptop, and that's when I smelled it. That gross baby-powder scent hung in the air over my desk. This was especially weird because Sarah had made a big point about dividing the room in half, and there were strict orders not to cross the invisible line. Just then, she darted behind me, through our room, and downstairs. The door slammed. Sarah was out on the corner, waiting to cross Elm Street.

"Sarah," I called out the window.

She stopped and looked up.

"Where are you going? Is everything OK?" I was worried that maybe something had happened to one of her dad's buildings.

She acted like she couldn't hear me. She headed up Christian Street, which was weird, because I knew she had squash. She didn't turn to go to Hill House, or the library, either. The only thing past the library was Archbold, which is where the dean's offices are. I went to dance class, and when I got back, I tried to talk to Sarah, but she wouldn't look at me. She spent that night downstairs in Marla's room.

A few days later, in the middle of English, Mrs. Ryan told me that I was to immediately report to Mr. Jessup's office. Sarah had English with me, and I instinctively turned to her. She quickly looked down. I knew then: that weird-smelling, yoga-pants-wearing New Yorker with the big diamond earrings had betrayed me.

In Mr. Jessup's office, there was Dad, telling me it was for the best that I leave Choate. It was hilarious watching Mr. Jessup and Dad dance around each other, with every sentence starting with "Because I care so much about Bee" or "Because Bee is such an extraordinary girl" or "For the good of Bee." It was decided that I'd leave Choate and they'd transfer my credits so I could go to Lakeside next year. (I'd apparently gotten accepted. Who knew?)

Out in the hallway, it was just me, Dad, and the bronze bust of Judge Choate. Dad demanded to see my book, but there was no way. I did show him the envelope that came in the mail, though. "Where did this come from?" "Mom," I said. But the writing on the envelope wasn't Mom's, and he knew it. "Why would she send this to you?" he asked. "Because she wants me to know." "Know what?" "The truth. It's not like you were ever going to tell me." Dad took a breath and said, "The only true thing is now you've read things you're not old enough to possibly understand."

That's when I made the executive decision: I hate him.

We took a charter plane from Santiago really early in the morning and landed in Ushuaia, Argentina. We rode a bus through the little plaster city. The houses had Spanish-style roofs and mud yards with rusty swing sets. When we arrived at the dock, we were ushered into a kind of hut, with a wall of glass dividing it the long way. This was immigration, so of course there was a line. Soon the other side of the glass filled up with old people decked out in travel clothing and carrying backpacks with blue-and-white ribbons. It was the group that had just gotten *off* the ship, our Ghosts of Travel Future. They were giving us the thumbs-up, mouthing, You're going to love it, you have no idea how great it is, you're so lucky. And then everyone on our side started literally buzzing. Buzz Aldrin, Buzz Aldrin, Buzz Aldrin. On the other side was a scrappy little guy wearing a leather bomber jacket covered with NASA patches, and his arms were bent in at the elbows like he was itching for a fight. He had a genuine smile, and he gamely stood on his side of the glass while people in our group stood next to him and took pictures. Dad took one of me and him, and I'm going to tell Kennedy, Here's me visiting Buzz Aldrin in prison.

When I got back to Seattle after leaving Choate, it was a Friday, so I went straight to Youth Group. I walked in on the middle of some stupid game called Hungry Birdies, where everyone was divided into two teams and the mommy birds had to pick up popcorn from a bowl using a piece of red licorice as a straw, then run it over to the chicks and feed it to them. I was shocked that Kennedy was playing something so babyish. I watched until they noticed me and then it turned quiet. Kennedy didn't even come over. Luke and Mae gave me a big Christian-style hug.

"We're so sorry about what happened to your mother," said Luke.

"Nothing happened to my mother," I said.

The silence got stiffer, then everyone looked at Kennedy, because she was my friend. But I could tell she, too, was afraid of me.

"Let's finish the game," she said to the floor. "Our team is up, ten–seven."

We got our passports stamped and emerged from the tent. A lady said to follow the white line to the captain, who will welcome us onboard. Just hearing the words "the captain" made me run along the splintery dock so fast I knew it wasn't my legs but my excitement carrying me. There, at the bottom of some stairs, stood a man in a navy suit and a white hat.

"Are you Captain Altdorf?" I said. "I'm Bee Branch." He had a confused smile. I gulped some air and said, "Bernadette Fox is my mother."

Then I saw his name badge. CAPTAIN JORGES VARELA. And under it, ARGENTINA.

"Wait—" I said. "Where's Captain Altdorf?"

"Ahh," said this false captain. "Captain Altdorf. He's before. He's now in Germany."

"Bee!" It was Dad, huffing and puffing. "You can't just run off like that."

"Sorry." My voice cracked and I started crying in my mouth. "I've seen so many pictures of the *Allegra* that it's making me feel a lot of closure."

That was a lie, because how can seeing a ship give you closure? But after Choate, I quickly learned that in the name of closure Dad would let me do anything. I could sleep in Mom's Airstream, not go back to school, and even come to Antarctica. Personally, I found the concept of closure totally offensive, because it would mean I was trying to forget about Mom. Really, I was going to Antarctica to find her.

When we got to our cabin, our bags were waiting for us. Dad and I each had two: one suitcase with normal clothes, plus a duffel with our expedition stuff. Dad immediately started unpacking.

"OK," he said. "I'll take the top two drawers, and you can have the bottom two. I'll take this side of the closet. Great! The bathroom has two drawers. I'll take the top one."

"You don't have to comment on every boring thing you do." I said. "This isn't Olympic curling. You're just unpacking a suitcase."

Dad pointed to himself. "What you are looking at is me ignoring you. That's what the experts told me to do, so that's what I'm doing." He sat down on his bed, dragged his duffel between his legs, and unzipped it in one clean swoosh. The first thing I saw was his neti pot, the thing he uses to irrigate his nasal passages. There was no way I was going to be in the same tiny room while Dad did that every day. He stuck it in a drawer, then continued unpacking. "Oh, God."

"What?"

"It's a travel humidifier." He opened a box. Inside was a machine the size of a mini cereal box. Then his face twisted and he turned to the wall.

"What?" I said.

"I asked Mom to get one for me, because the Antarctic air is so dry."

My eyes widened into saucers, and I thought, Oh, God, maybe it *wasn't* such a good idea to go on this trip if Dad was going to be crying the whole time.

"Well, ladies and gentlemen." Thankfully it was a Kiwi voice crackling over a speaker in the ceiling. "Welcome onboard. As soon as you're settled, please join us in the Shackleton Lounge for welcoming cocktails and hors d'oeuvres."

"I'm going." I dashed out of there, leaving Dad alone to blubber.

Whenever I lost a baby tooth, the tooth fairy used to leave me DVDs. My first three were *A Hard Day's Night, Funny Face,* and *That's Entertainment.* Then, for my left front tooth, the tooth fairy left me *Xanadu,* which became my favorite movie of all time. The best part was the final number in the brand-new roller disco, which was all shiny chrome with polished wood, curved velvet seats and walls made of shag carpet.

That's what the Shackleton Lounge looked like, plus it had bunches of flat-screen TVs hanging from the ceiling, and windows to look out. I had it all to myself because everyone else was still unpacking. A waiter put out potato chips on the tables, and I munched down one basket all by myself. A few minutes later, a pack of supertan people wearing shorts, flip-flops, and nametags ambled up to the bar. They were crew members, naturalists.

I walked over. "Can I ask you a question?" I said to one of them, Charlie.

"Sure." He popped an olive into his mouth. "Shoot."

"Were you on the trip that left just after Christmas?"

"No, I started mid-January." He dropped a couple more olives into his mouth. "Why?"

"I was wondering what you knew about one of the passengers. Her name is Bernadette Fox."

"That I wouldn't know." He spit a bunch of pits into his palm.

Another equally tan guide whose nametag said FROG asked, "What's your question?" He was Australian.

"It's nothing," the first naturalist, Charlie, said, and kind of shook his head.

"Were you on the New Year's trip?" I asked Frog. "Because there was a woman on it named Bernadette—"

"The lady who killed herself?" Frog said.

"She didn't kill herself," I said.

"Nobody knows *what* happened," Charlie said, widening his eyes at Frog.

"Eduardo was there." Frog reached into a bowl of peanuts. "Eduardo! You were here when the lady jumped. It was the New Year's trip. We were talking about it."

Eduardo had a big round Spanish-looking face and spoke with an English accent. "I believe they're still investigating."

A woman with curly black hair piled on top of her head got in on the conversation. KAREN, said her badge. "You were there, Eduardo?— aaagh!" Karen screamed and spit out a mouthful of beige pasty stuff into a bowl. "What's in there?"

"Shit, those are peanuts?" Charlie said. "I've been spitting my olive pits in there."

"Crap," Karen said. "I think I broke a tooth."

And then it all started happening really fast: "I heard she escaped from a mental institution before she got here." "I chipped a tooth." "How could they let someone like that onboard? is my question." "That's your tooth?" "They'd let anyone on if they have the twenty grand." "You fucker!" "Gee, I'm sorry." "Thank God she killed herself. What if she killed a passenger, or you, Eduardo—"

"She didn't kill herself!" I screamed. "She's my mother, and there was no way she'd ever do that."

"She's your mother," Frog muttered. "I didn't know."

"None of you knows *anything!*" I gave Karen's chair a kick, but it didn't move because it was bolted to the floor. I flew down the back stairs, but I had forgotten our room number and even what deck we were on so I kept walking and walking through these horrible narrow hallways with low ceilings and which reeked of diesel fuel. Finally one of the doors opened, and it was Dad.

"There you are!" he said. "You ready to head upstairs for orientation?"

I shoved my way past him into the room and slammed the door. I waited for him to come back in, but he didn't.

Off and on, throughout preschool and even the beginning of kindergarten, my skin was blue because of my heart. Most times you could hardly tell, but other times it was pretty bad, which meant it was time for another operation. Once, before my Fontan procedure, Mom took me to the Seattle Center and I was playing in the huge musical fountain. I had stripped down to my underwear, and I was running up and down the steep sides, trying to outsmart the shooting water. An older boy pointed. "Look," he told his friend. "It's Violet Beauregarde!" That was the bratty girl in *Willy Wonka and the Chocolate Factory* who turned blue and ballooned into a huge ball. I was puffy because they'd pumped me up with steroids to get me ready for surgery. I ran to Mom, who was sitting on the edge. I stuffed my face in her breasts. "What is it, Bee?" "They called me it," I squeaked. "It?" Mom's eyes were across from mine. "Violet Beauregarde," I managed to say, then burst into fresh tears. The mean boys huddled nearby, looking over, hoping my mom wouldn't rat them out to their moms. Mom called to them, "That's really original, I wish *I'd* thought of that." I can pinpoint that as the single happiest moment of my life, because I realized then that Mom would always have my back. It made me feel giant. I raced back down the concrete ramp, faster than I ever had before, so fast I should have fallen, but I didn't fall, because Mom was in the world.

I sat down on one of the narrow beds in our tiny room. The ship's engine began to rumble, and the Kiwi came over the PA.

"Well, ladies and gentlemen," he said. The sound cut out for a second, like he was about to announce something bad and he had to collect his thoughts. Then, he came back on. "Say good-bye to Ushuaia, because our Antarctic adventure has just begun. Chef Issey has prepared the traditional bon voyage roast beef and Yorkshire pudding to be served in the dining room, after our orientation."

There was no way I was going to that, because it would mean sitting with Dad, so I decided to get to work. I pulled out my backpack and took out the captain's report.

My plan was to follow in Mom's footsteps because I knew something would jump out, some kind of clue that nobody but me would notice. What, exactly? I had no idea.

The first thing Mom did was charge $433 at the gift shop a few hours after she got on board. The bill wasn't itemized, though. I headed out, then realized this was also my perfect opportunity to toss Dad's neti pot. I grabbed it, then walked toward the front of the ship. I passed a trash can in the wall and chucked the neti pot, then covered it with paper towels.

I turned the corner to the gift shop, and that's when—whoa—the seasickness hit. It was all I could do to keep it together to slowly turn around and back down the stairs, one by one, very gently, because I'd vomit if I jerked my body even a little. I'm not kidding, it took me, like, fifteen minutes. When I got to the landing, I carefully stepped into the hallway. I took a deep breath, or tried to, but all my muscles had seized up.

"Little girl, you sick?" a voice sliced into my ears. Even the sound of a voice made me feel like throwing up, that's how bad it was.

I turned stiffly. It was a housekeeper, her cart bungeed to a handrail.

"Here, lady, take this for seasick." She handed me a little white packet.

I just stood there, barely able to lower my eyes.

"Oh, you sick, lady." She handed me a bottle of water. I could only look at it.

"What cabin you in?" She picked up the ID badge around my neck. "I help you, little girl."

My room was a few doors away. She opened it with her key and propped open the door. It required fierce determination, but I slowly managed the steps. By the time I entered, she had closed the shades and turned down the beds. She put two pills into my hand and offered me the opened water bottle. I just stared at them, but then counted to three and summoned the concentration to swallow the pills, then sat on a bed. The woman kneeled and pulled off my boots.

"Take off your sweater. Take off pants. It's better."

I unzipped my hoodie, and she pulled it off by the cuffs. I squirmed out of my jeans. I shivered with the air against my bare skin.

"You lie down now. You sleep."

I gathered the strength to slip under the chilly covers. I curled up and stared at the wood paneling. My stomach was filled with the wobbly chrome eggs Dad had on his desk. I was alone with the rumbling of the engine, the tinkling of the hangers, and the opening and closing of drawers. It was just me and time. It was like when we had a backstage tour at the ballet, and I saw the hundreds of weighted ropes, the bank of video monitors, and the light board with one thousand lighting cues, which were all used for one small scenery change. I was lying there on the bed, seeing the backstage of time, how slowly it went, everything it's made up of, which is nothing. The walls were dark blue carpet on the bottom, then a metal strip, then shiny wood, and then beige plastic to the ceiling. And I thought, What horrible colors, they might kill me, I have to close my eyes. But even the effort of that seemed impossible. So, like the ballet stage manager, I pulled one rope in my brain, then the other, then five more, which closed my eyelids. My mouth hung open, but no words came out, just a crackly moan. If there were words to it, what they would say was, Anything but this.

Then it was fourteen hours later, and there was a note from Dad saying he was in the lounge, listening to a seabird lecture. I jumped out of bed, and my legs and stomach got sloshy again. I pulled the chain on the window shade. It was like we were on the inside of a washing machine. I got pitched back onto the bed. We were crossing the Drake Passage. I wanted to absorb it, but there was work to do.

The ship's hallway was festooned with barf bags, pleated like fans and tucked in the railing joints, behind hand-sanitizer dispensers, in door pockets. The ship was so tipped that one of my feet was walking on the wall and the other was on the floor. The reception area was really wide, which meant there were no railings to grab onto if you wanted to cross it, so they had rigged a Spider-Man web of ropes. I was the only person. Like sick animals, everyone else had retreated into their warrens of misery. I pulled on the door of the gift shop, but it was locked. A lady working behind the desk looked up. She was massaging something into the inside of her wrist.

"Are you open?" I mouthed.

She walked over and unlocked the bottom metal strip. "Are you here for the origami paper?" she said.

"Huh?" I said.

"The Japanese passengers are doing an origami demonstration at eleven. I have the paper if you'd like to participate."

I had noticed them, a group of Japanese tourists. They didn't speak a word of English, but they had their own interpreter, who got their attention by waving a stick with ribbons and a stuffed penguin dangling from it.

The boat jerked, and I fell into a basket of Harmsen & Heath sweatshirts. I tried to get up, but there was no way. "Is it always this bad?"

"This is pretty rough." She went behind the desk. "We're getting thirty-foot swells."

"Were you here for Christmas?" I asked.

"Yes, I was." She opened a little unlabeled jar and dipped her finger into it. She started rubbing the inside of her other wrist.

"What are you doing?" I asked. "What's that in the jar?"

"It's a cream for motion sickness. The crew couldn't function without it."

"ABHR?" I said.

"Actually, yes."

"What about tardive dyskinesia?"

"Wow," she said. "You know your stuff. The doctor tells us the dosage is so low there's no chance of it."

"A woman was on the Christmas trip," I said. "She bought a bunch of stuff from the gift shop on December twenty-sixth, in the evening. If I give you her name and room number, could you look up the receipt so I can see exactly what she bought?"

"Oh—" The woman gave me an odd look that I couldn't figure out.

"It's my mother," I said. "She bought four hundred dollars' worth of merchandise."

"Are you here with your dad?" she asked.

"Yeah."

"Why don't you go back to your cabin, and I'll dig up the receipt. It might take about ten minutes."

I gave her my room number and pulled myself along the ropes and back to my room. I had been all excited about having a TV, but then got less excited when the only two stations were showing *Happy Feet* and the seabird lecture. The door swung open. I jumped up. It was Dad... followed by the gift shop lady.

"Polly said you asked to see a copy of Mom's receipt?"

"We were instructed to get your father," she told me, shamefaced. "I did bring some origami paper."

I glowered at her, Kubrick style, and threw myself on the bed.

Dad gave Polly a look like, I'll take it from here. The door closed, and Dad sat across from me. "The naturalists felt really bad about last night," he said to my back. "They came to find me. The captain spoke to the whole crew." There was a long pause. "Talk to me, Bee. I want to know what you're thinking and feeling."

"I want to find Mom," I said into the pillow.

"I know you do, baby. So do I."

I turned my head. "Then why were you at a stupid seabird lecture? You're acting like she's dead. You should be trying to find her."

"Now?" he said. "On the ship?" The side table was crammed with Dad's eyedrops, reading glasses with one lens taped over, dark glasses with one lens taped over, those awful Croakie things that keep your glasses on, his heart-rate monitor, and a bunch of little tubes of vitamins you put under your tongue. I had to sit up.

"In Antarctica." I pulled the captain's report out of my backpack.

Dad took a deep breath. "What are you doing with that?"

"It's going to help me find Mom."

"That's not why we're here," he said. "We're here because you wanted closure."

"I just told you that to trick you." It's pretty obvious to me now that you can't say that to somebody and expect them to be fine with it. But I was too excited. "You're the one who made me think of it, Dad, when you said the letter from the Harmsen guy was just a lawyer talking. Because if you look at the captain's report with an open mind, it proves that Mom loved it down here. She was having such a good time, drinking and going out all day, that she decided to stay. And she wrote me a letter telling me that, so I wouldn't get worried."

"Can I give you another interpretation?" Dad said. "I see a woman who kept to herself and drank a bottle of wine at dinner, and then moved on to the hard stuff. That's not having a fun time. That's drinking yourself to death. And I'm sure Mom did write you a letter. But it was mainly full of paranoid rants about Audrey Griffin."

"It says, '*highly probable.*'"

"But we'll never know," Dad said. "Because she never mailed it."

"She gave it to a passenger to mail when they got back home, but it got lost."

"How come this passenger failed to report that during the interrogation?"

"Because Mom told them to keep quiet."

"There's a saying," Dad said. "When you hear hoofbeats, think horses, not zebras. Do you know what that means?"

"Yeah." I fell onto the pillow and gave a big puff.

"It means that when you're trying to figure something out, don't start off being too exotic in your reasoning."

"I know what it means." I moved my head because I had landed in a patch of drool.

"It's been six weeks, and nobody's heard from her," he said.

"She's somewhere waiting for me," I said. "It's a fact." A pulsing aura of energy attacked the right side of my face. It was emanating from Dad's junk on the table. There was so much of it, and it was so neatly arranged, it was worse than a girl, it just made me sick. I jerked myself up to get away from it.

"I don't know where you're getting this from, sweetheart, I really don't."

"Mom didn't kill herself, Dad."

"That doesn't mean she didn't have too much to drink one night and fell overboard."

"She wouldn't have let that happen," I said.

"I'm talking about an accident, Bee. By definition, nobody lets an accident happen."

A plume of smoke rose from behind the desk chair. It was the humidifier Mom had bought for Dad, now plugged in with an upside-down bottle of water sticking out of it. Just like Dad wanted.

"I know why it's convenient for *you* if Mom killed herself." Until I started saying the words, I had no idea they were tamped down in my stomach. "Because you were cheating on her, and it gets you off the hook because you can go, Blah blah blah, she was crazy all along."

"Bee, that's not true."

"*You* look for horses," I said. "While you spent your whole life at work, me and Mom were having the best, funnest time ever. Mom and I lived for each other. She wouldn't do anything *close* to getting drunk and walking next to a ship's balcony because it would mean she might never see me again. That you think she would shows how little you know her. *You* look for horses, Dad."

"Where is she hiding, then?" Dad asked, starting to blow. "On an iceberg? Floating on a raft? What's she been eating? How's she keeping warm?"

"That's why I wanted the receipt from the gift shop," I said really slowly, because maybe then he'd understand. "To prove that she bought warm clothes. They sell them there. I saw them. Parkas and boots and hats. They also sell granola bars—"

"Granola bars!" That was it for Dad. "Granola bars? That's what this is based on?" The skin on Dad's neck was translucent and a big vein trembled. "Parkas and granola bars? Have you been outside yet?"

"No—" I stammered.

He stood up. "Come with me."

"Why?"

"I want you to feel the temperature."

"No!" I said as emphatically as I could. "I know what cold feels like."

"Not this kind of cold." He grabbed the captain's report.

"That's mine," I yelled. "That's private property!"

"If you're so interested in facts, come with me." He grabbed me by the hood and dragged me out the door. I was grunting, "Let me go!" and he was grunting, "You're coming with me!" We elbowed each other up the steep and narrow staircase one level, then two levels, and we were clawing and cussing so fiercely it took us both a second to register that we had become the focus of attention. We were in the lounge. The Japanese people sat at origami-paper-covered tables, just staring at us.

"You here for origami?" said the Japanese translator with mixed emotion, because on the one hand it looked like nobody had shown up for their workshop, but on the other hand, who would want to teach origami to the two of us?

"No, thanks," Dad said, letting go of me.

I sprinted across the lounge and accidentally brushed against one of the chairs, which I had forgotten was bolted down, so instead of it tumbling out of the way, it nailed me in my ribs and I ricocheted into one of the tables, plus the boat started pitching.

Dad was on me. "Where do you think—"

"I'm not going outside with you!" We were a wrestling, scratching, slapping bundle of origami paper and brand-new Patagonia, tumbling toward the exit. I stuck my foot against the doorjamb so Dad couldn't push me any farther.

"What was Mom's big crime, anyway?" I screamed. "That she had an assistant in India doing errands for her? What's Samantha 2? It's just something so people can sit around and have a robot do all their shit for them. You spent ten years of your life and billions of dollars inventing something so people don't have to live their own lives. Mom found a way of doing it for seventy-five cents an hour, and you tried to have her committed to a mental hospital!"

"That's what you think?" he said.

"You were a real rock star, Dad, walking down the aisle of the Microsoft Connector."

"I didn't write that!"

"Your girlfriend did!" I said. "We all know the truth. Mom ran away because you fell in love with your admin."

"We're going outside." All Dad's working-out obviously had some effect, because he picked me up with one arm as if I were made of balsa wood, and with the other yanked open the door.

Right before it shut, I caught a glimpse of the poor Japanese people. Nobody had moved. Some hands were frozen in midair, in the middle of doing a fold. It looked like a wax museum diorama of an origami presentation.

I hadn't been outside yet the whole trip. Instantly my ears stung and my nose became a burning-cold stone at the end of my face. The wind blew so hard it froze the inside of my eyes. The tops of my cheeks felt like they might crack.

"We're not even in Antarctica yet!" Dad howled through the wind. "Do you feel how cold it is? Do you?"

I opened my mouth, and the saliva on the inside froze, like an ice cave. When I swallowed, which took all my effort, it tasted like death.

"How did Bernadette keep alive for five weeks in this? Look around! Feel the air! We're not even in Antarctica yet!"

I pulled my hands inside my cuffs and made fists with my numb fingers.

Dad shook the report at me. "The only truth here is that Mom was safely onboard January fifth at six p.m. and then she started drinking. The waters were too rough to anchor. And that was it. You're looking for facts? Feel this. This wind, this cold, these are the facts."

Dad was right. He's smarter than me, and he was right. I would never find Mom.

"Give me that," I said, and swiped at the report.

"I won't let you do this, Bee! It's not good for you, constantly searching for something that isn't there!" Dad shook the report at me, and I tried to grab it, but my joints were too stiff and my hands caught on my sleeves and then it was too late and every last piece of paper got sucked high into the heavens.

"No! It's all I have!" With each word, my icy breath knifed the inside of my lungs.

"It's not all you have," Dad said. "You have me, Bee."

"I hate you!"

I ran to our room and swallowed two more white pills, not because I was seasick, but because I knew they would knock me out, and I just slept. I woke up once and I wasn't tired anymore. I looked out the window. The sea was choppy and black and so was the sky. A lone seabird hung in the air. Something bobbed in the water. It was a huge chunk of ice, our first harbinger of the horrible land ahead. I took two more pills and fell back asleep.

Then music filled the room, ever so faintly, and over the span of a couple of minutes it gradually got louder. *I'm starting with the man in the mirror...* It was Michael Jackson, a wake-up call coming from the speakers, and there was a blazing crack between the window shade and wall.

"Well, good morning," said the voice over the PA. After his ominous pause, he continued, "For those of you who haven't had the pleasure of looking out the window, welcome to Antarctica." With those words, I shot up. "Many of you are already on deck relishing the clear, still morning. We got our first glimpse of land at six twenty-three, when we came upon Snow Hill Island. We're now making our way into Deception Bay." I yanked the cord on the shades.

There it was, a black rocky island with snow on top, black water under it, and a big gray sky above, Antarctica. I got a huge knot in my stomach because if Antarctica could talk, it would be saying only one thing: you don't belong here.

"The Zodiacs will be begin loading at nine thirty" the Kiwi continued. "Our naturalists and camera experts will be leading walks. And kayaks are always available for those who prefer to go kayaking. The temperature is minus thirteen degrees Celsius, eight degrees Fahrenheit. Good morning and, again, welcome to Antarctica."

Dad burst in. "You're up! How about a swim?"

"A swim?"

"It's a volcanic island," he said. "There's a hot spring, which warms a patch of water near the shore. What do you say? Do you want to take a dip in the Antarctic Ocean?"

"No." I was looking back at myself. It was like the old Bee was standing there saying to me, "What are you talking about? That's something you'd love to do. Kennedy would freak." But the new Bee was the one who controlled my voice and she answered, "You can go, Dad."

"I have a feeling you're going to change your mind," Dad said, all singsong. But we both knew he was faking.

Days passed. I could never tell what time it was because the sun never set, so I went by Dad. He'd set his alarm for six a.m. like at home, then go to the gym, then I'd hear Michael Jackson singing, and Dad would come back to shower. He figured out a system where he'd bring clean underwear into the bathroom and emerge in that, then get dressed the rest of the way in the room. Once he said, "It's the damndest thing. I can't find my neti pot anywhere." Then he'd head off to breakfast. He'd return with a plate of food for me and a Xerox of the six-page *New York Times Digest*, which had big hand-written letters across the top, FRONT DESK COPY ONLY—DO NOT BRING TO ROOM. It was printed on the back of the previous day's left-over menus. I liked seeing what fish they served the night before, because I'd never even heard of any of them, things like toothfish, hake, wreckfish, and red porgy. I saved them in case Kennedy doesn't believe me. Then Dad, the layer king, would elaborately get into his expedition clothes and salve himself with sunblock, lip stuff, and eyedrops, and head out.

Soon, black rubber boats with motors called Zodiacs would ferry the passengers ashore. After the last Zodiac headed out, I'd stir to life. It was just me and the vacuum cleaners. I'd go to the way-top floor, which is the library, where I kept tabs on an epic Settlers of

Catan game some passengers were playing. There were a bunch of jigsaw puzzles too, which got me excited because I love puzzles, but inside the boxes I'd find a note saying, "This puzzle is missing seven pieces" or some number, and I thought, Why would I do that puzzle? There was another lady there, too, who never got off the ship, I don't know why. She didn't talk to me, but was always working in a *Sudoku Easy Does It* book. On top of each page, she wrote the place where she did the puzzle, as a souvenir. They all said, "Antarctica." Mostly, though, I just sat in the library. It had glass on all sides, so I could see everything. All you need to know about Antarctica is it's three horizontal stripes. On the bottom, there's the stripe for the water, which is anywhere from black to dark gray. And on top of that, there's a stripe for the land, which is usually black or white. Then there's a stripe for the sky, which is some kind of gray or blue. Antarctica doesn't have a flag, but if it did it should be three horizontal stripes of different shades of gray. If you wanted to get really artsy, you could make it all gray, but say it was three stripes of gray, for the water, the land, and the sky, but that would probably take too much explaining.

Eventually, the flotilla of Zodiacs would head back to the ship. I couldn't tell which one Dad was on, because all the passengers were issued the same red hooded parkas and matching snow pants, probably because red makes them stick out best against the gray. The guides get to wear black. I made sure I was back in my room when the first Zodiac returned, so Dad would think I'd been moping. The housekeeper always left a towel twisted into the shape of a bunny on my pillow, and each day it got more elaborately accessorized. First, the towel bunny was wearing my dark glasses, then my hair band, then one of Dad's Breathe Right strips.

Dad would burst in, still carrying the cold on his clothes, full of information and stories. He'd show me pictures on his camera, and say the photos didn't do it justice. Then he'd go to the dining room for lunch, and bring me back something, then afterward he headed back out for the afternoon excursion. My favorite time was the evening recap, which I'd watch on TV in my room. Every day, the scuba divers went down and videotaped the seafloor. In this hostile, black water, it turns out there're millions of the craziest sea creatures I'd ever seen, things like glassy sea cucumbers, worms covered with graceful, foot-long spikes, fluorescent-colored sea stars, and copepods, which are spotted and striped, like out of *Yellow Submarine*. The reason I'm not calling any of them by their scientific names (not like I even would) is because they don't have names yet. Most of this stuff humans are seeing for the very first time.

I tried to love Dad and not hate him for his fake cheer and the way he gets dressed. I tried to imagine what Mom saw in him back when she was an architect. I tried to put myself in the shoes of someone who finds every little thing he does a total delight. It was sad, though, because the thought of him and all his accessories always made me sick. I wished I'd never made the connection about Dad being a gigantic girl, because once you realize something like that, it's hard to go back.

Sometimes it was so great I couldn't believe how lucky I was that I got to be me. We'd pass icebergs floating in the middle of the ocean. They were gigantic, with strange formations carved into them. They were so haunting and majestic you could feel your heart break, but really they're just chunks of ice and they mean nothing. There were ebony beaches dusted with snow, and sometimes there was a lone emperor penguin, giant, with orange cheeks, standing on an iceberg, and you had no idea how he got there, or how he was going to get off, or if he even wanted to get off. On another iceberg, a smiling leopard seal, sunning herself, looked like she wouldn't hurt a fly, but she's one of the most vicious predators on earth, and she'd think nothing of leaping up and grabbing a human in her razor teeth and pulling him into the freezing water and shaking him until his skin slid off. Sometimes I looked over the edge of the ship at the sea ice, like white jigsaw puzzle pieces that will never fit together, and passing through sounded like clinking cocktails. There were whales *everywhere*. Once, I saw a pod of fifty killer whales, mommies and babies, frolicking in a pack, blowing happily, and penguins hopping across the inky ocean like fleas, then propelling themselves to safety on an iceberg. If I had to choose, that would be my favorite part, the way the penguins pop out of the water and onto land. Hardly anyone in the world gets to see any of this, which put pressure on me to remember it especially well, and to try to find words for the magnificence. Then I'd think of something random, like how Mom used to write notes to put in my lunch. She'd sometimes include one for Kennedy, whose Mom never wrote her notes, and some were stories that would take weeks to play out. And then I'd get up from my seat in the library and look through the binoculars. But Mom was never there. Pretty soon, I stopped thinking about home, and my friends, because when you're on a boat in Antarctica and there's no night, who are you? I guess what I'm saying is, I was a ghost on a ghost ship in a ghost land.

One night, it was the evening recap and Dad brought me a plate of cheese puffs, then went back up to the lounge, and I watched it on TV. A scientist gave a presentation about counting penguin chicks as part of an ongoing study. Then it was time to announce the plan for tomorrow, which was going to Port Lockroy, to a British military outpost left over from World War II, which was now an Antarctic heritage museum where *people live* and run a *gift shop* and a *post office*. Where we are all encouraged to *buy Antarctic penguin stamps* and *mail letters home!*

My heart started doing gymnastics and I paced around wildly, repeating, Oh-my-God-Oh-my-God-Oh-my-God, waiting for Dad to burst through the door.

"Well, ladies and gentlemen," came the voice through the speakers. "That was another wonderful recap. Chef Issey has just informed me that dinner is ready. *Bon appétit*."

I flew up to the lounge because maybe Dad was sitting there stunned, but the gathering had broken up. A pack of people was shuffling down the stairs. I ran to the back and took the long way to the dining room. There was Dad, sitting at a table with some guy.

"Bee!" he said. "Would you like to join us for dinner?"

"Wait, weren't you at the recap?" I asked. "Didn't you hear—"

"Yes! And this is Nick, who's studying the penguin colonies. He was telling me he always needs helpers to count penguin chicks."

"Hi…" I was so scared of Dad in that moment that I took a step back and bumped into a waiter. "Sorry…hi…bye." I turned around and walked as fast as I could out of there.

I ran to the chart room, which is a gigantic table with a map of the Antarctic Peninsula laid across it. Each day, I'd watch crew members mark our ship's path with a dotted line, and afterward passengers would drop by and painstakingly copy it onto their maps. I pulled open a huge flat drawer and found the map of Mom's journey. I placed it on top and followed with my finger the dot-dot-dot. Sure enough, her ship had stopped at Port Lockroy.

The next morning, Dad was at the gym, and I went out on deck. Plunked onto the rocky shore was a black wooden building, L-shaped, like two Monopoly hotels, with white window trim and cheery red shutters. Penguins dotted the landscape. The backdrop was a field of snow, looming over which was one big, pointy mountain rising above seven smaller scrunched-together ones, Snow White and the Seven Dwarfs.

Dad had signed up to go kayaking with the first group, then to Port Lockroy with the second group. I waited until he was gone, then ripped the tags off my red parka and snow pants and suited up. I fell in with the stream of passengers clomping, astronaut-like, down the stairs to the mudroom. It was full of lockers and had two huge openings on either side where floating docks were tethered. I headed down a ramp to a sputtering Zodiac.

"Port Lockroy?" confirmed a crewman. "Did you scan out?"

He pointed me to a stand with a computer. I scanned my ID badge. My photo popped up on the screen, along with the words ENJOY YOUR TIME ASHORE, BALAKRISHNA! I felt a surge of annoyance at Manjula, who was supposed to have made sure I got called Bee, but then I remembered she was an Internet bandit.

A dozen red suits crammed into the Zodiac with Charlie at the motor. It was mostly women who had all seen enough penguins for one lifetime and felt the need to start *shopping*. They were bursting with questions about what there was to buy.

"I don't know," Charlie said with a tinge of resentment. "T-shirts."

It was the first time I'd been out on the glassy water. Bitter wind attacked me from all sides. My whole being instantly shrank, and any time I moved, my skin hit a new cold patch in my snowsuit, so I became trapped in stillness. I turned my head the teeniest bit possible, just enough to see the shore.

The closer we got to Port Lockroy, the building strangely got smaller and smaller, which was the first time I got scared. Charlie gunned the engine and drove the Zodiac onto the rocks. I belly-rolled off the big inflated side and dropped my life jacket. I scrambled across the big rocks, avoiding the singing gentoo penguins guarding their rock nests until I reached a wooden ramp leading to the entrance. A British flag flapped in the cold gray wind. I was the first one there, and I flung open the door. Two girls, college-aged, kind of goofy and enthusiastic, greeted us.

"Welcome to Port Lockroy!" they said in British accents.

It was one of those miserable situations where it was just as cold inside as it was outside. I was in a room with turquoise-painted walls. This was the gift shop, with colorful banners hanging from the ceiling; tables full of books, stuffed animals, and postcards; and glass cubbies of sweatshirts, baseball hats, and anything you could embroider a penguin on. There were no signs of Mom, but why would there be? This was just the gift shop.

Across this room was an opening leading to the rest of Port Lockroy, but the English girls blocked it. I kept it together and acted interested in the bulletin boards while the other passengers trickled in and oohed and aahed at the swag. Even the sudoku lady had torn herself away from the library for this outing.

"Welcome to Port Lockroy," alternated the girls. "Welcome to Port Lockroy."

It seemed like we had been standing there for an hour already. "Where is everyone who lives here?" I finally asked. "Where do you live?"

"You're looking at it," said one. "Let's wait for everyone to get in before we begin the lecture." Then they started up again, "Welcome to Port Lockroy."

"But where do you *sleep?*" I asked.

"Welcome to Port Lockroy. Is that everyone? Oh, we have some more coming."

"Is there, like, a dining hall where everyone else is?"

But the girls looked right over my head. "Welcome to Port Lockroy. OK, it looks like we're all here." One of them began her spiel. "During World War Two, Port Lockroy was a secret outpost for the

British military—" She stopped because the group of Japanese tourists had just entered, and with them, the usual low-grade confusion. I couldn't take it anymore. I squeezed past the English girls.

There were two small rooms. I went left, into an old-fashioned command center with desks and rusty machines full of dials and knobs. But no people. At the far end was a door marked DO NOT OPEN. I passed a wall of decaying books and pulled at the door. Blinding light blasted me back: it led outside to a snowfield. I closed the door and backtracked to the other room.

"In 1996 the U.K. Antarctic Heritage Trust paid to turn Port Lockroy into a living museum," one of the girls was saying.

This room was a kitchen, with rusty stoves and shelves full of weird food rations and British tins. There also was a door marked DO NOT OPEN. I raced to that and yanked it open. Again . . . eye-watering snow shock.

I quickly shut the door. Once my eyes readjusted, I returned to the main section and tried to figure things out. OK, there were only three doors. The front door where we came in, and these other two leading outside . . .

"During the war, Port Lockroy was home to Operation Tabarin—" the girls went on.

"I don't understand," I butted in. "How many people live here?"

"Just the two of us."

"Where do you *live* live?" I said. "Where do you sleep?"

"Here."

"What do you mean, *here?*"

"We roll our sleeping bags out in the gift shop."

"Where do you go to the bathroom?"

"We go outside—"

"Where do you do your laundry?"

"Well, we—"

"Where do you shower?"

"This is how they live," a tourist lady snapped at me. She had freckles, blue eyes, and a bunch of gray in her blond hair. "Stop being rude. These girls come down for three months and pee in a tin can for the adventure."

"It really *is* just the two of you?" I said weakly.

"And the cruise ship passengers like you who come visit."

"So nobody has, like, gotten off one of the ships to live with you...?" The sound of the words coming out of my mouth, and the whole idea that Mom would be here waiting for me, struck me as so babyish that all of a sudden I burst into the most babyish tears. Swirled into my humiliation was anger at myself for letting my hope gallop off so stupidly. Snot sheeted down my face and into my mouth and down my chin and onto my new red parka, which I had been excited about, because we got to keep it.

"Dear God," the freckled lady said. "What's wrong with her?"

I couldn't stop crying. I was trapped in the fun house of pemmican rations, photographs of Doris Day, crates of whiskey, a rusty can of Quaker Oats where the Quaker Oats guy is a young man, Morse code machines, long johns with butt flaps hanging from a clothesline, and baby bibs that read ANTARCTICA BEACH CLUB. Charlie, chin lowered, spoke into the radio clipped to his parka. Lots of concerned ladies asked, What's wrong?, something I now know how to say in Japanese, which is *Anata wa daijōbudesu?*

I burrowed through the gathering nylon mass and made it out the front door. I stumbled down the ramp and, when I got to the bottom, clambered over some big rocks as far as I could go and stopped at a little inlet. I looked back, and there were no people. I sat down and caught my breath. There was one elephant seal, swaddled in her own blubber, lolling on her side. I couldn't imagine how she was ever going to move. Her eyes were big black buttons, oozing black tears. Her nose, too, was oozing black. My breath was dense clouds. The cold seized me. I didn't know if I'd ever move again. Antarctica was truly a horrible place.

"Bee, darling?" It was Dad. "Thank you," he said quietly to a Japanese lady who must have led him to me. He sat down and handed me a handkerchief.

"I thought she was here, Dad."

"I can see why you might have thought that," he said.

I cried a little, but then stopped. Still, the crying continued. It was Dad.

"I miss her, too, Bee." His chest jerked violently. He was bad at crying. "I know you think you have a monopoly on missing her. But Mom was my best friend."

"She was *my* best friend," I said.

"I knew her longer." He wasn't even being funny.

Now that Dad was crying, I was, like, *both* of us can't be sitting on rocks in Antarctica crying. "It's going to be OK, Dad."

"You're absolutely right," he said, blowing his nose. "It all started with that letter I sent Dr. Kurtz. I was only trying to get Mom help. You have to believe me."

"I do."

"You're great, Bee. You've always been great. You're our biggest accomplishment."

"Not really."

"It's true." He put his arm around me and pulled me close. My shoulder fit perfectly under his shoulder. I could already feel the warmth from his armpit. I nestled in closer. "Here, try these." He reached into his parka and pulled out two of those pocket-warming heat biscuits. I yowled, they felt so good.

"I know this trip has been hard on you," Dad said. "It's not what you wanted it to be." He let out a big gooey sigh. "I'm sorry you had to read all those documents, Bee. They weren't meant for you. They weren't something a fifteen-year-old should have had to read."

"I'm glad I read them." I didn't know Mom had those other babies. It made me feel like there were all these children Mom would rather have had, and loved as much as she loved me, but I was the one who lived and I was broken, because of my heart.

"Paul Jellinek was right," Dad said. "He's a great guy, a true friend. I'd like us to go down to L.A. and spend some time with him one day. He knew Bernadette best. He realized that she needed to create."

"Or she'd become a menace to society," I said.

"That's where I really failed your mom," he said. "She was an artist who had stopped creating. I should have done everything I could to get her back."

"Why didn't you?"

"I didn't know how. Trying to get an artist to create...it's gigantic. I write code. I didn't understand it. I still don't. You know, I'd forgotten, until I read that *Artforum* article, that we used Mom's MacArthur money to buy Straight Gate. It was like Bernadette's hopes and dreams were literally crumbling around us."

"I don't know why everyone's so down on our house," I said.

"Have you ever heard that the brain is a discounting mechanism?"

"No."

"Let's say you get a present and open it and it's a fabulous diamond necklace. Initially, you're delirious with happiness, jumping up and down, you're so excited. The next day, the necklace still makes you happy, but less so. After a year, you see the necklace, and you think, Oh, that old thing. It's the same for negative emotions. Let's say you get a crack in your windshield and you're really upset.

Oh no, my windshield, it's ruined, I can hardly see out of it, this is a tragedy! But you don't have enough money to fix it, so you drive with it. In a month, someone asks you what happened to your windshield, and you say, What do you mean? Because your brain has *discounted* it."

"The first time I walked into Kennedy's house," I said, "it had that horrible Kennedy-house smell because her mother is always frying fish. I asked Kennedy, What's that gross smell? And she was, like, What smell?"

"Exactly," Dad said. "You know why your brain does that?"

"Nuh-uh."

"It's for survival. You need to be prepared for novel experiences because often they signal danger. If you live in a jungle full of fragrant flowers, you have to stop being so overwhelmed by the lovely smell because otherwise you couldn't smell a predator. That's why your brain is considered a discounting mechanism. It's literally a matter of survival."

"That's cool."

"It's the same with Straight Gate," he said. "We've discounted the holes in the ceilings, the wet patches in the floors, the cordoned-off rooms. I hate to break it to you, but that's not how people live."

"It's how we lived," I said.

"It *is* how we lived." A long time passed, which was nice. It was just us and the seal and Dad whipping out his ChapStick.

"We were like the Beatles, Dad."

"I know you think that, sweetie."

"Seriously. Mom is John, you're Paul, I'm George, and Ice Cream is Ringo."

"Ice Cream," Dad said with a laugh. ·

"Ice Cream," I said. "Resentful of the past, fearful of the future."

"What's that?" He asked, rubbing his lips together.

"Something Mom read in a book about Ringo Starr. They say that nowadays he's resentful of the past and fearful of the future. You've never seen Mom laugh so hard. Every time we saw Ice Cream sitting there with her mouth open, we'd say, Poor Ice Cream, resentful of the past, fearful of the future."

Dad smiled a big smile.

"Soo-Lin," I started to say, but even uttering her name made it difficult to keep talking. "She's nice. But she's like poop in the stew."

"Poop in the stew?" he said.

"Let's say you make some stew," I explained, "and it's really yummy and you want to eat it, right?"

"OK," Dad said.

"And then someone stirs a little bit of poop in it. Even if it's just a teeny-tiny amount, and even if you mix it in really well, would you want to eat it?"

"No," Dad said.

"So that's what Soo-Lin is. Poop in the stew."

"Well, I think that's rather unfair," he said. And we both had to laugh.

It's the first time during this whole trip that I let myself really look at Dad. He had on a fleece headband over his ears and zinc oxide on his nose. The rest of his face was shiny from sunblock and moisturizer. He wore dark mountain-climbing glasses with the flaps on the side. The one lens that was taped over didn't show because the other lens was just as dark. There was really nothing to hate him for.

"So you know," Dad said, "you're not the only one with wild ideas about what happened to Mom. I thought maybe she'd gotten off the ship, and when she saw me with Soo-Lin she somehow dodged us. So you know what I did?"

"What?"

"I hired a bounty hunter from Seattle to go to Ushuaia and look for her."

"You did?" I said. "A real-life bounty hunter?"

"They specialize in finding people far from home," he said. "Someone at work recommended this guy. He spent two weeks in Ushuaia looking for Bernadette, checking the boats coming in and out, the hotels. He couldn't find anything. And then we got the captain's report."

"Yeah," I said.

"Bee," he said carefully. "I have something to tell you. Have you noticed I haven't been frantic about not being able to get email?"

"Not really." I felt bad because only then did it occur to me that I hadn't thought about Dad at all. It was true, he's usually all into his email.

"There's a huge reorg they're probably announcing as we sit on these rocks." He checked his watch. "Is today the tenth?"

"I don't know," I said. "Maybe."

"As of the tenth, Samantha 2 is canceled."

"Canceled?" I didn't even understand how that word could apply.

"It's over. They're folding us into games."

"You mean for, like, the Xbox?"

"Pretty much," he said. "Walter Reed pulled out because of budget cuts. At Microsoft, you're nothing if you don't ship. If Samantha 2 is under games, at least they can ship millions of units."

"What about all those paraplegics you've been working with?"

"I'm in talks with the UW," he said. "I'm hoping to continue our work over there. It's complicated because Microsoft owns the patents."

"I thought you owned the patents," I said.

"I own the commemorative cubes. Microsoft owns the patents."

"So, like, you're going to leave Microsoft?"

"I *left* Microsoft. I turned in my badge last week."

I'd never known Dad without his badge. A terrible sadness poured in through my head and filled me to the brim, like I was a honey bear. I thought I might burst of sadness. "That's so weird," is all I could say.

"Is now a good time to tell you something even weirder?" he said.

"I guess," I said.

"Soo-Lin is pregnant."

"What?"

"You're too young to understand these things, but it was one night. I'd had too much to drink. It was over the moment it began. I know that probably seems really…what's a word you would use… gross?"

"I never say gross," I said.

"You just did," he said. "That's what you called the smell at Kennedy's house."

"She's really pregnant?" I said.

"Yep." Poor guy, he looked like he was going to barf.

"So basically," I said, "your life is ruined." I'm sorry, but something in me made me smile.

"I can't say that thought hasn't occurred to me," he said. "But I try not to think of it that way. I'm trying to frame it as my life being *different. Our* lives being different. Me and you."

"So me and Lincoln and Alexandra are going to have the *same* brother or sister?"

"Yep."

"That's so random."

"Random!" he said. "I've always hated when you used that word. But it is pretty random."

"Dad," I said. "I called her Yoko Ono that night because she was the one who broke up the Beatles. Not because she's Asian. I felt bad."

"I know that," he said.

It was good that sappy-eyed seal was there, because we could both just watch her. But then Dad started putting in eyedrops.

"Dad," I said. "I really don't mean to hurt your feelings, but..."

"But what?"

"You have way too many accessories. I can't keep track of all of them."

"It's a good thing you don't have to, isn't it?"

We were quiet for a while, and then I said, "I think my favorite part of Antarctica is just looking out."

"You know why?" Dad asked. "When your eyes are softly focused on the horizon for sustained periods, your brain releases endorphins. It's the same as a runner's high. These days, we all spend our lives staring at screens twelve inches in front of us. It's a nice change."

"I have an idea," I said. "You should invent an app so that when you're staring at your phone, it tricks your brain into thinking you're staring at the horizon, so you can get a runner's high from texting."

"What did you just say?" Dad spun his head to look at me, his mind in high gear.

"Don't you dare steal my idea!" I gave him a shove.

"Consider yourself warned."

I groaned and left it at that. Then Charlie came over and said it was time to head back.

At breakfast, Nick the penguin-counter asked me again if I'd be his assistant, which did sound pretty fun. We got to leave before everyone else, in our own Zodiac. Nick let me stand next to the outboard and steer. The best way to describe Nick would be to say that he didn't have any personality, which sounds mean, but it's kind of true. The closest he came to personality was when he told me to scan the horizon wide, like a searchlight, back and forth, back and forth. He said after he was down here the first time driving a Zodiac that he went back home and immediately got into a car accident because he was looking left to right, left to right, and ended up rear-ending the car directly in front of him. But that's not personality. That's just a car accident.

He dropped me off at an Adélie penguin colony and gave me a clipboard with a satellite map marked with some boundaries. This was a follow-up to a study a month back, where another scientist had counted the eggs. It was my job to see how many had successfully hatched into chicks. Nick sized up the colony.

"This looks like a complete breeding failure." He shrugged.

I was shocked by how casually he said this. "What do you mean, a complete failure?"

"Adélies are hardwired to lay their eggs in the exact same place each year," he said. "We had a late winter, so their nesting grounds were still covered with snow when they made their nests. So it looks like there's no chicks."

"How can you even tell?" Because there was no way *I* could see that.

"You tell me," he said. "Observe their behavior and tell me what you see."

He left me with a clicker and headed off to another colony, saying he'd return in two hours. Adélies may be the cutest penguins of all. Their heads are pure black except for perfect white circles, like a reinforcement, around their tiny black eyes. I started at the top left corner and clicked each time I saw a gray fuzz-ball sticking out from between an Adélie's feet. Click, click, click. I worked my way across the top of the mapped area, then dropped down and worked my way back. You have to make sure not to count the same nest twice, but it's almost impossible because they're not in a neat grid. When I was done I did it over again and got the same number.

Here's what surprised me about penguins: their chests aren't pure white but have patches of peach and green, which is partially digested krill and algae vomit, which splatters on them when they feed their chicks. Another thing is penguins stink! And they're loud. They coo sometimes, which is very soothing, but mostly they screech. The penguins I watched spent most of their time waddling over and stealing rocks from one another, then having vicious fights where they'd peck each other until they bled.

I climbed high on the rocks and looked out. There was ice, in every possible form, stretching forever. Glaciers, fast ice, icebergs, chunks of ice in the still water. The air was so cold and clean that even in the way distance, the ice was as vivid and sharp as if it were right in front of me. The immensity of it all, the peacefulness, the stillness and enormous silence, well, I could have sat there forever.

"What behavior did you observe?" Nick asked when he got back.

"The penguins that spent most of their time fighting were the ones with no chicks," I said.

"There you go," he said.

"It's like they're supposed to be taking care of their chicks. But because they don't have any, they have nothing to do with all their energy. So they just pick fights."

"I like that." He checked my work. "This looks good. I need your John Hancock." I signed at the bottom, to verify that I was the scientist.

When Nick and I arrived back at the ship, Dad was in the mudroom peeling off his layers. I scanned my ID card. It bonged, and the screen read: BALAKRISHNA, PLEASE SEE OFFICIAL. Hmm. I scanned it again. Another bong.

"That's because you didn't scan out," Nick said. "As far as it knows, you're still on the ship."

"Well, ladies and gentleman," said the overhead voice, followed by the big pause. "We hope you enjoyed your morning excursion and that you're hungry for some Argentinean barbecue, which is now being served in the dining room." I was halfway up the stairs when I realized Dad wasn't with me. He was standing at the scanner, with a puzzled look on his face.

"Dad!" I knew everyone would be charging the buffet line and I didn't want to get stuck at the end.

"OK, OK." Dad snapped to, and we beat the lunch crowd.

There was no afternoon excursion because we had to cover a huge distance and didn't have time to stop. Dad and I went to the library to look for a game to play.

Nick found us there. He handed me some papers. "Here's copies of your data, and past data, in case you're interested." So maybe that was his personality: nice.

"That's so cool," I said. "Do you want to play a game with us?"

"No," he said. "I have packing to do."

"Too bad," I told Dad. "Because I'd really like to play Risk, but we need three players."

"We'll play with you," a British girl's voice said. It was one of the two girls from Port Lockroy! She and the other girl had handwritten labels stuck to their shirts that said their names, and ASK ME ABOUT PORT LOCKROY. They were freshly showered, with gigantic smiles stretched across their shiny faces.

"What are you doing here?" I said.

"There's not a ship scheduled to visit Port Lockroy for two days," said Vivian.

"So the captain said we could spend the night on the *Allegra*," said Iris. They both wanted to talk so badly that they were like race-car drivers jockeying to cut each other off. It must have been from the lack of anyone else's company.

"How are you going to get back?" I asked.

"There was a change of plans involving Nick—" Vivian started.

"That's why there's no afternoon excursion." Iris finished.

"The *Allegra* has to take him to Palmer," Vivian said.

"So we'll end up crossing paths with the *next* ship to visit Port Lockroy, and Vivian and I will transfer to that—"

"The cruise companies like to keep it hush-hush, though—"

"They like to give the passengers the impression they're all alone in the vast Antarctic Ocean so these crew transfers are only ever done in the dead of night—"

"And you'll be pleased to know we've showered!" said Vivian, and they both burst into giggles, ending the talking derby.

"I'm really sorry if I was rude," I said.

I turned to Dad, but he was heading down to the bridge. I didn't call after him because Dad knows my strategy for Risk, which is to occupy Australia at the outset. Even though Australia is small, there's only one way in and out, so when it comes time to conquer the world, if you don't have Australia, you go in and your armies get trapped there until your next turn. Then the next player can gobble up the single armies you've left in your path. I had the three of us quickly pick our colors and distribute our armies before Dad came back. On my first four turns, I yoinked Australia.

Playing Risk with these girls was so fun because in my whole life I've never seen two people happier. That's what a hot shower and peeing in a proper toilet will do. Vivian and Iris told me a funny story about how one day they were sitting at Port Lockroy between cruise ships and a huge fancy yacht pulls up and it's Paul Allen's yacht, the *Octopus,* which he and Tom Hanks got off and then requested a tour. I asked the girls if they got to shower on the *Octopus,* but they said they were too afraid to ask.

The freckled lady who called me rude at Port Lockroy sat down with a book and saw me and Vivian and Iris laughing like we'd known one another forever.

"Helloooo," I said to her like a big smiling cat.

Before she could respond, the voice over the PA said, "Well, good evening." He was announcing a bunch of whales on the starboard side, which I'd already seen. A few more "Well, good evening"s came and went, announcing a photography lecture, and then dinner, and then *March of the Penguins,* but we didn't want to stop the game, so we took turns running plates of food from the dining room up to the library. With each announcement, Dad would pop up and give me the thumbs-up through the window, and I'd give him the thumbs-up in return. The sun was still blazing, so the only way to judge the passage of time was by the people trickling out of the library. Pretty soon, even Dad stopped appearing, and it was just the three of us playing Risk. Hours must have passed. It was just us and the cleaning crew. Then there seemed to be another "Well, good evening," but I couldn't be sure because of the vacuum. Then sleepy-eyed passengers with parkas over their pajamas appeared on the deck with their cameras.

"What's going on?" I said. It was two in the morning.

"Oh, we must be at Palmer," Vivian said with a hand flutter. It was her turn, and she actually thought she was about to seize Europe.

More people appeared on the deck, but I couldn't see over their heads. Finally, I stood on my chair. "Oh my God!"

There was a little city, if you'd call a bunch of shipping containers and a couple corrugated metal buildings a city. "What *is* that place?"

"That's Palmer," Iris said.

Palmer was short for Palmer *Station*. When Nick said he was packing, and when Iris said we were dropping Nick off at Palmer, I figured it was to count penguins on some island.

"That's where Nick is stationed for the next month," Vivian said.

I knew all about the three places in Antarctica where Americans can live. They are McMurdo Station, which looks like an awful dump with about a thousand people. There's, of course, the South Pole, which is way far inland and impossible to get to, with twenty people. And Palmer Station, with about forty-five people. All three are populated by scientists and support staff. But I had checked the chart room and asked the captain: the *Allegra* never stopped at Palmer Station.

Still, here we were.

"Are we getting off?" I asked the girls.

"Oh, no," Iris said.

"Scientists only," Vivian added. "They run a very tight operation."

I dashed out onto the deck. A few Zodiacs streamed back and forth the two hundred yards between our ship and Palmer Station. Nick was heading away from us on a Zodiac stacked with coolers and food crates.

"Who are those people coming aboard?" I wondered aloud.

"It's a tradition." Charlie the naturalist was standing next to me. "We let the scientists at Palmer come aboard for a drink. "

I must have had quite a look on my face, because Charlie quickly added, "Nope. People apply five years out to get to Palmer. Beds and supplies are extremely limited. Moms from Seattle don't end up there on a whim. I'm sorry to be like that. But, you know."

"Bee!" whispered a wild voice. It was Dad. I figured he was asleep because it was two in the morning. Before I could speak, he was shepherding me down the stairs. "I started thinking when your ID didn't scan," he said, his voice all trembly. "What if Bernadette got off the ship but *she didn't scan out?* Her ID card would show she was still onboard, so everyone would naturally conclude that she had disappeared from the ship itself. But if she got off the ship some-where and didn't scan out, she might still be there." He pulled open the door to the lounge, which was filling up with some pretty ratty-looking people, scientists from Palmer Station.

"Neko Harbor was the last place Mom got off," I said, trying to put it together. "And then she got back on."

"According to the scan of her ID card," Dad explained again. "But what if she slipped off the ship *later? Without* scanning out? I was at the bar just now, and some lady went up and ordered a pink penguin."

"A pink penguin?" My heart started quaking. That was the drink from the captain's report.

"It turns out the lady is a scientist at Palmer Station," Dad said. "And the pink penguin is their official drink."

I searched the faces of the new arrivals. They were young and scruffy, like they could all have worked at REI, and full of laughter. Mom's face wasn't among them.

"Look at that place," Dad said. "I didn't know it existed."

I kneeled on a window seat and peered out. A series of red walk-ways connected the blue metal buildings. There were a dozen elec-tricity poles sticking up, and a water tank with a killer whale painted on it. A gigantic orange ship was docked nearby, nothing like a cruise ship, but more like one of those industrial types that are always in Elliott Bay.

"According to the woman, Palmer Station is the plum assign-ment in all of Antarctica," Dad said. "They have a chef who was trained at the Cordon Bleu, for God's sake."

Below, Zodiacs were coming and going between our ship and the rocky shore. There was an Elvis mannequin in one of the Zodiacs, which the naturalists were videotaping to much hooting and hollering. Who knew. It must have been some inside joke.

"So the pink penguins on the captain's report...," I said, still trying to compute.

"They weren't for Bernadette," Dad said. "They must have been for a scientist, like Nick, who was being dropped off at Palmer Station, and who Bernadette befriended."

I was still stuck on something. "But Mom's ship didn't come anywhere near Palmer Station—" Then I realized. "I know how we can check!"

I ran out of the lounge and down the stairs to the chart room, Dad on my heels. On the shiny wooden block was the map of the Antarctic Peninsula, with the little red dotted line showing our journey. I opened the drawer and leafed through the maps until I found the one dated December 26.

"This is the trip Mom took." I laid it out and placed brass weights on the corners.

I traced the red dotted path of Mom's trip. From Tierra del Fuego, the *Allegra* stopped at Deception Island like we did. Then it looped up and around the Antarctic Peninsula and went deep into the Weddell Sea, and back around, to Neko Harbor and Adelaide Island, but after that it turned around and went back through the Bransfield Strait to King George Island and down to Ushuaia. "Her boat didn't come near Palmer Station." There was no way around it.

"What are these?" Dad pointed to gray dashes intersecting the red dotted line. It happened in three different spots.

"A current or something," I guessed.

"No...these aren't currents," Dad said. "Wait, they each have a symbol…” It was true. In these gray lines were a snowflake, a bell, and a triangle. “There’s got to be a key…”

There was, on the bottom left. Next to these symbols were the words SITKA STAR SOUTH, LAURENCE M. GOULD, and ANTARCTIC AVALON.

“I know the name Laurence M. Gould from somewhere,” I said.

“They sound like the names of ships,” Dad said.

“Where do I know it from—”

“Bee?” Dad said with a huge smile on his face. “Look up.”

I raised my head. Out the window, that huge ship, all orange hull, in blue block letters: RV LAURENCE M. GOULD.

“It crossed paths with Mom’s ship,” Dad said. “And look where it is now.”

I was afraid to say what I was thinking.

“She’s here, Bee!” Dad said. “Mom is here.”

“Hurry!” I said. “Let’s go ask one of those people in the lounge—”

Dad grabbed my arm. “No!” he said. “If Mom finds out, she might pull another disappearing act.”

“Dad, we’re in Antarctica. Where could she go?”

He gave me a look, like, Really?

“OK, OK, OK,” I said. “But tourists aren’t allowed off. How are we—”

“We’re going to steal a Zodiac,” he said. “We have exactly forty minutes.”

It was then that I realized he was holding our red parkas. He grabbed my hand and we twirled down one, two, three levels until we landed in the mudroom.

“How are you both doing tonight?” said a girl behind the counter. “Or is it morning already? It is!” She returned to her paperwork.

“We’re about to go back upstairs,” Dad said loudly.

I pushed him behind a bank of lockers. "Give me the jackets." I stuffed them in an empty locker and led him to the crew section, where I had been with Nick. On the wall was a line of black parkas. "Put one of those on," I whispered.

I strolled to the floating dock, where a Zodiac was tied up. The only crew member was a Filipino. His nametag said JACKO.

"I heard one of the sailors talking," I said. "The ship is picking up satellite signals from Palmer Station, so they're all on the bridge calling home for free."

Jacko disappeared up into the ship, two steps at a time. I whispered to Dad, "Now!"

I zipped myself into a gigantic crew parka and rolled up the sleeves. We grabbed two life vests and clambered into a Zodiac. I unlooped the rope from its cleat, then pushed a button on the motor. The engine coughed to life. We broke from the *Allegra* and headed across the sparkling black water.

I looked back. A few passengers were still on deck taking pictures, but most had retired inside. The sudoku lady was now in the library. Iris and Vivian sat at our Risk game, looking out the window. Most of the cabin shades were lowered. As far as the ship was concerned, Dad and I were cozily on board.

"Get down," Dad said. A Zodiac was now headed in our direction. "You're way smaller than anyone who should be out here." He stepped in front of the motor and grabbed hold of the wand. "Lower," he said. "All the way."

I lay belly-down on the plank bottom. "Take off your stupid glasses!" Dad was wearing his clear ones, and the taped-over lens was really noticeable.

"Shoot!" He fumbled to stuff his glasses into his pocket and zipped his jacket to above his nose.

"Who is it coming toward us?" I asked. "Can you tell?"

"Frog, Gilly, and Karen," Dad said all lockjawed. "I'm going to gently sway this way. Nothing too extreme, just getting a little distance." He waved at them.

I felt their Zodiac pass.

"OK, we're good," he said. "Now I'm looking for a place to dock..."

I peeked over the rubber edge. Palmer Station was all around us. "You just ram really fast up onto the rocks—" I said.

"No you don't—"

"Yes you do," I said, standing up. "Just full speed—"

Dad did, and I suddenly got pitched onto the inflated rubber edge. I grabbed onto the rope railing, and my body slammed against the outside. My feet and one knee got trapped between the hard rubber and the rocky shore. "Gaaah!" I screamed.

"Bee! Are you OK?"

I didn't think I was, actually. "I'm fine." I pulled free and stood up, wobbly. "Oh, no!" That other Zodiac had circled back around, and those onboard were waving their hands and shouting. At us. I ducked behind the boat.

"Go," Dad said.

"Where?"

"Just find her," he said. "I'll hold them off. Our ship leaves at three a.m. That's thirty minutes from now. Find someone. Ask for Mom. She'll either be here or she won't. If you want to return, you must radio our ship by two fifty. Got that? Two fifty."

"What do you mean, *if* I want to return?"

"I don't know what I mean," said Dad.

I took a big gulp and stared up at the corrugated sprawl.

"Make sure you"—Dad reached into his inside pocket and

pulled out a small black velvet bag with a gold silk rope—"give her this."

Without saying good-bye, I limped up the road, most of its gravel eaten away by erosion. On my left and right were shipping containers, different shades of blue, with stenciled signs. REEFER, VOLATILE, FLAM LOCKER, CORR LOCKER, THE BAT CAVE. On wooden decks, tents were set up. They had real doors, and funny flags, like a pirate, or Bart Simpson. Even though the sun was in the sky, I was walking through the silence of night. As I continued, the buildings became denser and connected by a Habitrail of red bridges and bundled pipes. To my left was an aquarium with squid and starfish pressed up against the glass, and strange sea creatures like from the evening recap. There was a big aluminum drum, and next to it a sign with a martini glass which read ABSOLUTELY NO GLASS CONTAINERS NEAR THE HOT TUB.

I arrived at the steps leading to the main building. Halfway up, I dared to look back.

The other Zodiac had pulled next to Dad's. One of the guides had climbed into it. There seemed to be some arguing going on. But Dad stayed positioned at the motor, which meant the guides had their backs to me. So far, I hadn't been spotted.

I opened the door and found myself alone in a big toasty room with carpet tiles and a row of aluminum picnic tables. It smelled like an ice rink. One wall was devoted to shelves filled with DVDs. Toward the back was a counter and an open stainless-steel kitchen. On a dry-erase board were the words WELCOME HOME, NICK!

Laughter erupted from somewhere. I ran down the hall and started opening doors. One room was nothing but walkie-talkies plugged into charging stations. A huge sign read NO COFFEE MUGS ALLOWED EXCEPT FOR JOYCE's. The next room was desks and computers and oxygen tanks. One was just weird scientific machines. Then there was a bathroom. I heard voices from around the corner. I ran toward them. Then I tripped.

On the floor was a spaghetti pot sitting atop a flattened-out trash bag. Inside the spaghetti pot was a T-shirt with something familiar on it...a rainbow handprint. I reached down and picked it out of the cold gray water. GALER STREET SCHOOL.

"Dad," I cried. "Daddy!" I ran back down the hall to the wall of windows.

Both Zodiacs were zooming away from Palmer Station, toward our ship. Dad was in one of them.

Then, at my back, "You little rotter."

It was Mom, standing there. She was wearing Carhartt pants and a fleece.

"Mom!" Tears sprang up in my eyes. I ran to her. She dropped to her knees, and I just hugged her so hard and buried my body in her. "I found you!"

She had to carry all my weight in her arms because I had just given up. I stared into her beautiful face, her blue eyes examining me like they always used to.

"What are you doing here?" she said. "How did you get here?" Her wrinkles radiated like sun rays from her smiling eyes. There was a big stripe of gray running down her part.

"Look at your hair," I said.

"You almost killed me," she said. "You know that." Then, with tears and confusion, "Why didn't you write?"

"I didn't know where you were!" I said.

"My letter," she said.

"Your letter?"

"I sent it weeks ago."

"I never got your stupid letter," I said. "Here. This is from Dad." I handed her the velvet bag. She knew what it was, and pressed it to her cheek and closed her eyes.

"Open it!" I said.

She untied the cord and pulled out a locket. In it was the photograph of Saint Bernadette. It was the necklace Dad had given her after she won her architecture prize. It was the first time I'd ever seen it.

"What's this?" She pulled out a card and held it away from her face. "I can't read what it says." I took it from her and read it aloud.

1. BEEBER BIFOCAL
2. TWENTY MILE HOUSE
3. BEE
4. YOUR ESCAPE
FOURTEEN MIRACLES TO GO.

"Elgie," Mom said, and breathed out a sweet relaxed smile.

"I knew I'd find you," I said, and hugged her my tightest. "Nobody believed me. But I knew."

"My letter," Mom said. "If you never got it—" She pulled my arms apart and looked into my face. "I don't understand, Bee. If you never got my letter, how are you here?"

"I did it like you," I said. "I slipped away."

PART SEVEN

The Runaway Bunny

MONDAY, FEBRUARY 21

My first day back at Galer Street, on the way to music, I passed my cubby. It was stuffed with notices from the past few months. Crammed in with all the flyers about the recycling challenge and Bike-to-School Day was an envelope, a stamped envelope, addressed to me in care of Galer Street. The return address was a contracting company in Denver and the writing: Mom's.

Kennedy saw my face and she started hanging on me, all "What is it? What is it? What is it?" I didn't want to open the envelope in front of her. But I couldn't open it alone. So I ran back to homeroom. Mr. Levy was with some teachers who were about to walk to Starbucks on their break. As soon as Mr. Levy saw me, he told the others to go on ahead. We shut the door, and I tried to tell him everything all at once, about the intervention and Audrey Griffin who saved Mom and Choate and my roommate who didn't like me and Antarctica and Soo-Lin's baby and finding Mom and now this, the missing letter. But it squirted out in a big jumble. So I did the next best thing. I went to my locker and gave him the book I wrote at Choate. Then I went to music.

At lunch recess, Mr. Levy found me. He said he liked my book OK, but in his mind, it needed more work. He had an idea. For my spring research project, how about I complete it? He suggested I ask Audrey and Paul Jellinek and Ms. Goodyear and anyone else to provide documents. And Mom, of course, but she wasn't going to be back from Antarctica for two weeks. Mr. Levy said he'd give me credit for the classes I'd missed so I could graduate with the rest of my class. And that's what this is.

Friday, January 7
The missing letter from Mom

Bee,

I write to you from a shipping container in Antarctica, where I'm waiting to have four wisdom teeth voluntarily extracted by a veterinarian. Let me back up.

Last thing you knew, I vanished while being chased around the living room with a butterfly net. Earlier that day, you'll recall, I was at World Celebration Day. To avoid actual "celebration" with occupants of said "world," I made busy at the coffee table, pouring, stirring, and slamming, in all, five cups of mud. The moment the performance was over, I hightailed it home (*not* to Dr. Neergaard's to get my teeth pulled, which was truly an insane idea, even I had come to realize that) and intervened in my own intervention, rendered much more painful by the fact that I had to pee something fierce. I went into the bathroom, and, hark, cameth a tap, tap, tap.

You know how we thought Audrey Griffin was the devil? Turns out Audrey Griffin is an angel. She plucked me off the balcony and whisked me to the safety of her kitchen, where she presented me with the dossier of my truly terrible behavior, which you have by now received via snail mail.

I know it seems like I just took off, but here's the thing: I didn't.

For all I knew, Elgie was still planning to take you to Antarctica. He was very adamant about that in the intervention. The next morning, I headed to the airport so I could talk to you both in person. (Be warned. I will never, ever email, text, or possibly phone anyone again. From now on, I'm the Mafia, only face-to-face contact or nuttin'.) I asked if you had checked in, but divulging such information was strictly forbidden — those 9/11 hijackers just keep on giving — so my only option was to check in and board the plane.

As you know, you weren't on the flight. I panicked, but then a pretty stewardess handed me a glass of orange juice over chipped ice. It tasted way better than it had any right to, so I took the trip to Miami, my mind on fire: a furious, injury-seeking missile. Elgie was the rat, I the misunderstood genius. The screeds I rehearsed were epic and airtight.

Stepping off the plane in Miami was like reentering the womb. Was it the welcoming voices of LeBron James and Gloria Estefan? No, it was the scent of Cinnabon. I ordered a large and headed down to a tram, which would deliver me to the ticket counter. There I'd buy passage home and accept my fate.

The Cinnabon wasn't going to eat itself, so I sat. Trams came and went as I pulled apart the puff of deliciousness, enjoying every bite, until I realized I'd forgotten napkins. Both my hands were plastered with icing. My face, too. In one of my vest pockets was a handkerchief. I held up my hands, surgeonlike, and asked a lady, "Please, could you unzip this?" The pocket she unzipped contained only a book on Antarctica. I lifted it out and wiped my hands and, yes, my face, with its clean pages.

A tram arrived. The doors jerked open and I took a seat. I glanced down at the book, now on my lap. It was *The Worst Journey in the World*, by Apsley Cherry-Garrard, one of the few survivors of Captain Scott's ill-fated attempt at the South Pole. The back read, "People don't go to Antarctica. They're called to Antarctica."

We pulled into the main terminal. I didn't get off. I went to Antarctica.

Of course, the first place you'd check for me would be the cruise company. They'd tell you I was on board and, therefore, you'd know I was safe. Added bonus: once I set sail, there was no way to communicate. It was what Dad and I desperately needed: a three-week time-out.

As soon as I boarded the *Allegra* — I'm still slightly shocked I wasn't yanked off at the last minute by some authority — I was greeted by a naturalist. I asked how he was.

"Fine," he answered. "As long as I'm headed back to the ice."

"Didn't you just come from the ice?" I asked.

"Three days ago," he answered wistfully.

I couldn't imagine what he was talking about. It was ice. How much can you love ice?

Well, I found out. After two days of heinous seasickness, I awoke in Antarctica. Out my window, three times as high as the ship, and twice as wide, was an iceberg. It was love at first sight. An announcement was made that we could go kayaking. I bundled up and was first in line. I had to commune, up close, with the Ice.

Ice. It's trippy, symphonies frozen, the unconscious come to life, and smacking of color: blue. (Snow is white; ice is blue. You'll know why, Bee, because you're knowledgeable about these things, but I had no idea.) It rarely snows because Antarctica is a desert. An iceberg means it's tens of millions of years old and has calved from a glacier. (This is why you must love life: one day you're offering up your social security number to the Russia Mafia; two weeks later you're using the word *calve* as a verb.) I saw hundreds of them, cathedrals of ice, rubbed like salt licks; shipwrecks, polished from wear like marble steps at the

Vatican; Lincoln Centers capsized and pockmarked; airplane hangars carved by Louise Nevelson; thirty-story buildings, impossibly arched like out of a world's fair; white, yes, but blue, too, every blue on the color wheel, deep like a navy blazer, incandescent like a neon sign, royal like a Frenchman's shirt, powder like Peter Rabbit's cloth coat, these icy monsters roaming the forbidding black.

There was something unspeakably noble about their age, their scale, their lack of consciousness, their right to exist. Every single iceberg filled me with feelings of sadness and wonder. Not *thoughts* of sadness and wonder, mind you, because thoughts require a thinker, and my head was a balloon, incapable of thoughts. I didn't think about Dad, I didn't think about you, and, the big one, I didn't think about myself. The effect was like heroin (I think), and I wanted to stretch it out as long as possible.

Even the simplest human interaction would send me crashing back to earthly thoughts. So I was the first one out in the morning, and the last one back. I only went kayaking, never stepped foot on the White Continent proper. I kept my head down, stayed in my room, and slept, but, mainly, I *was*. No racing heart, no flying thoughts.

At some point, I was paddling in the water, and a voice popped out of nowhere.

"Hello!" it said. "Are you here to help?" It might have been saying, Are you a good witch or a bad witch? It was that perky, the blues that Technicolor, the iceberg that spirally.

The greeting belonged to Becky, a marine biologist, who was out in a Zodiac, taking water samples. She was bunking on the *Allegra* en route to Palmer Station, a scientific research center, where, she explained, she was going to *live for the next several months*.

I thought, No way, you can actually *live* down here?

I climbed into her Zodiac and called out phytoplankton levels. She was a big talker. Her husband was a contractor who was back home in Ohio using a computer program called Quickie Architect (!) because he wanted to be put up for a project at the South Pole to dismantle a geodesic dome and replace it with a research station.

Whaaaaa…?

By now you've learned that I'm a certified genius. Don't say I never told you about my MacArthur grant, because I did. I just never stressed what a big deal it was. Really, who wants to admit to her daughter that she was once considered the most promising architect in the country, but now devotes her celebrated genius to maligning the driver in front of her for having Idaho plates?

I know how bad it must have been for you, Bee, all those years, strapped in the car, hostage to my careening moods. I tried. I'd resolve never to say anything bad about any of the drivers. Then I'd be waiting, waiting, for some minivan to pull out of a parking space. "I'm not going to say it," I'd remind myself. From the backseat, in your squeak: "I know what you were going to say. You were going to call her a fucking idiot."

Why I'm even mentioning this, I guess it's to say that I let you down in a hundred different ways. Did I say a hundred? A thousand is more like it.

What did Becky mean, dismantle the dome? What were they going to do with it? What was the new station being built from? What materials are even *found* at the South Pole? Isn't it just ice? I had a million questions. I asked Becky to have dinner with me. She was a drab type, with a ten-gallon ass, unctuous toward the waiters in some "see how well I treat the help" show of superiority. (I think it's a midwestern thing.) After dinner, Becky strongly suggested she'd like to hit the bar, where, between her questions to the bartender about the ages of his "*kinders*" back in Kashmir, I pumped her for more facts.

At the risk of being like Dad and overexplaining stuff you already know: Antarctica is the highest, driest, coldest, and windiest place on the planet. The South Pole averages sixty below zero, has hurricane-strength winds, and sits at an altitude of ten thousand feet. In other words, those original explorers didn't have to just *get* there, but had to climb serious mountains to do so. (Side note: Down here, you're either an Amundsen guy, a Shackleton guy, or a Scott guy. Amundsen was the first to reach the Pole, but he did it by feeding dogs to dogs, which makes Amundsen the Michael Vick of polar explorers: you can like him, but keep it to yourself, or you'll end up getting into arguments with a bunch of fanatics. Shackleton is the Charles Barkley of the bunch: he's a legend, all-star personality, but there's the asterisk that he never reached the Pole, i.e., won a championship. How this turned into a sports analogy, I don't know. Finally, there's Captain Scott, canonized for his failure, and to this day never fully embraced because he was terrible with people. He has my vote, you understand.) The South Pole is on a shifting ice sheet. Every year they have to relocate the official Pole marker because it can move one hundred feet! Would this mean my building would have to be a wind-powered crab-walking igloo? Maybe. I'm not worried about it. That's what ingenuity and insomnia are for.

Any structure built would have to be coordinated out of the United States. Every material, down to the nail, would have to be flown in. Getting the supplies there would be so costly that absolutely *nothing* could be wasted. Twenty years ago, I built a house with zero waste, using only materials from no farther than twenty miles. This would require using materials from no closer than nine thousand.

My heart started racing, not the bad kind of heart racing, like, I'm going to die. But the good kind of heart racing, like, Hello, can I help you with something? If not, please step aside because I'm about to kick the shit out of life.

The whole time I was thinking, What a fabulous idea of mine to take this family trip to Antarctica!

You know me, or maybe you don't, but from then on, every hour of my day became devoted to plotting my takeover of the new South Pole station. When I say every hour of my day, that would be twenty-four, because the sun never set.

If anyone asked me—which in his defense, that *Artforum* reporter valiantly attempted, but every time I saw his name in my in-box I frantically hit delete delete delete—I'd say I never considered myself a great architect. I'm more of a creative problem solver with good taste and a soft spot for logistical nightmares. I had to go. If for no other reason than to be able to put my hand on the South Pole marker and declare that the world literally revolved around me.

I didn't sleep for two days straight because it was all too *interesting*. The South Pole, McMurdo, and Palmer stations are all run by the same military contracting company out of Denver. The coordinator of all Antarctic operations happened to be at Palmer for the next month. My closest connection to any of this was Becky. I resolved then: I don't care how profusely Becky apologizes every time she asks a waiter for more dinner rolls, I'm going to stick with her.

One of those days, I was out on the water with Becky in our floating science lab, calling out numbers. Ever so casually, I mentioned that it might be fun for me to accompany her to Palmer Station. The tizzy that erupted! No civilians allowed! Only essential personnel! There's a five-year wait! It's the most competitive place in the world for scientists! She spent years writing a grant!

That evening, Becky bid me adieu. This was a shock, because we were nowhere near Palmer Station. But a ship was swinging by at three in the morning to get her. Turns out there's a whole shadow transportation network down here in Antarctica, much like the Microsoft Connector.

They're marine research vessels on a constant loop, transporting personnel and supplies to the various stations, often hooking up with cruise
ships, which also double as supply ships for these remote stations.

I had a measly six hours. There was no way I could persuade Becky
to bring me to Palmer Station. I was in bed despairing when, at the
stroke of three, up sidled a giant paprika-colored bucket, the *Laurence M.
Gould*.

I went down to the mudroom to get a front-row seat to my future
slipping away. Stacked on the floating dock were Becky's lockers and
fifty crates of fresh produce. I could make out oranges, squash, cabbage.
A sleepy Filipino loaded them onto a bobbing, unmanned Zodiac. Suddenly a crate of pineapples was thrust at me.

I realized: For days, I'd gone out with Becky on plankton-measuring
excursions. This guy thought I was a *scientist*. I took the crate and
jumped into the Zodiac and stayed there as he passed me more. After
we filled the Zodiac to capacity, the sailor hopped in and fired up the
engine.

Just like that, I was headed to the massive, utilitarian *Laurence M.
Gould*. We were met by an equally sleepy and resentful Russian sailor.
The Filipino stayed in the Zodiac and I climbed onto the *Gould*'s dock
and began unloading. The Russian's only concern was logging in the
crates. When the Zodiac was empty—and to test that this was actually
happening—I faintly waved to the Filipino. He motored back to the
Allegra by himself.

There I was, standing firmly on the *Laurence M. Gould*. The best
part: I hadn't scanned out of the *Allegra*. They'd have no record of me
leaving, and probably wouldn't know I was missing until they docked
in Ushuaia. By that time, I could get word to you.

I looked back at the *Allegra* and gave her a nod of thanks. Then, in
the maw, the shape of Becky started loading the remaining supplies

onto a Zodiac. My irrational dislike of her took hold again. And I thought, What do I need Becky for? Becky's not the boss of me.

I found my way into the belly of the ship and through a labyrinth of foul-smelling passages, a combination of diesel fuel, fried food, and cigarettes. I came upon a tiny lounge with pilly pastel sofas and a boxy TV. I sat there as the engine grumbled to life. I sat there as the boat pulled away. I sat there some more. And then I fell asleep.

I awoke to the screech of Becky. Around breakfast time, some sailors had seen me sleeping and asked around. Luckily, we were just six hours from Palmer Station. Becky decided the thing to do was deliver me to Ellen Idelson, the manager of Antarctic operations. For the rest of the journey, I was a prisoner in the lounge, an object of curiosity. Russian scientists would poke their heads in, watching me watch *Lorenzo's Oil*.

As soon as we reached Palmer, Becky dragged me by the scruff to dear leader, Ellen Idelson. To the chagrin of Becky, Ellen was *thrilled* when I declared I'd work for free and that no job was too demeaning.

"But how is she going to get home?" Becky wailed.

"We'll stick her on the *Gould*," Ellen said.

"But the beds are all accounted for," Becky said.

"Yeah," Ellen said. "That's what we always say."

"But she doesn't have her passport! It's on the *Allegra*."

"That's her problem, isn't it?"

We both watched Becky huff off.

"She's really good at writing grants," Ellen said with disgust. It was a case of "the enemy of my enemy is my friend." June was busting out all over.

I was turned over to Mike, a former state senator from Boston who had wanted so badly to spend time in Antarctica that he had trained to become a diesel mechanic. He put me to work sanding and painting the decks around the generator housing. He handed me a stack of industrial-grade sandpaper. Before I went through the grits, the wood needed to be scraped. I had a putty knife, which was dull, and I figured I could borrow a whetstone from the kitchen.

"There she is," said Ellen, who had been having a tête-à-tête with the chef when I entered. Ellen pointed to a picnic table. I obediently sat.

She walked over with an open laptop.

On the screen was my Wikipedia page. In a window behind it, *Artforum* dot-com. (On a side note, the Internet here is faster than I've ever seen, because it's military or something. The motto should be *Palmer Station: Come for the Ice. Stay for the Internet.*)

"It wasn't cool, what you did," Ellen said. "Stowing away on the *Gould*. I just didn't want to get Becky more excited. That's not good for morale."

"I understand."

"What do you want?" she asked. "Why are you here?"

"I need to get a letter to my daughter. Not an email, but a real letter. One that will arrive in Seattle by the seventeenth." It's imperative that you get this letter, Bee, before the ship returns to Ushuaia, so nobody will worry.

"The pouch goes out tomorrow," Ellen said. "The letter will make it."

"Also, I'd like a shot at designing the South Pole station. But I need to get there in person and catch a vibe."

"Ah," Ellen said. "I was wondering."

Ellen launched into the utter impossibility of this: planes to the Pole depart only from McMurdo Station, which is 2,100 nautical miles from Palmer. Getting to McMurdo was relatively easy. Flights to the Pole were a different beast. They were strictly reserved for EP, essential personnel, and I gave new meaning to the term non-EP.

Halfway through this speech, it dawned on me that Ellen Idelson was a contractor. She was performing contractor Kabuki. It's a ritual in which (a) the contractor explains in great detail the impossibility of the job you've asked him to do, (b) you demonstrate extreme remorse for even suggesting such a thing by withdrawing your request, and (c) he tells you he's found a way to do it, so (d) you owe him one for doing what he was hired to do in the first place.

We played our roles expertly, Ellen ticking off the difficulties, me abjectly apologizing for such an irrational and thoughtless request. I nodded gravely and retired to my sanding chores. Five hours later, Ellen whistled me into her office.

"Lucky for you," she said, "I'm partial to weirdos, enigmas, and geniuses. I got you a spot on a Herc from McMurdo to Ninety South. The plane leaves in six weeks. You'll leave Palmer in five. You'll have to stand up the whole three-hour flight. I've got it packed with weather balloons, powdered milk, and jet fuel."

"I'm fine with standing," I said.

"You say that now," Ellen said. "One question, though. Do you have all your wisdom teeth?"

"Yeah...," I answered. "Why would you ask?"

"Nobody with wisdom teeth is allowed at the South Pole. A couple years back we had to airlift out three people with infected wisdom teeth. Don't ask me how much that cost. We instituted a rule: no wisdom teeth."

"Shit!" I jumped up and down like Yosemite Sam, hopping mad that of all the reasons the South Pole would slip through my fingers, it'd be because I didn't go to that goddamn dentist appointment!

"Easy," Ellen said. "We can remove them. But we'll have to do it today."

My body gave a little jolt. Here was a woman who took can-do to an exciting new level.

"But," she said, "you need to know what you're getting yourself into.

The South Pole is considered the most stressful living environment in the world. You're trapped in a small space with twenty people you probably won't like. They're all pretty awful in my opinion, made worse by the isolation." She handed me a clipboard. "Here's a psych screening the overwinterers take. It's seven hundred questions, and it's mostly bullshit. At least look at it."

I sat down and flipped to a random page. "True or False: I line up all my shoes according to color. If I find them out of order, I can turn violent." She was right, it was bullshit.

More relevant was the cover sheet, which set forth the psychological profile of candidates best suited to withstand the extreme conditions at the South Pole. They are "individuals with blasé attitudes and antisocial tendencies," and people who "feel comfortable spending lots of time alone in small rooms," "don't feel the need to get outside and exercise," and the kicker, "can go long stretches without showering."

For the past twenty years I've been in training for overwintering at the South Pole! I knew I was up to something.

"I can handle it," I told Ellen. "As long as my daughter gives me her blessing. I must get word to her."

"That's the easy part," Ellen said, finally cracking a smile for me.

There's a guy here studying fur seals. He's also a veterinarian from Pasadena, with a degree in equine dentistry. He used to clean Zenyatta's teeth. (I'm telling you, there are all kinds down here. At lunch today, a Nobel Prize–winning physicist explained "the quilted universe." I'm not talking about Galer Street pickup, with the parents standing around in their North Face. It's a quantum physics concept where everything that *can* happen, is happening, in an infinite number of parallel universes. Shit, I can't explain it now. But I'm telling you, for a fleeting moment at lunch, I grasped it. Like everything else in my life—I got it, I lost it!)

So. The veterinarian is going to extract my wisdom teeth. The station doctor, Doug, will assist him. Doug is a surgeon from Aspen who came here as part of a lifelong quest to ski all seven continents. They're confident the extraction will be a cinch because my wisdom teeth have erupted through my gums and aren't at funky angles. For some reason, Cal, a genial neutrino specialist, wants in on the tooth action. Everyone seems to like me, which has everything to do with the fact that I came bearing fresh produce, and the paucity of women. I'm an Antarctic 10, a boat ride away from being a 5.

Bee, I have one shot to make it to the South Pole. The *Laurence M. Gould* is headed to McMurdo in five weeks. From there, if my streak continues, I can catch that sleigh to Ninety South. But I will go only if I hear back from you. Send word through Ellen Idelson to the email below. If I *don't* hear back, I'll take that ship to McMurdo and from there fly home.

XXXX

Doug the surgeon just gave me Novocain and Vicodin, which was the only reason Neutrino Cal was on hand, it turns out, because he heard they were unlocking the drug chest. He's gone now. I don't have much time before I get loopy. Now for the important stuff:

Bee, don't hate Dad. I hate him enough for the both of us. That being said, I may forgive him. Because I don't know what Dad and I would be without the other. Well, we know what *he'd* be: a guy shacking up with his admin. But I have no idea what I'd be.

Remember all those things you hated about me when you were little? You hated when I sang. You hated when I danced. You *really* hated when I referred to that homeless guy with the dreadlocks who walked around the streets with a stack of blankets across his shoulders as "my brother." You hated when I said you were my best friend.

I now agree with you on that last one. I'm not your best friend. I'm your mother. As your mother, I have two proclamations.

First, we're moving out of Straight Gate. That place was a decades-long bad dream, and all three of us will awake from it when I snap my fingers.

I got a phone call a few months ago from some freak named Ollie-O, who was raising money for a new Galer Street campus. How about we give them Straight Gate, or sell it to them for a dollar? The unutterable truth: Galer Street was the best thing that ever happened to me, because they took fantastic care of you. The teachers adored you, and there you blossomed into my flute-playing Krishna, Bala no more. They need a campus, and we need to start living like normal people.

I'll miss the afternoons when I'd go out on our lawn and throw my head back. The sky in Seattle is so low, it felt like God had lowered a silk parachute over us. Every feeling I ever knew was up in that sky. Twinkling joyous sunlight; airy, giggling cloud wisps; blinding columns of sun. Orbs of gold, pink, flesh, utterly cheesy in their luminosity. Gigantic puffy clouds, welcoming, forgiving, repeating infinitely across the horizon as if between mirrors; and slices of rain, pounding wet misery in the distance now, but soon on us, and in another part of the sky, a black stain, rainless.

The sky, it came in patches, it came in layers, it came swirled together, and always on the move, churning, sometimes whizzing by. It was so low, some days I'd reach out for the flow, like you, Bee, at your first 3-D movie, so convinced was I that I could grab it, and then what — become it.

All those ninnies have it wrong. The *best* thing about Seattle is the weather. The world over, people have ocean views. But across *our* ocean is Bainbridge Island, an evergreen curb, and over it the exploding, craggy, snow-scraped Olympics. I guess what I'm saying: I miss it, the mountains and the water.

My second proclamation: you are not going away to boarding school. Yes, I selfishly can't bear life without you. But mostly, and I mean this, I hate the idea for you. You will simply not fit in with those snobby rich kids. They're not like you. To quote the admin, "I don't want to use the word *sophistication*." (OK, we need to double-swear to *never* tease Dad about the emails from the admin. You may have a hard time seeing it now, but trust me, it meant nothing. No doubt poor Dad is already dying of mortification. If he hasn't ditched her by the time I return, have no fear, I will swat her away myself.)

Bee, darling, you're a child of the earth, the United States, Washington State, and Seattle. Those East Coast rich kids are a different breed, on a fast track to nowhere. Your friends in Seattle are downright Canadian in their niceness. None of you has a cell phone. The girls wear hoodies and big cotton underpants and walk around with tangled hair and smiling, adorned backpacks. Do you know how absolutely exotic it is that you haven't been corrupted by fashion and pop culture? A month ago I mentioned Ben Stiller, and do you remember how you responded? "Who's that?" I loved you all over again.

I blame myself. None of what's become of me was Seattle's fault. Well, it might be Seattle's fault. The people are pretty boring. But let's withhold final judgment until I start being more of an artist and less of a menace. I make you only one promise, I will move forward.

Sorry, but you have no choice. You're sticking with me, with us, close to home. And I don't want to hear it from the Runaway Bunny. The Runaway Bunny stays.

Say yes, and I'll be gone an extra month. I'll return and work on my plans for the new South Pole Station, you'll graduate Galer Street and go to Lakeside, Dad will continue making the world a better place at Microsoft, and we'll move into a normal house, dare I say, a Craftsman?

Say yes. And know I'm always,

Mom

Acknowledgments

Thank you...

Anna Stein, fierce and elegant agent, dear friend.

Judy Clain, true believer, full of kindness and sparkle.

To my parents. Joyce, for the near-embarrassing belief in me, and Lorenzo, for making me want to become a writer.

For the hands-on help: Blaise Agüera y Arcas, Heather Barbieri, Kate Beyrer, Ryan Boudinot, Carol Cassella, Gigi Davis, Richard Day, Claire Dederer, Patrick deWitt, Mark Driscoll, Robin Driscoll, Sarah Dunn, Jonathan Evison, Holly Goldberg Sloan, Carolyne Heldman, Barbara Heller—I shudder to think what a mess I'd have on my hands without your notes—Johanna Herwitz, Jay Jacobs, Andrew Kidd, Matthew Kneale—my Roman star, twinkling—Paul Lubowicki—especially, especially!—Cliff Mass, John McElwee, Jason Richman, Sally Riley, Maher Saba, Howie Sanders, Lorenzo Semple III, Garth Stein, Phil Stutz, Arzu Tahin, Wink Thorne, Chrystol White, John Yunker.

The Cassella girls: Elise, Julia, and Sara, without whose decency and charm, there'd be no Bee.

At Little, Brown: Terry Adams, Reagan Arthur, Amanda Brower, Emily Cavedon, Nicole Dewey—rockstar!—Heather Fain, Keith Hayes, Morgan Moroney, Michael Pietsch, Nathan Rostron—sometimes I think my whole writing career is an elaborate ruse to make you take my calls—Geoff Shandler, Amanda Tobier, Jayne Yaffe Kemp.

Deep, lifelong thanks to: Nicholas Callaway, Mia Farrow, Merrill Markoe, Peter Mensch, Sue Naegle, Ann Roth, James Salter, Larry Salz, Bruce Wagner, Leta Warner.

For the Seattle embrace: the parents, faculty, and staff of the ___ school, Mr. Levys all, gnats not a one. Huge thanks to my comrades at Seattle7Writers, Elliott Bay Book Company, University Books, and the Richard Hugo House.

Most of all: George Meyer, who, with kindness and minimal complaint, suffers the arrows so I can wall off and write. Thanks for sticking with me, baby.

Reading Group Guide

Where'd You Go,
BERNADETTE

A NOVEL BY

MARIA SEMPLE

Dear Mountain Room Parents

Hi, everyone!

The Mountain Room is gearing up for its Day of the Dead celebration on Friday. Please send in photos of loved ones for our altar. All parents are welcome to come by on Wednesday afternoon to help us make candles and decorate skulls.

Thanks!

Emily

Hi again.

Because I've gotten some questions about my last email, there is nothing "wrong" with Halloween. The Day of the Dead is the Mexican version, a time of remembrance. Many of you chose Little Learners because of our emphasis on global awareness. Our celebration on Friday is an example of that. The skulls we're decorating are sugar skulls. I should have made that more clear.

Emily

Parents:

Some of you have expressed concern about your children celebrating a holiday with the word "dead" in it. I asked Eleanor's mom, who's a pediatrician, and here's what she said: "Preschoolers tend to see death as temporary and reversible. Therefore, I see nothing traumatic about the Day of the Dead." I hope this helps.

Emily

Dear Parents:

In response to the email we all received from Maddie's parents, in which they shared their decision to raise their daughter dogma-free, yes, there will be an altar, but please be assured that the Day of the Dead is a pagan celebration of life and has nothing to do with God. Keep those photos coming!

Emily

Hello.

Perhaps "pagan" was a poor word choice. I feel like we're veering a bit off track, so here's what I'll do. I'll start setting up our altar now, so that today at pickup you can see for yourselves how colorful and harmless the Day of the Dead truly is.

Emily

Parents:

The photos should be of loved ones who have passed. Max's grandma was understandably shaken when she came in and saw a photo of herself on our altar. But the candles and skulls were cute, right?

Emily

Mountain Room Parents:

It's late and I can't possibly respond to each and every email. (Not that it comes up a lot in conversation, but I have children, too.) As the skulls have clearly become a distraction, I decided to throw them away. They're in the compost. I'm looking at them now. You can, too, tomorrow at drop-off. I just placed a "NO BASURA" card on the bin to make sure it doesn't get emptied. Finally, to those parents who are offended by our Day of the Dead celebration, I'd like to point out that there are parents who are offended that you are offended.

Emily

Dear Parents:

Thanks to their group email, we now know that the families of Millie and Jaden M. recognize Jesus Christ as their Savior. There still seems to be some confusion about why, if we want to celebrate life, we're actually celebrating death. To better explain this "bewildering detour," I've asked Adela, who works in the office and makes waffles for us on Wednesdays, and who was born in Mexico, to write you directly.

Emily

Hola a los Padres:

El Día de los Muertos begins with a parade through the zócalo, where we toss oranges into decorated coffins. The skeletons drive us in the bus to the cemetery and we molest the spirits from under the ground with candy and traditional Mexican music. We write poems called calaveras, which laugh at the living. In Mexico, it is a rejoicing time of ofrendas, picnics, and dancing on graves.

Adela

Parents:

I sincerely apologize for Adela's email. I would have looked it over, but I was at my daughter's piano recital. (Three kids, in case you're wondering, one who's allergic to everything, even wind.) For now, let's agree that email has reached its limits. How about we process our feelings face to face? 9 A.M. tomorrow?

Emily

Dear Parents:

Some of you chose to engage in our dialogue. Some chose to form a human chain. Others had jobs (!) to go to. So we're all up to speed, let me recap this morning's discussion:

—Satan isn't driving our bus. Little Learners does not have a bus. If we did, I wouldn't still need parent drivers for the field trip to the cider mill. Anyone? I didn't think so.

—*Ofrenda* means "offering." It's just a thing we put on the altar. Any random thing. A bottle of Fanta. Unopened, not poisoned. Just a bottle of Fanta.

—We're moving past the word "altar" and calling it what it really is: a Seahawks blanket draped over some cinder blocks.

—Adela will not be preparing food anymore and Waffle Wednesdays will be suspended. (That didn't make us any new friends in the Rainbow and Sunshine Rooms!)

—On Friday morning, I will divide the Mountain Room into three groups: those who wish to celebrate the Day of the Dead; those who wish to celebrate Halloween; and Maddie, who will make nondenominational potato prints in the corner.

Dear Mountain Room Parents:

Today I learned not to have open flames in the same room as a costume parade. I learned that a five-dollar belly-dancer outfit purchased at a pop-up costume store can easily catch fire, but, really, I knew that just by looking at it. I learned that Fanta is effective in putting out fires. I learned that a child's emerging completely unscathed from a burning costume isn't a good enough outcome for some parents. I learned that I will be unemployed on Monday. For me, the Day of the Dead will always be a time of remembrance.

Happy Halloween!

Emily

"Dear Mountain Room Parents" originally appeared in *The New Yorker*.

Questions and Topics for Discussion

1. *Where'd You Go, Bernadette* is told from the point of view of a daughter trying to find her missing mother. Why do you think the author chose to tell the story from Bee's perspective? What light does it shed on the bond between Bernadette and Bee?

2. What are your thoughts on Bernadette's character? Has she become unhinged or has she always been a little crazy? What, if anything, do you think sent her over the edge? Have you ever had a moment in your own life that utterly changed you, or made you call into question your own sanity?

3. When Bernadette relocates from Los Angeles to Seattle, she must cope with being a transplant in a new city. Have you ever moved, or even stayed put but switched jobs, and had to adjust to an entirely different culture? What was it like?

4. The idea of going to Antarctica becomes too much for an already frazzled Bernadette to bear, but the trip itself, surprisingly, turns out to be exactly what she needs to get back on track. How do other characters in the novel experience their own breakthroughs? Which character is most transformed?

5. How are Audrey Griffin and Bernadette Fox more alike than they realize?

6. Bernadette often behaves as if she is an outsider. Do you think she is? If so, do you think her feelings of being an outsider are self-imposed, or is she truly different from the other members of her community? Do you ever feel like an outsider?

7. The book has a very playful structure. Do you think it works? Why do you think the author chose it rather than a more straightforward, traditional structure? Think about other books with unusual structures and how their formats influenced your reading experience.

8. What do you think of Bernadette and Elgie's marriage? Is it dysfunctional? Is there real love there? How has their marriage changed over time? Think about romantic relationships you've been in that have evolved, positively or negatively, and why.

9. *Where'd You Go, Bernadette* is, at its core, a story about a woman who disappears, both literally and figuratively. Were you able to relate to the book? How and why? Do you feel Bernadette's disappearance was unique, or do all women, in a sense, disappear into motherhood and marriage?

About the Author...

Maria Semple is the author of *This One Is Mine* and *Where'd You Go, Bernadette,* which has been translated into eighteen languages. She lives in Seattle.

...And Her Newest Book

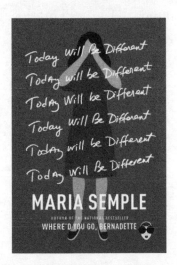

Today Will Be Different is a brilliant and hilarious novel about a day in the life of a woman forced to abandon her small ambitions and awake to a strange new future.

Following is an excerpt from the opening pages.

Today will be different. Today I will be present. Today, anyone I speak to, I will look them in the eye and listen deeply. Today I'll play a board game with Timby. I'll initiate sex with Joe. Today I will take pride in my appearance. I'll shower, get dressed in proper clothes, and change into yoga clothes only for yoga, which today I will actually attend. Today I won't swear. I won't talk about money. Today there will be an ease about me. My face will be relaxed, its resting place a smile. Today I will radiate calm. Kindness and self-control will abound. Today I will buy local. Today I will be my best self, the person I'm capable of being. Today will be different.

Because the other way wasn't working. The waking up just to get the day over with until it was time for bed. The grinding it out was a disgrace, an affront to the honor and long shot of being alive at all. The ghost-walking, the short-tempered distraction, the hurried fog. (All of this I'm just assuming, because I have no idea how I come across, my consciousness is that underground, like a toad in winter.) The leaving the world a worse place just by being in it. The blindness to the destruction in my wake. The Mr. Magoo.

If I'm forced to be honest, here's an account of how I left the world last week: worse, worse, better, worse, same, worse, same. Not an inventory to make one swell with pride. I don't necessarily need to make the world a better place, mind you. Today, I will live by the Hippocratic oath: first do no harm.

How hard can it be? Dropping off Timby, having my poetry lesson (my favorite part of life!), taking a yoga class, eating lunch with Sydney Madsen, whom I can't stand but at least I can check her off the list (more on that later), picking up Timby, and giving back to Joe, the underwriter of all this mad abundance.

You're trying to figure out, why the *agita* surrounding one normal day of white-people problems? Because there's me and there's the beast in me. It would be kind of brilliant if the beast in me played out on a giant canvas, shocking and awe-ing, causing fabulous destruction, talked about forever. If I could swing that, I just might:

3

self-immolate gloriously for the performance-art spectacle. The sad truth? The beast in me plays out on a painfully small scale: regrettable micro-transactions usually involving Timby, my friends, or Joe. I'm irritable and consumed by anxiety when I'm with them; maudlin and shit-talking when I'm not. Ha! Aren't you glad you're at a safe distance, doors locked, windows rolled up? Aw, come on. I'm nice. I'm exaggerating for effect. It's not really like that.

And so the day began, the minute I whipped off my sheets. The *click-click-click* of Yo-Yo's nails across the hardwood, stopping outside the bedroom. Why, when Joe whips off his sheets, doesn't Yo-Yo *trot-trot-trot* and wait in abject hope? How can Yo-Yo, on the other side of a closed door, tell it's me and not Joe? It was once depressingly explained by a dog trainer: it's my smell Yo-Yo's caught whiff of. That his idea of nirvana is a dead seal washed up on the beach leaves me asking, Is it time for bed yet? Nope, I'm not doing that. Not today.

I didn't mean to be coy about Sydney Madsen.

When Joe and I arrived in Seattle from New York ten years ago, we were ready to start a family. I'd just wrapped five wearying years at *Looper Wash*. Everywhere you looked it was *Looper Wash* T-shirts, bumper stickers, mouse pads. *I'm a Vivian. I'm a Dot.* You remember. If not, check your nearest dollar store, the two-for-one bin, it's been a while.

Joe, a hand surgeon, had become a legend of sorts for reconstructing the hand of that quarterback whose thumb bent back and nobody thought he'd ever play again but the next year he went on to win the Super Bowl. (I can't remember his name, but even if I did, I couldn't say, due to doctor/patient/nosy-wife confidentiality.)

Joe had job offers everywhere. Why pick Seattle? Joe, a nice Catholic boy from outside Buffalo, couldn't see raising kids in Manhattan, my first choice. We struck a deal. We'd move anywhere he wanted for ten years, and back to New York for ten; his city for ten, my city for ten, back and forth, unto death. (A deal he's conveniently forgotten his end of, I might add, seeing as we're coming up on year ten and not a peep on packing up.)

As everybody knows, being raised Catholic with half a brain means becoming an atheist. At one of our skeptics' conventions (yes, our early years were actually spent doing things like driving to Philadelphia to watch Penn Jillette debate a rabbi! Oh, to be childless again...or not), Joe heard that Seattle was the least religious city in America. Seattle it was.

A Doctors Without Borders board member threw Joe and me a welcome-to-town party. I swanned into her Lake Washington mansion filled with modern art and future friends, mine for the taking. My whole life, I've been liked. Okay, I'll say it: I've been adored. I don't understand why, on account of my disgraceful personality, but somehow it works. Joe says it's because I'm the most guy-like woman he's ever met, but sexy and with no emotional membrane. (A compliment!) I went from room to room, being introduced to a series of women, interchangeable in their decency and warmth. It was that thing where you meet somebody who tells you they like camping and you say, "Oh! I was just talking to someone who's going on a ten-day rafting trip down the Snake River, you should totally meet them," and the person says, "That was me."

What can I say? I'm terrible with faces. And names. And numbers. And times. And dates.

The whole party was a blur, with one woman eager to show me funky shops, another hidden hikes, another Mario Batali's father's Italian restaurant in Pioneer Square, another the best dentist in town who has a glitter painting on his ceiling of a parachuting tiger, yet another willing to share her housekeeper. One of them, Sydney Madsen, invited me to lunch the next day at the Tamarind Tree in the International District.

(Joe has a thing he calls the magazine test. It's the reaction you have when you open the mailbox and pull out a magazine. Instantly, you know if you're happy to see this magazine or bummed. Which is why I don't subscribe to *The New Yorker* and do subscribe to *Us Weekly*. Put to the magazine test, Sydney Madsen is the human equivalent of *Tinnitus Today*.)

That first lunch: She was so careful with her words, so sincere in her gaze, noticed a small spot on her fork and was overly solicitous toward the waiter when asking for a new one, brought her own tea bag and asked for hot water, said she wasn't very hungry so how about we split my green papaya salad, told me she'd never seen *Looper Wash* but would put a hold on the DVDs at the library.

Am I painting a clear enough picture of the tight-assed dreariness, the selfish cluelessness, the cheap creepiness? A water-stained fork never killed anybody! *Buy* the DVDs, how about? Eat the food at the restaurant, that's how they stay in business! Worst of all, Sydney Madsen was steady, earnest, without a speck of humor, and talked... very... slowly... as... if... her... platitudes... were... little... gold... coins.

I was in shock. Living too long in New York does that to a girl, gives her the false sense that the world is full of interesting people. Or at least people who are crazy in an interesting way.

At one point I writhed so violently in my chair that Sydney actually asked, "Do you need to use the powder room?" (Powder room? *Powder room?* Kill her!) The worst part? All those women with whom I'd gladly agreed to go hiking and shopping? They weren't a bunch of women. They were all Sydney Madsen! Damn that blur! It took everything I had to kink her fire hose of new invitations: a weekend at her beach house on Vashon Island, introducing me to the wife of someone for this, the playwright of something for that.

I ran home screaming to Joe.

Joe: You should have been suspicious of someone so eager to make friends, because it probably means she doesn't have any.

Me: This is why I love you, Joe. You just boil it all down. (Joe the boiler. Don't we just love him?)

Forgive me for long-hauling you on Sydney Madsen. My point is: for ten years I haven't been able to shake her. She's the friend I don't like, the friend I don't know what she does for a living because I was too stultified to ask the first time and it would be rude to ask now (because I'm not rude), the friend I can't be mean enough to so she gets the message (because I'm not mean), the friend to whom I keep saying no, no, no, yet she still chases me. She's like Parkinson's, you can't cure her, you can just manage the symptoms.

For today, the lunch bell tolls.

Please know I'm aware that lunch with a boring person *is* a boutique problem. When I say I have problems, I'm not talking about Sydney Madsen.

Yo-Yo trotting down the street, the prince of Belltown. Oh, Yo-Yo, you foolish creature with your pep and your blind devotion and your busted ear flapping with every prance. How poignant it is, the pride you take in being walked by me, your immortal beloved. If only you knew.

What a disheartening spectacle it's been, a new month, a new condo higher than the last, each packed with blue-badged Amazon squids, every morning squirting by the thousands from their studio apartments onto my block, heads in devices, never looking up. (They work for Amazon, so you know they're soulless. The only question, how soulless?) It makes me pine for the days when Third Ave. was just me, empty storefronts and the one tweaker yelling, "*That's* how you spell America!"

Outside our building, Dennis stood by his wheelie trash can and refilled the poop-bag dispenser. "Good morning, you two."

"Good morning, Dennis!" Instead of my usual breezing past, I stopped and looked him in the eye. "How's your day so far?"

"Oh, can't complain," he said. "You?"

"Can complain, but won't."

Dennis chuckled.

Today, already a net gain.

I opened the front door of our apartment. At the end of the hallway: Joe face down at the table, his forehead flat on the newspaper, arms splayed with bent elbows as if under arrest.

It was a jarring image, one of pure defeat, the last thing I'd ever associate with Joe—

Thunk.

The door shut. I unclipped Yo-Yo's harness. By the time I straightened, my stricken husband had gotten up and disappeared into his office. Whatever it was, he didn't want to talk about it.

My attitude? Works for me!

Yo-Yo raced to his food, greyhound-style, back legs vaulting past his front. Realizing it was the same dry food that had been there before his walk, he became overwhelmed with confusion and betrayal. He took one step and stared at a spot on the floor.

Timby's light clicked on. God bless him, up before the alarm. I went into his bathroom and found him on the step stool in his PJs.

"Morning, darling. Look at you, up and awake."

He stopped what he was doing. "Can we have bacon?"

Timby, in the mirror, waited for me to leave. I lowered my eyes. The little Quick Draw McGraw beat my glance. He pushed something into the sink before I could see it. The unmistakable clang of lightweight plastic. The Sephora 200!

It was nobody's fault but my own, Santa putting a makeup kit in Timby's stocking. It's how I'd buy myself extra time at Nordstrom, telling Timby to roam cosmetics. The girls there loved his gentle nature, his sugar-sack body, his squeaky voice. Soon enough, they were making him up. I don't know if he liked the makeup as much as being doted on by a gaggle of blondes. On a lark, I picked up a kit the size of a paperback that unfolded and fanned out to reveal six different makeup trays (!) holding two hundred (!) shadows, glosses, blushes, and whatever-they-weres. The person who'd found a way to cram so much into so little should seriously be working for NASA. If they still have that.

"You do realize you're not wearing makeup to school," I told him.

"I know, Mom." The sigh and shoulder heave right out of the Disney Channel. Again, my bad for letting it take root. After school, a jigsaw puzzle!

I emerged from Timby's room. Yo-Yo, standing anxiously,

shivered with relief upon seeing that I still existed. Knowing I'd be heading to the kitchen to make breakfast, he raced me to his food bowl. This time he deigned to eat some, one eye on me.

Joe was back and making himself tea.

"How's things?" I asked.

"Don't you look nice," he said.

True to my grand scheme for the day, I'd showered and put on a dress and oxfords. If you beheld my closet, you'd see a woman of specific style. Dresses from France and Belgium, price tags ripped off before I got home because Joe would have an aneurysm, and every iteration of flat black shoe... again, no need to discuss price. Buy them? Yes. Put them on? On most days, too much energy.

"Olivia's coming tonight," I said with a wink, already tasting the wine flight and rigatoni at Tavolàta.

"How about she takes Timby out so we can have a little alone time?" Joe grabbed me by the waist and pulled me in as if we weren't a couple of fifty-year-olds.

Here's who I envy: lesbians. Why? Lesbian bed death. Apparently, after a lesbian couple's initial flush of hot sex, they stop having it altogether. It makes perfect sense. Left to their own devices, women would stop having sex after they have children. There's no evolutionary need for it. Our brains know it, our body knows it. Who feels sexy during the slog of motherhood, the middle-aged fat roll and the flattening butt? What woman wants anyone to see her naked, let alone fondle her breasts, squishy now like bags of cake batter, or touch her stomach, spongy like breadfruit? Who wants to pretend they're all sexed up when the honeypot is dry?

Me, that's who, if I don't want to get switched out for a younger model.

"Alone time it is," I said to Joe.

"Mom, this broke." Timby came in with his ukulele and plonked it down on the counter. Suspiciously near the trash. "The sound's all messed up."

"What do you propose we do?" I asked, daring him to say, *Buy a new one.*

Joe picked up the ukulele and strummed. "It's a little out of tune, that's all." He began to adjust the strings.

"Hey," I said. "Since when can you tune a ukulele?"

"I'm a man of many mysteries," Joe said and gave the instrument a final dulcet strum.

The bacon and French toast were being wolfed, the smoothies being drunk. Timby was deep into an *Archie Double Digest.* My smile was on lockdown.

Two years ago when I was getting all martyr-y about having to make breakfast every morning, Joe said, "I pay for this circus. Can you please climb down off your cross and make breakfast without the constant sighing?"

I know what you're going to say: *What a jerk! What a sexist thug!* But Joe had a point. Lots of women would gladly do worse for a closet full of Antwerp. From that moment on, it was service with a smile. It's called knowing when you've got a weak hand.

Joe showed Timby the newspaper. "The Pinball Expo is coming back to town. Wanna go?"

"Do you think the Evel Knievel machine will still be broken?"

"Almost certainly," Joe said.

I handed over the poem I'd printed out and heavily annotated. "Okay, who's going to help me?" I asked.

Timby didn't look up from his *Archie.*

Joe took it. "Ooh, Robert Lowell."

Skunk Hour

[handwritten note in cloud: 8:30 Thursday Lola, Oct. 8th]

By Robert Lowell

(For Elizabeth Bishop)

Nautilus Island's hermit
heiress still lives through winter in her Spartan cottage;
her sheep still graze above the sea.
Her son's a bishop. Her farmer
is first selectman in our village;
she's in her dotage.

[handwritten: showing or characterized by austerity; Ancient Sparta]

[handwritten: HER]

Thirsting for
the hierarchic privacy
of Queen Victoria's century,
she buys up all
the eyesores facing her shore,
and lets them fall.

[handwritten: impressions of a sea village after summer — heading into winter]

The season's ill—
we've lost our summer millionaire,
who seemed to leap from an L. L. Bean
catalogue. His nine-knot yawl
was auctioned off to lobstermen.
A red fox stain covers Blue Hill.

[handwritten: OUR]

And now our fairy
decorator brightens his shop for fall;
his fishnet's filled with orange cork,
orange, his cobbler's bench and awl;
there is no money in his work,
he'd rather marry.

[handwritten: tool for piercing holes in leather]

One dark night,
my Tudor Ford climbed the hill's skull;
I watched for love-cars. Lights turned down,
they lay together, hull to hull,
where the graveyard shelves on the town. . . .
My mind's not right.

A car radio bleats,
"Love, O careless Love. . . ." I hear
my ill-spirit sob in each blood cell,
as if my hand were at its throat. . . .
I myself am hell;
nobody's here—

only skunks, that search
in the moonlight for a bite to eat.
They march on their soles up Main Street:
white stripes, moonstruck eyes' red fire
under the chalk-dry and spar spire
of the Trinitarian Church.

I stand on top
of our back steps and breathe the rich air—
a mother skunk with her column of kittens swills the garbage pail
She jabs her wedge-head in a cup
of sour cream, drops her ostrich tail,
and will not scare.

[handwritten annotations: MY; thick strong pole used for a mast; military formation; I → OUR?]

I began from memory: "'Nautical Island's hermit heiress still lives through winter in her Spartan cottage; her sheep still graze above the sea. Her son's a bishop. Her farmer's first selectman'—"

"'Her farmer *is* first selectman,'" Joe said.

"Shoot. 'Her farmer *is* first selectman.'"

"Mom!"

I shushed Timby and continued with eyes closed. "'...in our village; she's in her dotage. Thirsting for the hierarchic privacy of Queen Victoria's century, she buys up all the eyesores facing her shore, and lets them fall. The season's ill—we've lost our summer millionaire, who seemed to leap from an L. L. Bean catalogue'—"

"Mommy, look at Yo-Yo. See how his chin is sitting on his paws?"

Yo-Yo was positioned on his pink lozenge so he could watch for dropped food, his little white paws delicately crossed.

"Aww," I said.

"Can I have your phone?" Timby asked.

"Just enjoy your pet," I said. "This doesn't have to turn into electronics."

"It's very cool what Mom is doing," Joe said to Timby. "Always learning."

"Learning and forgetting," I said. "But thank you."

He shot me an air kiss.

I pressed onward. "'His nine-knot yawl was auctioned off to lobstermen'—"

"Don't we love Yo-Yo?" Timby asked.

"We do." The simple truth. Yo-Yo is the world's cutest dog, part Boston terrier, part pug, part something else...brindle-and-white with a black patch on one eye, bat ears, smooshed face, and curlicue tail. Before the Amazon invasion, when it was just me and hookers on the street, one remarked, "It's like if Barbie had a pit bull."

"Daddy," Timby said. "Don't you love Yo-Yo?"

Joe looked at Yo-Yo and considered the question. (More evidence of Joe's superiority: he thinks before he speaks.)

"He's a little weird," Joe said and returned to the poem.

Timby dropped his fork. I dropped my jaw.

"Weird?" Timby cried.

Joe looked up. "Yeah. What?"

"Oh, Daddy! How can you say that?"

"He just sits there all day looking depressed," Joe said. "When we come home, he doesn't greet us at the door. When we are here, he just sleeps, waits for food to drop, or stares at the front door like he has a migraine."

For Timby and me, there were simply no words.

"I know what he's getting out of *us,*" Joe said. "I just don't know what we're getting out of *him.*"

Timby jumped out of his chair and lay across Yo-Yo, his version of a hug. "Oh, Yo-Yo! *I* love you."

"Keep going." Joe flicked the poem. "You're doing great. 'The season's ill' . . ."

" 'The season's ill,' " I said. " 'We've lost our summer millionaire, who seemed to leap from an L. L. Bean catalogue' —" To Timby: "You. Get ready."

"Are we driving through or are you walking me in?"

"Driving. I have Alonzo at eight thirty."

Our breakfast over, Yo-Yo got up from his pillow. Joe and I watched as he walked to the front door and stared at it.

"I didn't realize I was being controversial," Joe said. " 'The season's ill.' "